ITALIAN

AMERICAN

This book is dedicated to my mama, the real Mariella, whose strength and courage transcended distance as she raised five daughters far from home.

Italian American

Front cover by Ebooklaunch

Editing by Rose McCaffrey

Interior Design by Usman Ali

Published by Dennyloo Publishing

77 Charlton Street

New York, NY 10014

Author's website www.luiginavecchione.com

Acknowledgements

First, I would like to thank everyone who enjoyed Greetings from Asbury Park and asked for the sequel. I wasn't planning on writing this book, but once I delved into the world of Mariella's America, I was hooked. I want to thank my dear friend Cynthia. We've known each other since our twenties, and you have always been one of my biggest supporters. Rosie, it's been so lovely to work with you again. You add depth and nuance to my writing. My wonderful betas - thanks for reading my work! To the Curcoopione's- I love you all. Carla, I don't know what I would do without my morning calls to you! Jolie and Kelly, thanks for your encouragement. Writing can be a solitary pursuit, but it's nice to bounce things off you two. And finally, thank you to my husband Dennis. You've always been my ride-or-die, and I will always be yours.

ITALIAN
AMERICAN

By

Luigina Vecchione

PART ONE

Chapter One

She's running out of time, Elisa thought, steering her beat-up Volkswagen into Wanamassa Gardens as the last rays of sun dipped below the horizon. The streetlights flickered alive, casting soft circles onto the sidewalk. She drove up Darlene Avenue, passing ranch-style houses with expansive, grassy lawns, then turned down Interlaken Avenue. As she pulled up to her childhood home, a familiar sadness settled in her chest.

She gazed at the sweet, yellow house fronted by a neat, trimmed lawn. Nothing had changed except for the towering oak tree standing in front. The developers had planted it as a gift when her parents first moved in. Elisa and her younger sister,

Olivia, had spent hours sitting on its branches, swinging their legs back and forth. Up in the tree, they played card games, got lost in the world of Nancy Drew and Hardy Boys books, and confessed middle school crushes. Its rustling leaves protected their deepest, darkest secrets from nosy ears below. During summer, the oak shaded the house from the blazing sun, and in the midst of harsh winters it became a shield against wind and snow. But after decades of growth, the tree's thick roots pushed through the sidewalk, causing it to crack, and its twisted branches hung bare, casting an unwelcoming shadow over the once-inviting scene.

"Hello? Mama?" Elisa called out as she entered the house. The aroma of simmering tomato sauce overwhelmed her. For a second, she imagined her mother standing at the stove in her red-checkered apron, sprinkling basil and oregano into the pot. But then she remembered.

Olivia popped her head out of the kitchen. "Hey, sissy! Filming again?"

"Liv! I didn't know you were here."

"Joey dropped me off an hour ago," Olivia said, wiping her hands on a dish towel. "No Sharon today."

"Is something wrong?"

"Nah, just a cold."

Sharon was the helper they'd insisted on getting after their father died. Although she resisted, Elisa was able to convince their mother that she could use the help. But she only agreed if it was on her terms.

In the beginning, she kept Sharon at arm's length. The woman spent 9 a.m. to 5 p.m. cooking, cleaning, doing the shopping, and ironing the laundry without a word from her charge. But one day, while waiting for her lift home, Sharon asked about the painting of the Roman Colosseum that hung prominently above the couch. Sharon told Elisa how her mother's eyes lit up while she recounted meeting her love for the first time in the arena, then explained that after he returned from the war, art had been therapeutic and he created the painting from memory. After that exchange, Sharon showed interest in the other paintings peppered around the house. She recalled to the sisters how lovingly their mother described each one, and how her expressive face told their story as much as her words.

As they grew close, Elisa took advantage of the situation. She asked Sharon to figure out a way to get her mother back into the kitchen. After moving to America, cooking had been the one thing that helped her connect to her roots. Without her husband around, she hadn't seen the point in cooking for herself. But once Sharon asked about a few recipes, their mother agreed to teach her. Her weathered hands skillfully kneaded dough, then fed it through the pasta maker until it was almost transparent. She cut tomatoes, onions, and basil for sauce, stuffed artichokes with butter and breadcrumbs, and layered noodles with béchamel sauce and sausage to make lasagna. After a few years, when arthritis settled into her joints, Sharon was ready to take over.

"Who is here?" A feeble voice drifted down the stairs.

"It's me, Mama. I'll be right up!"

"Who?"

"Me! Ellie!"

"Ah, okay."

"I'll be up in a sec," Elisa said. She joined Olivia in the kitchen, making a beeline for the large pot of red sauce gently bubbling on the stove. She dipped a wooden spoon in and tasted it. "Mmm. Just like Mama's. But why are you making sauce? The doctor said acid isn't good for her stomach."

"Calm down." Olivia waved her away. "The sauce is for me. I make it here because the smell brings her back to, you know, happier times." She pointed to a smaller pot of broth as it came to a boil on the front burner. "The soup is for Mama. She's forgetting more and more. Today, it took her a few minutes to remember the kids' names. I was showing her pictures from Mathew's graduation. She had a hard time understanding why she should be interested in someone she didn't know," Olivia said, punctuating her disappointment with a sigh.

Elisa pointed to her camera bag. "That's exactly why I

started this project."

"It's still jarring seeing her like that." Olivia stirred a handful of pastina into the broth. The water bubbled up, then settled. As they waited for the soup to cook, a clock chimed six p.m., then another, then a cuckoo clock tweeted. Ever since their father died, their mother was preoccupied with the little bird that chirped the time. She had become obsessed with many things: taking walks to see the stars at night, watching the Italian news channel, and dying. Although she was still able to get around, dying was something she couldn't wait to do.

When the pastina finished cooking, Olivia set it on a bed tray and headed upstairs. Elisa followed with her film equipment, careful not to knock into the electric chair that took their mother up and down the stairs when needed.

"Mama, Ellie's here," Olivia announced loudly when they entered the bedroom.

Mariella was in her recliner set up against the foot of the bed facing a TV on the wall.

"What?" she asked. Although their father's hearing aids still sat on the night table by his side of the bed, their mother had been reluctant to use hers.

"I'm here, Mama." Elisa gave her a kiss, then unpacked her camera bag as Olivia set up the TV table for lunch.

Mariella squinted so she could focus her tired eyes on her eldest daughter. "Hello, Tesoro. Come, sit by me." She patted the recliner next to hers that had sat empty for years, a solemn reminder of what once was.

"Just a moment, Mama. Let me get my tripod centered."

"What is that for?" Mariella asked, watching Elisa make adjustments until the tripod sat squarely in front of her.

"Mama, you remember Ellie filming you, don't you?" Olivia asked.

"Yeah, Mama, remember you were going to tell me about when you arrived here in America?"

Confusion etched wrinkles into Mariella's forehead. But she relaxed when she glimpsed the painting on the wall across from her. The girls had ordered it online for their parents' fiftieth anniversary. They'd found a service in China that created masterpieces from old photos.

"Do you know your father and I took that picture on the boardwalk?" Mariella said, her voice filled with longing. "There was a photo booth just outside a candy shop, and you could get a strip of four photos for just twenty-five cents. It was my first week in America. Everything felt so new. I was so hopeful." Her voice trailed off.

"I can't imagine what it was like for you," Elisa said. She placed a small microphone next to her mother. "Tell us, Mama. I wanna know all about it."

Mariella bristled. "Let me tell you about when your father and I met. Right after the war, the Americans came in like angels and saved us from those evil German soldiers. I was selling postcards at the Colosseum."

Elisa exchanged a knowing glance with her sister. They had heard the story so many times it was family lore. They couldn't understand why their mother avoided discussing those initial years living in America.

Mariella pointed to a framed canvas above her bed, Piazza Navona and its three magnificent fountains painted in great detail onto it. "That is one of your father's creations."

"Yes, Mama. We know," Olivia said gently. "And he did the one of the Colosseum in the living room and the one of Piazza di Spagna in the dining room. I love that one."

Elisa reached out and touched her mother's arm. "We've already filmed you talking about how you and Papa met. Don't you remember? I filmed you last week."

Slumping back in her chair, Mariella waved the soup away. "I do not think I can eat. My stomach is a little funny."

Olivia hesitated a moment. Her mother hadn't been eating much lately, blaming her "funny stomach." But she knew she couldn't force her to eat either. She took it back to the kitchen. When she returned, her mother's demeanor had changed.

"You know," Mariella began, a slight twinkle in her eyes, "I had such expectations of America. With everything I saw in the movies, I just thought it would be so easy. But nothing ever is, is it?" Sighing, she gazed at the withering oak right outside her window. She had told her daughters how the tree always felt like a promise of hope with each year it grew, marking not only its own life but the lives of their family. Now, with its cracked bark and brown leaves, Elisa wondered if her mother felt like her beginning was coming to an end. "No, it never is easy. But," she continued, "I would never have had the two of you beautiful girls if I did not come. And I would never have had the love of such a wonderful man." She blew a kiss to the painting.

"I bet leaving your family was tough." Elisa prodded for more.

With a dramatic sigh, Mariella nodded. "I would not wish that pain on anyone else. Of course, now you have your Skype and Face nonsense, but back then, all we had was airmail and our monthly calls. Not enough. Never enough. Especially when things … happen." Caught up in her memories, Mariella's voice drifted off once more. "What was it I was talking about?"

Olivia patted her mother's arm. "You were telling us about how hard it was to move to America. Mama, you've never said anything about it."

Elisa looked at her sister and realized Olivia was probably too young to remember. But visions from childhood of her mother's face full of worry, her heartbreaking cries echoing through the house when she had to say goodbye to her parents on the phone, these things were tattooed onto Elisa's heart. She knew it hadn't been easy for her mother. What she wanted to find out was how her mother found the strength to stay.

Mariella glanced over at her daughters' expectant faces. "Ah, yes, I remember when your father returned for me after months of waiting for my visa to be issued. Of course, I made sure I dressed like a movie star when I met him at the port that day because I worried he might not like me anymore. He had not seen me in seven months. He could have strayed while we were apart. But your father ... his love was never-ending."

Chapter Two

When the towering ship came into view, dwarfing the horizon, Mariella felt dizzy with excitement. Her husband was finally returning to her. Thick gray smoke billowed from its towering stacks while the resounding blast of its horns echoed throughout the city of Naples, announcing the arrival of SS *Andrea Doria*. As she watched the ship steadily grow larger in its approach, her anticipation grew. It was only a matter of minutes. After ten long months, after all of the doubt, and longing, and letters written with care then flown across the ocean, after praying he wouldn't forget her and wishing on his stars that he would safely come back to her—after all of that, it was only a matter of minutes before she would be in Jack's arms again.

Mariella's visa had taken much longer to secure than he'd initially thought. The devastation caused by the war brought thousands of refugees to the States, resulting in stricter requirements. Fortunately, Jack's father had a friend at city hall who sped up the process. But for Mariella, those ten months felt like an eternity. She would pass neighborhood gossips gathered on the street, whispering various theories about why they thought he had taken so long to return. Some believed that once he arrived back in America, the reality of marrying someone so far away must have come into play. Others were more cruel, suggesting he just wanted her for the honeymoon fun and that the marriage probably wouldn't be recognized in the United States. But Mariella taunted herself as well, assuming he'd simply come to his senses. Why would he want to be with a peasant from Italy when he had those beautiful women untouched by war at home?

Pushing away her fears, she searched the throngs of people waving down to their loved ones from the upper deck of the ship. For a few seconds, Mariella worried she might not remember Jack, but when his lovably crooked smile came into view, she knew everything would be okay.

Jack fixed his eyes on her as he traveled down the gangplank, then scooped her into his arms. "Why, hello, Mrs. Valentino," he whispered into her ear.

"Welcome back, amore," she said, unable to stop the tears that spilled from her eyes.

"Hey, what's with the crying?" he joked, but he didn't wait for an answer. It was clear he understood how months of being apart had taken a toll on her. "I'm so happy to have you in my arms. Finally."

A porter appeared beside them, interrupting their intimate moment. "Mr. Jack Valentino?"

Jack ran his hand through his hair, then nodded.

"I believe this is yours." The porter held out a dark leather suitcase.

"Ah, yeah." Jack took it and slipped the man a quarter. "Thank you very much."

The porter tipped his hat and then disappeared back into the crowd.

"Now, tell me." Jack turned his attention back to his wife. "How can you be more beautiful than the day I left?"

Mariella touched his face. "Oh, Jack, please do not ever leave me again."

After a two-hour train ride, Jack and Mariella arrived in Rome. They took a taxi to the bottom of her street and then walked up to her apartment building. Passing a group of women gathered at by the fountain, Mariella made sure they saw her then flashed a victorious smile.

As Jack and Mariella ascended the stairs to her family's apartment, familiar voices filled the air, cheering and laughing.

"Ciao! Ciao! You are here!" Giada's voice speaking English echoed from the fourth-floor landing, followed by Lia's enthusiastic greeting.

"Benvenuto, Americano!"

"Children, get inside, for goodness' sake, or the entire building will know our business!" Mama cried just as Signora Manetto stepped into the hall, wondering what all the commotion was about.

She peered down the stairwell. "Has Mariella's Jack returned?"

"Yes, he has," Mama said. "But he's had a long trip. Please give them space."

"Oh, of course I will! I only wanted to say hello."

"Ciao, signora," Jack said, arriving on their landing.

Signora Manetto pulled him in for a hug. "Ciao! Ciao, Jack! Ciao! Benvenuto."

"Grazie." He grinned as he followed Mariella into their apartment.

Papa rose from his chair, tucked his newspaper under his arm, and shook Jack's hand. "It took you long enough," he said in a stern voice, then kissed him on each cheek.

Although it was clear Jack didn't understand, he smiled politely. "I'm so happy, uh, felice? I felice to be con ... uh ... Mariella?"

Charmed at his attempt at Italian, Mariella squeezed his hand. "Jack is saying that he is so happy to be with all of us."

"We …eh…" Matteo began, speaking in his schoolboy English. "We no wait for returning, eh. Returning you." He gave Jack a big smile, exposing two missing front teeth.

Jack patted him on the shoulder. "Grazie!"

"Hello, Jack!" Giada waved from the dining table while filling the glasses with water as Lia followed behind placing small plates at each setting. "It is nice to see you again."

"Hello! Gee, your English is good."

"That's because she studies hard," Mariella said, giving Lia a jab.

"I study!" Lia stopped a moment to rattle off some English. "Eh … hot dog, John Wayne, sandwich … eh, Hollywood."

"Bravo!" Jack cheered.

Mama disappeared into the kitchen and returned with a platter of hard cheese cut into triangles, thin, feathery slices of prosciutto, rounds of salami, and baskets of crusty bread for the antipasti.

"Okay, okay!" she said, shooing everyone to the table. "I've roasted a beautiful chicken. Let's sit down. I don't want Jack's first meal to be cold."

When they finished eating, Mariella brought Jack to her room. Mama had insisted they stay at home instead of a hotel so that she could cherish every last minute left with her daughter.

Giada, Lia, and Matteo were happy to camp in the living room, giving her and Jack privacy. But the thought of being alone with him made Mariella anxious. They had only been married for two weeks before he left her, barely enough time to get to know each other in private. And sleeping with him in her childhood bed was certainly not ideal.

Mariella slipped into the bathroom and changed into a silky pink nightgown, the neckline delicately trimmed in lace. It was the same one she'd worn on her wedding night. Looking in the mirror to freshen her makeup, she noticed someone else looking back at her. Someone daring enough to travel across the ocean for love, but still terrified of what was to come. She lined her lips with pale pink lipstick, took a deep breath, then wrapped herself in a white cotton bathrobe.

When Mariella returned to the bedroom, she found Jack, already dressed in striped blue pajamas, waiting patiently on the bed.

"Uh, I wasn't sure which side you like to sleep on, so…" he quickly said.

Mariella took a deep breath, then allowed her robe to slip off her shoulders and fall to the ground.

As Jack took her in, electricity traveled through her, ending in her fingertips. She sat down. He wrapped his arms around her, and for the first time in months, Mariella felt like everything was going to be alright.

"I love you, darling," he whispered, then kissed her on the lips. At first, he was gentle. Then his kisses became hungrier until Mariella pulled back. "What is it?" he asked, catching his breath.

Mariella glanced over at the door.

"Oh." He nodded. "I'm sorry. I forgot where we were for a moment."

"It does not feel right with my family so close," she said.

Jack lay back on his pillow, the disappointment in his voice obvious. "That's okay. We've waited ten months. What's another week?"

Mariella slipped next to him, resting her head on his chest. Once they were under the covers, she felt more protected, as if they were in a different universe. She kissed him softly along his neck, across his cheek, then on his lips. Every part of her ached as she melted into him. They quietly made love, their limbs intertwined, moving in synch proving they were meant for each other.

Afterward, Jack fell asleep, but with so much to think about, Mariella was restless. She inched her way out from under the covers, carefully stepped over Jack, and opened the large casement window above her bed; the same window through which she'd spent countless hours searching for Jack's stars when she thought she'd lost him for good.

As she crawled onto the roof, gathering clouds made her hesitate a moment, but she continued. A chilling tune floated up to her from the alleyway below, echoing between the buildings. It was the song "Bella Ciao," an anthem of the anti-fascist resistance. Mariella glanced down to see an elderly man in a tan hat weaving back and forth between the buildings.

"Another one," she mumbled. In the past ten years, most had moved on from the war, but some couldn't escape the horrors they'd experienced.

She slid over to her familiar spot, allowing her mind to become consumed with visions of her sister clinging to her arm as her legs dangled off the roof, her face frozen, eyes filled with fear. The memory of the night they discovered Elisa's illness couldn't be erased. She lay back on the cool ceramic tile, her gaze drawn across a series of rooftops and chimneys, and considered the journey she was about to take. After all the American movies she had seen, a two-week voyage across the ocean thrilled her. She had never been at sea, let alone on a ship of such a high standard. And traveling in first class, the tickets part of a wedding gift from Jack's parents, was intimidating. But the real apprehension crept in as she pondered what would come after the journey.

"Penny for your thoughts," Jack whispered, popping his head out the window.

Mariella blushed. *Would I disappoint him if he bought my*

thoughts for a penny? she wondered. "That is okay, I can come in."

A mischievous smile formed on Jack's face, making him look like a child. "No, no. You stay there. I'll come to you!" He climbed out one leg at a time, peered over the edge, and quickly gripped the tile. "Oh boy. I didn't know we were so high. I guess I forgot to tell you I'm a little afraid of heights."

Watching Jack try to focus on the horizon made Mariella laugh. It was nice to have something she could do better. "It is not so high, amore. You will be fine."

"Oh, really? Will you catch me if I fall?"

Mariella's smile vanished. "No, I cannot catch you. We should go in."

"Sweetheart, that was a joke," Jack said, searching her face. "Is something wrong?"

It suddenly dawned on Mariella that she hadn't told Jack everything about her sister's illness. "Elisa and me," she began carefully picking her words, "we ... were here when she have a seizure. That is how we find out she was sick."

"She had a seizure? Up here? Did she fall?"

Mariella shook her head. "It was un miracolo I catch her," she said, picking at a roof tile.

"It certainly was a miracle." Jack scooted closer to Mariella. "I'm sorry. I remember how close you two were."

Tears dotted Mariella's cheeks. Jack wiped her face with his sleeve then gazed up at the sky. "I bet she's right up there in heaven, looking after you."

"I know this," Mariella said, forcing a smile. "But that is not the only reason I cry. It is everything. Leaving here where her memory lives. Like here, or in the bedroom, or the dining table, or Villa Borghese, and ... all of the places."

"I understand. I'll never forget how I felt before shipping out to Africa. All the long walks I took on the boardwalk and around town, past my school and church, knowing that I may never come home. But," Jack leaned in and placed his hand over her heart, "Elisa will always be here, with you."

Mariella nodded, but wasn't convinced her sister wouldn't become a distant memory without the surrounding reminders.

"Sweetheart, you're allowed to feel sad. You're leaving everything for me. I wish I could do the same for you."

"It is no problem. I want to come with you. I want a life in America. With you, amore."

A loud crack of thunder made them jump.

"I guess that's our cue," Jack joked, lifting the mood between them.

Or it is God saying, "Go be in America!" Mariella thought as she followed Jack through the window. After surviving the war, then the death of her sister and the loss of her dear friend Helena, living in a new country should be easy.

Back in bed, they curled up into each other.

"Darling, I promise to do everything possible to make life in America good for you," Jack whispered before falling asleep with his lips against her ear.

Chapter Three

The rest of the week was spent saying goodbye. Signora Manetto had the whole family over to her tiny apartment for dinner one evening. Since she only had a small dinette with space for two, everyone carried a chair over. Papa and Matteo also brought their kitchen table, carefully positioning it on an angle so there was room for everyone. Signora made a beautiful lasagna and sat next to Jack. Once he finished his first serving, she offered another, then tried to serve him a third.

Mama stepped in. "Sylvia, he's had enough,"

"What are you talking about? He's a growing boy!" Signora Manetto insisted, turning to Jack. "Go on. It's a small piece!"

"He can't understand a word you are saying."

"Yes, he can." Signora Manetto pointed to the plate of food, then drew her arms up to show her muscles. "You'll need your energy for the trip home."

Mama threw her hands in the air. "What do you think? He's rowing the boat all the way back to America?"

The interaction brought a smile to Mariella's face but she couldn't fight the sadness of knowing it would probably be years before she would sit at her dear neighbor's table again.

Mariella also played tour guide during those final days, bringing Jack to all his favorite spots, and saying goodbye to hers. They threw lire coins over their shoulders and into Fontana di Trevi. Instead of a happy life with Jack, she thought of her family. She had never lived away from them and except for her wedding night, never slept somewhere other than home. And being the oldest, her parents had always depended on her to help out. Worry about how they would fare without her had been at the forefront of her mind, so she threw her coin for them. *I wish Mama, Papa, Giada, Lia, and Matteo will be okay when I'm gone.*

On their last day in Rome, she and Jack went to the bank of the Tiber River for a picnic of focaccia, salami, and provolone. Then, they took a stroll past Piazza di Spagna, Piazza del Popolo, and over to the Vatican, where Mariella lit votive candles for those who had died and those who were lost. Despite regular calls to the Office of Missing People, there was no more information about her friend Helena. All they knew after ten years was that the soldiers had taken her away in the back of a truck.

While the atmosphere during the week had felt more like a

celebration, their final day in Rome became heavy and mournful. After dinner with her family, Mariella needed air.

"Are you okay?" Jack asked as they walked out onto the street. The night air was cool and clear, with a canopy of shimmery stars hanging above.

"Si, I just want to be alone … with you."

She and Jack walked through Piazza Navona, her arm woven through his like the first time she brought him there. He had been so taken with the drama and beauty of her city, it wasn't surprising that she fell in love with him.

Jack's face lit up when they passed the majestic fountains. "It's exactly the way I remember," he said.

They took one last look at the gods and mermen that occupied the three fountains, cutting the piazza down the middle, then headed for the Colosseum. It was something she had put off all week, but time was running out. On their way, they stopped at a florist and bought a tiny bouquet of roses.

"It never gets old, does it?" Jack said when they entered.

The full moon's glow bathed the arena in a dusky light, illuminating everything. But when they went underground, a single candle Mariella had slipped into her purse before leaving was the only way to see. Mosquitoes flew haphazardly in and out of the stream of light. At that time of night, there was no one around.

Mariella took Jack's hand when they stepped into the room with the names. Each one carved into the walls, they came alive in the flickering light. But this time, there were so many more. *Miriam, Eva, Leora, Asher, Caleb, Aviva, Danielle, Marco, Eli, Davide, Ezra, Mendel, Ariana,* and so on until the whole wall screamed the names of the lost.

"Where did they all come from?" Jack asked, touching the name Francesco.

Mariella sighed. "I suppose everyone had the same idea. They want to keep their memory living."

She ran her finger along the wall until she found Helena, then plucked three roses from the bouquet and laid them on the ground at the foot of the wall.

Her sister's name was harder to look at.

"There it is," Mariella said, holding the candle against a section of the stone wall. But she found that seeing Elisa's name scrawled out along with the others was comforting, in a way. "I am happy she is not alone."

She traced it one last time, allowing herself to remember the night she'd carved it into the stone. At that point, Mariella was the only one who knew Elisa was gone. The loss only became real when her parents found out a few hours later.

"At least she die from the cancer," Mariella said. "Not like the others. They die from the men who hated them."

Jack nodded, but didn't seem to have any words.

Mariella laid the rest of the roses underneath, whispered a prayer, then took a deep breath. She turned to Jack and smiled. "I am ready now."

As they made their way home, she began to count her lasts: the last time walking up their cobblestone street, the last time telling her parents and siblings goodnight, the last time curling up in her featherbed. *I'll be back to visit,* Mariella reminded herself.

In the quiet early morning hours, Mariella was unable to sleep and realized she had one last goodbye to make. Tiptoeing past Lia, Matteo, and Giada sleeping in the living room, she went to the mantel where the photo of her late baby brother sat. Looking at his lifeless body laid to rest in a coffin, her days with him seemed like a lifetime ago, but the hole it had bored in her heart still felt new. She kissed his picture and whispered that no matter where she went, just like with her sister, she would hold on to his memory forever. After setting the frame back on the mantel, just the way Mama liked it, she slipped back into bed. Everything would change in a matter of hours and while she was nervous about the unknown, another part of her couldn't wait.

Chapter Four

A few hours later, Mariella and Jack left with her parents for the train station. A stillness blanketed the streets, making her feel like she had already said goodbye to her dear city. They boarded a train for Naples at 6 a.m. On the two-hour trip, Mama reassured Mariella that everything would be fine at home, speaking in whispers so as not to disrupt the quiet train car. She told Mariella about how wonderful her life in America was going to be, reiterated all the advice about keeping a happy marriage with humor, love, and understanding she had given on her wedding night, and reminded her to write as often as possible. Mariella took it in and nodded and smiled where she could. Yet, when the train churned to a stop and the massive ship sitting in the port came into view, ready to take her away from everything she knew, Mariella clung to her mother.

"Here's my suitcase. And that one is ours too."

Jack gestured toward Mariella's large, brown trunk for the ship's porter to load. It held everything she owned: cherished photos of the family she was leaving and the ones that died too soon, a large blanket crocheted with lamb's wool lovingly crafted by Signora Manetto, silver candlesticks from the Rossi family, and a silver tea set her father's boss gave them. All gifts from their wedding, plus a few more gifts given to Mariella to remind her of home.

The trunk also contained several exquisitely tailored suits and a few gowns made for her by Mama, who insisted her daughter present herself like royalty while traveling first class. Mariella had helped Mama choose the fabrics—a shiny, pale blue raw silk for a ball gown to wear at the wedding dinner Jack's parents were hosting, another gown in ivory lace for a much more demure look, then a few fancy suits made of linen and one in wool. Each outfit had been carefully paired with hats and gloves, something Mama knew was popular in the States after reading various magazines. Mariella was touched that her mother had given her something she'd never been able to afford for herself.

"How can I repay you, Mama?" she asked, choking on her tears as she said goodbye.

Mama didn't respond, but her silence was enough for Mariella to feel loved.

Papa's clenched jaw made it obvious he was biting the sides of his mouth to keep from crying. He turned to Jack and firmly shook his hand, then pulled Mariella against his chest and enveloped her in his arms. As he whispered in her ear about how proud he was of her, she could feel his body tremble.

"I love you too, Papa," she said, burying her face in his neck. Once he let go, he avoided her gaze.

Jack led Mariella up the gangplank and onto the ship. She stopped at the top to search for her parents down below. They waved up to her, looking lost and small surrounded by the throngs of people in the port. She blew kisses down until they turned to leave. Her chest ached as she watched Papa lead Mama through the crowd until they were out of sight.

Once they arrived in their suite, Mariella collapsed into sobs. Jack said nothing; just let her feel what she was feeling. She cried until she fell asleep.

Waking a few hours later to the gentle rhythm of waves rolling underneath was an odd sensation. Mariella looked out of the porthole window, but the sun had already set. Only a single beam of moonlight hitting the dark waters was visible.

"I've got us booked at the nine o'clock seating, okay, sweetheart?" Jack asked.

"Si, amore," she said, still groggy from sleep. "Yes, of course."

"Come with me, I drew a bath for you."

Jack led her to the Carrera marble bathroom with a large porcelain tub in the center. Translucent bubbles floated atop the water's surface while a short, stout candle in the corner filled the room with the soothing scent of lavender. Jack gave Mariella time alone to get ready. She eased into the hot, soapy water, submerging one foot at a time. Memories of her grandmother's old claw-foot tub on the farm came to mind. Mariella had loved to fill it with cold water during the muggy summer days, then jump in with her siblings, splashing everywhere until Nonno would come in from the stables and chase them out.

A pang of longing coursed through her. Unable to get her parents' heartbroken faces out of her mind, Mariella slipped under the water to wash away the pain.

"Va va va voom!" Jack said as Mariella stepped into the sitting room.

She wore a sheath gown made of a luxurious, dusky-rose-colored satin. It accentuated her curves, and Mariella knew she looked expensive. "You look handsome too," she said, admiring how dashing a figure he cut in a black tuxedo.

Jack pulled her into his arms and dipped her back. "Are you sure you're hungry? I know some other things we could occupy our time with," he said, nuzzling his face against her neck.

Mariella blushed. "Amore, I think we cannot be late to dinner."

The first-class restaurant was stunning. In the center of the room was a line of glass cylinders giving off soft light—intimate round tables nestled beneath oval windows offered captivating views of the horizon. Plush club chairs made everything feel chic. A tuxedoed host accompanied Jack and Mariella to their table.

"Madam," he said, pulling out Mariella's chair. Once she sat, he took a linen napkin from the table and shook it with flair before delicately laying it in her lap. "Your waiter will be with you momentarily."

Jack looked over at her and laughed. "I know, it's very fancy."

"I am not sure if I will ever get used to this," Mariella confessed.

"Well, darling, get used to it. You deserve all this and more. Now, if you don't mind, I need to go to the restroom."

After Jack left, Mariella surveyed the room. The other tables were filled with married couples and a few families enjoying dinner. An attractive woman about Mariella's age sitting across from a much older man caught her eye. With dark brown hair, dark eyes, and a simple yet elegant gown, she had a familiar look. Compared to the other women with their light complexions and sparkly jewels adorning their necks, this woman stood out.

Italiano! Mariella thought. The woman glanced her way and Mariella quickly offered a knowing smile, but it was met with a scowl.

"She may not want to acknowledge you," the waiter said, speaking in Italian.

Mariella jumped, putting a hand to her heart. "You scared me."

"I'm sorry, signora, I just saw you looking at that woman." Tall with curly black hair and a sharp Roman nose, the waiter gave her a sympathetic look.

"But isn't she from Italy?"

He nodded. "From the south. I could hear her accent when I saw her saying goodbye to her parents on the dock. But during lunch, when I tried to take her order in Italian, she refused to respond."

Mariella wrinkled her brow. "I don't understand. I know I won't be speaking my language when I arrive in America so speaking Italian to you is a relief."

"Yes, but some women are eager to wash the 'Italian' off of them as quickly as possible."

The waiter's demeanor suddenly changed as his supervisor passed by. He stood erect and pulled on the bottom of his jacket to straighten it out, then presented Mariella with the menu, an intricate illustration of red bougainvillea decorating the cover.

"Our selections for this evening, madam," he said in English.

"Thank you." As Mariella placed the menu on the table, she noticed her place setting. On either side of her plate, there was an array of spoons and forks, some regular size and others tiny. She felt a twinge of anxiety.

The waiter understood her concern. Once the supervisor disappeared into the kitchen, he spoke Italian again.

"You start on the outside and work your way in, you see?" he said, then explained which utensil was used for what.

"Grazie." Mariella surveyed the room, hoping no one could understand their conversation.

"Don't worry, signora. Many women are leaving Italy for a better life."

"I see." She wondered if maybe it was a mistake to speak Italian. Maybe it would be better for her to do the same and try to erase all of the Italian in her. But hiding it would be like hiding every part of Mariella—or worse, making her family disappear.

Jack returned to the table, prompting the waiter to switch to English again. "Here is your menu, sir. Chef Mario Bougattini will be cooking for you tonight. Can I offer you an aperitivo?"

"Yes, sir. Two coupes of Champagne would be perfect."

"But of course." The waiter disappeared briefly, then returned with two crystal glasses filled to the brim.

Jack raised his glass, fixing his gaze on Mariella. "I want to make a toast to the most wonderful woman in the world. Your sacrifice means everything to me."

Mariella blushed. "Amore, I would not do it for anyone but you."

After dinner, they took a stroll along the first-class deck. Jack wrapped his arms around her and pointed out to sea.

"See that?" he asked.

Mariella searched the darkness but didn't see anything. "What?"

"On the other side of this ocean is a wonderful place called Asbury Park. Aw, honey, you're gonna love it." He leaned his chin on her shoulder and grinned. "The boardwalk, the salty air, the Palace amusements—all of it."

Although Mariella wanted to share in his excitement, her nagging worries continued to taunt her. *What if I don't like it? What if nobody likes me? What if I can't understand anyone? Or I misunderstand and look like a fool? Or make someone mad?* Everything would be different, and—apart from the things Jack talked about, like the beach and the restaurant—it was hard to imagine a life there.

"Do you see our stars?" Jack asked, pulling Mariella from her spiraling thoughts.

She gazed up at the clear night sky. The Big Dipper shone brighter than all the other stars, or at least it did to her. "Your grande spoon!"

Jack laughed. "I guess you're right. It is a big spoon!"

"And you are my big spoon," she said, laying her head on his shoulder. When she looked back out over the vast expanse of the shadowy sea, the uncertainty of her future loomed in the darkness, but in his arms, Mariella was hopeful.

Chapter Five

Jack and Mariella spent the following week on the sun deck talking about the future while lounging on teak recliners. He briefed her on the people in his family. His father was stern but kindhearted. His mother was the opposite. She liked to joke a lot but also had a bite to her humor.

"She means well," Jack quickly followed up.

"And your brothers?"

"Carl is a lot like my pop. I swear he carries the weight of the world on his shoulders."

"And your brother Will? You said he is, eh, funny man, no?"

Jack let out a somber laugh, then told her about the tragic events that unfolded while he was home. "His wife, Jean, remember I told you she was pregnant? Well, she went into labor after four months. There was no way to save the baby. Will understood these things happen, but she couldn't get over it. A month later, she left."

"I do not understand. Where did she go?"

"That was the weird part. He thought she'd just gone home to Maryland to be with her parents but they hadn't heard from her. He was going crazy trying to figure out what happened to her."

"And what happened?"

"She ran off with a cousin. Apparently, they'd been carrying on for the past year and rumor has it the baby was his too. Poor Willie, he had no idea. Thank god she's in California and he doesn't have to see her around town."

Sitting back in her chair, Mariella shook her head in disbelief. "Is he okay?"

"The funny thing is," Jack said, leaning in, "I actually think he's happier."

"Good." Mariella walked her fingers up Jack's arm. "And you are the sweet, handsome one."

He grinned. "Why yes, yes I am!"

Just then, the ship's loudspeaker crackled to life.

"Attention, please, attention. The horses are at the starting line ready to go, go, go! Come join the fun and win valuable prizes at the races! If you want to participate, please make your way over to the lido deck. All bets are in American currency. Thank you."

"Horses?" Mariella said, eyes darting around the ship. "Here? That cannot be!"

"Oh, but there are, Mrs. Valentino. C'mon, let's go check it out."

Jack waited for Mariella to slip on her tan mules, then led her upstairs.

When they arrived at the activities section, Mariella was perplexed. "I do not see these horses."

"Sure you do."

Jack pointed over to the far corner, which had been roped off. There stood six brightly painted wooden horses in different colors, each with a number inscribed on the side. They walked over to get a closer look at the contenders.

"I think I like number five. He looks sturdy!" Jack nodded toward one with a deep red body and cartoon face.

Mariella was quiet while she inspected each horse. "Hmmm, I like three. Viola, it is the color of kings."

"Purple it is! We'll put money on both three and five. Let's see who wins!" Jack strode to the betting station and dropped twenty-five cents on each number.

"Now what happens?" Mariella asked as they took a seat with the rest of the spectators along a very short racetrack. "This does not make sense. How they can run?"

"The horses, see, they come alive and scoot across the track in no time!" Jack stood, mimicking a jockey racing on a horse.

Mariella gave him a doubtful look. "Amore..."

Addressing the crowd through a microphone, a middle-aged man in khaki pants and a white-collared shirt took center stage. "Good afternoon, ladies and gentlemen, and welcome to the races! My name is Gene, and I'll be your MC. We have six terrific thoroughbreds racing this afternoon. In the first position, we have Henrietta Hudson. Second is a wonderful horse named Pal Joey. Number three is Royal Roy."

"Bravo!" Mariella cheered, clapping her hands. "That is my horse!"

"In fourth, we have Martini Rossi. Number five is Sweet Caroline, and in our sixth position is Grey Gardens."

Jack stroked his chin. "Oh boy, my number five might be more delicate than sturdy."

"She is bella, too," Mariella teased.

A younger man she recognized as their porter stepped forward and blew into a horn to start the race. But none of the horses moved. Instead, the MC spun a gold cage and pulled out numbers. Then, a third attendant picked up the horse whose number matched and moved it ahead one step. The MC kept the crowd cheering them on with his colorful commentary.

"Number three, that's Royal Roy pulling ahead. What's this? Number five—Sweet, Sweet Caroline—has joined the race.

But our Royal Roy won't have it! Number three ahead again. This one's athletic! And, of course, why not? He's royalty."

"Go, Roy, go!" Mariella cheered.

After a few more spins, number two had pulled ahead.

"Okay, ladies and gentlemen. We have a real humdinger on our hands. No one could have predicted such a tight race as Royal Roy and Pal Joey are neck and neck. The others aren't even close. If either one wins this spin, they win the whole kit and kaboodle! And away we go!"

The crowd watched in anticipation as the MC cranked the gold cage a few times, then made a grand gesture as he pulled out the final number, keeping it hidden in the palm of his hand. He strolled over to Pal Joey, but then at the last moment turned toward Royal Roy and, with a flourish, moved him across the finish line. Everyone cheered.

"Ho vinto! I won!" Mariella waved her ticket in the air. "I never won in my life."

"Well, whaddya know? Congratulations!" Jack said, giving her a big hug.

"All of my winners, please step forward," the MC announced. "Don't be shy. I won't bite!"

A tall, older woman with a flowery hat stepped forward, followed by a lanky boy with bright orange hair and freckles on either side of his face. Mariella quickly joined them.

"Wouldja look at all these lucky people? What a fine-looking group. Let's see, who do we have here?" The MC shoved the microphone in front of the older woman's face.

"Hello, I am Mrs. Jeffcott of the Albany Jeffcotts," she said proudly.

"Well, hello, Mrs. Jeffcott. What made you bet on our boy Roy?"

The woman puffed out her chest. "Our family crest, the Jeffcott family crest, has purple throughout it."

"Ah, I see. A connection to your family certainly was a lucky one. Here's your prize." The MC handed her a bottle of Scotch, shook her hand, then shifted his attention to the boy. "And who is this little man?"

"I ain't a man," the boy said, kicking the ground. "I'm just a kid."

The MC chuckled, stooping down to the boy's level. "Sure you are. So, what's your name, kiddo?"

"Marvin."

"Hiya, Marvin. I suppose purple is your favorite color?"

"Nah." The boy shoved his hands deep into his pockets.

"No? I see. Maybe you're a fan of grape jelly?"

"Nah."

"Okay, well, why don't you tell me why you chose ole Roy."

"My ma told me to pick it."

"Well then, give this to your parents. Maybe they can hold onto it until you're grown." The MC handed the boy a bottle of cabernet. "That is if they don't drink it first!"

A round of laughter rang out as the boy wandered off the stage, looking dejected.

"And last but not least. Who is this beautiful woman?" The MC pointed the microphone in Mariella's direction.

"Mrs. Valentino. Eh. Of Asbury Park." She glanced over at Jack, who beamed back at her with pride.

"Mrs. Valentino of Asbury Park! And who do you belong to? Wait a minute," he said, making his way over to Jack. "I see you smiling at this beauty. How did you manage to find such a stunning souvenir? All I brought back from Italy was a lousy ceramic bowl and a statue of the Trevi Fountain. I would like one of these, please! Yowza!"

Jack let out a hearty chuckle. "Sorry, she's not up for grabs."

"Ha! Can't say I blame you, sir." The MC presented Jack with a bottle of Dom Pérignon. "Here you are, sir. Celebrate your wife's win with this!"

Everyone applauded except for Mariella, who quietly rejoined Jack in the audience.

As they strolled back to their cabin, the MC's words whirled around in her head.

"What's got you so quiet, darling?" Jack asked, sensing her

worry. He slipped his arm around her and pulled her close.

"I am not understanding."

Jack searched her eyes. "What don't you understand?"

"Why did that man say I am, eh, souvenir? As if you buy me. I did not like that."

"Aw, gee." He slumped against the railing, drew out a cigarette, and lit it. "It's all in good fun. He's just jealous that I've got the most beautiful woman on my arm, and he could never find someone like you."

"But I am no prize from a contest. I am a person."

"Of course you are." Jack gave her his lit cigarette, then lit one for himself.

Mariella looked out at the endless stretch of sea. "Where you think we are now?"

Jack shrugged. "I'm not sure. But we should probably go back to our cabin and get ready. We have that dinner tonight."

"What dinner?"

"Did I forget to mention it? We've been invited to a very special dinner with Mr. Evans. He's a friend of my pop's but also a very important businessman. I guess he got wind that we were on the ship and invited us to dinner with some other guests."

"Other guests?"

"Yes," Jack said, taking a drag of his cigarette. "It seems like he knows a lot of people on this ship. It should be fun and I bet you'll be the most beautiful woman there."

Mariella tried to mask her doubt with a smile. Before they boarded the ship, Jack had been in her world. A world she was confident navigating, a language she knew. Now, Mariella was in uncharted waters, losing any familiarity with each mile they drifted further away from home and closer to America.

Chapter Six

Mariella emerged from the bedroom dressed in a velvet number with a sweetheart neckline and a full skirt of black toile. With her hair parted deep to one side and cascading curls on the other, she looked stunning. Jack proudly escorted her to the first class ballroom.

"Bella," Mariella said as she took in a painted mural depicting the feast of Neptune that spanned the room's length.

"Good evening, Mr. and Mrs. Valentino. It's nice to see you tonight," the host greeted them warmly. Despite getting to know Jack and Mariella after several days at sea, he never referred to them by their first names. "I understand you are both guests of Mr. Evans tonight. Right this way."

He escorted them to a large table, elegant bouquets of birds of paradise displayed in the center. Noticing they were the last to be seated, Mariella's face grew hot.

Mr. Evans stood up, offering a slight bow. The man was striking with gray streaks in his slicked-back chestnut-brown hair, piercing blue eyes, and fanciful mustache. "It's a pleasure to make your acquaintance, Mrs. Valentino."

"The pleasure is mine." Mariella spoke slowly, hoping to hide her accent.

Jack quickly stepped in and shook the man's hand. "Nice to meet you. I'm Domenico's son Jack, and, of course, her better half."

"Nice to meet you, Jack. I was happy to see your name on the passenger list. How is your father?"

"Oh, you know my pop, same as always. Just focused on keeping the business booming."

"He always has been," Mr. Evans said with a grin, then turned to Mariella and pulled out the chair next to him. "Please, sit next to me. Jack, you can sit on her other side."

They both sat while he began the introductions. "I'd like you to meet Mr. and Mrs. Klein, they own Klein's Furniture in Manhattan."

"How do you do." An older woman wearing a fox fur around her shoulders greeted them with a smile as the gray-haired man next to her stood formally and bowed.

"And next to you, Jack, are our newlyweds, Mr. and Mrs. Sanderson."

Mr. Sanderson, a young man about their age, shook Jack's hand. "Hi there! I'm Joseph Sanderson. My wife, Julia, and I are just returning from our honeymoon. Actually, it was a trip to see her family."

"Sei Italiano?" Mariella asked, a hopeful smile brightening her face. With olive skin and dark eyes, Julia could have been a relative.

Julia let out a laugh. "Oh no, I can't speak a lick. Thank heavens my grandmother speaks English or my husband and I would have been lost over there!"

"Ah, too bad," Jack said, giving Mariella's hand a squeeze.

"Well, I've seen an awful lot of Italy during this past month," Mr. Evans said.

Honored to be seated next to such an important businessman, Mariella tried her hardest to impress; listening intently to his stories, smiling and nodding when appropriate, and giving a hearty laugh at his jokes, even when she didn't understand what he meant.

Their host regaled the table with stories of his travels through Italy. Most of the places Mariella hadn't ever been to. When the Oysters Rockefeller were served, topped with bacon, onions, spinach, and breadcrumbs, he spoke of eating the freshest seafood in Sardinia. Although Mariella didn't like the look of their rough shells, a smile never left her face as she choked the oysters down in one bite. Then came the Oxtail Consommé and his story of touring a vineyard in Montepulciano.

"This right here is the king of wines," he said, giving Mariella a wink while swirling the deep red liquid in his glass. "And I'll let you in on a secret: there are five cases coming home with me stored in the bowels of this ship."

Afterwards was a course of lobster ravioli in a simple but elegant tomato sauce. For this, he got personal, asking Mariella if she would be making her husband Italian delicacies while living in the United States.

"Of course." Mariella turned to Jack and realized she'd never had a chance to cook for him. "I am certain you will like my food."

"What's that?" Jack asked, adjusting his hearing aid.

Mr. Evans leaned in. "I was just asking your wife here if she'll be cooking Italian for you in the States."

"I certainly hope so. If my wife cooks anything like her mother, boy, I sure will."

"Lucky man!"

Next came the veal loin with a side dish of au gratin potatoes accompanied by his story of a visit to an olive farm with the most delicious oil he had ever tasted. Mr. Evans bragged about the bargain he made with the old man who produced it.

"I've bought seven barrels of it. Made a fantastic deal, too.

Don't think the man knew its value," he said under his breath. Hearing him boast about taking advantage of someone who had worked so hard to create a superior product made Mariella's smile stiffen.

At the end of the meal, when a lemon pudding soufflé was served, he bragged about the Maiolica tiles he'd found in Deruta that would decorate the large pizza oven under construction in his newest Manhattan restaurant.

By the time they said their goodbyes and returned to their suite, Mariella was exhausted from being so agreeable, but Jack was unusually quiet.

"Is something wrong?"

"Ah, it's nothing. It's just that I didn't like seeing another man give you so much attention."

"What?" She was proud of her performance at dinner. She assumed he would be happy too.

Jack sat down on the bed and loosened his tie. "Well, in my book, an honorable man doesn't spend the whole dinner talking to another man's wife. I think that guy could have been more respectful. I mean, you're mine, not his."

For the first time since she'd met him, Mariella saw Jack in a different light. She had never known his jealous side. "Amore. He talk to everyone."

"But he was looking at you when he spoke."

"He knows I am your wife. I think he is just being nice."

"Was he 'just being nice' by seating you right next to him? No, that man only had eyes for you."

Mariella sat at the vanity, pulled off her heels, and rubbed her feet. "And why is that wrong? At least he is not clapping to you for bringing home uno regalo Italiano."

"You mean souvenir?"

"I know what I mean!" Mariella snapped back.

"Oh, come on. That's not the same."

"No? One person is nice, make me feel good when everything is strange. The other make me look stupido." Mariella turned around and Jack unzipped her dress. She slipped out of it, then hung it in the closet. "I do not want to talk anymore."

"Aw, sweetheart, I'm sorry." Jack followed her to the bathroom, but she locked him out. "I guess I need to put myself in your shoes," he said, speaking through the door.

"You do."

"I know. But I'm not used to other men looking at you."

"Many men have interest in me back home."

"Oh, honey, I know that." Jack leaned against the wall. "But don't you see? In America, you'll be new and exotic."

Mariella cracked the door open. "That do not mean I run away with the first man who like me." Her face softened despite the tears in her eyes. "I feel so, eh, how do you say..."

"Out of place?"

"Yes, that. It will be worse in Asbury Park. Patienza, amore."

Jack wiped a tear from her cheek. "I'll try not to be such a heel next time."

"No," Mariella said, searching his face for understanding. "You need patience," she repeated in English.

During the final week of their voyage, the weather turned. The sea became choppy and rain fell sideways, pelting their porthole window. Before long, seasickness got the best of Mariella, confining her to their room. With her head pounding and bile rising, she had never felt worse. Although queasy the first day, Jack was used to traveling by sea and recovered quickly. He offered to stay with her, but Mariella didn't want him to see her in such a state. She sent him away even when he attempted to bring her soup and crackers.

By the time they reached Nova Scotia, the seas had calmed, and sunny skies brought Mariella out on deck again. She stretched lazily on a lounge chair, hoping to get some color back to her face before docking in New York City.

"Here you are, darling." Jack stood over her, holding a small espresso cup. "It's three o'clock. I know you like to have your afternoon coffee."

"That is kind, but it still may not be good for my stomach."

"That's quite alright. I can always get another when you're ready for one." He sat next to her and sipped the coffee. "I'm so happy you're feeling better. I would hate for you to miss it."

"Miss what?"

Jack turned to her, his face filled with anticipation. "The skyline."

"Skyline? What is this?"

"The skyline," he repeated. "The New York City skyline! We'll see it as soon as we pull into the harbor. Aw, it's terrific! Buildings and people and yellow cabs everywhere!"

"What time we arrive tomorrow?"

Jack nodded. "First thing in the morning. I think we pull into port at eight a.m."

Knowing that she would finally meet her in-laws, a surge of excitement quickly followed by a hint of uncertainty coursed through Mariella. The seasickness had caused her to lose a lot of weight and with it she'd lost her curves. When she dreamt of her arrival in America, she'd hoped to look put together, not like a scrawny mess.

"Should I wear my blue suit? The one Mama sewed, with the hat? Or maybe I wear a dress?" Mariella asked, nervously chewing on her thumbnail.

"Sweetheart, you could wear a potato sack and still look beautiful."

"Jack, I am serious. I want to make a good impression."

"Hmmm." Jack tapped his chin, playfully contemplating her question. "What to do, what to do."

Removing her oversized sunglasses, Mariella glowered at him. "Amore, please."

"Okay, okay. I think the suit would be the best. But remember, my family isn't very fancy."

Mariella didn't care how fancy her new in-laws were. She would be the one on display, not anyone else.

The following morning, she woke well before dawn, quickly turning off her alarm clock to avoid waking Jack. She went into the bathroom, where she had laid her beauty supplies out on the counter the night before. A plastic cap kept her hair dry as she showered, the steaming hot water melting away any tension in her body. Afterward, she carefully applied makeup and arranged her hair into soft curls with a generous amount of setting spray. Once happy with how it looked, she pulled on pantyhose and slipped into a skirt, a shirt, and a jacket before pinning her hat into place so it would stay perfectly positioned. By the time she emerged, the sun was starting to peek over the horizon, but Jack remained in a deep sleep.

She sat on the couch and thought about how she would soon leave their stateroom, the only place she'd lived away from her parents. During the past two weeks, she had become comfortable in her own skin. But now, another reality was settling in. One that had no familiarity, nothing except the dozens of American movies she'd studied to help prepare. Mariella smoothed her skirt, running her fingertips along the hem Mama sewed not more than a month before. Memories of her mother, sitting hunched over, a few pins held between her lips as she guided the material through the machine powered by her pedaling feet, made Mariella's heart feel like an orange being squeezed for juice. She would give anything to sit next to Mama in their home that now felt so far away. But then she wouldn't have Jack.

Mariella glanced out the window. Now, the sun was higher, casting a ray of golden light into the room, and her nerves began to prick at her. She paced the room to relieve herself from excess energy. It was only a matter of time before her world would change all over again.

An hour later, Jack woke up to find Mariella on the couch sitting completely still with her purse in her lap.

"What are you doing?"

She gave him a sheepish look. "Making sure not to get my clothing wrinkled."

"Oh, sweetheart, they're going to love you," Jack said. He tried to kiss her, but she quickly moved away.

"Please, amore, I spend much time to look perfect. I do not want to ruin my makeup."

Jack sighed. "Okay."

After showering and getting dressed, he called the porter to retrieve the luggage he had insisted on packing the evening before so they could get a premium spot on deck. They arrived just as the ship pulled into Hudson Bay.

The sky was gray, and thick fog hugged the coast, making the air humid and sticky. But when the Statue of Liberty came into view through the mist, the crowd gasped.

"There it is!"

"Isn't it the most beautiful thing you've ever seen?"

"I'm just so happy to be back in the good ole US!"

"Viva America!"

While everyone around her cheered, Mariella was quiet. She gazed up at the towering statue. It meant more to her than a new beginning. Without the strength of America, her beloved city would never have been liberated. She shuddered at the thought of what would have happened if they weren't saved. Her family may have all died of starvation, or worse, they could have lived the rest of their lives as secondhand citizens at the hands of the Germans. She had seen what those men were capable of. As the ship glided by, the statue's shadow enveloped Mariella, making her feel like anything was possible. America wasn't just the place she would live with the love of her life. It was the land of dreams. A place for everyone no matter where you came from.

"What do ya think?" Jack whispered in Mariella's ear.

"I have never seen anything so beautiful in my life."

"Oh yeah? Well, look over there!"

Jack pointed to the island of Manhattan; buildings impossibly stacked on top of one another stretched into the distance. Another large ship passed them, blowing its horn. Smaller boats and a few ferries dotted the bay. Along the island, cars and yellow cabs drove in clusters. And crisscrossing the river were bridges, each one more impressive than the next. It was exhilarating.

"Oh, Jack. Pinch me. I cannot believe I am here."

Chapter Seven

While waiting for the ship to dock, Mariella checked her makeup and applied more lipstick, then freshened it again as the gangplank was lowered.

"Don't be so nervous," Jack said. "I told you they're going to love you just as much as I do."

I hope so, she thought.

He began waving wildly at a group of people in the crowd below them.

"Ma! Pop!" he shouted, then grabbed Mariella's hand, hurried down the gangplank, and weaved through the crowd until he reached his mother. She was squat and plump with short curly hair.

Napolitano, Mariella thought.

Jack's father stood tall with an air of authority. "Good to

see you, Giacomo," Pop said, using Jack's Italian name instead of his American nickname. He waited patiently for his son to make the introductions.

"It's good to see ya, Pop!" Jack shook his father's hand, then turned to Mariella. "This is my father. Pop, this is Mariella."

"Signora," Jack's father said, formally extending a hand. "Benvenuta."

"Piacere di conoscerti," Mariella answered almost in a whisper.

Although his expression was stern, his kind eyes promised a warmer side. Before she could react, he'd drawn her into his arms and kissed both cheeks. "Welcome. Welcome."

"And this is my dear ole ma." Jack grinned widely at his mother. "Ma, this is your new daughter-in-law."

Mariella nervously touched the back of her neck as Jack's mother eyed her, a stiff smile on her face.

"Hello," Ma said without making a move.

Mariella hesitated, then kissed her on the cheek. "It is very nice to meet you."

The porter rolled a cart over, holding their belongings. Jack and his father quickly gathered the suitcases and Mariella's trunk before heading for their car.

"Boy, you don't travel light!" Ma exclaimed with a hearty laugh. "I thought you were poor!"

"Eh, well, I—" Mariella stuttered. "My mama, she make dresses for me and I have my matrimony dress and pictures of my familia, and well, it is my whole life in that trunk."

Ma gave her a curious look. "I was only joking. C'mon, you sit in the back seat with me; let the boys up front."

The Cadillac was black with sleek taillights and a cream leather interior. Mariella had never been in such a luxurious car before. As she scooted into the backseat, the smell of leather overwhelmed her senses, making her queasy. Jack and his father finished loading the luggage and got into the car.

"Here we go!" Jack exclaimed, pulling a paper map from the glove compartment. "Should I guide you over to the new parkway? It should save us a good amount of time."

Pop nodded, and Jack got to work figuring out the best route to Asbury Park.

"What do you think? I bet ya don't have fancy cars like this back home," Ma said.

Jack turned around to check on Mariella. Her face was flushed and beads of sweat dotted her forehead. "Gee, Ma, everything is going to feel strange to her. Honey, why don't you roll down the window and get some fresh air."

Mariella nodded, then struggled with the handle a few times before Ma leaned over and rolled the window down for her. The rush of cool autumn air was just what she needed.

When they got onto the Garden State Parkway, all she saw was green; tall pines, blankets of grass, and the occasional field of wildflowers. Mariella was happy to see that America was lush and lovely. The earthy smell of dirt and the sweet scent of honeysuckle drifted in through the open window.

Every so often, Mariella felt her mother-in-law's eyes on her. It was as if the woman was assessing every bit of her new daughter-in-law.

"America is so beautiful," she said, an enthusiastic smile on her face.

"It sure is," Ma responded with a haughty laugh.

Mariella also admired the car's interior. Ignoring the pungent, woodsy smell, she ran her fingers along the leather seat as if she were touching the delicate wings of a butterfly. "It is so soft. I love the color. Is this, eh"—for a moment, she almost forgot the word but quickly remembered—"leather?"

"It better be, we paid enough for it," Ma sniped.

After about an hour, they turned off at an exit. Quaint houses with grand porches lined the streets, and laundry hung from clotheslines in grassy backyards. A big yellow school bus passed them and Mariella was charmed by the excited faces of young children peering out from inside.

"Now we're turning into Asbury Park," Jack said, smiling back at her. "Pop, why don't you drive us by the ocean so she can see what I've been talking about!"

"Oh, c'mon," Ma complained. "She'll have plenty of time to see the boardwalk."

"It not gonna take long," Pop assured her, then turned left down Sunset Avenue and right onto Ocean Avenue.

The sight of the weathered boardwalk made Mariella smile. Even though it stretched along the shore, she caught glimpses of waves crashing against the shoreline. The day was bright and clear, but the ocean seemed agitated. They drove past an impressive building with ornate carvings of sea creatures draped above its grand entrance.

"See over there? That's Convention Hall. It's where all the big bands play. Let's see, Benny Goodman, and Glenn Miller, even Louis Armstrong played there. It sure is a beauty," Jack said proudly.

Mariella felt like she was dreaming. After so many years of imagining what Jack's beloved Asbury Park would be like, she was finally here.

"And this is my favorite building." As they rounded a bend, turning away from the ocean, Jack pointed to a circular building at the far end of the boardwalk. There were men and women entering and exiting, while their children ran excited circles around them. "It's the casino."

Mariella leaned out of the window to get a better look.

"What is moving inside?" she asked.

"That's a merry-go-round. It plays music as the horses pump up and down like you're riding a real horse."

"Wow." Mariella had read about similar rides called carousels but had never seen one. "Can we ride one day?"

"Sure! But first, we have to ride that."

Jack nodded toward a building one block inland as they waited for a stoplight to change. Another carousel, this one rotating vertically with people sitting in baskets, taking them up through the roof then back down again. A narrow lake ran along the other side with large paddle boats shaped like elegant white swans gliding through the water. The thrill of experiencing so many new things made Mariella optimistic.

Ma shook her head. "You're a lucky girl. Getting out of Italy and coming to live in America. Not everyone gets that chance. I hope you appreciate it." She patted Mariella's hand, offering her a forced smile. The glint of a gold tooth at the side of her mouth reminded Mariella of the one Mama had pulled out at the start of the war so her children would have a bit of food in their bellies. Jack's mother was right. She was lucky.

Once the light turned green, they drove past the Palace amusements, a giant clown face painted on the side of the building.

Jack chuckled. "And there's ole Tillie! Isn't he great? And

this is…" He trailed off as they pulled up to a building at the end of the block.

"The Villa Pensa!" Mariella exclaimed.

She had received many postcards with various drawings of the family restaurant, and it was just as she imagined. A red awning softened the facade while large, illuminated letters written in fancy script spelled out *Villa Pensa* across the front of the building. A fish tank with slow-moving lobsters inside sat in the window. There were doors on either side of the building, then an ornate set of double glass doors at the main entrance on the corner. It was beautiful.

"What the heck is that?" Pop asked. "Who left garbage out like that?"

Ma clicked her tongue. "It's that fool, Marvin. He's a drunk. I told ya not to hire him! Once a drunk, always a drunk."

"Don't worry, Pop," Jack said. "I'll talk with him."

"No, you don' talk to him. I talk to him," he bellowed as he put the car in park and got out. Ma quickly followed after him.

Glancing over at Mariella, sitting alone in the back seat, Jack gave her an apologetic smile. "That's life in the restaurant biz."

Before he could say any more, a loud thud jolted them. Mariella looked up to see a tall, slim man lying on the car's hood as another man, this one short and stocky, pounded on the driver's side window until Jack rolled it down.

"Hey there, buddy boy! Get on out here. We wanna meet your better half!" the shorter one shouted, peering in to get a look at Mariella.

The other one jumped off of the hood and opened Mariella's door. He extended his hand and helped her out of the car.

"Well, hello there!" he sang. "I'm your new brother-in-law Willie."

"And I'm Carl! Nice to meet ya." Carl gave her a quick kiss on the cheek.

Jack hurried out of the car and ran to her side. "Okay, boys. She's had a long trip. Let's give her a little breathing room."

"Yeah, Carl, give her some air, buddy," Willie joked, stepping in to give her a hug.

The group stood on the sidewalk as a few seagulls circled above them.

"Jack told me about you," Mariella said.

Carl shot Jack a look. "What's that supposed to mean?"

Jack shrugged. "It's not too hard to figure out who's who. You two are like Mutt and Jeff!"

"Thanks a lot, fella," Carl grumbled as he led everyone into the restaurant.

Willie held the door open for Mariella. "*Mutt and Jeff* is a comic strip, ya see? It isn't a compliment."

"Oh?" She turned back to Jack.

He winked, then escorted her past the lighted host podium and into the bar area. "Welcome to the Villa Pensa. What do you think?"

Mariella took it in. The checkered blue and white tile flooring gave the room a bright, airy atmosphere. In the center stood a grand oval bar covered in turquoise tufting and a white melamine top. On the walls hung ornately framed photographs of various scenes in Naples: waves against a stone wall, Mount Vesuvius sitting proudly in the distant horizon, and the Obelisco di San Gennaro carved out of marble.

"Che bella," she said, feeling more at home already.

They continued to the main dining hall, which hadn't opened yet. A couple of waitresses sitting at a table folding napkins spared a glance in her direction, and a heavyset black man wearing yellow rubber gloves up to his elbows peered out from the kitchen.

Square tables draped with white tablecloths and wooden slat chairs on each side filled the large room. Along the walls hung family photographs: Jack's grandmother holding a baby with her husband at her side and two suitcases at their feet on their first day in America; Ma sitting on a porch surrounded by Jack and his siblings; the Asbury Park boardwalk stretching out into the distance with buildings along one side and the ocean on the other;

people on the beach dressed in one-piece swimsuits and ladies under parasols.

"Come! Sit!" Ma hollered as she entered from the kitchen, carrying a huge bowl of spaghetti, red sauce, and large pink claws with the tails mixed in. Jack pulled out a seat for Mariella and then sat beside her.

A tall, slim woman with neatly pinned, reddish-brown hair scurried into the restaurant, carrying a large bag from Steinbach's department store. "Sorry, everyone! I had to get my dress tailored." She kissed Carl, then went to Mariella. "Hello there! I'm your new sister-in-law, Rachel. I belong to this one," she said, elbowing Carl as she sat down across from Mariella.

Carl eyed Rachel's shopping bag and frowned. "Not if you keep shopping!"

"This is necessary. It's for the reception." She turned to Mariella, a warm smile on her face. "Boy, is it going to be fabulous! Good food, drinks, and they hired that big band to play so we can all dance! You'll get to meet the whole gang!"

"Yes, it will be nice," Mariella said, unaware that his parents' small dinner to celebrate their wedding would be so lavish.

"Enough of talking. Eat, everyone! Eat," Mama ordered.

"Have ya ever had a lobster?" Carl asked, pointing to the bowl. "Don't worry, they won't bite!"

Willie smacked Carl on the back of the head. "She's Italian, not an alien!"

"Of course she's not, you bozos!" Rachel agreed.

But Carl was right; Mariella had never tasted lobster before. She had seen smaller versions of them, ones without claws in the front, at a seaside market in Naples and was repulsed. While the lobsters didn't look appetizing, the red sauce reminded her of home. With a hesitant smile, Mariella shook her head.

"See that, ya dope," Carl chided. "She's never seen one before."

"Okay, fellas, let's not scare her away," Jack interjected.

Mariella loved Jack's easy way. He had a calming presence, even with his family. She squeezed his hand. "I'm not afraid, amore."

"What does she have to be afraid of?" Ma griped as she served the pasta. "Mariella just arrived in the greatest country on Earth. She doesn't have anything to complain about. Now, eat, everyone! Eat!"

Chapter Eight

After lunch, Jack and Mariella drove to his sister's house—a charming blue Victorian with a wraparound porch and ferns hanging on either side of the door. It was the house he grew up in, the same one in the photograph hanging on the wall at the restaurant. Julia had inherited it once the business became a booming success and Pop had built a larger home a few blocks from the beach.

Despite being heavy with her third child, Julia went out of her way to make Mariella feel welcomed. "It's so nice to have another sister-in-law!" she said, giving Mariella a hug. "Come in, come in. Let's visit before the boys get home and all hell breaks loose!"

"Where are those little rascals?" Jack said.

"Who knows?" Julia said, throwing her hands up in the air.

"After school those boys leave on their bicycles and don't come home until the sun sets! I did tell them to come back early and meet their new auntie, but you never know with those two."

Her bubbly personality was infectious and Mariella quickly felt at ease.

"Isn't that the way with boys?" Jack said. "Me, Carl, and Willie would ride our bikes all around town until we burned holes in our tires!"

"I remember! Ma had her hands full with you three." Julia turned to Mariella and spread her arms out wide. "Come, make yourself comfortable."

Mariella glanced around the living room. A worn couch sat in front of a small brick fireplace and a rocking chair in the corner. Several green army men strewn on the floor, small metal cars arranged in a line against the wall, and a baseball bat propped up on the couch made it obvious that boys lived there. "I cannot believe you, eh, grew in this house. It is so big," she said.

Julia wiped her hands on the yellow apron hanging over her baby bump. "It's home. But I did spruce up the place since we've moved in."

"Let me give you a tour!" Jack brought her upstairs while Julia finished up in the kitchen. They went into the boys' bedroom. It was a good size with three bay windows letting in the light and thick-planked wood floors. "Willie, Carl, and I shared this room from when we were babies until we left for the war."

Mariella looked out the window. A tall apple tree, its branches laden with budding fruit, sat proudly in a large backyard.

"Oh!" Jack opened the closet, moved the hanging clothes aside, and pointed to the wall. On it were paintings of horses, men in Native American headdresses holding tomahawks, and a war scene with a mountainous backdrop and soldiers waving guns. "I guess you could say this was my first canvas."

Thinking of Jack as a child holed up in his closet so he could draw made Mariella smile. "And your mother? What did she think?"

Jack smirked. "Let's just say she was not too happy."

"Okay, you two lovebirds, come on down for dessert!" Julia called up.

When they got to the kitchen, Julia had set the table with pretty ceramic dishes and a small vase of pink roses in the middle. They sat down and she filled their mugs with American drip coffee.

"I hope you'll like this. I wanted to make you something American." Julia placed a pineapple upside-down cake in the center, then gently lowered herself into a chair. She cut a large slice topped with a pineapple ring for Mariella, then another for her brother.

"Grazie."

"Yeah, thanks a lot, sis," Jack said, digging into his cake.

Mariella ate a small piece and was surprised at how sweet it was.

"You like it?" Julia asked.

Mariella nodded. "It is lovely. But you are ready to have your baby, no?"

Julia rubbed her stomach. "Not for another two and a half months. Let's just say I make big babies."

"Oh, but you must be tired."

"Ha! I'm used to being tired. How about you two? After such a long trip, I bet you're exhausted. Leave it to Ma to have lunch planned the minute you get in. I bet you haven't even seen the house you're going to be living in, have you?"

"We're headed there right after this," Jack said, then turned to Mariella. "You're gonna love it."

"I know I will," Mariella said.

The truth was, she had been so preoccupied with meeting her new family she hadn't given much thought to where they would be staying. Anywhere by Jack's side seemed fine when there was distance between them, but now she worried. It wasn't possible to have their own place straightaway, but she didn't want to be a burden on anyone, let alone her new in-laws.

"Pop isn't just a businessman; he was a mason back in the old country," Julia told Mariella, then in a loud whisper she added, "I just hope I get that house in the will!"

"Not on your life!" Jack joked.

Julia let out a hearty laugh. "Not my life, Ma and Pop's life!"

Although unsure what was funny, Mariella joined in. It warmed her that Jack had such a nice relationship with his sister. She was looking forward to having one too, but didn't have to worry. By the time they said their goodbyes, Julia and Mariella had become fast friends.

"Here we are," Jack announced, pulling into the bluestone driveway. "Your new abode, Mrs. Valentino."

The house, a center-hall colonial, was made of red brick. Although there was no porch, the front was inviting with rose bushes in various shades of red. Jack left the luggage in the foyer so he could give his wife a quick tour.

"Good thing my parents are at the restaurant tonight, I'm pooped," he said, holding the door open for her.

Mariella glanced around the first floor. On one side of a grand staircase was the living room furnished with a loveseat, settee, and fireplace, while on the other was a sitting room with four club chairs, a small bar, and a coffee table. To Mariella it looked more like a palace than a home. They went upstairs. After showing her the bathroom with its porcelain tub and separate green-tiled shower, Jack took her to their bedroom. Mariella had never seen such a large bed. Made of stained oak and surrounded by four posts, it was covered with a beautiful white eyelet quilt. She sat down carefully, not wanting to wrinkle the smooth surface.

Jack joined her on the bed. Sensing her mood, he laced his fingers into hers. "Are you okay?"

Tears began to travel down Mariella's cheek but she quickly wiped them away. The realization that she wasn't going home anytime soon had finally sunk in, and although she was happy to be with him, she was certainly overwhelmed. Without words to describe how she felt, Mariella kept quiet.

"It's okay, sweetheart. I'm sure this will need a little getting used to."

She leaned her head on his shoulder and nodded. Glancing around the room that was now theirs, everything felt odd. And although it was nice to have a big bed to share with Jack, she suddenly craved her lumpy old featherbed.

Jack gathered her hands in his. "Whadya say we go to sleep? We've had a long day and it's already nine o'clock. Let's get a good night's sleep, you'll feel better in the morning."

Mariella leaned in and kissed him, then waited for him to bring up the luggage so she could change into her nightgown. Once they crawled into bed, Jack wrapped his arms around her.

The warmth of his body against hers was comforting and she quickly drifted off to sleep.

The following day, Julia came calling with her husband, Tony, excited to go dress shopping. Mariella was surprised at how Sicilian he looked with his dark skin, bushy eyebrows, and shorter stature. Although he greeted her warmly, it was clear he had places to go. Tony rushed her into the car, then drove them over to Steinbach's on Cookman Avenue.

As they entered the department store, Mariella didn't know where to look first. In Rome, she went to one store for lingerie, another for shoes, and another for clothes her mother hadn't made. At Steinbach's, everything was under one roof. Bright, colored glass perfume dispensers lined the counters while the smell of sandalwood and flowers tickled her nose. The employees were glamorous, from the doorman welcoming them to the stylish women in perfect makeup and set hair working behind the counters to the sharp-dressed gentleman manning the elevator. They passed through the jewelry section, women's handbags and shoes, then arrived at a wooden escalator.

"You okay?" Julia asked, noticing Mariella's hesitation.

"Yes, thank you," she said before stumbling onto the escalator. She hoped it wasn't obvious she hadn't ridden one before.

"I booked the wedding suite, so you can try on as many

gowns as you want. Oh, they have the most beautiful things! Wait until you see."

"Okay." Mariella didn't think she needed another dress for the reception. Mama had made her a beautiful gown, but when her mother-in-law glimpsed it, her face had changed. Mariella suspected it wasn't fancy enough.

When they arrived on the bridal floor, a chic older woman doused in expensive-smelling perfume directed them to the wedding suite. It had a chaise lounge, two upholstered chairs, a carpeted platform surrounded by mirrors, and a separate room to change in. Five gorgeous dresses, loaded with sequins, sashes, and silk, hung on a clothing rack against the wall. Mariella chose the simplest one—a beautiful satin-topped pale pink dress with a full toile skirt.

"That dress looks gorgeous on you!" Julia exclaimed when she emerged from the dressing room. "When my brother sees you in that number, he'll want to marry you all over again!"

Mariella gazed at herself in the mirror and spun around.

"Isn't she going to try the others on?" the saleswoman asked Julia. "I spent all morning pulling dresses."

"But I like this best," Mariella said, offering a polite smile.

The woman clicked her tongue. "How would you know without trying the others?"

"Because she knows," Julia said firmly. "Have it delivered to

LUIGINA VECCHIONE

this address as soon as possible. We need it for tomorrow night." She handed the woman a business card with the Villa Pensa's address embossed on it. "You can bill us at the same address."

With pursed lips, the woman took the card and left to write up the bill.

"And that, my dear sister-in-law, is how you deal with old cows like her," Julia joked. "Now, get changed so we can have lunch. There's a darling luncheonette on Main that has a pastrami sandwich to die for!"

As Jack and Mariella entered the ballroom at the St. Regis Hotel, everyone erupted in cheers. A hundred friends and various family members were gathered to celebrate their marriage. Mariella blushed as Jack led her onto the dance floor while a seven-piece band played Perry Como's "Girl of My Dreams." Afterward, they sat at a dais with Jack's parents on one side and his godparents, Mr. and Mrs. Prevete, on the other. They dined on shrimp cocktail, something she'd never had and didn't care for but ate all the same, followed by Beef Wellington, which she adored. Dessert was a towering seven-layer cake with white buttercream frosting and raspberry filling. Once dinner was over, the guests were invited to the dance floor. Will took center stage, jitterbugging across the room as the crowd cheered him on. All the while, Jack brought Mariella around to each table for introductions.

"This is Anthony Caruso and his wife, Marion."

The dark-haired man with a barrel chest smiled broadly. "Hello, young lady. Nice to meet you."

"And this is Johnny, my ole buddy from high school."

Johnny sported a thick scar on the right side of his forehead, down to his neck and disappearing under his shirt collar. Mariella knew he had a story to tell.

"Gee, I'm sorry my wife, Betty, couldn't come. She's about to pop with our fourth child," he said in a weary voice.

"Auguri!" Mariella congratulated before moving on.

"Hey, Jack!" A man with a buzzcut and broad shoulders called him over. "Aren't ya gonna introduce us to your new bride?"

Jack shook his hand. "Glad you could make it!" He turned to Mariella. "Sweetheart, this is Mikey. We went to high school together, and he and his family live a few doors over."

"Yes, but you can call me Butch!" Butch said, pumping her hand up and down. "It's real nice to meetcha!"

A tall, lean blonde wearing an elaborate royal-blue sequin gown joined him. "Hiya! I'm Millicent, but people call me Millie. Or Butchie's better half!" She let out a throaty laugh.

Mariella smiled. "Hello, Butch, hello, Millie...cent? I am Mariella."

"Well then," Millie said, stepping back to size her up. "All

84

this time, Jack kept goin' on about you, Mary this and Mary that, and what a stunner you were, but I just assumed since...well, you're comin' from, well...you know... I keep hearin' about how everyone is so poor over there. I didn't expect you to look like this."

Mariella didn't respond, unsure if she was being complimented or insulted.

"Now, Millie, you know I have excellent taste in women," Jack said, snaking his arm around Mariella's waist.

"I sure do," Millie replied, her eyes brightening as if they held a secret. "We all know how beautiful your last girl was." Jack shot her a look, but she ignored him and turned to Mariella. "By the way, we can't pronounce your name so we'll call you Mary. Hope that's okay."

Mariella hadn't realized that anyone could change your name as they pleased in America. She didn't like it much, but nodded anyway.

The introductions continued for a while. Mariella's face hurt from the polite smile she wore. The last hour was spent dancing cheek to cheek with her new husband. At moments, when the music was smooth and Jack held her close, she felt optimistic about their future. It didn't matter that she felt out of place; she had him.

When the night came to an end, Mariella was ready to go

home. Jack pulled the Cadillac up and she quickly slid in, her feet throbbing, head foggy from too much champagne. As they drove along the ocean, it seemed as if the whole world was asleep but Mariella knew somewhere out in the horizon, her family had already started their day. She pushed away the longing to be with them.

"They must be in bed," Jack said when he pulled up to the dark house. The Prevetes had driven his parents' home after dessert, leaving the younger people to enjoy the dance floor. Besides, they had closed the restaurant for the evening and Ma was itching to get an early start the following day.

At the front door, Jack turned to Mariella. "Shhhh." He slipped out of his shoes and she did the same. They tiptoed into the living room to find it filled with gifts wrapped in colorful paper, big bows, and ribbons.

"What is this, amore?" Mariella whispered, making space on the couch.

Jack closed the door so they could talk. "These are our wedding gifts." He shuffled through a pile of greeting cards. "My parents brought them home earlier. Hey! This one's from my Uncle Joey. He couldn't make it tonight."

Mariella's curiosity was piqued. "What could this be?" she asked, picking up a cylindrical package.

"Open it up!"

As she pulled back the silver wrapping, a set of silver candlesticks poked out. Next to her, a brightly covered square package had a tear in it, so she opened it too and found a beautiful wooden breadbox.

"Lovely."

"This one looks interesting," Jack said, pulling an elaborate blue bow off an oddly shaped package. "It's from my parents." He ripped at the paper, exposing an upright Kirby vacuum machine. "This'll come in handy!"

"And what is this?"

Jack pushed the machine around and gave a silly smile. "Any guesses?"

"Eh." Mariella sat up, always happy to play a game. "It is for cleaning the floor?"

"Ding, ding, ding! We have a winner!" Jack pushed the vacuum cleaner to the side, then picked up another gift, ripped off the paper, and unboxed it. "Aha! What about this gadget?" He held out a silver appliance with two rectangular holes in the top and a lever on the side.

Mariella was stumped. "Is it to cook the hotdogs?"

"Hotdogs?" Jack collapsed onto the floor laughing himself into hysterics, but Mariella didn't find it funny. When he noticed her go silent, he composed himself. "Aw gee, honey, I'm sorry."

"I do no, eh, understand what is funny," Mariella said, her

English faltering from exhaustion.

"Oh, sweetheart, I just thought it was cute. I wasn't making fun, honest."

"Well," Mariella began, her lips tight, "it is not cute for me."

"I understand." Jack nodded, then put his hand to his heart. "I promise to explain things you don't know. Okay? You can ask me anything."

Gazing down at Jack, kneeling on the floor with a hangdog look on his face, Mariella couldn't help but feel sorry for him. Yes, it was hard for her, but he too had to deal with their cultural differences.

She nodded. "So, tell to me, what do it do?"

"It toasts bread. Oh, uh, you may not know that word. Let me demonstrate for you. C'mon!"

They went into the kitchen and he plugged it in then slid two pieces of Wonder bread inside. After a minute, the darkened slices popped up, making Mariella jump.

"Toast!" Jack said triumphantly.

"Ah. Yes! We have this on the boat," Mariella recalled, having tried her first American breakfast on the ship—sunny-side-up eggs, bacon, and toast with jam. Although it wasn't bad, she preferred a simple pastry and espresso.

For the rest of the night, Jack and Mariella found reasons to open each package. They received ceramic bowls, marble ashtrays, a bar set from his brothers, two more sets of candlesticks, at least twenty lace doilies and twelve tablecloths, dish towels, silverware, three sets of martini glasses, two sets of champagne glasses, and a set of green glass tumblers. In the cards was money—$1,225 to be exact.

Crawling under the sheets as the sun began to rise, Mariella considered all the gifts they'd received. The ceremony and reception her parents gave them in Rome was small in comparison, the gifts more personal, some even handed down from generation to generation. But the shiny, new home goods piled high in the living room were exciting. Mariella felt wealthy just having them.

"You friends and you family are so, how do you say, eh … giving."

"Ah, you mean generous," Jack said. "They sure were."

She rolled over to face him. "I just have one question."

"Uh-huh," Jack said, his eyelids heavy.

"Where will we go to put it all? We do not have a home."

Jack kissed her neck, then yawned. "One day, darling. One day."

Chapter Nine

Watching Jack sleep, Mariella was filled with jealousy. She had only slept a few hours each night since arriving in America the week before, and it had begun to take a toll on her. She wasn't just missing her family. She had begun to worry she might not be able to fit into Jack's life.

Every evening, they would come together with a sense of urgency, as if trying to make up for moments missed while they were apart. In his arms, she couldn't imagine being anywhere else. But as soon as he disappeared into sleep, all she could feel was envy. Jack had his family close while hers felt like they were in another universe. It was easy for him to sleep because life was perfect. And each day, he left home with a purpose while she spent most of the day alone.

"Can I come to the restaurant?" Mariella asked one morning while Jack slapped aftershave on his face.

"Why, Mrs. Valentino, you're the wife of a successful restaurateur. This is your time to relax!"

"I guess."

He turned to her, a playful frown on his face. "Don't you want to be my wife?"

"Amore, it is not that. I love to be your wife. I just, eh … want there to have more for me. When your mother leave for the restaurant and I am done with the housework, I do nothing. I am bored."

"After all you've been through, maybe being bored is a good thing!"

Mariella's forehead creased. "What do you mean being bored is good?"

"Sweetheart," Jack said, looping his tie around his neck, "this is why I fell in love with you. I've never known anyone who worked harder. When I met you at fifteen years old you were selling postcards in the Colosseum and dealing with those rude soldiers. After that it was your job at the bank. I remember you writing about those horrible women treating you like dirt. Ha! If they could see you know."

Jack beamed as if he were picturing his wife walking into the office back in Rome and bragging about her American life. Mariella quickly understood. He was proud he could give his wife the luxury of boredom like the other wives in their neighborhood.

And so, each morning, she tried to follow the protocol. She woke early to put on makeup and pull curlers from her hair, then returned to bed just before Jack woke. While he dressed, she got busy in the kitchen to organize breakfast and get the paper. Since they lived with his parents, Ma insisted on cooking for him. Mariella didn't mind, though, since fried eggs weren't her specialty. Once he finished breakfast, she'd hand him his hat and briefcase and see him off with one last kiss. While the mornings left her glum, the other wives seemed energized, watching their husbands disappear down the street.

Ma put Mariella to work shining silverware, vacuuming carpets, and washing dishes. Without her son around, his mother's personality changed.

"Make sure you don't skip the living room when you dust today. I swear it's like you've never done any of this before!" Ma would tease, her voice light and airy as if her words were harmless.

It didn't help that she only spoke to Mariella in English, a cruel reminder she needed to perfect hers. If that wasn't enough, Ma's comments were clear.

"How will you raise my grandchildren if your English isn't perfect?" she scolded. "You live in America now. We speak English here."

But when Ma left for the restaurant, the boredom really set in. Sometimes, Mariella read articles in the fashion magazines

Jack brought home to help her work on her English. It wasn't so much the language that gave her problems—although it was clear her accent made it hard for people to understand her. It was the colloquialisms that were troublesome. She mostly read advertisements, relying on pictures for context. An image of a beautiful woman with glossy hair, a man standing next to her, and a bottle labeled "shampoo" beside them was easy to understand. But the headline—STEPPING OUT WITH LUXURIOUS HAIR KEEPS MY DREAMBOAT FROM STRAYING— didn't make sense. If she couldn't figure it out, she earmarked the page so when Jack returned home he could explain it. Then, the next time someone spoke about their "dreamboat" or someone "straying," she would understand.

Mariella hoped she wasn't being unappreciative. Jack did work very hard and never complained. She wondered if maybe she didn't know how to relax, but promised herself she would try. Adjusting Jack's tie one morning so it lay perfectly straight, Mariella kissed his nose.

"What was that for?" he asked, grinning down at her.

"For always thinking of me."

"Sweetheart, I've thought of you for the past eight years, why would I stop now?"

"Eh, I mean…" She fiddled with one of his shirt buttons. "I am so used to working, I need to get used to not."

"I promise you will." He kissed her, then turned to go. "Don't wait up for me. But if you do, you know I won't complain!"

Once the screen door slammed shut, Ma called out from the kitchen. "What are ya hiding out? You've got dishes to wash."

Suddenly Mariella felt foolish for complaining about being bored.

One lazy afternoon Mariella climbed one of the apple trees that lined the backyard. As she dangled her feet from a high branch, her mind returned to nights sitting on the roof with her sister. Mariella had just ended her engagement to Lorenzo one time they were out there. She remembered how comforting it was to have Elisa, always willing to listen and offer advice she desperately needed.

When her chest began to ache at the memory, she distracted herself with an inchworm struggling to climb a branch. Wallowing in nostalgia would only leave her in a mess of tears and regret.

Suddenly, a voice called up to her. "Yoo-hoo! Whose feet are those? Is that you, Mary?"

Mariella peered down to see her neighbor smiling up at her. She wore pink pedal pushers with ballet flats, a white shirt with cap sleeves, and a baby-blue cardigan draped around her shoulders.

"Hello, Mary, remember me? Millie? My husband, Butch, and I were at your wedding party."

When Mariella didn't answer right away, Millie's smile faded.

"You do speak English, don't you? I thought you could speak English."

"Yes. I speak English," Mariella quickly said.

"Well then, would you mind coming down from the tree so we can speak properly?"

Mariella's face flushed with embarrassment as she gathered her skirt between her legs and shimmied down. "Hello," she said, offering her hand, hoping not to seem too foreign.

Millie shook it awkwardly. "Where've ya been? I haven't seen ya much around the neighborhood. Is Jack hiding you? I mean, he does have a lot of exes around here. Is he hiding you so you won't run into them? Maybe one in particular?"

Mariella shook her head. "No. Eh, I have been here."

"Well, we shoulda had you over long ago! How 'bout you and Jack come over for a BBQ Friday night?" Millie babbled her words so quickly they seemed to connect.

"BBQ?"

"Oh, right!" Millie laughed. "I guess ya got a lot to learn. Bar-be-cue. It's a big grill, you know? Cooking over fire?"

"Yes, yes. I know this party," Mariella said, remembering

the barbecue party Julia threw in her backyard the first weekend she arrived. The name was so odd she'd forgotten about it.

"Great! And, don't worry about dressing. It's a shorts and sandals sort of thing."

Mariella followed Millie to the front lawn. She gestured toward a pretty blue house on the corner with a wraparound porch and flower boxes spilling over with vibrant pink and violet petunias.

"That's my house over there!"

"It is lovely," Mariella said, longing for a place she could call her own. She would fill the yard with flowers and bushes of lavender and birdhouses galore.

"Tell Jackie all the boys will come, too. It'll be a hoot. See ya then!"

Millie ran across the street, but instead of going to her house, she made a beeline for the white house beside it, sprinting up the stairs and calling out "Yoo-hoo!" before quickly disappearing inside.

Staring at her reflection a few days later, Mariella frowned. She straightened out her crisp white cotton blouse with a boat neck collar accented in red. Paired with the red-checked capri pants and white ballet flats she'd bought at Steinbach's the day before, Mariella felt uncomfortable. She would have never gone to a party dressed so casually back home.

Jack wrapped his arms around her waist and leaned his chin on her shoulder. "Why the long face, sweetheart?" he asked, kissing her neck between his words.

"Amore," she said, "I look like a country girl."

"You look beautiful."

"I like the clothings, but it is odd to go for a party dressed so casual, no?"

"Not around here. Besides, it's a casual party. Like a picnic." Jack let her go and ran a comb through his hair, then smoothed it out with pomade. "It's just a casual get-together in their backyard. Don't they have parties like this in Italy?"

Mariella thought about it a moment before nodding. "Yes, but always with family. I remember when we were children on the farm. My cousins, aunts, and uncles would go for Easter dinner. Papa always help Nonno butcher a lamb and Nonna would make mozzarella using the milk from their cows." As she spoke, the thought of cream spilled all over the farmhouse floor as her grandfather tried to bring her brother back to life so many years ago soured her happy memory.

"Having the whole family together sounds swell," Jack said. "But this is different. It's a good ole American tradition."

Mariella looked in the mirror and shrugged. "I guess there is much I need to get used to."

Chapter Ten

As Jack and Mariella arrived at the BBQ, children raced back and forth in a lively game of hide and seek. Tiki torches burned brightly on the patio where a group of women lounged on colorful chairs and chatted, Pall Mall cigarettes perched between their lips, while the men gathered around the grill as it spewed billowy plumes of smoke.

"Yoo-hoo! There you kids are!" Millie cried, hurrying over to them

"Hiya, Millie," Jack said.

"Hey, you two lovebirds!" Millie hugged Jack quickly, then looped her arm through Mariella's. "Your wife needs some girl time! You go on and visit with the fellas. They're all watching Butch cook at the grill," she said, then turned to Mariella and laughed. "Of course they are. Where there's meat and fire, there's a man!"

Mariella waved goodbye to Jack as Mille dragged her over to the patio.

"Hey, girls, I'd like you to meet our new neighbor, Mari—What is it?" Millie asked Mariella, her face screwed up.

"It is okay. You can call me Mary," she said, trying to be accommodating.

Millie let out a drawn-out sigh. "Oh, right. Mary is much easier! Anyhoo, this is Jack's new wife. Let me introduce you to the girls. That's Susan over there, but we call her Suze. She lives in the gray Cape across the street." Millie pointed to a buxom woman with mousy brown hair and pencil-thin eyebrows. "And that's Betty over there with the third martini in her hand!"

Betty was what Mariella thought all Americans would look like—platinum blonde and big blue eyes.

"Don't listen to her! It's only my second!" Betty whispered loudly, raising her glass. "But it won't be my last!"

"Keep kidding yourself, dear," Millie said with a smirk. "And last, but not least, this is my sister Clara."

She gestured to a thin, shy-looking woman with dark curly hair. Clara didn't look anything like her sister. She gave Mariella a quick smile.

"Well," Millie continued, "let's just say we have the same father."

All the women laughed except for Clara, who lit a cigarette and ignored them.

"Hey, Mary! Come sit over here!" Betty patted the space beside her.

As soon as Mariella sat down, the women turned their attention on her.

"So, you and Jack?" Suze said.

"Yes," Betty leaned in, "quite a catch you've got there, haven't you?"

"Oh boy, does she," Millie said. "I bet all those women in Italy want to marry an American!"

Suze nodded. "I read that it's still not so great over there."

"I hear it's a royal mess." Millie took a drag of her cigarette, then continued. "My cousin Clark works as a buyer for Gimbels department store and he hears the place is still chaotic, even though the war's been over for almost a decade. It's their way of life, you see. All those long lunches and afternoon naps—it's no wonder they can't get anything done."

Mariella tried to keep up with their conversation but only got the gist. She wasn't sure if they were genuinely concerned or judging the entire population of Italy.

Suze clicked her tongue in disapproval. "What a shame! I honestly don't understand how anyone can live that way."

"Excuse me," Clara said, narrowing her eyes at the women.

"She's sitting right here, for God's sake. Why don't you ask her what it's like in Italy instead of gossiping about it."

Millie shot her sister a look, then turned to Mariella, sweetening her voice. "So, Mary. What's it been like over there? Dreadful, I bet!"

Mariella searched for the words to explain the state of her country. How they spent months under German occupation, facing death at every turn. Or the nights spent huddled with her family in their cold apartment, trying to ignore the pains cramping their stomachs from too little to eat. Or having to travel with her father through back alleys in the dark of night only to discover the black market a friend had told them about was out of lighter fluid, or fruit, or meat, or blankets. Or spending her youth fending off advances of Allied soldiers just to sell a few postcards. Lazy? She would like to know how they would survive any better. But before Mariella could answer, Jack called her over.

"Boo!" Millie jeered. "We were just getting to know Mary, and now you're taking her away from us!"

"I will be back soon," Mariella said as she hurried off to join her husband.

Millie watched her walk away, then spun around to the other women and rolled her eyes.

"You better watch out for that one, Mill," Clara said slyly. "I think Butch likes what he sees."

Millie scoffed. "Phooey."

"Sure," Clara pressed, unable to contain her glee. "I bet you thought she'd come over barefoot with raggedy clothes, balancing a basket full of fruit on her head like some old-world peasant!"

Suze let out a sigh. "I certainly didn't think she'd look like that!"

"She is stunning," Betty conceded.

The women quietly watched as their husbands stumbled over each other to meet Jack's new wife.

Millie's husband shook her hand. "Remember me? I'm Butch."

"He's married to Millie," Jack reminded her.

Mariella offered Butch a polite smile. "Yes, I remember you."

"And this here's Tom," Jack said.

A tall, lean man with eyes as blue as the sea stepped forward and gently shook Mariella's hand. "Betty's my wife. It's nice to meet you."

"It is nice to meet you too."

"And Pat here belongs to Susan." Jack gestured to a short man with thinning hair and a cheery smile.

"Do you mean Suza?" Mariella tried to be clever but got the nickname wrong. The men laughed.

"That's a cute accent you have there," Pat said. "I just call her Pinky."

"Pinky?"

"Oh, right!" Jack explained. "Those two were sweethearts all through high school."

"Couldn't get rid of her. She always wore this bright pink sweater that, well, let's just say, accented her assets." Pat laughed as he elbowed Jack in the ribs. But Mariella's stone-faced expression killed his laughter. He turned to Jack. "Can't she understand me?"

"Sure," Jack said, his hesitation making him sound unsure. "You understand what he's saying, don't you, dear?"

Mariella pursed her lips a moment, then gave him a reassuring smile. "Yes, of course I do."

"Grub's on!" Butch announced. He carried a large tray of burgers and hotdogs over to a folding table by the patio. Everyone stubbed out their cigarettes and began forming a line.

"Grub?" Mariella asked Jack as they made their way over.

"Food. He means the food is ready."

Why couldn't he say that? she wondered.

"Wait until you try his ribs. They're terrific!"

They walked to the back of the line where Millie handed them a plate, fork, knife, and paper napkin each. Mariella was surprised but assumed it was customary for guests to set their own place at the table.

"Now, grab some food and sit wherever you can find a seat!" Millie instructed before moving on to the next person in line.

When they reached the table, a woman who looked like an older version of Millie scurried around, making sure the food was set. There was a large bowl filled with something that had potatoes and mayonnaise. Mariella took a scoopful. Next to that were an array of pickled vegetables and something called "cornbread." She took a bit of both. Then there was another large bowl with mayonnaise and some sort of chopped vegetable.

"Jack, what is this?"

"It's coleslaw." He took a scoop and plopped it onto her plate.

"What is a cole-slaw?"

"Let's see, it's cabbage and mayonnaise and something sweet and something tangy like vinegar. Try it!"

As Millie passed, she pointed to the potato salad on Mariella's plate. "Oh, honey, stay away from that stuff. It'll turn your hourglass shape into a big, fat ball!"

"Okay," Mariella said, but before she could ask Jack what an hourglass was, she noticed a large tray of yellow corn with red and blue skewers poking out of each. It was familiar because corn was what they fed to fatten up the pigs on her grandmother's farm, but she couldn't understand why they were on the table.

Jack picked up one and topped it with a square of butter.

"Aren't you going to take one? Jersey corn is the best!"

Mariella's eyes grew wide. "You eat it like this?"

"Sure we do. It's very American. Here." Jack placed a small ear of corn on her plate. "It's best with this!" He cut another square of butter and popped it on top. "Now, how do you like your burger? Cheese? No cheese? Or maybe you want to try a hotdog?"

"Can I share one with you?" she asked, looking at the tray of sandwiches. She wanted to be polite, but her stomach had soured.

"Whatever you like, sweetheart. I'll take one of each so you can have a taste."

Once their plates were full, Mariella glanced around the backyard, looking for a spot to eat. A few children had already taken up the benches at the picnic table, and most of the women had returned to their lounge chairs, balancing their plates on their knees.

"Jack, where can we eat?" she whispered.

"Come with me." Jack brought her to a table tucked away underneath a weeping willow tree in the corner of the yard. It was a nice reprieve from the crowd.

"So, what do ya think of the gang?" he asked, rubbing the butter into the corn with his knife.

Mariella thought for a moment. "They are very nice.

Sometimes, I do not understand what they are meaning. But if I ask, they think I do not speak English well."

"Don't worry, Pat was just ribbing you. He didn't mean anything by it."

"See, this is what I talk about. What is 'ribbing'?"

"Ah." Jack laughed, but Mariella wasn't smiling. "I'm sorry, sweetheart. I know this is a lot to take in."

"But then why these people always talk in code? Maybe if they talk slower—"

"Gee, this must be awfully hard for you. But I promise things will get better." Jack picked up his corn. "Now, are you ready for your first taste of an American delicacy?"

"How do you eat it?"

"Ha! It's an art, really. See, you pretend you are a typewriter. Let me demonstrate." Jack put the corn between his teeth and nibbled it, edging his way from one end to the other.

The sight of her sophisticated husband eating like a cow looked so ridiculous, Mariella dissolved into giggles. "I am sorry, it is very funny."

"Funny? Well, at least I got you to smile. Now, take a bite of yours."

Mariella cautiously picked up her corn.

"Oh, come now, what are you afraid of?"

She hesitated a moment, then took a small bite. It tasted

mostly of butter. "It is very good."

"Really?" Jack asked, shooting her a skeptical look.

"Amore, I have a funny stomach."

"Yeah? Is it the food? Or maybe just nerves?"

Mariella wiped her mouth with a napkin and shrugged. "I think both. But I do not want to be a rude person."

"Don't worry, honey. You've tried enough new things. Let me take care of it." Jack turned away from everybody, took a bite of the hot dog, then yelled over at Butch, waving it in the air. "My wife is enjoying your dogs!"

Mariella waved at her host too. "It is delicious!"

Butch waved back, although it wasn't clear if he knew what they had said. Jack leaned in to Mariella. "You can try the hotdog another day. I don't think your funny stomach can handle it."

"Thank you." Mariella took a few more bites of the coleslaw, which she liked, then watched everyone mingle while Jack finished eating.

She was surprised that the women stayed away from the men and the children were mostly ignored. At her family parties, everyone sat together at a long table for hours. They had lively conversations, ate food in courses—taking breaks to smoke their cigarettes—and drank local wine, all while the children moved around the table, getting attention from everyone. She made sure to stand by her grandfather as he carved the prosciutto and passed every second slice to her. By the end of the night, when the moon and stars were high in the sky, they would join the adults, already loose from wine, to sing and dance. On special occasions, her Uncle Vito would pull out the spoons to play "Che La Luna" on his knee while a few tambourines were passed around to shake.

"Hey, you two lovebirds!" Butch shouted from across the yard, pulling Mariella away from her memory. "Why are you hiding back there? You two still honeymooning? Why don't you get a room!"

Mariella turned to Jack, shaking her head. "Why do we need to get a room?"

"Oh, uh." Jack did his best to keep from laughing. "He doesn't mean anything. Honest. C'mon, let's get some dessert. Millie's apple pie is outta this world!"

Chapter Eleven

After dreaming of a life in America with her husband by her side, Mariella soon discovered how different the reality would be. By the middle of July, most days Jack was working into the early morning hours. She tried to stay up for him, waiting to remove her makeup and brush out her hair, but Mariella often fell asleep before he returned.

It didn't help that her mother-in-law became even more demanding.

"Be sure to finish all those chores I've given you," Ma would complain, "and for goodness' sake, wash those sheets separately! They look dingy when you wash them with dark colors."

I could do better if I didn't have to use those complicated appliances, Mariella thought. Although she knew the wringer machine was popular with Americans, she preferred using a washboard to clean her clothes.

When Ma left for work at noon, Mariella was filled with a sense of relief. It was short-lived, though as the loneliness soon returned. Julia visited every so often, taking her to lunch in town. But once she delivered her baby, another boy, it was hard for her to come around.

One sticky afternoon, as she hung wet laundry on the line, Mariella's thoughts drifted to Rome. She had finally gotten her first letter from her mother a few days before. Although Mama tried to sound upbeat, Mariella could tell without her around, something was missing. She wrote about how Signora Manetto had gotten in trouble with the neighbors when she started feeding the mice that had taken up residence in a corner of her kitchen. Before long, they began invading the hallways, making their way into the apartment below theirs. It didn't surprise Mariella. Signora Manetto had always worn her loneliness like a coat in winter. Now, with no one to talk to, Mariella understood her just a little bit more.

After receiving the letter, she was transported to their tiny kitchen in Rome. She could almost smell the aroma of rich tomato sauce as Mama doled out her homemade linguini. For a moment, she thought she might be imagining the voice calling out to her. But then she spotted a petite figure standing at the back gate and quickly composed herself.

"Hi there. Do you remember me? I'm Clara, your neighbor's sister."

Mariella quickly waved her in. "Of course I remember you!"

Clara's smile lit up her whole face. "I'm so relieved you're home. Gee, I hope I didn't scare you," she said, letting the gate slam behind her.

"Scare me? Why? It is nice to have a visitor!" Mariella's voice croaked. She hadn't talked with anyone for hours.

"Believe me, it's nice to visit. My sister has those cackling hens over for lunch, and I couldn't listen to them gossip anymore."

"Hens?" Mariella asked.

Clara laughed, making her dark curls fall into her face. She pushed them out of her eyes. "I live with Millie and her family. She has those women over, the ones you met at the barbecue. Aren't they horrendous?"

Although Mariella didn't know them well, she certainly knew the type. They reminded her of the women she'd worked with at the Bank of Italy and how they picked on her when she was newly hired.

"Mind if I hide out here for a while?" Clara asked, clasping her hands together as if she were begging.

"Yes, yes! Of course." Mariella tried not to sound too eager. "Would you like a coffee?"

"Only if you make me the Italian kind. I love a good, strong coffee."

Mariella beamed. "You make my day." It wasn't three o'clock yet but she was more than happy to share her espresso at any time. Especially since, of late, the rich smell had become a vivid reminder of home.

They went into the kitchen. Mariella pulled apart her espresso pot and spooned the coffee into the bottom. "You say you live with Millie?"

"Yes," Clara grumbled, plopping down in a chair at the kitchen table. "I've actually lived in the house longer than her. See, it was our father's. He got sick a few years ago." She leaned in and whispered the word "cancer" as if one could catch it by saying it out loud.

"Oh." After watching her sister Elisa die from brain cancer, Mariella knew how devastating the illness could be.

"Anyway," Clara continued, "he never had a will. Millie was living in a tiny apartment with her family and knew I couldn't afford to keep up the house on my own. So, we made a compromise. They moved in and I can stay as long as I'm available for babysitting. Good thing her mother is around most of the time so I don't have to take care of those little runts too often."

Although Mariella didn't know what "runts" meant, Clara

made clear she didn't care for them. "Have you ever had espresso?"

"Never. But I had Turkish coffee when I traveled there," Clara said, her face brightening.

Mariella shot her new friend a curious look. She was different from the other women she had met, more carefree and interesting. Her curly, unruly hair was messy but in a beautiful way. Her dark brown eyes were sympathetic, and despite being American, Clara felt strangely familiar.

"You go to Turkey?"

Clara laughed. "Don't look so shocked. We Americans aren't all the same!"

"Oh, no." Mariella frowned, worried she had offended her new friend. "I did not mean…"

"It's okay. I *am* different from most people around here. Let's see, I've traveled to Turkey and Greece. They were both wonderful, but my favorite was the island of Corfu. I've never seen water look so blue."

Mariella tied an apron around her waist and disappeared into the pantry. "And how do you go to these places?" she asked.

"My father. He was in the import business and liked to have company when he traveled." She smiled. "I guess I'm lucky."

"I never been anywhere but Rome," Mariella admitted as she emerged with two espresso cups, saucers, and a silver sugar pot. "Oh, and my grandparents' farm in the country. And, eh, Naples a few times."

"Well, those sound like interesting places. I've always wanted to visit Italy."

"Oh, you must. I know it is home, but it is so beautiful. I can show you the Colosseo and Piazza di Spagna and, of course, Piazza Navona. This is Jack's favorite of places. I can show you all the sights."

"I'd like that. Is the Vatican as big as they say?"

Mariella nodded. "And so beautiful. We can climb on the top of the Duomo."

"That would be wonderful! I believe seeing how other people live in the world is an eye-opener."

"Eh, what is this?"

"Oh, sorry. It means something that makes you understand people better."

"I see. Then living in America is an eye-opening for me."

Clara stifled a laugh, then nodded. "I'm sure it is!"

The espresso pot bubbled over its spout, making a high-pitched whine. Mariella swiftly took it off the stove before coffee dripped onto the burner. She poured the dark liquid into each cup and brought them to the table.

"Thank you." Clara closed her eyes and inhaled. "I love the smell of this coffee. I bet it brings back fond memories of home for you."

Mariella swallowed hard. It was the first time anyone other than Jack had asked her about home. "Yes, it does make me think of my family."

Clara leaned over and patted Mariella's hand. "Oh, you poor thing. You must be so homesick."

The tears came fast and furious before Mariella could stop them. She fought to gather herself. "I am sorry. I never live away from my family before."

Clara nodded sympathetically. "Can I ask you something? Do you like it here?"

"Yes, of course," Mariella replied a little too quickly. "I mean, I try my best. When Jack is with me, all is perfect. Just like I dream. But when he works I am lonely."

"Well, then, we must do something about that. How about I come by this time every day? We can have coffee and go for a walk to the beach, or just sit and chat? I'm going crazy staying at Ozzie and Harriet's house." Clara paused. "Oh, sorry, you probably don't know Ozzie and Harriet. They're a couple in a TV show. Anyway, I don't have anyone to talk to either. Anyone with substance, that is. Would that be good?"

Clara peered through her curls but didn't have to wait for a response. Mariella hugged her. Having a friend was just the thing she needed.

True to her word, Clara came by every afternoon. On nice days, they walked to the beach and combed the sand for seashells or got ice cream cones on Main Street, or Clara would help hang laundry as they got to know each other. It turned out her mother had died in a horrible car accident when Clara was eight years old. Her father married Millie's mother, but the woman never treated Clara like a daughter. She wasn't horrible to her. It was worse— she was indifferent. Only a year apart in age, Clara and Millie were close as children, but once Millie hit puberty, she ignored Clara too.

"It's okay, though," Clara said, unconvincingly. "At least I had my dad. I loved him so much. He only married the witch because he needed someone to take care of us. There was never any love there. They divorced when I graduated high school."

"Oh." Mariella hadn't ever met anyone who was divorced or had divorced parents. It wasn't common in Italy.

"But the witch's loss was my gain! Dad started taking me on his cross-country business trips. We went all the way to California and back. Then, of course, we went overseas. It worked out fine because I wasn't leaving anyone behind. And, in my book, the adventure was better than sticking around here. But last year, when Dad got sick, we came back. That's when my father began to worry about me."

"Why?"

"I've never really dated and he thought my chances of getting married and having a family of my own were dwindling. So, to make him happy, I agreed to go on a date with the son of a business acquaintance. The fella wasn't bad looking, just boring. But when he asked me to marry, I said yes." Clara gazed into her espresso cup. "I'll never forget how happy my dad was when I told him. At that point, he could barely speak, but I could see it in his eyes."

Mariella couldn't help but think of the faraway look in her own sister's eyes during those days she was more sick than alive. "What happened?"

Coming back to the present, Clara shrugged. "I broke it off the minute Dad died. Let's face it, I was never going to marry him. It's okay, though. He married another woman a few months later and seems happy."

"And so are you," Mariella said, more as a question than statement.

Clara looked away and smiled. "And so am I."

The fact that Millie was so awful to Clara made Mariella angry, so when Millie came searching for her sister, it didn't take much for Mariella to lie.

One particular afternoon, Millie knocked at her screen door, more agitated than ever. After hiding Clara in the pantry, Mariella answered the door.

"Have you seen that sister of mine?" Millie said in a huff. "I swear, I don't know where that girl goes. Between you and me, I think she's having an affair. That would explain all the sneaking around, wouldn't it?"

Mariella's eyebrows knit together. "I am sorry, but I do not understand."

"Oh, right." Millie sighed, folding her arms as she leaned against the doorframe. "You know, you should really take some English lessons. It's not easy talking to you when I have to explain things all the time. Anyway, if you see my sister, please tell her I have a salon appointment I cannot miss, and she needs to come home to take care of the children." Millie paused as though she wanted to say more, then thought better of it. "Well, okay, I'll go. Maybe she's already home. Toodles!" she said, hurrying across the street.

"Is she gone yet?" Clara whispered, peeking out from the kitchen.

Mariella nodded. "She needs you to care for the children."

"What else is new? I'd better go, or she'll work herself into a tizzy! Can you imagine me having an affair? With these bozos around here? Not on your life! See you tomorrow. Ciao bella!" Clara said, blowing Mariella a kiss before slipping out the back door.

Chapter Twelve

Jack stood in the doorway, watching his wife sleep. The moonlight streaming through their window against Mariella's long, dark eyelashes and olive skin made her look like a photograph. She was curled up into a ball, knees pulled against her stomach, hands clasped at her heart. Taking shallow breaths, her lips parted each time she exhaled. Although she was asleep most nights he returned from work, he never really noticed. It was as if he were seeing her for the first time. Jack wondered if her wounds from the war were more profound than his own.

Since returning from his final post in Japan, Jack was haunted by one recurring nightmare. One that sent him right back to the day he injured his ear. It was always the same.

He would find himself standing on the boardwalk, surrounded by happy families and the restaurant in the distance, well-lit with lively music drifting out. Suddenly, the skies would darken. Although he'd try to take a step, he'd be unable to move. Again, again, again, he'd try and fail. Then a voice crying from somewhere further down on the beach would release him and he'd go to investigate. Running along the sand, he'd find a foot, then a leg, then a head—eyes opened wide in agony. That was when the terror set in. But the part that scared him most was when the body's head cried out in a desperate howl.

The first nightmare occurred a few days after his return from the war. He'd flown out of bed, unable to get his bearings. Pop's personal experience allowed him to understand what the evils of war did to a young mind. During those months, he would join his son in the hallway, help him catch his breath and then guide him back to bed. Jack couldn't understand why these nightmares hadn't begun until he'd returned home. His best guess was that while overseas, he was still in the chaos of combat; the safety of home allowed him to finally process the trauma.

His hearing aid had become a constant reminder of the day a bomb exploded right by him in Algiers. The sound vibrated throughout every part of his body, then the world went silent. He touched one ear and saw the blood, then checked other parts of his body. Somehow he was still in one piece. Slowly, the sound, although fuzzy and faint, began to come back. He wished it hadn't, because then the cries of agony wouldn't haunt him. But the boy he saw blown into pieces became fodder for his nightmares. Jack's heart broke listening to the boy whine for his mother. How he cried like a baby for her while writhing in pain lying in the mud so far away from home. It was easy to fall into despair, mulling these things over. The guilt of having survived and returned to his own family could have easily destroyed Jack. But when his mind went there, when he woke up in a sweat from the terror, he learned to push those memories back into the dark corners of his mind. It was the only way.

A few nights after they returned from Italy, Jack woke up to Mariella coaxing him back to bed. Initially, he thought he was still in a dream. Everything felt foggy during those nights. But the next morning, she explained how she woke to his erratic breathing, legs kicking at nothing. She tried to soothe him, talking in whispers telling him he was safe, but he didn't seem to hear her. He eventually got out of bed and crept into the hallway as if trying to get away from something. She followed and guided him back to their room. After four or five of these occurrences, he stopped. *Funny*, Jack thought, being close to Mariella, someone he met in the thick of the war, brought these hidden memories forward again. But she was also the one to help tamp them down.

"What are you doing?" Mariella whispered, rubbing her eyes from sleep.

Jack hadn't seen her wake. He sat beside her and ran his fingers down her arm before leaning in to kiss her lips. "You're so beautiful in the moonlight."

Mariella held onto him. He knew she missed him at night, but there wasn't anything he could do about it. During the summer, reservations filled up from opening until ten p.m., then came the late-night crowd after concerts at Convention Hall. That was when things became chaotic. Most people were interested in keeping the party going, which meant some nights they didn't close until two or three. If she was sleeping when he returned, Jack fought the urge to wake her, just for a few minutes. She may have been missing him, but the feeling was mutual.

"Hey, why don't you get dressed and come out with me?" Jack asked.

"What time is it?"

"One thirty. But if we hurry, we'll catch him before he leaves."

Mariella turned on her bedside lamp. "Catch who?"

"Never mind, sweetheart." Jack went to her closet and took out a shift dress and some sandals. "Just put this on. C'mon, you'll be happy you did."

As they drove along the ocean, a gentle breeze cooled the warm night air. It was the route he always took, especially after he returned from the war. During those years, knowing Mariella was somewhere out on the horizon made him feel closer to her.

When they reached the casino, Jack turned inland.

"Are we going to the restaurant?" Mariella asked, sounding worried.

Jack offered her a smile but kept quiet until he pulled up to the Palace Amusements.

"Perfect timing," he said, noticing the light on in the office. "Come on!" He helped Mariella out of the car and led her in through the back door. "Hello? You in there?"

Jack's friend Johnny shuffled out of the office. "Hey, Jack, whatcha doing here so late at night?"

"I should be asking you the same thing!"

Johnny rubbed the scar on one side of his face, as if to remind himself it was there. "Betty had the baby a week ago. We have another boy. But I can't get any sleep at my house. Between the other three and a crying baby, it can drive a man crazy."

"Well, congratulations, buddy. Your daughter is gonna have a hard time dating with three brothers! You remember how we kept the boys away from my sister. Julia's lucky there was a war or she'd never be married."

"Ain't that the truth! Now tell me, why are you two here?"

"Well pal," Jack said, slinging his arm around Mariella, "I was hoping you'd give my bride and me a ride on the Ferris wheel. You know she's never been on one."

Mariella turned to him, a giddy smile on her face. "Really?"

"Haven't you noticed the full moon? We can't go wasting such a beautiful night, now, can we?"

"It is okay?" Mariella turned to Johnny, crossing her fingers.

Jack noticed the heaviness in his friend's eyes and knew it wasn't just the new baby keeping him up at night. Since returning from the war, a dark cloud had taken residence over his head. One night when Johnny was drunk, he told Jack something awful that happened overseas. Knowing they all had horrific experiences, Jack tried to change the conversation, but Johnny couldn't be deterred. It was as if to punish himself, he needed to keep it in the forefront of his mind. It had taken place while in France, during one of the many battles they fought. As Johnny slurred his words, making everything harder to understand, Jack got only a portion of the story. German soldiers used the town's citizens as human shields, and in a heated battle, Johnny shot a mother holding her baby. The night was dark and rainy and he thought she had a gun. The baby was crushed under its mother's body as she fell to the ground. At the end of his story, he just kept mumbling, "I couldn't save the baby. It was too late. I killed the baby." Without a way to cope, he had turned to the bottle. Alcohol eased his mind—until it caused even more problems. The first time Jack noticed the light on at two a.m. in the Palace office, he went in and found Johnny and a bottle of whiskey. His friend looked destroyed, but this time wouldn't talk without some coaxing. It turned out he'd had an argument about his drinking with his wife the night before. Tears filled his eyes when he admitted he took it out on her with his fists. The guilt and shame he'd carried seemed unbearable. He wasn't staying late at night to escape his family; he was doing it to protect them.

"Whaddya say? A couple spins before bed?" Jack asked.

Johnny gave him a weary smile. "Sure."

He led them over to the giant Ferris wheel. Suspended from the rim were colorful baskets, each with a wooden bench for two.

"Let me go first," Jack said, pointing to his ear. "My battery is dying and I can hear better out of this one."

Mariella slid in next to him. Once Johnny latched the door, he pulled back on the lever, and away they went.

Clinging to Jack, Mariella buried her face in his neck. "I cannot look!" she cried as they climbed out of the building and dipped back in.

"But you have to. That's the best part."

After several turns, Jack gave Johnny a sign, and soon they were suspended at the top. It took a few minutes, but Jack convinced Mariella to uncover her eyes.

The lights from the casino cast an ominous glow on the dark, rolling ocean. "How lovely," she cooed.

"Isn't it? Look, you can see all the way to Bradley Beach! And would ya look at those waves? They're tremendous!"

"Amore, your Asbury Park is beautiful."

"My Asbury Park? It's yours now too."

Mariella put her head on his shoulder. "I miss you when you are not home."

"I'm here now, darling," Jack said, brushing his lips against her forehead.

"Will it be like this always? All the summers will be lonely?"

Jack watched as the wind blew softly, causing slight ripples on the lake dividing Asbury Park from Ocean Grove. He had never thought about the logistics of having Mariella with him in America. He'd just wanted her by his side. Suddenly, he felt selfish. "Gee, we need to take advantage of the summer tourists, especially with the parkway expansion opening. It'll be easier for people to go to beaches further south. Plus, they keep talking about some big investor building a large shopping center over in Eatontown. I'm not sure they'll actually do it, but Harvey from the commerce is worried about what it will do to business."

"Why do they go there?"

"They say these shopping centers are all the rage in California."

"But I do not understand. I can shop here."

"Sure, but these centers have a big variety of stores all in one place. Plus there's large parking lots surrounding it so you don't have to lug your packages all around town."

"That does sound nice."

"Hey, why don't you come to the restaurant on weekend nights?"

Mariella sat up and gave him a curious look. "To do what?"

"I bet we can find something. You can help me host. Our customers would love to be greeted by a beautiful woman." Jack grinned.

"And what would your mother think?" Mariella asked, the tension in her voice not going unnoticed by Jack.

He had felt the friction between them since the first day she arrived, but figured it was a passing thing, like with Willie's and Carl's wives. This seemed different, more personal. Ma had already dealt with being an outsider since arriving in America at age six. She had paid her dues and wasn't going to give someone new to the country any slack. Jack didn't like it but if he were to push back on Ma, she would get defensive. Instead, he hoped it would get better with time.

"She's cooking weekend nights. She'll be so busy in the kitchen she won't have time to bother with you."

Mariella thought for a moment, then nodded. "I would like that very much!" She hugged him and felt something in his jacket pocket. "What is this?"

"Oh, right! I was going to give it to you in the morning." Jack slid a cheery yellow envelope out of his pocket. "Millie and

Butch were in tonight. Boy, did those two tie one on." He shook his head, then realized Mariella didn't understand. "We say that when someone is drunk."

She creased her forehead.

Jack thought a moment. "I think the word is umbrago."

"Umbriago?" She put her thumb to her mouth and pretended she was drinking from a bottle, then crossed her eyes.

He laughed. "Yes, Millie said this is for you. She told me it was important." He handed her the card.

Mariella looked at the envelope. The border was decorated with pink and purple flowers dancing along a green vine. She pulled out a notecard with the same design.

"Ladies Lunch…e… on," she read out loud. "What is this?"

"Looks like she's having a lunch in your honor. How nice. This'll give you a chance to make more friends." Jack leaned over the side of the basket and yelled down to Johnny, who had fallen asleep. "Hey, buddy! Wake up!"

Johnny groggily lifted his head. "I'm awake. You want down?"

Jack nodded. Johnny pulled the lever, and they were back on the ground in a few seconds.

"You should get home, Johnny. Go get some sleep." Jack patted him on the back.

"Thank you," Mariella said.

Johnny waved goodbye, then retreated into his office once again.

On the ride home, Asbury's roads were empty. Jack enjoyed feeling like he was the only one in town, like he had special access to all of the city's nooks and crannies. He and Mariella snuck back into the house like teenagers. They washed up and slipped into bed, but the night wasn't over until they made love, melting into each other seamlessly.

Chapter Thirteen

"You decent?" Julia called out as she climbed the stairs to the second floor. "I just got this number back from the dry cleaners. I nearly forgot it was there. But I think it's perfect for the occasion. And I'm sure it'll fit you. I know it wouldn't get past my big belly!" she said, letting out a weary laugh. After delivering her third boy nearly three months before, Julia had yet to lose her baby weight.

Mariella popped her head out of the bathroom. "Here I am!"

Arriving at the top of the landing, Julia ceremoniously held out the dress. "Tada!"

"Oh my, it is beautiful!"

"Want me to help ya get it on?"

"I can do it." Mariella quickly dipped back into the

bathroom. "Thank you, Julia. You saved me today," she said through the door.

"Think nothing of it." Julia leaned against the wall. "Hurry up! I can't wait to see you in it."

Mariella opened the door and turned around. "Can you zip me up?"

"Sure." Julia zipped up the back, then buttoned the top. When Mariella turned back around, she smiled. "I don't think I ever looked like that wearing this dress. It really suits you!"

"It does?" Mariella went to her bedroom for a look in the full-length mirror. Julia was right. The pale blue dress fit like a glove. Its full, crinoline-filled skirt added the drama she'd hoped for. With her hair set in smooth curls at the nape of her neck and bangs swept to one side, she looked stunning.

Julia followed her in. "I wish I could see the faces on those old cows when they see you!"

"Cows?"

"Listen, Mariella, I went to school with those women, and I tell you, they can be nasty as anything. Of course, being Jack's younger sister, they spared me their wrath, but I know some girls they were awful to." She sighed. "What I'm saying is, these are mean women. They're older now, but I haven't seen a change. Just … be careful. Don't talk about your personal life. Nothing about Jack or any of us, or it will be town gossip for the next month."

"Do not worry, Julia," Mariella said. "I will be fine." She had heard the same advice from Clara when they had coffee the day before. And although she was going to be there too, Clara couldn't promise she could protect her. The reality was, Mariella didn't care. She was just happy to have something to break the monotony no matter how nasty the women were.

Despite Jack's offer to drive her on his way to work, Mariella chose to walk. It was a clear shot along the lake to Main Street, then five blocks over the bridge to the Deal Lake Country Club—about fifteen minutes. Walking always helped clear her head. But that day the wind had kicked into high gear, blowing everything around. Despite covering her hair in a silk scarf, Mariella's perfect curls had descended into chaos. She planned to make a beeline for the bathroom when she arrived, but couldn't avoid Millie greeting guests at the entrance.

"There she is!" she squealed. "Oh my, did you walk all the way here?"

Mariella slipped out of her scarf and smoothed her hair. "Yes, it is not a long walk."

"But that wind is just awful today. You're lucky it didn't blow you away. Never mind, you can freshen up later. Come and meet the women." Millie led her to where the other women were sitting and clapped her hands. "Girls. Attention, please! Our VIP guest has arrived. This is Jack Valentino's wife, Mary," Millie said, throwing up her arms like a carnival barker.

Mariella stood in the center of the room as the women eyed her, like the prize for a contest she had no knowledge of.

"Now, let me introduce you to each of the girls." Millie brought her around the table and made the introductions. This time she spoke slowly, and Mariella realized that Jack had something to do with it. She wished she hadn't told him that she struggled to understand when everyone spoke so quickly. "Mary, this is Louann. She's an old friend from elementary school."

Louann was a petite woman with freckles on her nose and thick red hair. Mariella had never seen someone so pale.

"Nice to meet you," Louann said, offering her hand limply. Mariella gave it a shake.

"And this is Carolyn. She lives two blocks away from us."

Carolyn rubbed her pregnant belly as though she were hoping to be granted wishes. She gave Mariella a quick smile, then returned to her conversation with Louann.

Millie continued, "And, of course, you remember Betty, Suze is over there, and of course my sister Clara?"

"Come sit by me," Clara said, pulling out the chair next to her.

"Oh no, no, you're in the wrong seat. I've got place cards in front of each setting. Your seat is where Carolyn is and she needs to sit where Betty is. Now Betty, you scoot over one. Then, Mary, you sit right where my sister was sitting."

Standing up reluctantly, Clara and Carolyn moved to their new seats. As Mariella went to her assigned seat she noticed a glamorous woman sitting in the chair next to hers.

"Oh, my lord! I almost forgot!" Suddenly, Millie's voice had a bite, drawing everyone's attention. "I have one more introduction. Mary, this is Lauren."

Lauren sat stiffly. Her platinum blonde hair was gathered neatly behind her ears and fastened with diamond-encrusted silver clips. She wore a pink dress with multicolored flowers decorating the bodice. Coupled with her porcelain skin and blue eyes, she looked like royalty.

For a moment, the woman's name swirled in Mariella's head until everything clicked. Lauren was Jack's ex-fiancée. Mariella's insecurities quickly flooded back.

"Lauren, this beautiful woman is Mary, Jack Valentino's new wife," Millie said, excitedly tripping over her words. "You remember Jack, don't you?"

Glaring at Millie with the force of a laser that could slice her in half, Lauren pursed her lips. "Of course I do." She glanced up at Mariella, a forced smile on her face. "Hello."

Mariella nodded but didn't respond. Either real or imagined, she felt everything about her screamed immigrant. She refused to add her horrible accent.

"I sat you two next to each other because I'm sure you'll have lots to discuss." Millie sang her words cheerily.

Mariella noticed the women at the table whispering to each other—all but one. Clara sat quietly, glaring at her sister.

As soon as she sat down, Lauren's perfume overwhelmed her. It was lavender, a favorite of her mother's, and a rush of longing for home made everything worse.

Thoroughly pleased with herself, Millie returned to her seat and tapped a knife against her champagne coupe. "Girls. Could you please pause your conversations for a moment? Thank you. I'm so happy all of you could make it! It's really wonderful to gather together and welcome our new foreign friend. For lunch today, I ordered cucumber and salmon sandwiches. Is that okay, Mary? Do you eat sandwiches in your country? Or is it always spaghetti and meatballs or something with red sauce?"

"Italy is not a third-world country, Mill," Clara said curtly. "I'm sure they eat sandwiches there. Right?" She gave Mariella a hopeful look.

Mariella nodded.

"How would I know?" Millie said, puffing her chest out. "I live in America, the best country in the world!"

Thankfully, a waitress arrived with a two-tiered serving platter, keeping Millie from climbing onto her patriotic soapbox. Mariella took one of each to prove she wasn't a barbarian.

"So, Lauren," Millie said across the table, "I think you and Mary have something in common, don't you?"

"Oh, Millie, you're always so thoughtful," Lauren said, her voice dripping with sarcasm.

Millie grinned. "Think nothing of it." She watched as Lauren ate her sandwich and grew frustrated. "Oh, go on! Why don't you tell her? I'm sure she wants to know everything about her husband. I would want to know if my Butch had been engaged to a stylish woman like yourself. We all want to know about our husbands' past lives. Don't we, girls?"

The ladies roared with laughter, some genuine, some uncomfortable.

Lauren's frustration caused Mariella to feel less intimidated. "I know who you are," she said in a friendly voice. "You are Jack, eh, old girl. I am sorry, um, I do not know the word for this." Suddenly, Mariella regretted being so bold.

"Fiancée," Lauren said firmly. "I was his fiancée."

"Fee-an-say?" Mariella repeated.

"Yes." Lauren turned to the rest of the women. "Only because I didn't know Jack had left someone overseas. If I had, I wouldn't have ever gotten involved."

"Oh, come now, Lauren, I don't think Mariella was the reason for your breakup," Suze joked.

Lauren pursed her lips again. "Of course not."

Millie leaned in. "Then whaddya mean, Laur?"

"What I mean is that only a certain type of man chased those women over there. If I had known he was one of them, I would have never gotten involved."

The uncomfortable quiet that descended over the room was only worsened by the sound of cutlery clinking against china plates as the women nervously pretended to be more invested in their food.

"Hmmm," Millie finally said, a sly smile spreading across her face. "Then I guess it all worked out for the best. You're happily married, and Jack has this Italian beauty!"

"Yes," Betty said, "and who would've thought! We all assumed Mary would arrive uncivilized like those dirty gypsies we saw on the newsreels."

As the women broke into laughter again, Mariella couldn't sit quietly any longer.

"They are not dirty," she said softly, but no one heard, so she stood up to get their attention. "They are not dirty."

Everyone quieted.

"What's that, dear?" Millie asked.

"The Roma Gypsies. I mean, maybe they are, but that was from what was done to them, to us."

"Sure." Millie narrowed her eyes at Mariella. "But ... they were dirty, right?"

Mariella's heart raced. She never thought she would have to defend herself after being a victim of war, let alone defend those helpless people who had been the real targets of Hitler's regime. *Uncivilized?* she thought. *War is uncivilized.* But explaining it to women who only experienced it on the silver screen was impossible. Mariella sat down.

"That's what I thought," Millie chirped. "You have no idea how horrible it was for *us* to sit through those awful newsreels. Thank God we don't have to watch those dreary reports anymore. It was bad enough that we had to ration things here..." She waved her napkin to get the waitress's attention. "Yoo-hoo! Miss! Can you please get us a fresh pitcher of ice water? The ice in this one has already melted, and I like my water just a touch above freezing."

The waitress quickly carried the pitcher away, water sloshing over the sides from moving too fast.

"I guess it's true," Lauren said.

Suze leaned in. "What's true?"

"You can take a horse out of the country, dress her up and line her lips with lipstick, but she's still a horse."

"Lauren!" Clara said, tightening her jaw.

"I'm not talking about her. I'm just saying in a general sense."

"You're being rude is what you are."

"Oh please, she doesn't understand what I was saying, right?" Lauren turned to Mariella. "You no understand me, right?"

Mariella looked at her in disbelief. "I-I don't...."

Lauren turned back to Clara. "See? Trust me, these foreigners aren't very smart."

Chapter Fourteen

For the remainder of the meal, Mariella was happy to be left out of their conversation as the women gossiped about former schoolmates. As she ate her bland sandwich, Clara made eye contact and cocked her head toward the restroom. Mariella quickly excused herself. Clara followed close behind.

"I'm sorry," she said, leaning against the sink while Mariella reapplied her lipstick. "But I warned you. You know it's no accident that Lauren is here, right? This lunch is a total setup."

"I am fine," Mariella said, trying not to sound bothered.

"Girls!" Millie said, bursting through the door. "I've ordered Cherries Jubilee for dessert! The chef is ready with it, but we can't eat until you two return to the table. Stop dilly-dallying around!"

"Listen, Millie, you can tell them to hold their horses," Clara said impatiently. "We're not done powdering our noses."

Millie's eyes flicked over to Mariella then back to Clara. "Well, hurry up!" she snipped, before leaving.

"Ugh! My sister is maddening!"

"It is okay, really." Mariella tucked her lipstick back into her purse and forced a smile. "I am happy to be here."

"Just don't be so *nice* to everyone. These women don't understand nice."

Mariella returned to the table and found Lauren in her seat whispering with Suze. Neither one acknowledged her.

"Okay, everyone," Millie sang to the women. "It's time for our dessert, and boy, is it a doozy! You're all going to love it. Now, let's all sit down. Come on, Mary!" Millie said, louder than necessary. "You need to sit. In your chair?"

Everyone stared as Mariella's face heated with embarrassment. She quickly sat in Lauren's chair instead, then preoccupied herself with the contents of her purse. Other than the tube of lipstick, it didn't hold much; a powder rouge and puff for applications, a plastic coin purse with two quarters inside and a picture she'd tucked in the side pocket before leaving for America. It was of her class, the only school picture taken before the war. She must have been about thirteen years old and insisted on standing in front holding hands with her dear friend Helena. They wore matching braids with ribbons at the ends. Although the photo was black-and-white, she remembered the powder-blue silk Mama made the ribbons with. Hitler and Mussolini had already formed the Rome-Berlin axis, and at first, her mother refused to make a bow for her daughter's Jewish friend. If found out, the repercussions would have been severe. But Mariella insisted Helena's mother would take the blame. Despite her fear for the woman's safety, Mama gave in and made the bow. It was a simple show of solidarity for the girls.

Stuck in the past, Mariella didn't notice the plates with cherries and ice cream being paraded to the table. The chef, dressed in white with a tall, mushroom-topped hat, lit the cherries on fire. While everyone clapped at the spectacle, Mariella quickly shut her purse, pushing the comfort of her memories away.

"Well, Mary, I hope you enjoyed yourself today," Millie said as Mariella headed for the door. "It was a lot of work, to be honest, I'm happy it's over. But I did it so that you can make friends. I hope it was worth it. I—" She was suddenly distracted by the waitstaff clearing a table. "Excuse me! Excuse me! If there are leftovers, I would like to take them home. This luncheon cost my husband a pretty penny, and it would be nice if he got a little taste of the food."

Holding a melted bowl of ice cream with a scant amount of strawberry sauce, the waitress gave her a blank look. "Uh, sure, ma'am. I'll get this in an icebox container right away."

Millie turned back to Mariella and sighed. "It's so hard for these restaurants to get good help. I'm sure you know. That must be why you need to work with Jack on the weekends."

Mariella had worked as a hostess the night before while Millie and Butch drank martinis at the bar until they couldn't see straight. She'd overhead Jack explaining how she had been lonely, which was why she was there. They both pretended to understand, but now it was obvious it had become gossip.

Suze joined in the conversation. "Millie told me about you working. I thought it was so odd. My husband would never put me to work." She turned to Lauren, who was waiting by the entrance for her ride. "What about you, Laur? Wouldn't your husband just *die* if he needed you to go out there and earn a living?"

Lauren offered a cunning grin. "My father would have had his head." She brushed a stray hair behind her ear just as a red Cadillac pulled up to the door. "Of course, I would never be with a man who allowed his wife to work, now would I?"

It was obvious Lauren knew her words stung, but she let them float casually in her wake as she got into the car.

"Wanna lift home?" Suze asked Mariella.

"No, thank you. I like to walk."

"Suit yourself."

Another car pulled up, this time a black sedan. Pat leaned out of the driver's window. "Hiya, girls! How was lunch?"

Suze ran around to the passenger side. "It was okay, but the Cherries Jubilee! That was fantastic."

Slipping her scarf over her head, Mariella walked past their car and started down the long driveway.

"Hey, Mary, wanna ride?" Pat yelled out to her.

Suze shook her head. "She likes to walk."

"Strange," he muttered as he drove away.

Mariella hugged herself to keep warm as she walked home. A mist had rolled in, blocking the sun, and a cool breeze blew against her skin. She scolded herself for not saying more to Lauren, but didn't understand why someone as sweet as Jack would want to marry such a woman. She wondered if maybe there was more to him than she knew. They had written for almost eight years before he came back for her. During that time, he'd shared the news about his engagement to Lauren. He seemed proud of her, spoke of how they shared a lot in common. Now the thought terrified her. *How can this nasty woman have anything to do with my Jack?* she wondered. Then she remembered her engagement to Lorenzo. She, too, had bragged in her letters about meeting a wonderful man. Did she agree to marry him because Jack was engaged too? Possibly. Lorenzo had shown who he was time and time again, but she pretended not to see until she was forced to. Mariella decided Jack must have done the same. Besides, she couldn't continue to love her husband without having complete faith in him.

"You still awake?" Jack asked, as he loosened his tie. "It's two a.m." He sat on the bed beside her and turned on the light. "How was the luncheon? Make any new friends?"

She had gone over the events of the day for hours, and had every intention of telling Jack, but his kind eyes were filled with love and hope and suddenly, she didn't want to disappoint him.

"Yes, amore, it was nice. I meet a few new women," she said.

Jack kissed her lips. "See, before you know it, you'll have plenty of American girlfriends."

"I know, amore, I know," Mariella said, watching him change his clothing. When he crawled next to her in bed she curled up as close as possible.

Chapter Fifteen

Under a tree filled with green leaves and orange fruit, Mariella watched a butterfly form a perfect figure eight until it landed on her lap. It looked up at her, but she couldn't see the face. Its cellophane wings fluttered back and forth gracefully. She tried to focus, but couldn't make out who it was. The butterfly flew by her ear and hovered. "Write Jack," it whispered, mimicking her sister's words from long ago. Electricity ran through Mariella. "What? What? Who are you?" she cried. The butterfly flitted around her head, then came close again. Mariella kept still. "Write your letter," it whispered. Suddenly, the fruit suspended above transformed into bright red blossoms of bougainvillea. *Elisa!* Mariella thought. She tried to call out, but her mouth was dry and words formed without sound. The butterfly flew close once more and the feeling of Elisa's thin hands stroking her hair caused a pang of longing to run through her. *I miss you*, she thought. *I miss you so much.*

"What's wrong, sweetheart?" Mariella opened her eyes and found Jack gazing down at her. He took her in his arms, brushing away her tears. "Another bad dream?"

It wasn't a bad dream; it was reality. Mariella couldn't help but feel the sting of her sister's absence. Sometimes, the pain took her breath away, but she didn't want Jack to worry about her.

"I am used to them," she said.

"Honey." Jack looked deep in her eyes. "You don't have to face them alone anymore. You have me, now. Besides, what hurts you hurts me."

Mariella let out a soft laugh. "I never want to hurt you, amore."

"Do you want to talk about it? Maybe we can call Italy today."

"I wish we could, but Mama wrote that they will not have a telephone in until next month." Mariella had been thrilled to hear that her parents would install one in their apartment. Keeping in touch by airmail was tedious. Her letters took at least a month to get from New Jersey to Rome and it was worse in the reverse. Although international phone calls were expensive, especially when they were made during the week, Jack worked one five-minute call a month into their budget. Mariella couldn't wait.

Later that morning, Jack lingered in the kitchen acting strange. He usually left by eleven, but that morning he read the paper cover to cover. Ma kept eyeing them, as if they were two teenagers waiting for her to leave so they could make love.

"Jackie, you're gonna be late for work," she finally said.

Jack winked at Mariella. "I'm not going in until later today."

"What are you talking about?" Putting her hands on her hips, Ma's face hardened. "You can't hang around here taking care of your wife. She's a big girl. She can be alone. Besides, she's got silverware to polish."

"Well, Ma," Jack said, folding his newspaper, "it will have to wait. I've already talked to Pop. It's only for a few hours, they'll be fine at the restaurant. Mariella and I have somewhere to go."

"Why doesn't anyone tell me things?" Ma complained. "You two have been married for over a year. You're not newlyweds anymore!" She removed her apron, laid it on the stove, and left the kitchen in a huff.

Mariella looked over at Jack, worry etched on her face. "I do not think your ma likes me."

"She's never cared for any of the women in my life." Jack said, "But she's furious at you because you're not going anywhere. It's nothing to worry about. We've got bigger fish to fry!" He took her by the hand and led her to the driveway where his father's Cadillac convertible sat with the top down. "Your chariot awaits."

Mariella touched her hair. She had set it in curlers overnight, brushed it out that morning, then sprayed it with AquaNet. "Amore, I just did my hair. Let me get a scarf."

"I'll wait," he responded breezily.

As Jack drove down Corlies Avenue, the crisp fall air felt good on Mariella's skin. She asked him several times where they were going, but he just smiled and whistled a cheery tune. They drove along Wickapecka Avenue, passing a substantial house that made her think of the White House, with pillars on either side of the door and a white picket fence around the front lawn. Then, they made a right onto Darlene Avenue, where a large, colorful sign on the corner greeted them. Big block letters at the top read LIFE IS GOOD IN WANAMASSA GARDENS. Below it was a painting of a house with a Chevrolet in the driveway. A husband, wife, and two blond children, a boy and girl, waved happily from the porch. Jack and Mariella continued down the road where newly built houses, more modest than the faux White House, lined one side of the street while on the other, men riding tractors were hard at work digging up trees to make room for additional homes.

At the end of the street, Jack turned onto an unpaved road punctuated by a small makeshift sign that read "Interlaken

Avenue." A new build stood on the corner, but the rest was pines and oaks and dirt. Halfway down the road, Jack pulled the car over.

"Well, what do you think?" He grinned, getting out of the car.

"What do I think?" she repeated, following him. "I think we are in the middle of a forest."

Jack laughed. "Well then you need to use your imagination! Picture this as your driveway," he said, pointing to a dirt trail leading into the woods.

"My driveway?"

"Sure." Jack offered his arm, and Mariella weaved hers into it. They walked to a small clearing. "And this right here can be your front door." He drew a line in the dirt with his foot.

Mariella shook her head. "I do not understand."

"This, Signora Valentino"—Jack stretched his arms out wide—"is where we will build our new home!"

It took a few seconds for his words to register. Mariella never thought they would own their own house. Being from Rome, she had only pictured them in an apartment, but a house was never on her radar. Suddenly, though, she *could* picture it; children running across a grassy lawn, a laundry line in the back with sheets of her own drying, the familiar aroma of sauce using basil and tomatoes from her garden drifting out from the kitchen window. She searched his eyes, wondering if he was joking, but his expression was all too familiar. It was the same when he told her he loved her at the Colosseum and again when he professed his love standing in her family's apartment in Rome.

"Our own home?" she asked in a whisper.

Jack didn't respond. Instead, he led her deeper into the woods until they arrived at a stake in the ground with a ribbon tied to it. "Our own home on our own property that goes all the way to here. Can you picture it?"

Mariella's eyes grew wide as she looked back to where he'd drawn the line for their front door. "Amore, are we building a mansion?"

"Why not! Or better yet, we'll build a castle!" He pulled her close. "Just for you and me. And of course," he kissed her, "all the little Valentinos we can make!"

"Children?"

"Not just any ole children. Our family. Sweetheart, can't you just picture it?"

At that moment, Mariella couldn't picture anything else.

Over the next several months, Jack and Mariella attended Sunday mass, then drove to Wanamassa Gardens to check on the progress of their new home. At first, it was disappointing. The process was much slower than Mariella had hoped—trees cleared one week, tunnels dug for various piping the next. Still, knowing they would have a place of their own made it all worth it. Although Pop was happy for them, Ma felt differently. Her jabs at Mariella became more cruel, like switching from a butter knife to one used for carving a roast.

"You need to scrub the toilet," she would yell from the bathroom. "If you don't, that house of yours will smell to high heavens. And for God's sake, hang the towels properly. Where were you living before, a barn?"

In those moments, Mariella had to swallow her anger. Her own mother had always taken pride in their sparkling-clean apartment, even when they had nothing, and she'd taught her daughter well. Mariella used lemon and vinegar to scrub the kitchen and got down on her hands and knees to polish the wooden floors. She found herself lost in daydreams of setting up her own house with beautiful furniture they would pick out together. They would finally be able to use the many wedding gifts they'd received. She would plant a vegetable garden in the backyard and hang a long laundry line for their clothing to dry. In the front she planned an array of colorful flowers to welcome friends and neighbors. Mariella also imagined the different seasons in the house. During summer, they could set up a table in the back and have dinners outside like she did on her grandparents' farm. During the winters, she imagined a cozy house with snow falling gently past their windows.

When Ma carried on about what an awful job Mariella did, she would never talk back. Instead, she retreated further into her daydreams. *Soon*, Mariella thought, watching her mother-in-law inspect her work. *Soon I'll be in my own house, and you will have nothing to say about it.*

Chapter Sixteen

Clara peered through the screen door. "Is it time to move in already?" she asked, her voice tinged with sadness.

"Come in, I will make you a coffee!" Mariella said, trying to hide her excitement as they went into the kitchen. After a year in the United States and nine months waiting for their home to be built, she and Jack were finally moving out of his parents' house.

"I guess it was inevitable. The one friend I make here runs off as fast as she came."

"Stop being dramatic. You are always welcome at my house."

"What am I going to do without you here? I suppose I'll have to get used to drinking American coffee. And let's face it, I don't drive, and your house will take me at least a half hour to walk to. Thirty minutes there, then thirty minutes back. It's not like popping over."

During Mariella's lonely first months in America, Clara's company had kept her from falling into a depression. Now, she was abandoning her. Suddenly she got an idea.

"Wait here." Mariella ran up the stairs to her bedroom, then returned with a sealed cardboard box. She held it out to Clara, her face beaming. "For when I am not around."

"What's this?" Clara asked, opening the box. She pulled out a black-handled espresso pot shaped like a woman; a large top for the coffee to bubble up into, thin middle, and an equally large bottom for the grinds and water.

"My neighbor give it to me before I come here," Mariella explained. "She want to make sure I have two if one is lost. Now it is yours."

Clara held the gift to her heart and smiled. "Thank you. I promise to take good care of it."

"Come on. I show you how to make perfect espresso." Mariella gave her a quick lesson on how to use the pot—filling the basket, tapping down the grinds, then pouring water into the bottom. "Now, you need fire." She placed the pot on the stove. "Voila!"

"It looks simple enough," Clara joked, "but Lord knows I'll screw it up!"

"You will be fine."

"I guess. Oh, Mariella, I've got to get out of that house. Living with my sister and her family is hell. You've made life so much better."

As Mariella listened to Clara's words, the familiar feeling of guilt washed over her.

Clara looked out the window. The sky had grown dark, and gathering clouds promised a storm. "I guess I can ride my nephew's bike to your house when it's not raining."

"That would be wonderful!" Mariella held up her espresso cup in celebration. "To friendship!"

Clara sighed. "To keeping in touch."

Mariella tapped her chin and thought for a moment. "To sisters."

"To sisters!" Clara said, smiling through her tears.

"Penny for your thoughts," Jack asked Mariella as they stood on the front lawn admiring their new house. Painted in a cheery yellow, it had square windows framed by white shutters in the front and one on the side, plus a large window in the living room. Shrubs flanked the property and a newly poured asphalt driveway leading to a one-car garage was roped off for protection.

It was perfect.

Tears pricked at Mariella's eyes. She laid her head on his

shoulder. "I cannot believe it is ours."

"Well, believe it, Mrs. Valentino."

They held onto each other, readying themselves to take a giant leap into their new life.

Carl and Will drove up in a trailer with a few pieces of furniture including a green Formica kitchen table with four chairs donated by Jack's parents. They'd also bought them an oak bedroom set with a beautiful design carved into the headboard. The day before, Jack had brought Mariella to pick out a mattress.

"How do we choose?" she asked, gazing out at the vast showroom.

"I guess we'll have to try them out," Jack teased, but Mariella thought it was a great idea. She spent a few minutes bouncing on each mattress until she found one most like her featherbed back home.

"Is this all you two have, Jackie boy?" Will asked, staring into the half-empty trailer.

Jack shrugged. "It's a start. We want to move in first, then decide what we need."

"C'mon, we don't have all day," Carl said. "Now, tell us where you want to put all this stuff."

Jack and his brothers moved everything into the house, then left for the restaurant, giving Mariella time to settle in. She got to work, sorting out boxes stacked on the kitchen table. The first was filled with silverware—all wedding gifts from their reception. She organized the top drawer with forks, knives, and spoons, then used the drawer below for cooking utensils. At the bottom of the box, she found a long, thin package Mama had instructed her to open when she had a kitchen of her own. Mariella tore off the paper to find one of her mother's stained wooden spoons with a note attached. It read: *Always cook with love.* Mariella smiled at Mama's flowery handwriting and the thoughtful reminder of home.

That evening was like their wedding night all over again. Everything felt new, even Jack. It made sense; they were starting a fresh chapter of their lives. At his parents' house, Mariella worried about being heard during their intimate moments. A lot of times, her nerves led to mindless chatter. Now, they were able to express themselves freely.

After they made love, Mariella was too excited to sleep. The slight rise and fall of Jack's chest confirmed he had quickly drifted off. Watching the newly hung sheer curtains move with the breeze, Mariella imagined they were dancing a ballet to the chirping crickets outside. She took stock of all that had happened in the past two years. Before Jack's return, after breaking it off with Lorenzo and her sister's death, she had resigned herself to a life without love. Now, she was living the American dream.

Mariella slipped out of bed and went into the room next to theirs. Tiptoeing across the floor, she counted one, two, three, and so on until she reached eight. Approximately three hundred and sixty-five centimeters across. The bedroom she'd shared with her three sisters was half of that. Mariella pictured a crib in the corner under the window, shadowed by a sycamore tree, and a rocking chair for nighttime feedings right beside it. *Amazing!* she thought.

The third room, just past the landing, was much smaller. Jack planned to make it an office to store their important papers. Mariella shuffled downstairs to their living room and the large picture window overlooking the street. Most of the land had been cleared and skeletons of houses stood in their place, making things look stark. Luckily, the house directly across from hers and the one next door were almost completed. She insisted they not hang curtains on the window; it felt friendlier that way. Walking through their dining room, which sat empty, ready for the delivery of a dining set the following day, Mariella went into the kitchen. In the still night, she noticed the soft hum of their new refrigerator. She opened the door and looked inside. After growing up with a small icebox, the thought that they could fill all of the shelves seemed impossible. But there was also a compartment for vegetables and fruits and a separate one for butter and eggs. Then, at the bottom, was a bin for frozen things.

Mariella couldn't wait to tell her mother all about it.

Glancing around the kitchen, she imagined making Christmas dinner for her family. She opened the oven, pulled out an imaginary roast, and placed it on the kitchen table.

"What are you doing, sweetheart?" Jack asked, leaning against the wall watching her. Mariella blushed as if caught nosing around someone else's house, then remembered it was all hers. "Couldn't sleep?"

"I think I am too excited."

"Same here. Can't wait to fill this house with children."

Mariella took his hand and kissed the palm where his scars from the war intersected. "Not just children. Our children."

"Then I guess we better get started," Jack whispered, a sly smile on his face. He took her by the hand and led her back up the stairs to bed.

Chapter Seventeen

Over the following month, Jack and Mariella settled into their new house. She busied herself making tablecloths and curtains, organizing her laundry room, and hanging a few of Jack's paintings. Although he'd created several before the war, she preferred the ones made after his return. He had painted Piazza di Spagna, adding colorful flowers for sale along each step, another with a view of the road leading up to her apartment in gray and black, and a third featuring the center fountain in his favorite square—Piazza Navona. But the one she liked most was a large painting of the Colosseum in all its glory. Hung above the couch in their living room, it was a beautiful reminder of the fateful day they met.

When everything was in its place and the excitement faded, loneliness set in once again. Clara made good on her promise and visited several times, but she was right. It wasn't the same. A lot of planning had to go into her visits, especially after Clara took a job at the library.

One warm June morning, Mariella decided to explore her new neighborhood. As she walked outside, the smell of lilacs and cotton filled the air, making her smile. She had recently trimmed the fragrant bush in her garden and used the clippings for sachets to put in their clothes drawers.

Mariella passed the house next to hers. The builders had finished it a few weeks prior, and an older couple had moved in. She planned to welcome them with some homemade biscotti the day they arrived, but when the woman saw her walking over, she hurried back inside. The house next to it was partly finished, but construction had stalled. The one after that, a different style and slightly larger than Jack and Mariella's, was almost done. Three men, precariously balanced on ladders, painted it an eggshell blue.

She continued, passing two empty lots and a lovely white house on the corner that served as the model home for Wanamassa Gardens. But it was something on the other side of the street that caught Mariella's eye.

A shiny, brass Jewish star hung prominently from a brick building on the corner. She crossed the road and walked along a pebble-covered path that led to the entrance. Since the door was open, she went inside. The temple was expansive, with pews lined down the center and large stained-glass windows on either side, much like her church in Rome. Mariella walked up to the front, a peaceful feeling washing over her.

"Can I help you?" a voice, deep like her father's, asked.

She hadn't noticed the man standing off to the side. He was middle-aged, with a long, dark beard and a few strands of hair hidden underneath his yarmulke.

"Oh, I am sorry. I hope I can be here. I live down the street, eh, I thought, I mean, I come because—" Mariella paused, surprised at the emotion in her voice. "I had a friend…"

"Please, sit." The man waved her over to a pew, and they both sat down. "Where are you from?"

Mariella pursed her lips, frustrated that her foreignness made her stick out like a sore thumb.

"I'm sorry, dear. I noticed your accent, and I'm certain it is not from Israel, but Argentinian, maybe?"

"No, I am from Italy."

"Ah." The man extended his hand. "I'm Rabbi Sheridan."

"Oh, I did not know." She hesitated, then shook his hand. "I-I thought because—"

"Because I dress like any other man, I couldn't possibly be a rabbi?"

"I am sorry."

"You don't need to apologize. We rabbis don't have special

powers like your priests do." He smiled as he stroked his beard. "We are just ordinary people educated in the Jewish faith, like guides for the community."

"Oh."

"And what brings you here?"

"I had a friend back home. Helena." As her name fell out of Mariella's mouth, so did the tears from her eyes. "I am sorry, Rabbi, it was not long ago."

"It's okay. War has affected us all. Take your time, dear." He patted her arm, his gaze filled with concern.

"I grew up in Rome. And my friend Helena, she was Jewish. Oh, Rabbi, she was kind and sweet, and funny. And her parents, they try to protect her. They hide for months in an attic on top of a restaurant. I cannot know what that was like. But the Germans still catch them. They took her parents. Thanks to God, she got away." Mariella swallowed hard. "She hid with us for a time, then with nuns across the street. They were good to her and she was not alone. They hid many children in the annex. I know because I watch them celebrate the sabbath." The memory of flickering light in a sea of darkness brought her right back to that night. "I can never forget how scared I was when they come. Those Nazis, they are bad people. When they find the children, they shoot Mother Superior. She had courage—even when they put a gun at her head, she did not cry."

"And what happened to the others?" the rabbi asked.

Mariella noticed the hurt and pain so many had carried during those times clouding his eyes. She would have thought he had been in Europe during the war, if he hadn't had such a strong New York accent. "They took the nuns and the children in a truck, like animals. I do not know where."

Rabbi Sheridan nodded. "You may never find out. My father's family were living in Poland. Now they are all gone— every single one, except for my father. He was lucky. He and my mother moved here in their twenties when I was just a baby. He tried convincing his family to come before the borders closed, but no one would believe it could get that bad. We assume they were taken to camps, but there is no record. Jews didn't matter."

"I do not think anyone mattered to the Nazis."

Mariella and the rabbi sat silently, allowing the words too painful to speak to go unsaid. She knew her friend was probably dead. They had all died.

"How can your father live knowing his family suffered?" Mariella finally asked.

"Ah, that is the million-dollar question." He let out a soft laugh. "But how can you not when your life was spared? If God allows you to live, you must do it fully. My father never let grass grow underneath his feet, as they say. He was always doing. His jewelry business was one of the best in the city because he worked hard to get the finest pieces for his customers. When he wasn't working, he joined the Jewish Aid Coalition to help those resettling in the US. He called it his year-round Mitzvah. A good deed, that is."

Mariella spent the rest of the afternoon chatting with the rabbi. They spoke about the neighborhood and how it was changing. The rabbi had been at the synagogue since it was built ten years before, when the only thing surrounding it were woods. He loved having more people around and said because of the new homes his congregation grew. They spoke about God and eventually Mariella began to tell him how she lost her faith for a while.

"How can he let this happen? Not only war, but my sister, he let a tumor grow in her brain. She die so young. Why would he let this happen?" she said, her eyes searching for answers.

The rabbi stroked his beard as if it helped him think. "Have you ever heard of the saying 'God had his reasons'?"

Mariella sighed. "I hear this many times."

"Yes, yes, of course you would. But it is true. If you think about your sister and her goodness, wouldn't it make sense her place would be by his side?"

"Without her family? So young?"

"Ahhh," the rabbi said, raising his finger, "our physical bodies have limited time on Earth, but there is some Jewish thought that the afterlife is also spent here. And you have to trust that your sister is by your side in spirit."

"How can that be? I left her in Rome."

"Of course, dear, her body is in Rome, but not her spirit. Her spirit is all around us. She is the leaf that fell from the tree during fall to nourish the ground. Or the bee that makes the honey. Or the cloud that is filled with water ready to rain on the dry earth."

His words made Mariella hopeful. Up until their conversation, she had always thought of her sister visiting in the form of birds back home. The idea that Elisa could also be around her in America took some of the loneliness away.

They talked more about family and how Mariella couldn't wait to start her own. The rabbi had three, all boys. He said, "The most wonderful thing about raising children is best said in a Jewish proverb. 'As you teach, you learn.' I've learned so many things about life while raising my boys. It's a wonderful experience. God bless you with many children of your own."

"Thank you, Rabbi," Mariella said, noticing the time. "Oh! It has gotten late. I need to go home. The restaurant is closed on Monday, so Jack is home early, and I like to have his dinner waiting."

Rabbi Sheridan smiled at her. "Please don't keep your husband waiting. But," he leaned in, "don't be a stranger either. You are always welcome in this temple."

Chapter Eighteen

"Hello, operator? Yes, we are trying to call Rome, Italy," Jack said. "Yes. Yes, we've tried a few times, but when you connect us the call gets dropped."

Mariella bit at her thumbnail as she waited. Even though it was costly, now that her parents had a phone, Jack worked monthly calls into their budget. But it hadn't ever taken this long to get through. Thoughts of Italy thrown into another war they knew nothing about plagued her mind.

"Yes, yes, my wife is Italian. She can speak to the operator there, but we're not getting through."

"Ask if maybe something is happening over there?"

Jack raked his hand through his hair. "She wouldn't know, sweetheart. But don't worry, I'm sure everything is fine. Excuse me, operator? You got through? Oh, okay, here is my wife."

Mariella quickly took the phone, relaxing when she heard her language spoken on the other end. "Hello? Yes. Is everything okay in Italy?" she asked.

"It depends on what you think okay is," the operator said with a laugh, "Okay, I'll put you through."

"Pronto?" A worried voice picked up on the first ring.

"Mama, it's me, Mariella."

Once she began to talk, Jack pressed the timer on his watch for five minutes.

"What took you so long? You're fifteen minutes late. I thought maybe something was wrong."

"The operator couldn't get through at all today. We had to try three times." Mariella gesticulated as if Mama could see. She was surprised that speaking Italian took some getting used to.

"Well, at least you are okay. And how is your house? Are you settled in?"

"Yes, Mama. It's a dream. There are so many rooms, I don't know what to do with them! Jack has taken some pictures I will send when he develops them."

"That would be wonderful. And how is he?"

Mariella turned to Jack. "She wants to know how you are."

He leaned into the phone. "I'm doing bene, Mama. Just swell! And I'm sending kisses, uh, tanti baci to all of you!"

Mama laughed on the other end. "Oh, he's such a beautiful

man. Please, tell him I send all my love."

"She sends her love," Mariella told Jack.

"And how are you, Tesoro?" Mama continued. "Any baby news yet?"

Mariella knew her mother couldn't wait to have grandchildren. She was getting anxious about it, too. Every Sunday at church she said prayers hoping God would intervene. "Not yet, Mama. I'm sorry to disappoint you. It just hasn't happened yet." Eager to change the subject, Mariella asked, "Where's Papa?"

"I am here, Tesoro!" Papa's deep voice vibrated with emotion. He could never get through their monthly phone calls without choking up. "I miss you so!"

His longing brought out hers. "Oh, Papa, I miss you too."

"Three more minutes," Jack interrupted. Pointing to his watch, he shot Mariella an apologetic look.

"Mama, I don't have much time. Is everyone there?"

"Of course, Tesoro. We are getting ready for lunch."

"Oh," Mariella was suddenly transported to their apartment in Rome. Smelling Mama's sauce, setting the table, and filling a carafe with the jug of homemade wine they kept under the kitchen sink. "And what did you make?"

"I made cappelletti with peas and prosciutto and cream. Sylvia is coming over."

"Signora Manetto? What's wrong?"

Mama sighed. "I don't know. I think she has just gotten more lonely in her old age. The other night it was so hot we had all of the windows opened. But I couldn't sleep, so I went to the kitchen for a glass of water. That's when I heard some sort of whining. It sounded so sad. I didn't figure out what it was until I went into the hallway. Poor thing must cry herself to sleep at night."

The idea that her dear neighbor was so painfully lonely made Mariella feel like her own loneliness was superficial. She had her husband and the prospect of a family to look forward to. Signora Manetto didn't have anyone but her friends, and they weren't around in the early morning hours when loneliness took hold the tightest.

"I'm so happy you're having her over, Mama. She'll enjoy being with the family. Please send her my love."

"I will, Tesoro," Mama said, a commotion erupting in the background. "Okay, okay," she shouted then returned to the phone. "Everyone wants to speak to you so I will hand the phone over, but I will be back to say goodbye."

"Here I am, Mariella! How is America?"

"Hi, Giada! America is wonderful," Mariella responded, a little too enthusiastically. "It's so nice to hear your voice. How are you?"

"I'm good, but I wish you were here."

"One day. But it better be a Sunday because I can smell Mama's cooking from across the ocean!" Mariella let out a soft laugh. "Now, tell me, how's your boyfriend?"

"Oh, he's always so busy with his work. I hate to say it, but he's become an absolute bore!"

"Two minutes," Jack said.

Mariella tried to ignore him. "Sometimes men can be bores."

"And sometimes there are too many fish in the sea to put up with a bore!"

"That is true!" Mariella said. Her sister would rather be alone with a book than with someone she wasn't madly in love with.

"I wanna say hi!" a muffled, high-pitched voice called out in the background.

"Okay," said Giada, "I have to give the phone to Matteo. I'm sending gigantic kisses to you and Jack!"

Before Mariella could respond, Matteo got on the phone. "Hi, Mariella!"

"Matteo? Is that you? You sound so grown up!"

"That's because I am! You know I play soccer and I am the star of the team."

"You are?"

"Yup. And I scored five goals in the match I played yesterday. We won, of course."

"That's terrific!" Mariella turned to Jack. "My brother is a soccer star."

Jack clapped. "'Well, whaddya know! Bravo, Matteo! Bravo!"

"Your zio Jack says well done!"

"Tell zio thank you!" Matteo said. "When are you coming home?"

Mariella winced. "One day," she said softly.

Jack tapped her on the shoulder and mouthed, "One minute."

"Can I speak to Lia?"

"Sure," Matteo said, handing the phone over.

"I don't know why I have to be last! I miss you just as much as everyone else."

"Oh, Lia!" Mariella laughed. Although Matteo was the youngest, Lia had always been the baby. "How are you?"

"I'm good. Just going to school and then coming home to study. I don't know why Mama and Papa are making school such a big deal. I'm just going to get married and become a mother."

"Yes, and they want you educated so you are not a stupid mother."

"Of course, you would say that. You always liked school."

"Exactly," Mariella said, firmly. "You would appreciate it too if it had been kept from you. I had to drop out during the war, but you have it available, so don't be a donkey. Study and become the best student you can. For me."

"Okay," Lia said, reluctantly. "Hey, tell your Americano he needs to send some more chocolate. Matteo and I like the Hershey's."

"We've already sent a large package to all of you. It should arrive in a few weeks."

"Thanks sister. Oh, Mama wants the phone. I love you!"

"I love you too."

Mama returned to the phone. "You sent a package?"

"Yes, Mama. Jack's mother added a few sleeves of those crackers you like with the cheese baked in."

"Oh, please thank her. Your father and I love those. We just finished the ones you sent a few months ago. And of course, the Hershey's has been gone since the day it was received. Your brother and sisters are animals!"

Jack leaned in. "Ten seconds."

"I don't have much time left."

"Okay," Mama said in a small voice. "I love you, Tesoro."

"Me too," Papa chimed in. "I miss you so much. I wish you were here so I could hug you."

"I promise to call next month." Mariella spoke quickly, trying to put words to everything she felt in her heart. "I love you! I miss you too! Bye! Bye! I love you! Bye. I'm sending a million kisses. I love you. Bye. Goodbye."

Once the phone went back on the cradle, she fell apart. It wasn't unusual. Every month, when her time was up, she felt she was saying goodbye all over again. Jack held her tight while she shook with grief until she was numb. Sometimes, she wondered if it might be easier not to be reminded of her old life.

Most Sundays after their calls, Jack spent hours trying to cheer Mariella up. First they would go to morning mass, then he would take her on a drive along the ocean. They passed Deal, Long Branch, Monmouth Beach, and Atlantic Highlands, winding up the hill and moving inland. Usually, they turned around and followed the same route back. But this morning, Jack kept driving until he was on the Garden State Parkway.

"What are we doing?" Mariella asked.

A dense fog had gripped the coast but it was beginning to dissipate as they climbed over the Raritan Bridge.

Jack smiled. "You'll see. Just be patient. We won't get there for a while."

Listening to the hum of the car's motor, Mariella closed her eyes. After an emotionally draining morning, she was exhausted.

It didn't take long before she drifted off to sleep.

After about forty-five minutes, Jack nudged Mariella gently on the shoulder.

"Wake up, sweetheart," he whispered. "We're here."

"What?" Mariella sat up and looked around. "Where?"

They were in a parking garage. Jack got out of the car and handed his keys to an attendant, then waved for her to come. After checking her makeup in the rearview mirror, she joined him. They walked onto a city street where a bright yellow taxi sped by.

Mariella's eyes grew wide. "Is this—"

"New York City!" Jack announced. "But that's not the best part."

He slipped his hand into hers, and they walked across Broadway. The whole city vibrated with life. Couples strolled down the sidewalk arm in arm, while stylish women had their hands full with hat boxes from Bloomingdale's and bags from Macy's department store. Some hailed taxis while others kept their treasured purchases close as they made their way home. Three young children ran in between their parents, playing hide and seek until their father scolded them. A sweet, salty scent from a cart nearby where a man was roasting nuts filled the air. They crossed Lafayette Street and turned down a narrow road. Car horns blared and jazz music drifted out of a bar as a tipsy man stumbled onto the street. It was overwhelming and exhilarating at the same time. But what Mariella saw next made her stop in her tracks—at the end of the street an Italian flag waved proudly atop a sidewalk produce stand.

"Verdure e Frutta Qui!" the dark-haired, mustachioed man called out.

Mariella smiled. "Boun giorno, signore. Sei Italiano?"

The man pinched his fingers together and explained that, of course, he was Italian, the entire area was filled with Italians. "Bienvenuta, signora. E' Piccola Italia!" he said, but was quickly distracted by an older woman squeezing his peaches.

Across the street she eyed a storefront with a large sign that read "Ferrara's." Breathing in the smell of freshly baked bread and pastries and espresso, Mariella looked at Jack. "This is Little Italy?"

He nodded, a satisfied smile on his face. "I thought if I can't take you home, at least I can give you a little piece of it."

Home, she thought. A lump formed in her throat. She reveled in the sound of people speaking her language on the street. One woman bargained with a man selling seafood from the back of his truck. Another woman sat in her window calling out to her children playing stickball in the street to order them home for lunch. Two grandmothers dressed in black walked arm in arm, heads turned toward each other as they conversed. Although most spoke in dialect, the scene was familiar.

She and Jack went to a restaurant with red-checked tablecloths and basket-bottomed bottles of Chianti for lunch. The food was the most authentic she'd had since arriving in America. They lingered over linguini and clam sauce, indulged in creamy cannolis, and topped it all off with tiny cups of espresso.

"I have one more place to take you," Jack said as they left the restaurant.

Mariella could hardly contain her joy when she entered Di Palo's deli. There were legs of prosciutto hanging from the ceilings, enormous wheels of golden-hued Parmesan in a glass case, shelves full of Perugina chocolates, tins of peeled tomatoes, boxes of homemade biscotti, jars of anchovies and artichokes, and several barrels of olives. She wanted to buy everything, so Jack gave her an unlimited budget. Mariella placed her order—a half pound of prosciutto and a half pound of Mortadella, a pint of olives, a large tin of imported olive oil, a chunk of Parmesan, and a loaf of bread stuffed with meat—all speaking in Italian. She felt so at home that when the deli man quoted the cost, she bargained the price down.

As they drove back across the George Washington Bridge on their way home, Mariella laid her head on Jack's shoulder. She had already thanked him multiple times throughout the day. But what touched her most was that Jack's thoughtfulness proved he understood how she felt.

Chapter Nineteen

As August stretched on, the air that had been fresh at the beginning of summer was now sticky and oppressive. Mariella spent particularly humid days fanning herself as she prayed for rain to cool everything off. With tourist season in full swing, she only saw glimpses of Jack in the morning and then late at night. Every Saturday evening, she would pull her hair into a tight bun and join him at the restaurant to work as a hostess. But they were often so busy that she wouldn't see him until the end of the night when she was ready for a foot soak and bed.

Jack carved a little plot out of the right-hand corner of their backyard for Mariella when they moved in. She grew bunches of basil, parsley, and oregano, plus tomatoes planted in a row like soldiers in formation supported with wooden stakes. It wasn't long until their green limbs crept up high, reaching for the sky while balancing juicy plum tomatoes Mariella canned to use for sauce in the winter. Crisp heads of escarole and radicchio emerged from the ground, promising fresh salads dressed in vinegar and olive oil. A line of green and yellow zucchini grew in the last row, their vines curling around themselves. The squash made an excellent soup, but it was the delicate flowers poking out of their tops she was most excited about. Once they bloomed, Mariella carefully stuffed each one with ricotta cheese and then fried them to a golden brown. After several visits from the neighborhood rabbits nibbling, Jack built a fence covered in chicken wire with a hinged gate at the front to protect it.

Early one evening, Mariella had just finished watering her garden and dragged the hose to the front. Although humidity hung in the air, rain had evaded them for days. Their withering oak sapling needed to be brought back to life. Once the ground was saturated, she moved on to the planters along the driveway and noticed two men walking by.

"Good afternoon," she said, speaking slowly to hide her accent.

The men nodded politely and continued along. Then, a young family of five passed. The father walked proudly with his two boys while his wife trailed behind, pushing a baby carriage. A toddler sat inside, wiggling her finger. Mariella wiggled her finger back, wishing they would stop to chat, but they continued. It wasn't until several more people passed that she remembered it was Friday.

Shabbat services, Mariella thought, wrapping up the hose. She went inside, changed her clothes and freshened her makeup, then headed to the temple.

"Shabbat Shalom," a man wearing a yarmulke greeted Mariella in the lobby. He smiled warmly, then handed her a prayer book.

Mariella ran her fingers over its embossed letters as she quietly took a seat in the back.

When the cantor began to sing, the haunting, familiar words made her stomach drop.

During her call home the prior Sunday, Mama had news about the missing nuns. Sister Gabriella mysteriously returned to the convent one day. She said it was like seeing a ghost. Although the nun was physically present, her light, free-spirited personality had disappeared. And there was something more significant: her left eye was fused closed, leaving her face disfigured. Mariella could only assume the terrors she had endured. Mama asked about Helena and the children, but Sister Gabriella said they had been sent to a camp in the north, then separated. That was all she knew.

When candles were lit for the Sabbath, Mariella prayed for

every soul lost during those months. A sudden jolt of guilt ran through her. *Who am I to live in a house with more rooms than I can use while my family makes do in a cramped two-bedroom apartment? How can I enjoy a lavish life while those sweet children and kind nuns are still missing?*

On her way out of the temple, Mariella bumped into an older woman wearing a black scarf. "Excuse me," she said as they both tried to exit the same door. "Please, after you."

The woman smiled. "Oh, thank you, dear."

When she pushed the door open, Mariella noticed a series of tattooed numbers on her arm and a rush of sadness and anger soured her stomach. She followed the woman out.

"Excuse me," Mariella said softly, then repeated, "Excuse me, miss."

The woman turned around and looked up at her. "Yes, dear?"

"I am sorry to bother you."

"I can't tell," the woman said, touching her ear, "is your accent French or Italian? I think you look Italian, no?"

"Yes, I am Italian." Mariella smiled. Hearing the woman's accent, she didn't mind being asked about hers. "And you? If you do not mind, I hear your accent as well."

"I am from Poland. Many of us are here… for obvious reasons," she said, gesturing toward the temple. "But I hope to keep my accent. It is a part of me—a part of my history."

After a year of trying to erase her rolling R's and change the way she drew out the end of each word, Mariella felt foolish.

"And you, dear?" the woman asked.

"Excuse me?"

"Why are you here in America?"

Mariella blushed. "I come for love."

"Ah, love!" the woman said, her face brightening. "And you are married?"

"Yes, I live down the street with my husband, Jack. I am Mariella."

"Mariella," she repeated without any trouble. "What a beautiful name. I am Ada. It is nice to meet you, dear."

"Eh ... I have seen markings like this before," Mariella said, pointing to her arm.

Ada quietly nodded, then rolled up her sleeve exposing more numbers. "You mean this, no?"

"Yes, those."

"I was at Auschwitz. But I was one of the lucky ones. I arrived a few days before the Allied forces liberated the camp. This number here was supposed to identify my dead body. Now, I use it as a reminder of how cruel man can be." She looked up at the sky. "And how fortunate I am."

Before Mariella could stop herself, she threw her arms

around the woman. They stood for a moment, holding each other. The woman smelled like garlic and yeast, as if she had been baking. Her small body felt sturdy and strong, a total contradiction to her wrinkled, tired face. *This is what war does to a person,* Mariella thought, reminded of how her own mother had become a shell of her former self, but still kept a strong façade for her family during those horrible times.

When they parted, Mariella felt the need to explain. "That was a horrible time. I am missing people I love too. My best friend. Do you know what happened to people in the camps?"

Ada patted Mariella's hand. "I wish I knew. Many of my neighbors, almost all of my cousins, even my brother-in-law, are still missing. We had to leave because, well, living with their ghosts became too much."

"I am sorry. Is there no information of them?"

Ada shook her head somberly.

"But I do not understand. There have to be some record for the family," Mariella said, a sense of inequality burning inside of her.

"They did not keep records of the dead. Why would they care? We are just Jews. My family did not mean a thing to them. They just piled their bodies into pits and burned them."

"But how they can do this?"

"I do not know," Ada said, gazing up at the sky again. "I do, however, hope they have prayed to God to forgive them, because I know I never will."

As Mariella lay in bed that night, watching the empty space beside her, she thought about sacrifices. Everyone made them. Rabbi Sheridan's father dedicated his life to serving others, honoring those who had been lost. Ada left her beloved Poland at a ripe old age when she should have been settled in a familiar place. The place she had created memories, like grooves carved into marble. But she'd had to sacrifice everything she knew for a life worth living.

Helena's parents, who'd given up their lives to ensure their daughter would have one. Although Mariella had grown accustomed to a comfortable life, without her family close by, something was always missing. Still, her sacrifices seemed small in comparison. After speaking with the rabbi, she had promised herself to keep looking for signs of her sister in nature. Her conversation with Ada reminded her to be proud of her culture. She vowed to stop hiding her accent. And after her visits to the temple, she refused to allow Helena's parents' sacrifices to fade away into nothingness.

"I swear on my grave and everything I know, I will never give up looking   :o herself.

PART TWO

Chapter Twenty

Pushing a silver cart through the aisles of Foodtown, Mariella searched for a bottle of extra virgin olive oil. The large tin they'd bought on their trip to Little Italy lasted her months, but now she needed to make do with what their local grocery store offered. Instead of waiting for Monday, when Jack could drive her, she ventured out alone and found the market, a ten-minute walk from their house. She passed an aisle of canned goods. Then, the meat counter where a butcher stood in front of a glass display containing trays of chicken breasts, pork chops, sausage, and steaks. A sudden wave of nausea ran through her. Growing pale, she quickly pushed her cart down the spices and condiments aisle, trying to breathe through it. It wasn't the first time she had felt this way. For several weeks, her stomach had been exceptionally sour. The nausea usually happened in the morning, but some days, it stayed with her until evening.

Mama's voice had filled with joy on their telephone call the week before. "It's a baby! I know it is! You children all got me so sick. I couldn't keep anything down."

Although she hoped her mother was right, it was hard to get excited when she felt so miserable.

Mariella finally found a small bottle of olive oil at the end of the aisle and put it in her cart. She didn't care that it came from Parsippany, New Jersey. She just needed to get home.

Later that evening, Mariella waited in bed for Jack to return from work. It was almost November, and powerful gusts of wind whooshed against the window above their bed. She rubbed her stomach, wondering if maybe she wasn't alone.

A sudden, loud bang sounded downstairs. Adrenaline coursed through her body.

More banging sounds from the first floor forced her out of bed. *Is someone trying to get in?* Mariella wondered, her heart racing. She grabbed a shoehorn with a long steel handle hanging from Jack's suit valet, then reconsidered and instead rifled through her dresser drawer and found a hat pin. She would aim for the intruder's eye. As footsteps came up the stairs, she quietly slipped into the closet.

"Sweetheart?" Jack called out, switching on the bedroom

light. "Where are you?"

Mariella threw the closet door open and fell into his arms. "Thank God it is you!"

"Of course it's me!" Jack laughed, then pulled her closer. "You're shaking. Who did you think it was?"

She looked up at him sheepishly and shrugged. At times she felt ashamed not to be past her fears brought on by the war. After all, it had been almost ten years; enough time for her to process all of it. And now, she was miles away from all the memories she held on to. She should be feeling safer than ever, but panic and terror still lived inside.

"I heard some banging. I guess my mind played tricks on me."

Jack held her tight as if suddenly reminded of her past. "I'm sorry, honey. It's that darn wind. I forgot to latch the screen door and it blew open a few times. Come on." He brought her back to bed, then changed into his pajamas.

"How was the restaurant?"

"Now that it's fall, business is slowing down." He slipped under the covers, giving her a curious look. "Is something else wrong?"

"No, amore." Mariella twirled a tuft of his chest hair with her finger, holding onto her secret for a few more seconds.

"Are you sure?"

"Well… there is something I have to ask you."

"Alright, I'm all ears."

"I should see a doctor."

Jack sat up. "Why? What's wrong? Is something wrong?"

A wave of warmth, sticky and sweet, traveled through her like honey. Jack's unwavering care and love reminded her of why she'd followed him to America. "No, I do not think so."

"Well, then? Why a doctor?"

Gazing up at him, her fingers tenderly caressed her abdomen. She knew it was written all over her face, her brown eyes filled with a mixture of fear and excitement.

"Oh, wait a minute. Hold on a minute." Jack pulled her chin up and studied her. "Are you telling me…?"

"I am not positive, but I am sick all the day. Today, I almost vomit in the market. I think I should go. Just in case."

Jack jumped up on the bed and clapped. "Well, hot diggity dog! I'm going to be a father! A father! A father! I'm going to be a father!" he sang, dancing around. "And you, my dear, will be a mommy!"

"Okay, okay, amore. Let us be sure." Mariella smiled, allowing herself to dream.

"Okie dokie," Jack said, settling back in bed, "we'll call Dr. Berg tomorrow."

"Good. But you have one thing wrong."

"What's that?"

"I am not going to be Mommy."

"No?"

Looking down at her belly, Mariella smiled. "No, I am going to be Mama."

"Terrific!" Jack laughed. "Then call me Papa!"

After Mariella vomited her toast the following morning, Jack dropped her off at his family doctor. He had some business at the restaurant, but it was only a few blocks away. Mariella assured him she would be fine walking over once she was done with her appointment.

A stern, older man, dressed in a long white coat with a stethoscope hanging from his neck, entered the waiting room. "Marilla Valentino?"

"Yes, that is me," Mariella said, too exhausted to correct his pronunciation.

"I'm Dr. Berg. You can come this way."

She followed him to an examination room with a steel table against the wall, a desk, and two chairs. She was relieved when he directed her to one of the chairs.

"Now, Jack tells me you may be expecting?" Dr. Berg asked, sitting down at his desk.

"I have been sick for almost two months now."

He began taking notes. "And when did you have your last menstrual period?"

"Eh," Mariella muttered.

Dr. Berg looked over the top of his glasses and frowned. "Well? Don't you know?"

"I ... I do not know this word."

Dr. Berg sighed. "Menstruate? When you bleed once a month?"

"Ah. Yes, I have not since July."

"You had it in July?"

"No, eh, from July."

Dr. Berg removed his glasses and narrowed his eyes on her. "You either had it in July or not. Which is it?"

"Eh. No, I did not have it in July."

The doctor ignored Mariella as he jotted a few more things down on the pad, then handed it to her. "Go to the building next door, number one-fifteen. Then give this to the receptionist. *Receptionist.* The lady that sits behind the desk in the front. You understand?"

Mariella nodded politely, took the paper, and left.

The next building was like a small hospital. Nurses in starched white hats bustled about while a few people sat patiently waiting their turn. After fifteen minutes, a nurse with a clipboard led Mariella to another examination room, this one much smaller than at the doctor's office.

"Hello, dear. I hear someone might be expecting!" the middle-aged nurse said sweetly, putting Mariella at ease.

"Yes. I think so."

"I'm Nurse Betty. And you are," she looked down at the clipboard, "Mar-ella?"

"Actually, it is Mariella."

"What's that? Spanish?"

Mariella smiled. She had never been to Spain but always wanted to visit. "No, I am Italian."

"Ah! There are lots of Italians here. Have you ever been to the Villa Pensa restaurant? Now, that's real authentic Italian food. At least, that's what they say. I've never been to Italy myself. Okay, honey," Nurse Betty said, taking out a plastic cup with a lid. "I'm going to give you a cup. You need to urinate in it."

"Urinate?"

"Sure."

Mariella shifted in her seat. "Eh, I do not know this word."

"Oh, I'm sorry, honey. Urinate means to go to the bathroom. You know, pee?" The nurse took the cup and put it underneath her skirt. "You see?"

Looking around the room, Mariella blushed. "Here?"

Nurse Betty laughed. "Oh, heavens no! I'll show you to the bathroom."

Relieved, Mariella followed the nurse to the bathroom and locked herself in, then checked the lock to be sure. She had never been asked to pee in a cup and it all seemed so strange. She just thought the doctor could tell if she was pregnant by examining her stomach; she didn't know there was a test. After checking the lock a third time, she pulled her pantyhose and panties down, squatted, and filled the cup with urine. After screwing on the top and finishing up, she opened the door.

"Here it is," she said, quickly handing it to the nurse. Mariella hoped no one was watching as she held it up and inspected it.

"Looking good!" Nurse Betty said cheerily. "Now, in a few weeks, we'll know if you should start painting that baby's room!"

Another nurse passed by with a tray, a large needle laid upon it with a long, yellow tube and a jar connected on the other end. There was a smaller jar next to it emitting a sharp smell of disinfectant. Mariella's stomach turned at the scent, not only because everything lately made her sick. It reminded her of visiting her sister in the hospital during her final days. When they had hoped a miracle could happen, the smell didn't bother Mariella. But as soon as the end was inevitable, everything became a nuisance: the clanking radiator, the cheery morning nurse, and the sharp smell of sterilizing fluid. The edges of her vision grew blurry and her knees weak.

"Are you okay?"

Mariella nodded, clutching the nurse's arm.

"Come with me." Nurse Betty led her back to the room and sat her down, then brought her a paper cup of water. "Here you are, dear. I'm sure it's just the pregnancy."

"I am okay." Mariella tried to stand up, but the nurse stopped her.

"First, drink up and rest a moment." Folding her arms, the nurse waited to be sure Mariella drank the whole cup. "So, tell me, what do you want?"

"Excuse me?"

"Boy or girl? What's your preference?"

Mariella hadn't given it any thought. Babies were born regardless of what you wanted and it all was a blessing to her. "I will take either."

Nurse Betty smiled. "That's a good attitude to have. So many women want a boy to please their husbands. Not me, I was hoping for a girl. Ha! Five girls later, I really wish I could have one more try."

"Five children! How wonderful." Mariella thought about having a bevy of children running in and out of the house, letting the screen door slam behind them, giggling and shouting. She couldn't imagine anything sweeter.

"You feeling better?"

"Yes, thank you."

"It's my pleasure. Just you wait, it should only take a few weeks." Nurse Betty winked.

Mariella headed for the door but turned back. "I am sorry, eh, can I ask a question?"

"Of course you can, dear."

"What do they do, eh, with the urinate?"

"You'll never believe it if I tell you but … they take the urine and put it in a syringe, then inject it into a rabbit."

"A rabbit?" Mariella studied the woman's face, wondering if she was telling lies to make her feel stupid.

"Yes," the nurse continued. "I don't know how, but something happens to the rabbit's ovaries and I think, if it dies, then it means you're pregnant. But from my mouth to God's ears, I think you're going to be getting good news with these results!"

"Thank you." Although a wave of nausea ran through Mariella, she gave the nurse a cheery smile as she left, then threw up on the sidewalk in front of the medical center.

Chapter Twenty-One

Several weeks later, Jack returned home from work around dinnertime with a large bouquet of roses.

"Sweetheart? Where are you?"

"Jack?" Mariella called down from the bedroom.

Jack bounded up the stairs two at a time.

"Honey, what's wrong? Is your stomach still giving you problems?" he asked, when he found her in bed. He sat beside her.

"Yes. All the day long. Oh, Jack, I must look awful. I do not have any makeup on."

"Mrs. Valentino," he said, brushing the hair out of her eyes, "you couldn't look more beautiful if you tried."

Mariella eyed the flowers he held. "Roses, compliments, and a kiss? Amore, what is going on with you?"

"Gee, I don't know. I just received some news today.

198

Important news. Actually, world-changing news."

Intrigued, she sat up in bed. "About what?"

He leaned in and whispered in her ear, "…And baby makes three."

"What?"

"Sweetheart, you're finally 'on the nest'!"

Confusion screwed up Mariella's face. "On the nest? What does this mean, 'on the nest'?"

"The rabbit died!"

"The rabbit died? Why do you say such strange things?"

"Because, beautiful wife of mine," Jack said, cradling the roses, "we're having a baby!"

Mariella looked down at her swollen stomach, then back up at him. "How do you know?"

"Doc called me at the restaurant. How about that? We're gonna get a visit from the stork!"

Tears began to stream down Mariella's cheeks. Jack searched her face. "Are these happy tears?"

"No." The idea that the doctor had dismissed Mariella in this way was aggravating. *Would he have called me instead if I were American? Shouldn't I know what is going on in my body before my husband?*

"No? You aren't happy?"

Mariella shook her head. "I want to be telling you. It is my news to share. Why did he not call me?"

"Oh, honey, he didn't think you would understand him over the phone."

"I am Italian, not stupid!!!" she sobbed, her anger at the man boiling up inside.

"You're right. You are not stupid. I should have suggested he contact you directly. Gee, I'm sorry, sweetheart. But let's not let that keep us from celebrating the fact that we're going to be parents!"

Once Mariella had time to think things through, reality set in. She was on the verge of being a mother, something she and Jack had been hoping for ever since getting married in Rome two years prior. The flutters in her stomach over the past weeks hinted that her wish was coming true, and even though she knew it was considered bad luck, she had been secretly planning a nursery in the room adjacent to theirs. She smiled. But then, her constantly shifting hormones caused her eyes to fill with tears again.

Jack plucked his handkerchief from his jacket pocket and dabbed at them. "What is it this time?" he asked gently.

"I wish my family was here."

Before she could say any more, he led her downstairs to the telephone table and lifted the handset from its cradle. "Hello, operator? Can you put me through to Rome, Italy?"

"But Jack, we called this past Sunday."

"Operator? Operator?"

Mariella tapped his shoulder. "Can we afford it? It is so expensive."

Jack gave her a wink, then fiddled with his hearing aid. "Operator? Yes, now I can hear you! Yes, we would like to call Rome, Italy. That's right. Sure, I'll wait." He put his hand over the receiver. "She's connecting me."

"Thank you," Mariella said in a small voice.

"Oh, yes. Un momento." Jack handed the phone to her.

Mariella spoke through her tears as she gave the operator her parents' phone number. It felt like an eternity waiting for her mother's voice to finally echo through the receiver.

"Mariella?"

"Yes, Mama, it's me," she said, wishing she could climb through the phone and tell her joyful news in person.

"It's three o'clock in the morning! Who died?"

Mariella gave Jack a sly smile. "She wants to know what is wrong!"

"Tell her!"

"Mama. No. No, nothing is wrong. No, Mama. It's just that, well, I'm going to have a baby!" Hearing herself say the words she'd longed to say felt strange. She'd dreamed of being a mother since she was a child. But after her brother died while he was in her care, she felt unworthy.

The other end of the phone went silent.

"Mama?"

Suddenly, she heard her mother shouting at Papa. "Wake up! Wake up! Mariella is going to have a baby!"

Mariella listened to her father grumbling. "Who's having a baby?"

"Your daughter, that's who."

"My baby is having a baby?"

"Oh, Tesoro! We are all so proud of you!" Mama said, returning to the phone. Her voice was tight, and Mariella knew she was holding back tears.

"I miss you, Mama."

"I miss you too, Tesoro."

Jack twirled his finger in the air, indicating she needed to wrap up the call. In those moments, saying goodbye made Mariella resent him, but it was only temporary. "Ciao, Mama, ciao, ciao, I'll write, yes, I promise, I love you, ciao … ciao … ciao."

Before she could say another word, Jack hung up the phone. "Sorry, darling. That was costing us a small fortune."

Mariella smiled at the thought of her parents' joy. "I never hear Mama so happy! They will have celebrations from now until morning!"

"Do you think the neighbors know already?"

"I can imagine Signora Manetto will run around the building announcing my news before Mama can!"

"Oh boy, I doubt your mother would allow it!" Jack said, laughing as he headed for the kitchen. "I bet you're hungry."

Mariella shot him a weary smile. Making dinner was the last thing she wanted to do.

"I've got an idea. Let me cook for a change. You need your strength."

"Amore, *you*? Cook?"

Jack grinned. "Of course I can cook. I'll make some eggs. How about that? Breakfast for dinner." Mariella watched Jack open the cabinet underneath the sink and stare into the abyss before asking, "Now, where do you keep the pots?"

Chapter Twenty-Two

Pregnancy was not easy for Mariella. Although she stopped vomiting over the next several weeks, the nausea continued. When Clara visited, she brought her a box of saltine crackers. They didn't have much taste, but they helped settle her stomach. In the afternoons, she put on a thick wool sweater and sat on her front porch, hoping the cold air would calm her stomach. That was when her imagination ran wild. She had conversations with her fagiolo piccolo—little bean—imagining her dark eyes and Jack's lopsided smile looking up at her. Since her child would be American, she felt the need to speak Italian. Mariella spoke about the tiny apartment in Rome that had witnessed so much tragedy but also became the keeper of wonderful memories. She described the sweet little courtyard between buildings where they'd played with balls and spoon-faced dolls and the Colosseum where she and her siblings imagined they were kings and queens. She fought tears as she spoke about her father's warm hugs and how he let her hide away until she felt better. How her mother was tough, because otherwise she would have crumbled—how inside Mama's hard shell was warm and fuzzy and everything a daughter needed. She explained how the memory of her late sister's laugh always brought joy to her heart. Or the giggles of her poor little brother who didn't make it past age two. And she talked about the living; sweet Giada, who always had her nose in a book, bold Lia who never shied away from anything, and funny Matteo, who found humor in everything. Hiding away in her memories allowed Mariella's days to go by faster.

One Friday afternoon, she noticed a familiar face walking arm in arm with a much younger girl, about ten years old. She waved. "Hello, Ada!"

Ada stopped, wrinkling her eyebrows until her face relaxed. "You're that lovely lady I met at the temple a while ago. Uh, Mariella, isn't it? It's nice to see you."

"It is nice to see you, too. Are you going to services?"

"Yes. With my granddaughter, Evie."

Evie offered a timid smile.

"Would I be wrong to say you are with child?" Ada asked, an expectant grin spreading across her face.

Although Mariella wasn't that big, her thin frame made it hard to hide that she was pregnant. She rubbed her belly. "I am!"

"Mazel tov!" Ada cheered before continuing on to the temple.

As Mariella turned to go inside, she noticed a woman watching her from the house across the street. She remembered seeing a couple move in the month prior but had been too sick to introduce herself. Taking a chance, she headed toward the house but the woman quickly closed her curtains. Mariella stood in the street, unsure what to do next.

The woman poked her head out of her front door and waved.

"Hello!" she said.

"Hello! I am Mariella."

"Good to meet you, Mariella. I'm Louise. It's quite chilly out today. Would you like to come in for a cuppa tea?"

Mariella was pleased to hear her British accent. "Yes, thank you."

Louise's house was warm and welcoming, but the sweet smell of baked goods made her stomach turn.

"Have a seat, I'll make us a pot."

She glanced around the living room as Louise busied herself in the kitchen. The layout was similar to her own home, except the stairs were on the right instead of the left. Her couch and loveseat were upholstered in flowery patterns, there was a thin-legged coffee table, and framed drawings of charming English villages covered the walls.

"That one is where I grew up." Louise nodded toward the largest one as she returned with a silver tea tray. "Yorkshire. England, that is." She poured two cups and handed one to Mariella. "I am sorry, I meant to introduce myself when we first arrived. I knew you weren't from around here, either!"

As Louise ducked back into the kitchen, Mariella smiled. It wasn't that she liked being told she didn't fit in. When it came from another foreigner, it was as if she were part of a special group; an outsiders' club.

"And here," Louise said as she returned with a colorful tin, "a little taste of home." She took off the lid, exposing a dozen shortbread cookies. "Go on, take one! I baked them this morning. They're more buttery than sweet. My goodness, Americans do like sweet things, don't they?"

Mariella took a small bite of the crumbly cookie, hoping her stomach behaved. Louise was right. It was buttery and light and delicious, but one bite was enough.

"The pregnancy?" Louise asked, raising an eyebrow. Mariella nodded. "That is quite alright. I'll save a tin for when your nausea goes away."

"Thank you," Mariella said, wishing she'd brought something Italian to share with Louise.

"So, you're from where? Oh, let me guess—Italy?"

"Yes. Roma," Mariella said.

"Rome! I love Rome. We went on holiday there when I was little. I remember the Colosseum. It was so majestic!"

"That is where I met Jack during the war. He is my husband."

"Then we have something in common." Louise picked a framed black-and-white photo off the telephone table and handed it to Mariella. In it, two lanky soldiers stood in front of an army tent, arms swung around each other. "The one on the right is my Charles. We met during the war. I volunteered at the hospital, mostly bringing the patients magazines and water. But when they were short-staffed, I assisted the doctors. He was there for observation after hitting his head getting out of an aeroplane. Had to have stitches too. The poor chap was missing home so I found a few out-of-date *Ladies' Home Journals* a girlfriend was sent by an American cousin. He didn't seem to mind the subject matter, though. Every time I went in that room his nose was buried in between those pages! He told me later on that he had been riveted by the 'Can this marriage be saved' column."

Mariella laughed. "Was it love at the first sight?"

"Oh, no," Louise said. "It wasn't until a few months later. See, the soldiers were treated to Friday night dances in my town. And let me tell you, they needed it. Those boys were desperate for some company. Of course, my girlfriends and I couldn't resist going. Dancing was all we had for nightlife, especially during those years."

"Anything we do for fun mean so much back then," Mariella agreed. "Did you see him there?"

Louise nodded. "The first time I went, he was leaning against the wall, keeping to himself. I think the war had gotten to him. He told me later he wasn't in the mood to dance. Until I showed up. That was the night we fell in love. But he was a part of the third bomb division. He went on weekly missions, sometimes daily. My goodness, I spent months worrying about him."

"I think it was the 'time of worry.'" Mariella said, letting out a soft laugh.

"Yes, it certainly was." Louise took the photo back and carefully positioned the frame on the telephone table. "At the end of the war, he got his papers to leave. But that night, he appeared at my front door wanting to speak to my father. That's when I knew he would ask me to marry him." The faraway look on Louise's face made it clear there was more to the story.

"Was your father not happy?"

"He didn't care for Charles. Not only because he wasn't British—I suppose the idea of me moving so far away crushed him. Mum had passed away from pneumonia years before. I was all he had. It wasn't until Charles found work in my town that my father agreed to the marriage."

"Oh. How lucky you could stay home." Mariella remembered the night Jack appeared at her apartment with a proposal and a quarry job in Naples. Although they would have been poor, she wouldn't have had to say goodbye to her family.

"Well, it was my duty to care for my father."

"I understand a daughter's duty all too well," Mariella quietly said. "How did you end up here?"

Louise sighed. "Father passed this January. He wasn't in the best health."

"Was he old?"

"Yes. My mother was his second wife. His first wife died during childbirth. The baby died, too. He didn't marry Mum until his early forties. He was seventy when he passed. I suppose he had a life of heartbreak. He fought in the Great War, then lived through the Second World War."

Mariella thought about her father and how his hair grayed during those years war raged. Back then, he was barely forty, but it was obvious the struggles they endured had taken a toll on him.

"Listen to me, chattering this whole time! I haven't learned a thing about you. When did you arrive in the United States?"

"Eh, per un anno e mezzo," she said, absentmindedly. "I am sorry, I mean to say a year and half."

"That's quite alright. Managing a new culture and a new

language at the same time can't be easy. But you seem to be doing quite well!" Louise offered her a warm smile. "Is your husband Italian too?"

"No, no. He grew up in Asbury Park. But he works for his family restaurant so we cannot stay in Italy. It is called Villa Pensa."

"I've been there! It has a wonderful lobster tank in the window. I thought that was so clever, but I couldn't eat those horrible-looking creatures! You know, we should get the boys together. Maybe for cocktails? Oh, but I guess you won't be having any cocktails in your condition. When do you think you'll deliver?"

Looking down at her stomach, Mariella's mind blanked. It happened often. When she was tired, her English suffered.

Louise reworded her question. "When is your little one due to arrive?"

"In April. At least that is what the doctor say." As Mariella spoke, she noticed the clouds darkening outside the window. "I am sorry, but I have to go. It look like it will rain and my laundry is on the line."

"Oh, you go!" Louise waved her hand. "That's happened to me too many times!"

Mariella went out the door and then turned back. "I am so happy you are here," she said, before rushing across the street.

England wasn't Italy, but it wasn't America, either. They were both strangers in a strange country.

"I'll see you again. Cheerio, neighbor!" Louise called out after her.

Mariella waved as the cold December wind picked up, blowing her skirt around. She made it to the backyard, plucked each piece of clothing off the line without removing the clothespins, and got her laundry inside just as the clouds opened up.

Chapter Twenty-Three

Mariella twisted the phone cord several times around her finger, waiting for someone to answer. The first Sunday of each month was highly anticipated. She woke up at dawn and waited until eight a.m., when her family had gotten home from church, before calling.

"Pronto?" her father answered, sounding tired.

"Ciao, Papa! It's me!" said, speaking through her usual tears.

"Who?"

"Papa, it's your Tesoro!"

"Who is this?"

"Stop being foolish," Mama said in the background. "It's your daughter, Mariella."

"Mariella?"

"Yes, Papa, don't you recognize my voice?"

"Of course I do," he said, sounding like himself again. "How are you?"

"Don't worry about me, Papa. How are you doing?"

"I am okay. But I miss you, Tesoro. Why can't you come home?"

Mariella's heart sank. It wasn't a secret that she couldn't come home, and he had never asked her to. She pressed her palm to her heart, feeling worry and disappointment breaking it in two. The phone went silent as if someone had put a hand on the receiver, then Mama's voice was in her ear.

"Don't you listen to your father. He's being silly."

"Is he okay, Mama?"

"Your father is fine, just a little tired."

"Tired?"

"Yes. He's been working a lot lately. I try to get him to slow down, but you know your father. Now, how is the baby?"

"Fine, Mama. I am getting bigger every day! He was kicking around my belly this morning. It felt like he was trying to get out!"

"He? Oh, Tesoro, you are having a girl. I'm certain of it."

"And how are you so certain?"

"I see your face has rounded from the pictures you've sent."

Mariella touched her face. Her mother liked to predict who was having what. She was right about fifty percent of the time.

"Okay, Mama. We will see in April."

"April? What do those doctors know? Were they there when you made the baby? No. Trust me. She can come at any time. You just take care of yourself."

"I wish you were here, Mama."

Mama laughed. "Me? In America? Oh, no. Your stories are so strange." When Mariella told her about the breakfast of fried eggs, bacon, and toast that she had grown accustomed to, Mama couldn't believe it. She felt the same about the corn eaten like a typewriter, or the backyard parties with bare tables. Her mother would never have someone over without a tablecloth covering their table. It had been strange to Mariella too, but was slowly becoming normal.

"I know some things are different, but some are wonderful too. Oh, Mama ... I miss you and Papa... and Lia and Giada and Matteo." She quietly gave in to her tears.

"We miss you too, Tesoro," Mama said, her voice cracking. "You're never far from our hearts. And we will talk when we can. I'm knitting a blanket for the baby—pink on one side and blue on the other, just in case."

"Thank you, Mama. How is Lia? Can I say hi to everyone?"

"Of course, they're all here."

Lia quickly got on the phone. "Ciao, Mariella! Are you fat?"

"Yes, little sister, I am."

"Sweetheart," Jack whispered, holding up two fingers.

"I only have two minutes left, can I speak with Giada?"

The phone exchanged hands again.

"Ciao, Mariella! How is your baby?"

"Growing every day! How is Salvatore?"

"Dreamy! Papa has finally accepted our relationship." After her years-long crush on the medical student, Giada decided the age difference was too much. She'd accepted a date from an old classmate, and now it was becoming something more.

"Thank God! If Papa is not happy, no one is." Mariella smiled through her tears. "Can I speak to Matteo?"

"Yes, okay. Love you, sister!"

"I love you too!"

Matteo's voice came through the receiver next. "Mariella, can you come home?"

"One day, my love. I promise. You take good care of the family, okay? Remember, you are the man of the house."

"Uh-huh."

"Can you put Mama on?"

"Mariella?" Mama's voice sounded deflated. "Is your time almost over?"

"Yes, Mama. I'm sorry. I will call next month. I promise."

"No," Mama said firmly. "You are expecting my grandchild. If I cannot see you, I will at least talk to you more often."

"But Mama—"

"No buts. I have money put aside from my job. I will call in two Sundays. Besides, I miss you too much to wait."

"Fifteen seconds," Jack said softly. Mariella began to panic. Time passed so quickly that she never got to say all that she needed.

"I love you, Mama."

"I love you too. Eat well and get lots of rest. The baby depends on you to help it grow."

"I will."

"Good. And go outside. Fresh air is good for you and the baby."

"Ten seconds."

"Okay, Mama, I will."

"And tell Jack that you need to give in to your cravings or your baby will be born with an ugly birthmark."

Mariella laughed at the old wives' tale. "Of course. Give Papa a big kiss from me and write soon."

"Five, four—"

"I miss you, Mama!"

"Three, two, one."

Jack hung up the phone, and the quiet room filled with Mariella's sobs.

Chapter Twenty-Four

A light flickered on in the house behind theirs, as Mariella placed the espresso pot on the stove. They hadn't noticed it until the thick woods were cleared the month prior. A silhouette shuffled around inside, then the house went dark. She yawned. It was seven a.m., but knowing Mama would call at eight, she wouldn't sleep. Waiting for the water to boil, Mariella checked on her birds. Just beyond their kitchen window stood a cherry tree. Although most were making an exodus for warmer climes, a few lingered on its bare branches. She watched a lone regal-blue one with a purplish-black beak perched happily on top. Before long, a few more joined him. They were mostly dove-like creatures that reminded her of the ones that visited after her sister died.

Is that you? she wondered. The birds pecked at some seed,

then flew off without looking her way.

At eight a.m., just as her house filled with the melodic chimes of their living room clock, the phone rang.

"Pronto? I mean, eh, hello?"

"Tesoro? Tesoro. Is that you?"

"Yes, Mama! It's me!" Mariella sank into the chair. "I've been waiting for your call all morning!"

"And I've been waiting all day to call!" Mama said with a laugh. "If I had known you were up, I would have called earlier. I couldn't think of anything else."

"Is Papa with you? I didn't talk to him much last time, I'd like to say hello."

The hesitation in her mother's voice did not go unnoticed.

"Mama? Is something wrong?"

"No! No, Tesoro. You don't need to worry." But her mother's words defied how she sounded.

"Mama, when people say don't worry, that means to worry!" Mariella could hear her father mumbling in the background. "Mama? He's there, isn't he? Why can't I talk to him?"

His voice quickly sounded through the phone. "Tesoro! How are you doing?"

"Papa! I'm so happy to talk to you finally. How have you been?"

"Me? I'm terrific. Why wouldn't I be?" He laughed. "And

how is the baby? Getting big?"

"I'm not sure about the baby, but I sure am getting big! My little one is moving around a lot now. I think he will be a soccer player."

"Like your brother!"

"Yes! Like Matteo!"

"And how is … uh…" Papa faltered. "Uh …that man, the one who brought you to America."

"You mean Jack?" Mariella asked.

Papa was quiet for a moment.

"Papa?"

"Yes, I'm here, Tesoro," he said, distracted.

Mariella heard muffled talking on the other end, then Mama came on. "I'm sorry, Tesoro, I had to send your father to the panificio for some bread."

"But why does he sound so strange? He forgot Jack's name."

Mama picked her words carefully. "Your father hasn't been himself lately."

"He hasn't?" It wasn't as if Mariella hadn't noticed his stuttering, or the funny way he pretended not to know her voice every so often. It was there in the back of her mind, but she hadn't been brave enough to address it. The usual feeling of helplessness settled in, magnified by the vast distance between them.

"He'll be fine. Now, are you getting enough sleep?"

LUIGINA VECCHIONE

"Mama," Mariella began, shifting in her seat, "should I be worried about Papa?"

Mama exhaled wearily. "Tesoro, we are getting old. We both need more rest. He will be fine. I will make him pastina this afternoon."

"Well, Papa may need more than pastina," Mariella joked.

"Of course! Tell me, what will you eat today? Do you have your appetite back?"

The nausea that plagued Mariella for months had suddenly disappeared, just like Nurse Betty promised. One morning, she woke up to the smell of Jack's pancakes and instead of wanting to vomit, she ate a full stack.

"Yes, Mama! We are going to the restaurant for lunch. They make a wonderful meatball submarine."

"A what?"

Although it wasn't anything she'd ever eaten in Rome, it was the only thing Mariella craved. The meatballs were moist, the bread had a nice crust, and while the sauce was sweeter than she was used to, Mariella had grown accustomed to it.

"Is it an American dish?"

"Yes, Mama. When you come, we'll share a large meatball sub. You will love it."

"Okay, Tesoro. Oh! The time. I haven't been keeping track."

"We should say goodbye, then."

"No, Tesoro. I miss your voice."

Mariella brushed away her tears, wondering if she could ever get through a phone call without crying. "I miss you too, Mama. I miss everyone and everything about home."

"You've always been a good daughter. Your brother and sisters miss you, too."

In the background, Giada, Lia, and Matteo shouted "Hello!" and "I love you!"

"I love you all, too!" Mariella sobbed into the phone. "I should go, Mama, this is expensive. I will call next, and it will only be two weeks that we'll have to wait."

"Yes, yes, okay. I love you, Tesoro! Take good care of my grandchild!"

Mariella nodded but couldn't speak. She quickly hung up the phone. It was for the best.

Chapter Twenty-Five

Spring came in like summer, hot and sticky. The gauzy cotton housecoat Julia had loaned Mariella stuck to her like a second layer of skin. Fanning herself, she shuffled out back one morning and carefully lowered herself into a lawn chair.

"Yoo-hoo!" A woman from the house behind theirs waved eagerly. She had chestnut-brown hair rolled up in pink curlers and wore a lime-green housecoat.

Mariella pulled herself out of the chair and went over to the chain-link fence that divided their properties.

"Why, hello, neighbor! I'm Janey Evans. We moved in about a month ago." She gestured to three planters and several garden tools piled against the back of the house. "Don't mind my mess. We haven't had a chance to organize. Boy, this weather is going to be the death of me. I've never heard of eighty-degree weather in May, have you?" Speaking quickly, making it hard to understand, Janey gave Mariella a curious look. "You're not from around here, are you?"

Mariella braced herself, unsure if she was genuinely interested or gearing up to insult her. "Yes, I am from Italy."

"Wait a second, are you Jack Valentino's wife?"

"You know him?"

"Sure I do!" Janey scratched her head, making her puffy curlers sway back and forth. "My husband, Hugh, played football with him in high school!"

"Really?"

"Sure! We heard Jack lived around here, just didn't know you two would be right behind us! He'll be tickled when he finds out. I moved here from upstate New York, but we spent the past ten years living in Asbury Park, so I know all about your husband. Boy, he's a gem. How did you two meet?"

Mariella rubbed her belly. The baby had just begun to push against her bladder. "We meet in Italy. During the war."

"Ha! You're the third neighbor I've met with that same story. Have you met Louise from across the street? And then there's the Weinbergs down on Clark Street. They got out of Germany before it got really bad. It's a small world, isn't it?"

Without warning, Mariella's legs grew weak and something dripped between her legs. She looked down and was horrified to see a small puddle around her feet. Her stomach tightened.

"The school is only five blocks from here, so your little one can go there." Janey continued talking. "You won't be seeing any baby booties on my line, though. Oh, no. We've tried for years but no luck. Turns out I can't have children."

Although the sadness in Janey's voice was clear, Mariella couldn't offer any sympathy. "Eh, I am sorry. I need to make dinner. It is nice to meet you," she said, feeling a heaviness in her pelvis.

"Sure, doll! It's so nice to have new people around! I'll be seeing you."

Mariella waved goodbye as she slowly lumbered toward the house, hoping Janey didn't notice her drenched legs. Once inside, she remembered her mother's water breaking, but wasn't sure how long she had before giving birth. Making short strides as if the baby could fall out at any moment, she made her way to the telephone table.

"Operator, what number, please?"

A sharp pain caused Mariella's mind to go blank. She tried to breathe through it.

"Number, please?" the operator repeated.

"Eh... I ...I am sorry. I forgot."

"Well, who are ya trying to call?"

"My husband. I think I... am having my... baby."

The operator's voice brightened. "You don't say! Well, where is your husband, hon? Maybe I can find the number for you."

Mariella gritted her teeth as her stomach tightened in another contraction.

"You still there?"

"Yes, eh ... he... he is...he is at the Villa... Pensa restaurant."

"And where is that?"

"Eh." Mariella sat down, hoping the pain disappeared, but it only got worse. "Asbury Park," she said in a thin voice.

"Okay! Now we're getting somewhere." The operator put her on hold just as Mariella let out a moan. A few seconds later, she got back on the phone. "I've got it, hon. You doing okay?"

"I think so," Mariella said, alarmed at how quickly the contractions had accelerated.

"Okay, I'm going to put you through. You take care now and congratulations!"

Mariella nervously waited as the phone rang.

"Good afternoon. You've reached the Villa Pensa. How can I help you?" Ma answered in an official-sounding tone.

"Eh, hello. Is Jack... there?" Mariella asked, her stomach tightening up for another round.

"Who's this? His girlfriend?" Ma loved to joke about the

women Jack had dated in the past. "Hey, Jackie! It's your girlfriend!" she called out, then got back on the phone. "He's coming. You know, you're pregnant, not sick. He can't take time out to run errands for you."

Unable to respond, Mariella blew short breaths out.

"You still there?" Ma asked.

"Yessss..." Noticing more blood dripping down her leg, Mariella grew lightheaded. "But... but I need hi...him."

"Alright, hold your horses. Jack, it's your wife!" she called out.

When Jack came on the phone, his voice sounded like he was in a wind tunnel. "Hey, sweetheart, everything okay?"

"Th ... the baby...it's... com..." she whispered before passing out.

Sirens rang in Mariella's ear. She tried to run to the nearest air raid shelter but her legs wouldn't move. Darkness surrounded her, pressing down as if someone had sewn her eyelids shut. She called out for Jack, hoping he would know where to go.

"It's okay. I'm right here." he said from far away.

Mariella tried to open her eyes again but couldn't.

"Okay, sir, we'll take it from here," a woman's voice instructed.

"I love you, sweetheart."

Mariella recognized Jack whispering into her ear. She

fluttered her eyes open only to see his blurry face disappear behind a door. Then a bright light was shining down on her.

"Huh?" she mumbled.

"Okay, dear, we'll have your baby out in no…."

Mariella drifted back to sleep.

Chapter Twenty-Six

Mariella slowly opened her eyes to see sparkling dust particles floating in rays of sun streaming through a large hospital window. At first, everything was foggy, as if she were looking through a thin piece of gauze, but after a few moments, her eyes focused. Outside, a pine tree swayed in the breeze, a sharp contrast to the cloying smell of antiseptic in the room. She wished someone would open the window and let the fresh air in.

A gray-haired nurse stood by her bed, smiling warmly. She cradled a tiny bundle as if it were a prize. "Are you ready to meet your daughter?"

"My what?" It took a moment for Mariella to process her words. She propped herself up in bed. "I have a baby?"

"We needed to get her out quickly. Your placenta detached, but Doc got those forceps in and pulled her out before she lost any more oxygen," the nurse said, placing the tiny bundle in Mariella's arms. "She's a beaut, isn't she? I'll leave you two alone to get acquainted."

A girl! Mariella thought, happy to see a tuft of jet-black hair peeking out. She pulled back the blanket to reveal healthy pink skin and long, dark eyelashes. The baby furiously sucked on two tiny fingers, stretched lazily, punching the air a few times, then settled back down.

"Hello, sweet, dear daughter of mine." Mariella held the baby against her chest, stroking her soft, dark hair.

"Sorry, dear." Another nurse appeared at her bedside. "I'll have to take this little one from you. Your husband is waiting in the Stork Club."

"Stork Club?"

"The room for fathers? He's been waiting awhile."

"Oh?"

"Sure, your little one needed to be whisked off for oxygen right away. He's been pacing the floors for a few hours."

"But couldn't he come back here?"

"On no, this area is off-limits for men. Besides, who would want them? This time is for *you* to recover. Lord knows you won't have time when you go home!" The nurse laughed as she lifted the baby from Mariella's arms. "Come with me, sweetie. Your daddy can't wait to see his new girl."

Once she was gone, tears formed in Mariella's eyes. She had only just met her daughter and now she was gone. It didn't make sense to her. When Mama gave birth, the baby never left her side. Then again, her mother birthed all of her children at home. Just as Mariella was about to dissolve into sobs, she realized she wasn't alone. Six more beds, each separated from the next by a beige curtain, line the room.

"Hey! Want a cigarette?" The woman in the bed across from her waved a packet of Pall Malls in the air. "Don't bother getting out of bed—I've been here all week, I'll come to you!" With auburn hair pulled back into a neat bun and a full face of make-up, Mariella was impressed at how put together she was. The woman threw on a silky pink bathrobe and fluffy slippers then shuffled over. She tapped out a cigarette and lit it. "Here ya go."

"Thank you. I am Mariella."

"Nice to meet ya. I'm Madge."

Mariella took a long drag of the cigarette, resulting in a fit of coughing. "Maybe I should not be smoking right now," she muttered.

"Oh, you're fine. You just sucked it in too quickly. So...pink or blue?"

"Eh?"

"What did you have? Girl or boy?"

Mariella smiled. "A girl."

"A girl? Congrats! I had twin boys."

"Twin?"

Madge lit another cigarette and took a drag, the smoke curling around her nose as she exhaled. "Yup! I think they're identical, too. Both boys were eight and a half pounds on the dot. No wonder my back was aching for the past nine months."

"Two children at one time, how lucky!"

"That's what they keep telling me. But honestly," Madge said, walking back to her bed, "my house is never clean as it is. I can only imagine what havoc these two will add to my life."

"Will you stop moaning?" someone from the far side of the room chimed in. "All you do is complain. Not everyone here is as lucky as you."

Mariella tried to get a look at the woman but she lay with her back to the room and only a swath of curly brown hair was visible.

"Don't mind Carol." The woman in the next bed over swung her curtain open and leaned toward Mariella. "One of her twins didn't survive. The boy one."

"Oh, my. That must be terrible." An array of emotions bubbled up inside, but she forced them back down. Mariella had always thought she understood what her mother felt losing a child. Now she realized how devastating it must have been.

"The real tragedy is the hysterectomy they gave her after

birth. Something to do with a tumor they found. Poor thing. All she does is cry. She's worried her husband will leave her because she never gave him a boy."

Mariella noticed Carol lying motionless, as if she was holding her breath. "Will he really leave her?" she asked her neighbor, but the woman had already drawn her curtains shut.

"Time to feed your baby, Mrs. Valentino."

Mariella woke up to an older nurse with a big bosom standing above her. As she struggled to sit up, the nurse quickly fluffed a pillow and wedged it behind her. With her own family so far away, she didn't mind being mothered. "I'm sorry, I guess I fell asleep."

"That's understandable. You've been through a lot, dear."

The nurse disappeared, then quickly returned, wheeling a clear plastic bassinet to the side of the bed. Inside, her daughter shook and cried while kicking her feet in the air.

"Oh, no no, mio Tesoro." Mariella lifted her out, made sure no one else but the nurse was watching, then opened her nightgown and held her daughter close. The baby latched on immediately.

"You're an old pro!" the nurse said. "Do you have a few at home?"

Mariella winced, then repositioned her daughter. "No, but I helped my mother with my sisters and brother."

"Well, I don't have to worry about you! I'll tell ya, some of these women don't know a baby from a handbag!"

"And my husband?" Mariella was anxious to see Jack. "Can I see him?"

"He left already. Said he had to go to work."

"Oh," Mariella said, her voice deflating. It was all so strange to her. In Italy, childbirth was simple; you labored, you delivered the baby, you went on with your day. Family was around to help out when you needed sleep or had to cook for your family. But in America childbirth was sterile and clinical, filled with strangers and loneliness. Mariella yearned to hear her mother's voice but there was no way to call from the hospital. The month before her due date, she wrote Jack a script in Italian and instructed him to call her family the minute the baby arrived, then made him rehearse it so there was no room for error.

"Don't worry. You can meet your husband in the nursery when he returns. Give him a call on the house phone." The nurse pointed to a metal telephone table in the corner of the room. "But I suggest you get yourself together before seeing him. Most men have no idea how hard delivering a child is. And believe me, they're not interested in knowing either!"

"Why can I not keep her here?" Mariella asked.

"Oh, honey, nobody wants to hear a baby crying all night. I told you, this is your time to rest. When you get home, well, that's when the real work begins."

When she finished nursing, Mariella hesitated before separating herself from her daughter. It wasn't fair that she couldn't stay with her. It didn't seem natural. She reluctantly set the baby back into her bassinet. The little one slept peacefully, lips coated with her mother's milk, as the nurse wheeled her away.

Mariella shuffled to the telephone table. The medicine had worn off, and her pelvis throbbed, making her legs weak. Looking down at her swollen stomach, she recalled Mama's appearance after her siblings were born. Mariella had asked when the extra baby would come out. "Not in this lifetime," Mama replied with a laugh that left no room for doubt.

When she dialed Jack's office number, Jack picked up on the first ring. "Sweetheart, how are you and my beautiful little daughter doing?"

Mariella was overcome with emotion. "Can you come, please?"

"What's wrong? Are you okay?"

"I want to go home."

"Aw, gee, honey, I want you home too, but that's not how it works," Jack said carefully.

"What do you mean?"

"Well, most women spend a week in the hospital after they give birth, to be safe."

"A week?" Mariella repeated, leaning against the wall to ease the pain. "A week? But I am not sick. I had a baby."

"Sure, but it's only been three days. Your body has gone through a lot. I don't want anything to happen to you, sweetheart."

"What will happen? I feel fine. Besides, they do not keep the baby with me. She is only here when I feed her."

"Gee, I didn't know that."

"There is a lot you do not know. Mama had us all at home and she was on her feet right after."

Jack chuckled. "I bet she was exhausted. But you get to rest. And the nurses can teach you the basics."

"Basics?"

"Sure, the basics like bathing, feeding, diapering, all of those things."

Mariella lowered her voice. "Amore, I help my mother raise my siblings. I know how to do all of that."

"Gee, I guess you would, wouldn't you? I'm sorry. I'll come to visit."

"Only if you bring us home," Mariella demanded.

Jack sighed. "Are you sure?"

"Yes, I am. Come as soon as you can."

Chapter Twenty-Seven

When Jack pulled the car up, his parents' Cadillac was already waiting in their driveway. Three more cars lined the street in front of the house. Mariella sighed.

"I'm sorry, honey. Ma saw me leaving my office and, well, I couldn't lie to her, now, could I? Don't worry, they won't be long. My family's just itching to meet our new addition."

The baby stirred in her mother's arms, furrowing her dark eyebrows. Mariella held her close.

Jack parked across the street and then raced over to the passenger's side to open the door for Mariella. "Don't worry, honey. They won't be staying long."

"But I want to call my family."

"I understand," Jack said, helping her out of the car. "Just remember, I told your mother you wouldn't be out until the end of the week."

Mariella stopped a moment, allowing her stare to translate her thoughts for Jack. He nodded.

"Okay, I'll get rid of my family as soon as I can."

"Auguri," Pop said, holding the door open. He helped Mariella into the house, then turned his attention to the baby. "Che bella!"

She watched her father-in-law gaze at the baby sweetly. He had always been so kind, always made sure she was comfortable, just like her own father. But while Jack's father was flowers and sunshine, dealing with his mother was like crawling through barb wire.

"Finally!" Ma said. "We've been waiting for almost an hour!"

Mariella pretended she didn't hear. Instead, she pulled the blanket down around her daughter's face for Pop to see.

"She looks like you," he said, continuing to speak in Italian. "And how are you, my dear?"

"I am feeling fine."

"And your family? I bet there was a big celebration when they heard." His eyes lit up, as if he could imagine the fireworks going off down her street. After all, he left Naples at seventeen, unlike Ma, who was only a child. Pop's identity had been baked into him.

Mariella smiled. "I haven't spoken to them yet, but I'm sure they celebrated with a bottle of Spumante."

Rachel slipped next to her. "Isn't she a doll! Lucky you. Come, sit down. You must be exhausted. I hope you don't mind, I made a pot of coffee."

"Of course not, thank you." As Mariella sank into the couch, Jack carefully took the baby in his arms and brought her over to his mother, who sat like a queen on the loveseat.

"Ma, meet our little petunia," he said.

Mariella watched nervously as Ma juggled the baby in one arm while holding a cup of coffee in the other. After a few perilous moments, she went to her.

"I can take the baby so you drink your coffee."

Ma shooed her away. "I've had four children. I know what I'm doing. How do ya suppose I got anything done when they were young?"

"Mariella just wanted you to be comfortable," Pop said.

"Pop's right," Jack agreed. "Hey, where's Julia?"

"Your sister's gonna stop by later, without the boys," Ma said, smirking over at Mariella. "She knows how 'neat' you keep your house. She didn't want any problems. Ha! Those boys would tear this place up."

Willie hovered over his mother's shoulder and tickled the

baby's chin. "Coochie coochie coo!" he said. "She sure is small. Good thing she isn't a boy."

"Yeah," Carl joked, propping himself on the arm of the loveseat to get a good look. "Thank God she doesn't look like her father!"

"Hey, hey, now," Jack protested.

The baby began to fuss, her face growing red as her lower lip quivered. Mariella happily took her from Ma's arms and rocked her back to sleep.

"Don't listen to these boys," Rachel said. "She's a beautiful baby. Tell me, what did you name her?"

"We will call her Elisa ... for my sister."

The disappointment that crossed Ma's face was clear.

"And Rose for her middle name—after you, Ma!" Jack said.

Ma's face relaxed. "Why not Rosa? That's my name, not Rose."

"We like Elisa Rose. Sounds pretty, don't ya think?"

She clicked her tongue. "Sounds flowery. With a name like that, she's gonna need a brother to toughen her up."

"Oh, come on, Ma," Rachel said, "we need a little girl in this family."

"What for?"

Rachel nodded at Jack and his brothers. "To keep the boys in line, for starters! Besides, she's your first granddaughter. You should be celebrating."

"She's cute," Ma said with a shrug. "But I'm not gonna lie, I've always preferred boys."

"True," Willie agreed. "You're a boy mom, for sure!"

But you have a daughter, Mariella thought.

"I love my girl. She is my cuore," Pop said, touching his heart with his hand. Mariella wondered if Jack's mother had some jealousy toward Julia for the attention her husband showered her with.

Rachel wistfully touched her stomach. After having a miscarriage almost a year before, she was hoping to become pregnant soon. "I've always wanted a girl."

Carl bristled. "I'm like Ma. Hoping for another boy, if it ever happens."

"Trust me, Rachel, you don't want a girl," Ma said. "They're too damn sensitive. Ya can't even joke without getting a face full of tears in return!"

"Ole Julia was like one of the boys when she was younger, wasn't she, Ma?" Carl asked.

"Damn right. I wouldn't let my daughter be a wilting flower. My Julia's a strong girl."

"Don't be so negative, Ma," Jack said, gazing down at his daughter cradled in Mariella's arms. "My girl's gonna be wonderful."

"She sure is. You're gonna need a baseball bat to keep the boys away!" Willie agreed, then turned to Mariella. "Now, what does a guy gotta do to get a piece of that Danish I brought over? Rachel took it to the kitchen and hid it."

"Where else is a Danish supposed to go?" Rachel asked. She began to get up, but Mariella stopped her.

"I can get it," she said, jumping at the chance to leave the room. "Here, visit with your nipote ... how do you call it in English?"

She looked to Pop, who quickly responded. "Niece. The word is niece."

"Ah, grazie. You visit your niece," Mariella laid the baby in Rachel's arms and disappeared into the kitchen. Lingering for a moment, she hoped they would get the hint and leave. If her family were visiting, the house would have been filled with nothing but love. Her mother would have whisked the baby away and urged Mariella to get some rest. But she wasn't in Rome anymore and the space in her heart that held their memories throbbed as if demanding to be noticed.

Balancing a plate of sliced Danish with smaller plates underneath and a pot of coffee in her other hand, Mariella returned to the living room.

"Who would like more coffee?"

"Never mind," Ma said, getting up. "These boys need to

return to work. Give it to Julia when she comes."

Mariella watched Jack walk his family out as she stood in the doorway, gently rocking Elisa in her arms. When he got to the driveway, his mother turned to him. From the look on her face, the few words they exchanged seemed terse. Then, she hurried into the car and Jack raked his fingers through his hair as they drove away.

"Is everything okay, amore?" she asked when Jack came back inside.

He shook his head. "It's nothing. She's just worried about the business. Things haven't been very good lately, and she wants me working on new promotions to get people in."

"*Today?*" Mariella's forehead creased with worry. Jack had promised to stay their first night home, but she knew his mother would meddle.

"Of course she does. But—" He put his arm around Mariella and kissed his daughter on the head. "She's gonna have to wait, 'cause I'm staying with my girls today."

Chapter Twenty-Eight

"Mama?"

Jack watched Mariella whisper into the receiver. Elisa had fallen asleep in her arms, but instead of putting the baby down, she insisted Jack make the call. Before she could say any more, tears welled in her eyes. Jack felt helpless. Although she spoke in Italian, he was surprised at how much the way she talked said about her conversation. When her words were soft and melodic, she was speaking about their beautiful, daughter. Sharp clicks of her tongue must be about the hospital and its procedures. And when her voice lowered, Jack knew she was complaining about his family, causing guilt to muddle his thoughts.

"Three minutes, darling."

Mariella nodded, then continued with her conversation. Every once in a while, he heard his name and wondered: *Is she complaining about life here? Or me? Are they kind words?* She liked to shield him from how much she missed her family, but he could see the hurt in her eyes, the yearning for her own mother when they were with his. And even though she went to great lengths to keep it hidden, he still felt terrible. When they married years before, he focused on getting her to the United States, optimistic things would fall into place when she arrived. And even though having Mariella close was as he'd imagined, the logistics of day-to-day life were hard to ignore. He needed to work; it was the one reason they couldn't stay in Italy. But that meant lonely nights for her. At first, the way she clung to him when he arrived home made him feel loved. He ignored the fact that she had been alone most of the day. But he thought that after working since she was fifteen years old, she would want a break. He'd never considered sitting around the house reading fashion magazines and cleaning would be tedious.

"Ninety seconds, honey."

Mariella's eyes looked into the distance as if she were imagining her family's faces before her. A tear traveled down her cheek, and she batted it away. When she mentioned Jack's name again, he knew he was to blame for her final goodbye. He watched her grip the telephone, holding on desperately. In that moment, it was painfully obvious she would do anything to be back in Italy. She nodded as she listened to her mother for the final thirty seconds of the call. He assumed Mama was advising her daughter on how to care for their newborn. Mariella let out a soft laugh, then nodded again. Time was running out, and her words became quick, curt, and emotionless so she could say all she needed.

"Ten seconds, sweetheart."

"Ciao Mama, ciao."

"Eight ... seven..."

Now, her words came in sobs. The baby stirred in Mariella's arms, but even that didn't seem to quell the pain.

"Six ... five ... four..." Jack laid his hand on her back and tried to comfort her. "Three ... two..."

"Ti amo."

"One." He took the phone and quietly placed it back on the receiver.

She tried to smile. "They were so happy."

"I bet they were."

She rocked the baby back and forth to help her settle. "I'm sorry, amore. I am only crying because I am so happy."

Mariella's effort to protect his feelings broke Jack's heart. "You're allowed to cry," he said, handing her a tissue. "I understand."

She wiped her tears and laughed. "After you called, Mama said all their friends came to celebrate with cakes and cookies and homemade wi—" She stopped mid-sentence.

"What is it?"

"Today is Sunday, no?"

Jack nodded, then watched the joy on her face change to worry. "What is it?"

"Papa was not there today."

"Oh? Maybe he was at church?"

"No." Mariella thought a moment longer, trying to piece events together. "Mama said he was working. Why would he work on a Sunday?"

"It could be to prepare for a special event or something like that," Jack said. "I wouldn't worry, dear."

"Yes, maybe."

Jack helped Mariella to her feet. "I'm sure he was in the thick of it for the celebration!"

"But when you called with the news, was Papa there?"

"Well, sure, he even got on the phone to say Auguri." It was a lie. Jack had only spoken to Mama, but didn't want Mariella to worry. He helped her up the stairs and led her into the bedroom. "Now, you need to take care of yourself."

"Oh, Jack. This is perfect," Mariella said, gazing at the bassinet he had set up next to the bed. "I am so happy to be home."

She laid Elisa onto the soft mattress inside the bassinet and covered her with a white eyelet blanket her mother had sent.

Jack pulled back the covers on their bed. "Try and get a little shut-eye, sweetheart."

Mariella didn't fight him. He drew the curtains shut and left the two of them for a much-needed nap.

As he walked back down into the living room, someone knocked on the front door. It was Julia holding a big bouquet of pink roses.

"Congratulations, Papa!" She said, searching the room as she stepped inside. "Where's the new mommy?"

"Shhh," Jack said, pointing up the stairs.

"Poor thing, childbirth takes a lot out of a gal." She went into the kitchen and began to take apart the bouquet. Jack followed. "Do you have something to put these in?"

He nodded, then reached into the cabinet above the stove and retrieved a green glass vase. "Here ya go."

Julia filled it with water, then got busy arranging the flowers. "Now, tell me, why didn't Mariella want to stay in the hospital? I loved my time in the maternity ward. Nothing to do but rest and chat with all the gals. I tell ya, it was a hoot."

"Well, she's not used to that." Leaning against the stove, Jack rubbed the back of his neck. "They're still doing births at home back in Italy. She didn't think it was necessary to be there."

"Really? She could have died if she hadn't gotten through to you."

"Sure, but she was fine after. Remember, Mariella's from the old world, she's not as delicate as you might think." He sighed, prompting Julia to give her brother a good look.

"What about you?" She tousled his hair. "Boy! You look tired. Have you gotten any sleep?"

"Hey," he said, pushing it back into place. "I'm fine. I guess I haven't slept well, that's all." Jack thought twice about telling his sister how he'd sat up the past few nights, thinking about Mariella bleeding on their living room floor. Being away from home, she must have felt so alone.

Julia placed the vase on the kitchen table, then pulled out a chair. "Sit. I'll make you a grilled cheese sandwich. You need to take care of yourself, too."

"Thanks, sis," Jack said, sinking into his chair.

"So, how was Ma today?"

"Oh, you know Ma."

"Yes, yes, I do. Boy, she can be a prickly pear, don't ya think?" Julia asked, placing a pan on the stove. She opened the refrigerator and pulled out a brick of yellow cheese and a tub of butter.

"She can be. Gee, I thought after all this time she would eventually warm up to Mariella."

"Me too. Hey, where do you keep the bread?"

"Next to the stove. You know, Ma is so hard on her."

Julia took out two slices of Wonder Bread and slathered butter on each side. "Sure she is. But you do know why, don't you? Ma's jealous."

"Jealous?"

"Of course she is. You're her baby boy. No one has ever been good enough for you. Or for her." She placed one slice of bread in the pan, layered it with cheese, and topped it with the second slice of bread.

The smell of melting cheddar and toasted bread caused pangs of hunger to jab at Jack's stomach and he realized he hadn't had a bite since the night before. After a few minutes, Julia laid it on a plate and placed it in front of Jack. He took a bite. It was everything he craved.

"I wish Ma wouldn't be that way. It isn't very pleasant for Mariella," he said, with his mouth full.

"How did she take to the baby?"

"Who, Ma?"

"Yes, Ma. You know how she feels about little girls. Was she at least kind?"

"It depends on what you mean by kind."

"I guess you're right." Julia began to wash the pan when a thin cry came from the second floor. "She's awake!" She quickly dried her hands, then ran up the stairs two at a time.

By the time Jack arrived in the bedroom, Julia was already

by Mariella's side.

"Hello, doll. Aren't you a beauty?" she cooed, allowing the baby's tiny fingers to grip her own. "Can I hold her?"

"Of course you can." Mariella gently placed her in Julia's arms and returned to bed.

Jack watched his sister rock on her feet, humming a lullaby to his daughter. He knew she craved her own little girl to dote on. While Ma celebrated each boy she delivered, Julia's disappointment was obvious.

A short while later, Julia left, but not before promising to stop by the next day with some groceries. Mariella fed Elisa, then laid her on the bed between her and Jack. The baby slept peacefully, sucking at nothing every once in a while, as if she were dreaming about her next feeding. Jack glanced over at his wife. Her eyes were puffy from lack of sleep, her hair out of place, but at that very moment, he'd never loved anyone more.

"She's so tiny," Jack said, running his fingers along the baby's nose.

"Yes." Mariella sighed.

"What's wrong?"

"I was thinking of my brother, Matteo. He was so, so skinny when he was born. I thought Mama did not eat enough food. It made sense. It was wartime." She laid her head next to Elisa's. "But I did not want my daughter skinny like that."

"Sweetheart, you made the most beautiful baby. She'll grow, you watch. We'll give her the best of everything. Do you hear that, my sweet Elisa?" He kissed the baby's cheek, and although Mariella had closed her eyes, she smiled. "I like that."

"Like what?"

"To hear her name. It is like when birds visit, I know my sister is around." She laid a protective hand over her baby's body. "Now, her memory will be everywhere this little one is."

Over the following months, Jack watched Mariella blossom as a mother. It came naturally, as if she had been waiting her entire life for a family. She woke all hours of the night to feed their daughter, careful not to disturb Jack. In the past, when he left for work in the mornings, Mariella would look lost. Now, she made his eggs and toast while holding Elisa in one arm then happily waved goodbye. He didn't mind, though. At that moment, his little girl's well-being was all that mattered.

Chapter Twenty-Nine

By the time Elisa turned two, Mariella was pregnant again. The news sent her over the moon. Her dream of a houseful of children would soon be a reality. But then the sickness set in. This time, it was something different from the stomach upset she had struggled with before. It occurred at all times of the day and more violently. In the morning, while preparing breakfast, she sprinted for the bathroom with Elisa at her heels. Through each lurching wave of nausea, her daughter chatted about their neighbor's cat. Later in the day, she kept a lined bin close by while dusting furniture, just in case. As she made dinner in the evenings, she avoided cooking certain foods, like raw chicken and garlic, that were most likely to turn her stomach. Instead, she ate unsauced spaghetti or a slice of toasted Italian bread smeared with a thin layer of cream cheese. When she finally crawled into bed at night, every muscle in her body ached. At almost five months pregnant, the vomiting still occurred.

One summer evening, Mariella followed Elisa as she shuffled up the stairs for bed. Smart as a whip, her baby daughter had learned to speak in complete sentences by a year and a half. Now, she practiced speaking in Italian.

"Uno, du, tree, qua-qua—Mama?" Elisa cocked her head back and looked up at Mariella.

"Quattro, Tesoro. It's quattro," Mariella said in a weary voice. While her daughter's curiosity was impressive, answering her questions from morning to bedtime was tiring.

"Quarro, uno, du..."

"No, Tesoro. Cinque, sei, and then sette."

"Chick-we, say, set!" Once the stairs had been conquered, she skipped cheerfully into her room and jumped on the bed.

"Okay, Tesoro, it's time to sleep, not play."

"But I no tired, Mama." Elisa folded her dimpled arms in front of her. "You read book? Pwease?"

Mariella sighed at her daughter's theatrics. "Oh, honey, I am so tired."

"But Mama!"

"Not tonight, Tesoro. Now, get under the covers." She pulled back the sheet and patted the mattress.

Elisa reluctantly shimmied in, thought of something, then tried to get out. "Oh, Mama! We need prayers!"

Mariella stopped her. "No, Tesoro, it is okay.

Praying in your bed is as good as kneeling. God will still be listening."

"Okay, Mama." Elisa clasped her hands together as Mariella sat down on the edge of her bed and recited the prayer:

"Angelino bellino bellino, vieni e stammi sempre vicino, fammi buono come sei tu, e poi portami da Gesù. Amen."

"Ayyyymen."

"Now, go to sleep, okay, Tesoro?"

"Okay, Mama."

Mariella gave her a kiss, tucked her in, then grasped the headboard and pulled herself up from the bed.

"Mama?" Elisa asked, twirling one of her dark curls.

Mariella stopped in the doorway. "Yes, my love."

"What it mean?"

"What?"

"The prayer!"

"What does the prayer mean?"

"Yes."

Mariella leaned against the doorframe as she considered her daughter's question. "Well, it is a prayer asking the beautiful angels in heaven to watch over you here on Earth. Then, when you are ready, the beautiful angels will take you to Jesus."

Elisa gasped, her mouth forming a perfect circle. She sat up in bed and whispered, "The angels take me? When, Mama? I wanna go!"

"Oh, Tesoro, you are not ready for Jesus," Mariella told her. "You need to live a whole life before you see can see him." Despite the hot, sticky weather, a chill ran through her. Many nights had been spent sitting on the roof with her sister planning their futures. They discussed their ideal husbands; kind, handsome men who were also friends, the children they imagined; a boy and girl for each, and how they would have apartments right across the hall so they would never miss any moments in each other's lives. Sadly, her sister had never gotten a chance to learn there was no such thing as perfect. "Now, it is time for sleep," Mariella said. "Buona notte, Tesoro."

Elisa popped her thumb in her mouth and rolled over. "Buona notte, Mama," she mumbled, then quickly drifted off to sleep.

Mariella lay in bed and listened to the crickets. She'd never heard them before moving to the United States. There were so many things she hadn't done, like cooking eggs for breakfast or buying her groceries in a supermarket instead of the fruit and meat stands set up in the piazza each morning. She realized this American life would be all her daughter knew. The thought brought tears to her eyes. She wept for her old life, where she had her family by her side, no matter how hard things were. Her children would never understand the horrors she'd experienced. Of course, Mariella would tell them one day, but it wouldn't be enough. She could never explain the desperation they'd felt during those years. Living under the threat of death at every turn made her prayers a necessity. By the time her sister died years later, death had become familiar.

Stop this, Mariella thought, willing herself not to spiral. But once those awful memories were unleashed, tucking them back into the dark corners of her mind was near impossible. Unable to keep her thoughts from spinning, she got out of bed and went downstairs.

Mariella considered calling her parents, but, after counting forward six hours, she calculated it had just turned 3:30 a.m. in Italy. A call at that time would certainly cause a panic. Instead, she picked up the phone and dialed the restaurant.

"Hello, Villa Pensa restaurant." It was Ma. She considered asking for Jack, but didn't want to deal with her mother-in-law's nasty remarks. She hung up and dragged herself back to bed. Jack wouldn't be home for a few more hours, so she stared up at the ceiling, hoping the crickets would lull her to sleep. Instead, she found herself wondering how they made their noises.

Suddenly, the sound of scrambling on the roof made her jump, then she remembered their neighbor Louise complaining about squirrels getting in her attic. Scenes from her other life continued to cycle through her mind.

It's just pregnancy, she told herself, trying not to give in to her shifting hormones. But nothing stopped her from longing for the days of her past. *What is wrong with me? All I dreamed of was to be here with Jack.*

Fumbling in the dark, Mariella turned on her lamp. She opened her night table drawer and searched for a tissue, but instead her fingers brushed against the edges of a photo, which sat unnoticed beneath her bible. She pulled it out and stared at its slightly faded and cracked surface. Mariella knew it all too well. It was a family photo taken just a year before the Germans arrived in Rome. Mama was seated at the front, holding baby Lia tightly to keep her from escaping; Lia's eyes were clenched shut in frustration as she cried. Giada stood behind them in a frilly babydoll dress, looking bored. Elisa was next to Giada, giving her usual cheery smile. Papa was beside Mama, staring straight into the camera, an intense expression on his face. And Mariella stood firmly by his side, claiming the coveted spot.

She touched their innocent faces. When they'd had the photo taken, they had no idea what was coming. She envied the people in the photo, wishing she could go back to that life before everything changed. Not knowing was a blessing, a life without care.

A few tears fell onto the photo, and Mariella slipped it back into the drawer. She wiped her face with her sleeve and lay back down, scolding herself. She lived a good life in the U.S. Mariella had a loving husband, a beautiful daughter, and a house grander than she'd ever imagined. But to gain all this, she'd had to give up her family. One family for another. It didn't seem fair when she saw women pushing strollers, their own mothers beside them, cooing over the babies.

But when is life ever fair? she wondered.

At that moment, Jack entered the bedroom, tugging at his tie.

"Darling, what are you doing up?" he asked.

Mariella had been so absorbed in her thoughts she hadn't heard him come in. She sat up. "Why are you home so early?"

"Early?" Jack laughed, pointing to his watch. "It's two a.m.!"

"It is?"

"Sure," he said, slipping out of his shoes. "How was my girl today?"

Since Elisa was born, she was always his first question. It was obvious he missed her terribly when he was at work. "She was a good girl, and very talking-tive."

"Talking-tive?" Jack let out a laugh as he continued to undress. "I think the word is talkative."

Mariella frowned, embarrassed that she was still mixing up her words. It was just another example of the difference between her and the family she created.

"Our little girl does love to talk, doesn't she?" he said pulling on his pajamas. When Mariella didn't answer, he looked at her. "Are you okay, sweetheart? You look exhausted."

She considered telling him how much she longed for her mother's guidance, her neighborhood's cobblestone streets, and the sounds of her childhood home when everyone was there, but she didn't have the words without making him feel responsible. "I am just having a hard time sleeping."

"We've gotta change that! How can you function tomorrow on just a few hours of sleep?"

"Oh, I have not been up long. I heard you come into the house and woke up," Mariella lied.

"Gee, I'm sorry about that. I try to be quiet, but that door sticks every time I open it. Don't worry, I have tomorrow off. I'll fix it right up."

Mariella turned to him. "But it is Thursday. You always work on Thursdays."

"Yeah, well, business has been slowing down." Jack slid into bed next to her. "It makes more sense to stay closed."

"Oh."

"That's not a bad thing. I can take care of my girl at night and you can get some much-needed sleep, okay?"

"Okay, amore. Goodnight."

"Goodnight."

Within a few minutes, Jack began to snore while a continuous loop of memories kept Mariella from the sleep she craved.

Chapter Thirty

Heavy snow cascaded down from the sky like heaps of wet cotton balls. Mariella watched anxiously from her living room window as the streets turned white. She knew she should have put her foot down and demanded Jack stay home when his mother called. Now all she could do was wait as thoughts of him stuck in a ditch nagged at her.

But it wasn't her worry that twisted her stomach into a tight ball, forcing her to bend over and take short breaths until it wore off. For the past hour, contractions had been coming in waves about ten minutes apart. Mariella fought the urge to call for help. If she could pretend they weren't happening, then no one would be able to convince her to go to the hospital.

She heard someone clomping up the steps and lumbered over to the door, hoping to see Jack's kind face on the other side. But it was her neighbor Louise, bundled up with a scarf.

"Oh my goodness." Mariella held the storm door open. "Please come inside!"

Louise kicked her boots against the doorsill, shaking off the snow, then stepped in.

"It's a mess out there!" she said, her voice quivering from the cold. Before taking off her coat, she handed Mariella a brown paper bag. "I made you shepherd's pie. You need your strength. I worried about you when I saw Jack leave earlier."

Mariella took the bag and shuffled to the kitchen. "That is so kind of you, but I do not have an appetite. I am sure Jack will enjoy this when he gets home!"

"Don't tell me he's at the restaurant?" Louise asked while unwrapping her outer layers.

"Of course he is."

"With his wife in her ninth month of pregnancy? Surely, it isn't open in the middle of a blizzard!"

Mariela shook her head.

"Then tell me, dear, what's going on?"

"It is that horrible mother of his!" Mariella carefully sank into the couch while supporting her stomach with one hand. "I swear she thinks up things for him to do to keep him away from me."

"How could she keep her son from his pregnant wife and child on a night like this?"

"Oh, Louise, she never cared for me."

"What?"

"It used to be a quiet thing, but now she makes it very clear."

"Oh my. How about a cup of tea?" Louise asked.

"Okay." Mariella felt weak. Uncomfortable with her burgeoning belly, she hadn't slept for more than a few hours at a time in the past week.

Louise went into the kitchen, put the teapot on the stove, then returned to the living room. "So, if the restaurant isn't open, why did he have to go?"

"His mother wanted the boys to make sure there was no damage to the building. I tell you, what could he do if there was?"

"Nothing, that's what. Listen, why don't we call and tell him to come home?"

Mariella waved her hand. "It is Carl's shift. Jack is on his way home now. At least, that is what he said when he called an hour ago."

"An *hour?*"

"I know," Mariella said, trying to ignore the alarm on her neighbor's face. "I start to worry thirty minutes ago, so I call the restaurant and Carl told me he must be driving slow so he would not slide off the road. How can a ten-minute drive turn into an hour?"

"Oh dear. Well, these snowstorms happen every year. It's

not the first time he's driving in weather like this." The teapot began to whine and Louise disappeared into the kitchen, emerging a few minutes later carrying two steaming cups of tea. "I know I'm English, but I swear there is nothing that a nice cup of tea can't make better!"

An urgent cry traveled downstairs, adding to Mariella's worries. She struggled to get up but Louise stopped her.

"I'll take care of it."

"Thank you," Mariella sighed, and sank further into the couch.

After a few minutes of trying to get her back to sleep, Louise returned holding Elisa in her arms.

"Mama! Miss Lou is here!" she declared, a devilish smile on her face.

Mariella doubled over in another contraction. This time, the pain was more intense.

"Oh no." Louise looked over at her nervously. "How long have they been happening?"

"Eh," was all Mariella could muster until the pain subsided enough for her to form a complete sentence. "Not too long. I will be okay."

"Don't you want me to call someone?"

"Jack will be here soon. Do not worry."

"Mama." Rubbing sleep out of her eyes, Elisa's lower lip

began trembling. "Mama!"

Mariella glanced at her, feeling overwhelmed. It was clear her daughter needed her. But as she curled over, bracing herself for another contraction, Mariella realized how desperately she longed for her own mother.

"It's okay, little one. How about we let your mama rest and you come home with me for a sleepover! Would you like that?" Louise asked Elisa.

"I can sleep in your bed?"

"Yes, of course. You and I can cuddle up together. Mr. Charles will sleep in the spare room."

"And Cally?"

Louise looked to Mariella for approval. The thought of Louise's cat, Cally, sleeping right next to her daughter usually scared Mariella, but she couldn't care less at that moment. She nodded, relieved she wouldn't have to think of anyone but herself for the next few hours.

"Cally can sleep with us too!"

Elisa clapped her hands. "Yay!"

After promising she would call as soon as Jack arrived home, Mariella watched Louise bundle her daughter into her pink snowsuit complete with hood, scarf, and mittens, then carry her across the street and into her house. She glanced over at the phone table, wishing she could make the call she longed for. Mama would know what to do. Mama always did. Shuffling back to the living room window, Mariella noticed two faint beams of light appearing at the top of the street. They grew stronger as they traveled closer and closer until—finally—she could make out Jack's car.

He's home, she thought, just as her stomach tightened again. She doubled over, taking short quick breaths until it was over.

Mariella anxiously watched Jack climb out of the car and trudge through the snowbanks. He had to step high through the drifts as if he were wading through water. When he finally reached their front door, her stomach clenched again.

"It's a bear out there!" Jack exclaimed as he pulled off his rubber boots. "Almost didn't make it home. Main Street was littered with cars that had conked out. I'm lucky to be—" He stopped when he saw Mariella bent over in pain, clenching the side of the couch to get her through. "Oh no."

"Do... not worry.. it...it is nothing. Just... just my funny stomach," Mariella said, speaking erratically until the pain subsided. She fell into his arms.

"Hold on a moment, let me take off my overcoat."

But she wouldn't let go, nuzzling her face into his chest until it grew cold and wet. "I do not mind. You are home, that is all that matters."

Jack held her close, kissing the top of her head. "Gee, I must have given you quite a fright. I'm sorry, sweetheart."

"I was so worried," she said, croaking out the last part. Another round of contractions, this time only minutes apart, made her catch her breath again. She clung to him, trying to hide it, but Jack figured it out quickly.

"The baby?"

Mariella shook her head but hot, jabbing pains running down her legs rendered her speechless.

Jack lowered himself to eye level. "I think we better get you to the hospital."

"No!" she cried the minute the pain left her body. "I do not want to go to the hospital. I can do this at home."

"What? No, you can't. You need a doctor."

"Why? Mama gave birth at home five times. She did not need anyone else."

"Well, sure, my ma gave birth in our house too, but that's not done here anymore. People go to the hospital just in case."

Mariella defiantly shook her head. "I do not want to go to the hospital."

"But what if something happens to you like last time?"

"I am not going back there!" Mariella declared. "They put me to sleep, and God knows what else they do. I did not even get to meet my baby until hours later. I do not want that."

"But—"

"Besides, it is too dangerous to go out. No! I will not risk my baby's life. I can do this here. At home."

Jack was quiet as Mariella bent over and dug her nails into the arm of the loveseat. Her tightening abdomen felt like a million fingers were squeezing her.

"Oh, honey," he said, rubbing her back while she breathed through the pain. "I hate to see you like this. I wish I could take this pain away from you."

When Mariella came up for air, she paced the room, grabbing onto the walls to keep her shaky legs from giving out on her.

"What can I do for you? Do you need to sit? Why don't you sit down."

Jack tried to lead her to the couch but she pulled back, bent over, and took quick, short breaths to get through another contraction. Although he was trying to help, Mariella grew agitated. Papa was never around for the births when her siblings came along. It was women's business.

When the pain subsided once more, she pulled herself together and looked up at him. "Amore, I love you but… I cannot have you here."

A sense of relief brightened Jack's face. "No?"

Mariella shook her head. "Go to Louise and Charles's house. Elisa is already there but"—the pain began to return, and panic made her stumble over her words—"ask...ask Louise for...for... to come here."

"Louise?"

"Yes." Mariella put up a finger until the contraction passed, then spoke. "She has worked in a hospital."

"Well, that'll come in handy," Jack agreed, then narrowed his eyes on her. "Are you sure?"

Mariella nodded. She knew he wasn't keen on seeing his wife in the throes of childbirth. Without further argument, he slipped back into his boots, kissed Mariella good luck, and headed across the street.

Chapter Thirty-One

Wind howled through Jack's overcoat, chilling his bones. But it was leaving his wife that bothered him most. Once across the street, he glanced back and noticed her silhouette in the doorway. She looked so vulnerable he wanted to run back home, scoop her up, and force her into the car. But she had a point. The roads were downright dangerous. He waved just as she bent over in another contraction. Time was not on their side.

Louise had been watching from the window and quickly opened the door. "What's wrong?"

"I wanted to take her to the hospital but she won't budge," Jack said as he shook snow off his coat and went in.

"Well, that makes sense. It's miserable out there."

"Papa! Papa!" Elisa cried, skipping into the room, holding Louise's calico cat under its front legs, allowing its hind legs to drag on the floor. "This is Cally."

"You don't say?" Jack quickly turned back to Louise. "Mariella could really use you."

"Hey there, Jack!" Charles appeared from the kitchen, holding a short glass of whiskey. "Are you here for happy hour?"

Jack laughed. "Hiya, Charles. Actually, we—"

"He came to visit me, right, Papa?" Elisa dropped the cat in order to cling to her father's leg.

"Sure, honey," he said, watching Louise button up her coat, then pull on her boots.

"Don't worry, Jack. I've seen a few births. I promise you she'll be fine. Cheerio!" Louise quickly slipped out the door.

"Where is Miss Louise going? She promised a sleepover!" Elisa asked, tears coming fast and furious as a full-blown temper tantrum unfolded. Watching his daughter writhe on the floor, screaming and crying, Jack felt helpless. Thankfully, Charles brought out a plate of Linzer tarts.

"What do we have here?" Jack said, as she quieted down. Her face was heated, cheeks bright red as she rubbed her sleepy, wet eyes. "Now, if you behave, you can have one of Mr. Charles's cookies. Whaddya say?"

Elisa looked back at the door as if she were weighing her options. She fingered a few of the cookies before she chose one, then bit into it and giggled. "Yummy!"

"And when she gets to bed, I suppose Daddy can have a treat

too?" Charles said, jiggling the ice in his glass.

Jack laughed. "I suppose so!"

After Jack entertained Elisa with a few stories, she curled up next to Cally the cat, her thumb firmly in her mouth, then quickly fell asleep. Jack joined Charles downstairs in the rumpus room.

"I appreciate you staying awake with me, pal."

"And leave you here pacing like a lion at the zoo? Not on your life!" Charles brought out another short crystal glass from his liquor cabinet, then poured some Irish whiskey into it. "I hope Jameson is okay for you?"

"Sure, thanks," Jack said, peering out the window. Across the street, all he could make out through the blinding snow was a faint light coming from their living room, then one from the upstairs bedroom. "I wish I knew how it was going."

"I'm sure Louise will call if there's an issue." Charles handed the whiskey to Jack. "Drink this. It'll calm your nerves." He clinked his glass against Jack's and sipped.

Jack threw his back then let out a breath. "Ah, that'll do it."

Charles poured Jack another whiskey. "So, what are you thinking? A boy this time?"

"Well," Jack began. It wasn't the first time he'd been asked about wanting a son. "I wouldn't mind a namesake. But honestly, I just want a healthy baby."

"Of course, of course." Charles leaned in. "But we all want

our boys, don't we?"

Jack gave Charles a curious look. A good ten years older, Charles was always put together, like a person whose life had fallen neatly into place. But, other than a few drinks parties, due to their opposite work schedules, he hadn't spent much time with his neighbor. Louise, on the other hand, had become fast friends with his wife. Jack was grateful for it. He knew that there were parts he couldn't fill in for Mariella. Someone who shared her experience as a foreigner had been priceless. Louise was also exceptionally helpful with their daughter, but he didn't know why they didn't have children of their own.

"What about you? Have you and Louise ever thought of having your own brood?"

Charles held up one hand, his fingers spread apart. "Five times. She was pregnant five times, but every time was worse than the first. Until the fifth." He paused a moment, as if to allow the information to sink in, then continued. "That's when my boy was born. We named him William. A proper British name. He was a beautiful boy. He had eyes as blue as the Caribbean Sea and blond hair."

Hearing his neighbor speak about his son in the past tense made Jack regret asking the question. He looked out the window again. The snow seemed to be letting up a little, and the lights in the house were shining brighter.

"We'll never know what happened," Charles continued. "The little guy came a month early. Didn't have enough strength, I guess. The doctor said his heart just stopped. We never tried again after that. It was too painful. That was seven years ago."

"I can't imagine how that must have felt," Jack said, glancing nervously out the window again. "When I was away during the war, my ma had a little boy. Luca, she named him. I saw the one picture they had of him when I came home. Cute little rascal. In any case, I think he was about a year when he died."

"Oh, what of?"

"Influenza. Ma wasn't herself for months. Once we returned, safe and sound, she was able to get her footing. How about Louise?"

"I tell ya, my Louise is a strong gal. It's something about that stiff upper lip the Brits have. She mourned for a few months, then got on with it. Sometimes I think it was harder for me." Charles sipped his whiskey as if he were soothing himself. Jack did the same.

Over the next several hours, Jack kept an eye on his house as he and Charles played a few games of chess, chatting the whole time. He learned about how Charles and Louise met and how he needed to fight for her hand in marriage. They certainly had similar stories. When they grew bored of chess, Charles took out cards and chips and they had a lively game of poker.

"It's my lucky day!" Jack crowed when he won a ten-dollar hand. "C'mon, let's play again! I've got another baby on the way. I'll need the extra cash!"

But when the sound of footsteps crunching through the snow passed by the window, Jack dropped his cards and bolted up the stairs.

"Well?" he asked, reaching Louise before she could take off her overcoat.

She let out a weary laugh. "Everything's fine. Mariella was a champ. She knew exactly what to do. And you, sir, are the lucky father of another beautiful baby girl."

"Hey, hey!" Jack cheered. "And the baby, she's okay?"

"Yes," she confirmed, pulling off her wet boots.

"How 'bout my wife? How's she doing?"

Louise nodded. "She's exhausted but fine."

"Papa?" Elisa stood at the top of the stairs, rubbing sleep from her eyes. "Where's Mama?"

Jack ran up two steps at a time, then scooped her into his arms. "Hello, peanut! Want to meet your new baby sister?"

Elisa's eyes grew wide. "Mama wif my sister? That no fair! Why she no here wif me?" Her face heated up, making her cheeks rosy.

"Now, now," Jack said, trying to soothe his daughter. "Your sister just arrived. Mama has to be with her. At least for now. But we can go meet her, okay?"

"No, no, no!" Elisa shook her head vehemently. "I no wanna meet her. I hate her." She buried her head in Jack's chest.

"That's okay, dear," Louise said. "You don't have to love her right now. But I bet you will when she gets older. You'll always have a best friend, even when no one else is around to play with."

Elisa peeked over her father's shoulder.

"Sure!" Jack chimed in. "And when you're old enough to go on the merry-go-round all by yourself, you can share a horse with her!"

Elisa giggled.

"And eat candy floss with her!" Louise continued. "And— and go to the carnival with her!"

Jack spun Elisa around. "Miss Lou is right! All of that. Now, let's go meet your new sister."

"Okay," Elisa said as they bundled her up for the snowy trek across the street.

Mariella sat in bed propped up by pillows. She gently rocked their newborn daughter as Jack entered the room, Elisa perched in his arms. Aside from her hair, slick with sweat, Mariella looked beautiful.

"Mama! I wanna see!" Elisa whined.

Jack sat Elisa next to Mariella and watched her quietly talk to the baby. "You and me can be friends, okay? And you ride the merry-'round only wif me, 'cause you too small to ride alone. You need do all the things wif me. Okay?" She finished with a yawn, laid against her mother, and popped a thumb in her mouth.

"Tesoro, you must be tired."

Elisa nodded, her eyes drooping closed.

Mariella looked up at Jack. "Would you like to hold your new daughter, Papa?"

"Of course I would," Jack said, gently gathering the baby up in his arms. With a round face, pinkish lips, and a patch of dark hair, she looked like a petite version of her older sister. When Mariella said she was expecting again, he couldn't imagine having any more room in his heart for another child. Now, it felt so full, it could burst. He swallowed hard. "She's perfect. What will we call her?"

Mariella searched his face. "It is your turn. What do you want to call her?"

"Well, now, let me take a good look at this little daisy." He gazed down at his daughter again and tilted his head. "Hmmmm."

"Amore, you said once you see the baby, you will know its name. Please, I named Elisa. It is only fair you make the name for this one."

"Okay, okay. Give me a moment." Jack scratched his jaw where a five o'clock shadow was turning into a full-blown beard. "I always liked the name Olivia." He looked down at her delicate features. "She's elegant like an Olivia, don't you think?"

"Yes." Mariella smiled. "I like that name too. It is very English. But do you mind if we give her the middle name Helena?"

Jack recognized the faraway look in her eyes. It was the same one she had when she spoke about the war and the horrible things that had happened. He wished he shared her memories. Then, maybe he could help take the pain away. Laying the baby back in her arms, he sat on the edge of the bed. "That's a good idea, but what about your mother? Don't you want her name for the middle?"

"Oh, no. Mama never liked Vittoria. She always said she would disown any of us if we named one of her grandchildren after her."

"I see. Hmmm. Olivia Helena Valentino. What do you think, darling?" Jack asked the baby. Her brow creased in the middle as she concentrated on sleeping, and then relaxed.

Chapter Thirty-Two

Mariella woke to the sound of sparrows chirping happily, as if they were saying goodbye before migrating for warmer weather. She yawned, then snuggled further beneath her sheets until she realized something felt off. She checked the clock; it read 7:43 a.m.

Rushing into her daughters' room, she found both girls asleep. Her worry wasn't for Elisa, who never woke before 8 a.m., but at only ten months old, Olivia should have been up already. Mariella leaned over the crib, watching for signs of movement. After a few seconds, she noticed a faint rise in the baby's chest, followed by silence, then another shallow breath.

"Olivia?" she whispered, giving her daughter a nudge.

There was no response. Mariella slipped her hands under Olivia and felt her body flop like a dead fish. Holding her close, she ran down to the phone. First, she dialed the restaurant, but remembered Jack had left with his father at 6 a.m. to drive up to New York City and buy a new stove for the restaurant. Instead, she called Louise.

"Please come… Something is wrong with the baby… Olivia… Yes, she is not breathing very well… Yes… Thank you."

Mariella opened the front door just as Louise sprinted out of her house in a long, silk bathrobe, her hair rolled in curlers and tied up with a scarf. She hurried in, took Olivia from Mariella's arms, and laid her on the couch.

"What happened?" Louise asked in between blowing little breaths into the baby's mouth.

Mariella stood helplessly by the door, afraid some other terrible thing would happen if she moved. "I-I woke up on my own. She never cried or made a noise."

"Call emergency services."

"What?"

"Mariella, please. Pick up the phone and ask the operator to contact emergency services."

"Okay, okay." Adrenaline coursed through Mariella as she explained the unfolding nightmare to the operator.

Within minutes, the whine of a siren woke up the neighborhood. Louise met the EMTs on the front lawn and gave them a full report. A short, burly paramedic stomped into the house first. The look of concern on his face was comforting. He took the baby into his arms.

"Step aside." A second man, wearing a bulky fireman's coat, pushed past Mariella. Feeling like a guest in her own home, she moved out of the way. He moved the coffee table over so the paramedic could lay Olivia on the floor and kneel beside her.

"Don't worry," Louise reassured her. "They'll take good care of her."

Mariella wanted to trust her friend, but she had seen this all before. Her sister's vacant stare into nothingness while dangling off their roof. *Could brain tumors be hereditary?* Fear made every part of her want to scream. Just when things were hopeful, tragedy had always struck. The thought of her young daughter losing a sister and growing her own cavernous space embedded in her heart was unbearable. As her thoughts spiraled, she wondered if Jack would blame her. Mariella had woken up late. If she had set an alarm instead of counting on the children to wake her, she could have prevented it. Her head began to throb.

The men crowded around the baby, obstructing Mariella's view. Although she should have been angry, she felt relief. Watching her daughter, blue and lifeless, would be hard to forget.

Suddenly there was a gurgle followed by a hearty cry. Mariella kissed the gold cross around her neck and said a prayer.

"Here you go, miss," the paramedic said as he carefully passed Olivia to Mariella. The baby cried some more before settling into her arms.

"What is wrong?" Mariella asked, keeping one eye on her daughter.

"These things happen sometimes with babies. They forget to breathe."

"Forget?"

"Trust me, I've seen this before. Lucky we got here in time. These things don't always resolve themselves." He scribbled onto a small pad of paper as he spoke, then ripped the page off and handed it to her. "Here, these are my notes," he said, packing up his bag. "Take her to your family doctor to be sure she has nothing else going on."

Once they left, Mariella sat on the couch with Olivia on her lap, afraid to let go. Louise sat down on the loveseat, her face pale and sweaty.

"Are you okay?" Mariella asked. When Louise looked away, she understood. "It brings back awful memories for you, no?"

"Yes," Louise said, quietly.

"It is okay ... if you want to talk."

A tear traveled down Louise's cheek but she quickly swatted it away. "It's over now, I'm okay."

Olivia had fallen asleep in Mariella's arms so she laid her on the couch and sat next to Louise. "I often wonder if it is hard for you to come help with the children."

"Oh heavens no, I love to be with your little ones. But, seeing Olivia lying there so lifeless, brought me back to that horrible day."

"Was it like this with your son? Did he not wake up?" Mariella asked, worried Olivia might have the same thing.

Louise pulled a handkerchief from her sleeve and dabbed at another tear. "Yes, but only because he was premature. They kept him in the hospital a whole month before coming home. Only two days later we woke to our boy not breathing. His poor little heart wasn't strong enough," she said in an unsteady voice. Every time Mariella thought her neighbor would fall apart, her face tensed and she forced a smile. "Never mind. That was long ago. But I love taking care of your daughters. I can't have any of my own so it's nice to have yours in my life. Olivia's cries and Elisa's little songs make my house sound lived in. That, to me, is comforting."

Mariella squeezed her hand. "You will always be a part of our family."

"Mama?" Elisa shuffled downstairs and leaned against her mother. "Why is Miss Louise here?"

"Tesoro, she is here to pick you up, isn't that right, Louise? So I can take the baby to the doctor's?"

Louise slipped her handkerchief back into her sleeve and set Elisa on her lap. "Would you like that, little squirrel?"

Elisa nodded.

"Thank you," Mariella said, giving Louise a hug. "I would not be too long. At least I hope so."

Louise sniffed the top of Elisa's head and kissed it. "It's my pleasure."

"I do not know what happened. Emergency services said she could have died," Mariella explained, watching Dr. Berg examine her daughter. Although she'd resisted going to him, Jack's ma insisted. He had taken care of her children and she refused to have anyone else care for her grandchildren.

Dr. Berg removed Olivia's cotton nightgown and placed his stethoscope on different points of her chest. She began to cry. "Now, now, you're okay," he told her, though it sounded more like a statement than reassurance.

"Eh, I think that is cold? Maybe if you warmed it up with your hand?" Mariella suggested.

But Dr. Berg ignored her, continuing the examination while the baby's cries became more intense.

"Doctor?" Mariella asked, watching Olivia grow more agitated. "Can I help?"

Suddenly, the doctor threw his hands up and stepped away from the table. "Your daughter is fine. Now calm her down so I can hear myself think!"

Mariella scooped her up. "Okay, Stellina. Mama's here," she

said, rocking her back and forth. Olivia sucked on her fingers and finally calmed.

"You know you are spoiling her," Dr. Berg said. Taking a seat at his desk, he opened up a file and began to write.

"What?"

He looked up at Mariella, cocking one eyebrow. "I said you are spoiling her."

"Spoiling her?"

"Yes. Do you understand? It means you let her do whatever she wants. If she cries, you don't stick to the rules. You give in. She needs structure and discipline."

"But she is only a baby."

"She's practically a toddler. Children need direction and consequences if they don't do as they are told. Give her a good swat on the backside, and she'll listen to anything you say. Trust me, they are never too young for a good spanking."

Mariella had never heard of such a thing. She thought it was impossible to spoil a baby. She'd grown up in a house full of love. Except for when her brother died and she was left at her grandparents' farm, there wasn't a day her parents hadn't given her hugs and kisses. They made her feel like the center of the universe—especially her papa. But maybe something else caused this. Maybe her parents wanted to fill in the holes that the insecurity and terror of the war dug out of them.

"Now," Dr. Berg continued, putting down his pen, "your child knows she can get your attention by simply crying or doing something more alarming, which is what happened this morning. It's called breath holding. Most spoiled children learn to manipulate their mothers by merely holding their breaths."

"I do not understand. She was not with me. She was in bed."

"What time did you finally wake up this morning, Mrs. Valentino?"

"Eh, I do not set an alarm because she usually cries for me, but this morning, it was almost eight o'clock. She never made a sound, so I-I guess I slept late." Guilt was beginning to settle in the pit of her stomach.

Dr. Berg smirked. "Never made a sound, huh? Or, maybe she had been crying for hours. Maybe she heard you coming and held her breath."

Mariella thought about the morning. Reveling in the crisp, late-fall weather, she was looking forward to the day. Could she have slept through her baby's cries? She had been exhausted lately, but never enough to ignore her children's needs. "No, I would have woken up. I-I, I know it."

"Are you taking anything, Mrs. Valentino? Anything for stress? Valium? Something else?"

Mariella shook her head. "Doctor, you have not prescribe anything for me."

"Yes," Dr. Berg said, peering at her. "But who's to say you are not going to another doctor for your 'needs.' I can tell something is happening with you. It makes sense. You're a stranger in this country, you don't speak the language well, you don't understand our ways. It's not uncommon to feel blue."

Mariella was taken aback. No one had ever talked to her with such disregard. "I am perfectly healthy. I might feel like a stranger, but how should I feel when everyone treats me that way? And I know I did not sleep through my baby's cries. It must be something different."

"Mrs. Valentino," Dr. Berg lowered his voice, "I'm the doctor here, not you. Now, I have another appointment in five minutes; please show yourself out."

His face soured as he watched Mariella collect her things, put Olivia back in her carriage, and leave.

Chapter Thirty-Three

Sitting against the crib, Mariella kept her eyes trained on Olivia's chest as it filled with air and quickly deflated. She wove her hand through the wooden slats and stroked her daughter's hair. If she could have curled up inside to protect her little one, she would have.

"Sweetheart," Jack whispered, sliding down on the floor next to her. "It's nearly two a.m. You haven't slept for days. C'mon, you can't keep this up." He put his arm around her, but she pulled away.

"Of course I can," she said curtly.

"Honey, Dr. Berg said she's fine."

Mariella turned to him. Her eyes flickered as she spoke. "No. No, this is not normal. Babies do not stop breathing for no reason."

"But the doc said children are always testing us."

"Testing us?" Mariella raised her voice, then pulled Jack into the hallway. "*Testing* us? Do you think our daughter was *testing* us? She is not even a year old. All she cares about is eating and sleeping and playing with her toys."

"But he's a doctor, wouldn't he—"

"No. He is an old man who does not seem to understand children. Do you know he told me I should start to hit her? My parents never hit us, and we are okay."

"Sure, but Ma always smacked us and we're okay too," Jack said, a slight smile on his face. "Boy, we were rascals back then. I remember hiding under my bed whenever I heard Ma open the kitchen drawer. When she wielded her wooden spoon, we knew she was angry. She'd hit us on our backsides—never too hard, though. Then, she rinsed that spoon off and used it to stir her Sunday sauce."

Mariella watched Jack laugh at the memory, confusing her even more. "I could never do that to my girls. We need to find a new doctor."

"Gee, honey, Berg's been our doc all our lives."

"That is fine for you. But when it comes to my children, he will not be our doctor anymore," she said firmly.

"But, honey, we can't just leave the guy."

"Oh no? Do you know he said Olivia stopped breathing

because of me?"

"What do you mean?"

Mariella narrowed her eyes on him. "He said I was a bad mother."

"What?"

"Your Dr. Berg said it was my fault that she was not breathing—that I was a bad mother," she said, her face growing red. "I did not want to tell you because I was so ashamed. I was afraid you might believe so too. But I had time to think about it, I know that is untrue. He is the bad one!" Anger spilled out of her like thick tar.

Jack pulled her close, but his silence was deafening. Maybe he secretly agreed with the doctor. The thought rattled her.

"You are a wonderful mother," he finally said. "Any child would be lucky to have you as their mother."

Pulling away, she scanned his face to be sure. The concern in his eyes was everything she needed to know he was on her team.

"Let's get some sleep now, okay? I can stay up with the baby. I promise to wake you if I notice anything wrong. Tomorrow morning we'll look into where to go for a second opinion."

Jack walked Mariella back to bed. She fell asleep quickly, but horrible dreams plagued her. One in particular found her standing on a chair in the middle of the restaurant. Jack's family surrounded her, pointing and jeering while he stood to the side, ignoring her. She felt herself shrinking until she was the size of a small child and now everyone hovered over her. It was suffocating. She tried to scream and yell and fight back. Her lungs filled and filled until they popped. The air escaped in words, punching back at each person as if she were breathing fire. But most of her venom was directed at Jack's mother and Mariella grew with each jab until she woke up, tired and anxious.

The following morning, Jack kept his promise, and they looked through the telephone book for a new physician to see.

"Hey, here's one. Dr. Steinem. I think I played football with his son. I'll make an appointment with him."

It turned out the office was on Highway 35, only a few blocks away from Wanamassa Gardens. Jack could only schedule an appointment for 3 p.m. when he was a work. Mariella couldn't imagine managing a baby and toddler while cars whooshed past her so she asked Louise to stay with Elisa then immediately questioned herself. *Would a good mother be able to handle both children? Am I focusing too much on Olivia and making Elisa feel unwanted?* She wished she could talk it out with Mama, but lately when they spoke, her mother seemed distracted. She insisted everything was fine even though Papa had been working long hours and never seemed to be around. Mariella had only spoken with him a handful of times in the past year. While it didn't make sense, she had too much going on in her life to worry.

Mariella pushed Olivia's stroller into the medical building and was immediately confused. Unlike Dr. Berg's office, with its worn carpet and peeling wallpaper, she was met with modern art hung on clean white walls, plush rugs, and sleek furniture. A young woman with an elaborate beehive hairdo sat behind a desk.

Assuming she was in the wrong building, Mariella turned to leave but the woman stopped her.

"Are you my three p.m.?" she said, her crude New York accent emphasizing each syllable.

"Three p.m.?"

"Yes."

"I ... I am Mrs. Valentino. I have an appointment with Dr. Steinem."

"Whaddya think I'm asking ya?" She pulled a pen from her ear and pointed to the clock on the wall. "Are you my three p.m.?"

"Oh," Mariella said. "Yes, yes, I am."

"Good." She took a manila folder off her desk and stood up. "Come with me."

Mariella lifted Olivia out of the stroller and followed the woman to a small room. It was stylish with a white melamine table for examinations, a modern art piece of red blobs on white canvas, and an orange chair.

"Go ahead and have a seat, the doctor will be with you in a moment," the woman said, then left them.

Mariella waited for twenty minutes, jostling Olivia on her knee as she became fussy. Just when she was growing impatient herself, a thin, balding doctor entered.

"Hello, I'm Dr. Steinem," he said, reading her file.

A nurse followed, carrying a baby scale. She lifted Olivia out of Mariella's arms and weighed her, then whispered something to the doctor and left.

"Eighteen point five pounds. That's an average weight for a girl this age, nothing to worry about." Dr. Steinem returned Olivia to her mother as she began to whimper.

"It's okay," Mariella whispered, rocking her gently. "You're okay."

Dr. Steinem gave her a curious look. "Do you always do that when she's fussy?"

"Well, no. She gets shy around strangers."

"And you don't allow her to work it out herself?"

Mariella watched nervously as the doctor wrote a few notes on his clipboard. "I want her to know I am here if she needs me."

The doctor clicked his tongue.

"Is that bad?" Mariella asked in a small voice.

"I would think so. Especially when she is whining. This only encourages bad behavior. Like these breathing spells. Did you know that children will hold their breath until they get what they want?"

Mariella felt defeated as she bundled Olivia back into her stroller and left the office. Dr. Steinem had echoed Dr. Berg's advice but went a step further: "Don't comfort her when she whines; don't even react. Let her cry out her frustration." It all seemed to go against everything her parents had done. Mama and Papa would walk to the ends of the Earth for their children. Even at mass, the priest said children were a gift from God. Maybe the Italian way was wrong? By the time she reached Lousie's house, uncertainty had paralyzed her.

"Mama!" Elisa exclaimed, greeting her at the doorway. "Mama! We made fairy cakes! Miss Lou let me stir the cake, um, what was it called?" Louise stooped to her level and whispered in her ear. Elisa nodded, then giggled. "I forgot, I stirred the badder!"

"Tea?" Louise offered.

Mariella realized she was never actually asking if she wanted tea, it was more her telling you what was about to come. "Okay."

They went into the kitchen as Elisa yanked on her mother's skirt. "Want to some fairy cake? I'll give you a big piece! Okay, Mama?"

"Yes, Tesoro," Mariella said, her nagging thoughts swarming her mind like bees. *Should I be calling my daughter Tesoro like my parents did? Is it bad to think your child is a treasure? Is that coddling? Or should I never show affection again?*

She sat at the kitchen table and set Olivia on her lap.

"Mama!" Elisa continued, trying to push her sister over to make room on her mother's lap. "No fair. You hold that baby all the time. You need to hold me." She stamped her foot to accent her frustration.

"Now, now," Louise said, setting a tea tray on the table. "How about you help me cut the cake."

Elisa's face lit up. "Look! Mama! I'm cutting it!" she sang as Louise helped her guide a knife through the layers. Setting a large slice on a plate, she let Elisa hand it to her mother.

"Here, Mama."

"Thank you, Tesoro."

Elisa waited until her mother took a bite.

"Mmm. It is delicious."

"I told you, Mama," Elisa boasted.

"Now, come on, little squirrel. You can have your piece in the rumpus room." Louise took the girls downstairs. She sat Olivia in a playpen she'd set up for their visits, then offered a few toys she'd held onto after her son died. Elisa sat on the couch, captivated by Howdy Doody singing and dancing on the television.

Relieved to finally have a moment's peace, Mariella sipped her tea.

"Now, we can have a proper conversation," Louise said,

walking back up the stairs to the kitchen. "Tell me, what did the doctor say? I can tell it wasn't what you wanted."

Tears streaked lines through Mariella's face powder. "I guess I am just a bad mother. But what these doctors suggest is cruel. You tell me, how can I not pick up my children when they cry? Or soothe them when they are scared? I do not know how to act anymore."

Louise handed Mariella a tissue. "I know I am not a nurse, but I'm certain your daughter's breathing spells are not behavioral. Something else is going on. Let's face it, we all have cultural differences. In England, our way is not to indulge, but that doesn't mean doing so is bad. Sometimes, I wish my mother had been more affectionate and comforting. Especially since we were all living through such desperate times."

Suddenly, Elisa appeared in the kitchen doorway, her eyes wide.

"What is it?" Mariella asked, but Elisa could only point downstairs.

She and Louise rushed to Olivia and found her lying in the playpen, gazing off into space and jerking intermittently.

"Olivia?" Mariella cried, quickly picking her up. But Olivia's expression stayed frozen. "Sweetheart? What's wrong?"

Louise gently took the baby and placed her on the sofa.

"What's wrong with her?" Mariella went to pick her up

again, but Louise stopped her.

"I think it's a seizure. We need to let her cycle through it."

"Seizure?"

Visions of her sister seizing on the roof propelled Mariella into prayer. Although she hadn't been to church in weeks, Mariella asked God to please make the nightmare stop.

Within seconds, the color returned to Olivia's face. She took a deep breath, then began to cry.

Chapter Thirty-Four

Over the following month, Mariella took Olivia to several more appointments looking for answers. One doctor, another old curmudgeon, didn't seem interested in what Mariella had to say. He examined Olivia quickly, then said she was blowing things out of proportion.

Another doctor, a kind-faced man in his fifties, seemed more promising. He had a gentle way about him when he spoke. But as soon as Olivia began to cry, he lost his patience.

"Quiet her down! I can't examine her if she's screaming," he complained.

Mariella became flustered, narrowing her eyes on Olivia. "Be quiet," she said in a voice that was not her own.

The baby's eyes widened, her mouth fixed in a perfect oval. For a moment, Mariella hoped her daughter would have a seizure right in front of the doctor so she would be vindicated, but she immediately regretted it. Olivia's forehead wrinkled, and her lower lip quivered before a wail louder than ever before filled the room, the hallway, the office, and probably drifted down to the lobby. It broke Mariella's heart. She quickly packed her baby back up in the stroller and walked out, holding off her own tears until she reached the sidewalk.

After that, she demanded Jack come along. He made an appointment with a doctor in another county about twenty minutes away. A family friend raved about how his office was equipped with all the latest gadgets. When Jack and Mariella entered the newly built medical center, they too were impressed. There were shining linoleum floors, a large desk to check in at, and a comfortable waiting room with ashtrays in the armrests of each chair. Although she resisted, Mariella became hopeful.

"Mr. and Mrs. Valentino," a gray-haired nurse greeted them. "Right this way."

She led them to an examination room with jars of cotton balls, Q-tips, and gauze lining the counters. Gently taking Olivia from Mariella, the nurse weighed the baby on a scale lined with sheepskin and took some measurements. As she left, the doctor, a tall man with a sharp chin and curly blond hair, entered.

"Hello, I'm Dr. Smith." He shook Jack's hand.

"I'm Jack Valentino, and this is my wife, Mariella."

"Ah, piacere Mariella," Dr. Smith said with a wink.

Mariella couldn't believe her ears. The only Italian she had spoken since arriving in America was with her father-in-law, and his dialect made it hard for conversation to flow. "Sei parla Italiano?" she asked eagerly.

Dr. Smith put his hands up and laughed. "No, no. I can only say a few things. But I remember my time in Naples fondly."

Jack's ears perked up. "Were you over in forty-three?"

"First Tangiers, then Naples. I was part of the 300th General Hospital'"

"Sure! I avoided you boys like the plague!" Jack chuckled. "Every time I passed your tent, I did the sign of the cross and prayed I'd never have any use for you!"

The doctor looked at Jack expectantly. "And did you?"

Jack pointed to his ear and nodded. "Just a bomb I got a little too friendly with. I remember the doctor I saw. Dr. DeSimone. A fella from Boston, you know him?"

"Don't think I do. And I see you brought yourself a nice souvenir home." Dr. Smith glanced over at Mariella with a grin. She smiled back, afraid to show how she really felt and distract him from her daughter. He quickly turned his attention to the baby. "And this is?"

"This is our little patient, Olivia," Jack said.

"Well, hello!" Dr. Smith sang in a cheery voice. He briefly

scanned the notes on his clipboard. "Is this little missy talking yet?"

"Not yet," Mariella said, insisting she be part of the conversation. "But we are very worried about her breathing spells. She has had one almost weekly now."

"Uh-huh." Dr. Smith jotted some notes on his clipboard. "And when is that?"

"Sometimes in the morning, but mostly during the day."

"Mr. Valentino, are you home for these spells?"

"She usually has them in the afternoon when I'm at work. Except for the first time. That was in the morning, but I was in New York City with my father. All the other times she had them, I was already at work."

"Ah." Humming a lullaby, the doctor began to examine Olivia. He took her socks off and inspected her feet. He pulled up her undershirt and pressed on her stomach. She squirmed but didn't make a sound. He gently looked in each eye with a light. When he was finished, Dr. Smith turned to Jack. "She's completely healthy."

"She is?" Jack asked, the relief in his voice angering Mariella.

"How can she have nothing wrong? I have seen the seizure with my own eyes," she said, growing exasperated.

"Hold on a second, who is talking about seizures?"

Mariella was reluctant to bring up her sister's illness, fearful of what he would say. "My neighbor Louise, she has worked in a hospital, and—"

"Well, now, I think you are getting ahead of yourself," Dr. Smith chuckled. "I know you mothers like to consider yourselves doctors too, but without the training, I'm afraid you are just guessing. Now, I know you're only looking out for your children, but I see nothing wrong with her, Mrs. Valentino. Although—"

Mariella leaned in. "Yes, Doctor?"

"What language do you speak to her during the day?"

"I speak Italian and ... some English. Why?"

He hesitated, choosing his words carefully. "I think maybe you should only speak English."

Mariella's heart sank. She looked over at Jack. He shifted on his feet.

"Gee, Doc, my wife's trying her best. She's a wonderful mother to the girls."

"Oh, no. No. I'm not saying she isn't. Please don't be offended, but when English is secondary and spoken with a strong accent to boot, sometimes children get confused. These situations can certainly cause delays."

"But our oldest daughter speaks very well," Jack interjected.

"Yes." Dr. Smith nodded as he leaned against the examination table. "This can happen when the child is intelligent. Even so, it isn't easy having a foreign parent. You see, children expend a lot of energy learning two languages. Italian while Mom's in charge then English when Dad's around. It also takes time away from learning other things. Let's face it: Italian is a beautiful language, but English is much more important. Come back in three months, and we'll recheck her." He turned to Mariella, his expression sympathetic. "It's probably best to speak English to your daughters. It will also help improve your accent, and there's nothing wrong with that."

Mariella pursed her lips, but said nothing.

"I see her first birthday is next month. How will you celebrate?" Dr. Smith asked.

"My mother's planning a party at our restaurant," Jack said.

"Ah, terrific. Mrs. Valentino, I bet if you focus on giving your daughter the best darn party possible, it will take your mind off all of this worry. You'll see, sweet little Olivia will be thriving before you know it!"

"Sweetheart," Jack said, trying to catch up with Mariella in the parking lot. "Wait up."

But Mariella continued, carrying Olivia to the car. Neither of them spoke during the ride home, but by the time the baby went down for her afternoon nap, Mariella's anger had cooled down to a few embers, allowing her to think straight. She wasn't only angry at the lack of answers from yet another medical professional; she had hoped Jack would defend her more.

Mariella prepared a pot of coffee in the kitchen while he read the news. "I am not very happy."

"I know you're not, but I think the doctor might have a point about the language."

"I do not understand. You said I was a wonderful mother and all the children in the world would want me for a mother."

Jack put his paper down. "Come on now, you know I meant what I said. But you are navigating all of this in a country that's foreign to you. You have to take some of that into consideration."

"But what does my speaking less Italian help with her seizures?"

"I guess hearing your mother speak a different language can be scary. Maybe this isn't good for their brains? But that doesn't matter. All that matters is he said we shouldn't worry."

"That's what all the doctors said!"

"Then maybe she *is* fine. Maybe it's just a passing thing. Something Olivia will grow out of. Please don't worry so much. Olivia will be just fine."

Once he left for work, Mariella tried to make sense of the day. *Maybe I am crazy,* she thought. She had been so angry at the doctors' dismissal that perhaps she was missing the point. It had been over a week since Olivia had a breathing spell. She seemed perfectly healthy. Although unable shake her doubt, Mariella decided to take the doctor's advice and focus on that.

Chapter Thirty-Five

The Marina Room was adorned with various shades of pink; from the raspberry tablecloths and the cotton-candy-pink roses tied with magenta ribbons and placed in tall vases atop each table to the handful of blush-colored balloons tied to Olivia's highchair. Despite Ma's lack of enthusiasm for girls, when it came to throwing a party, she never skimped. Nearly fifty people—family, friends, and business acquaintances—enjoyed a four-course feast. Louise and Charles were honored guests, but Ma placed them at another table. Everyone indulged in hand-pulled mozzarella and tomatoes, spaghetti carbonara, and Lobster Fra Diavolo.

Clara swung by with a large, stuffed elephant but Olivia wasn't interested. Ma insisted on starting the party at one and the exhausted birthday girl desperately needed a nap.

"It's okay, sweet pea, you can play with it when you're

rested," Clara said, then turned to Mariella with an apologetic look on her face.

"Do you have to go?"

Clara frowned. "You know that beast of a sister of mine, I have to babysit so she can go lunch with her girlfriends," she said, rolling her eyes as she left.

"It's your birf-day, baby," Elisa sang, pulling a balloon down to show her sister.

Olivia pushed it away.

"Mama?" Elisa pushed her bottom lip out, warning that a tantrum was on the horizon.

Jack quickly stepped in. "Petunia, your sister's tired. But you can have fun even if she wants to be a party pooper!" he whispered loudly.

Covering her mouth with her hands, Elisa giggled. "You said pooper!"

"Yes, I did. And I will say it again!"

Elisa's eyes brightened, her smile frozen as she waited for her father to say the forbidden word.

"Pooper!" Jack exclaimed as his daughter dissolved into giggles.

Although Olivia began to cry, Mariella smiled. She loved to see the bond Jack had formed with his eldest daughter. But Olivia's cries became more intense. She gently rocked her, popped a pacifier in her mouth, and gave her a bottle of milk to no avail.

"Put that baby down! For God's sake, let her cry it out!" Jack's mother shouted from across the table.

"Gee, Ma, she hasn't been feeling well," Jack said.

"Yeah! She is being poopy!" Elisa chimed in, slapping her knee to punctuate her funny joke.

"Why don't I take her?" Jack said. "I'm not that hungry."

Mariella sighed. "And allow your mother to complain about her poor son having to do all the parenting? No, thank you."

"Mariella," Pop said, speaking Italian, "is there anything I can do to help? Maybe I can show her the lobster tank?"

Mariella was so touched by his kindness, she handed Olivia over.

"Hello, angioletto," Pop said. Although his eyes were filled with love and understanding, his large stature and deep voice had never been a good combination for babies. Olivia's face screwed up tighter and grew more red as she reached for her mother.

"It is okay," Mariella told Pop. "She is just tired."

He gently handed Olivia back.

Just as Mariella was about to give up and take the baby home, Louise appeared.

"Oh! I had that lovely dish with those awful-looking lobsters. Who would have thought those things would be so tasty? You must try it. Hello, little squirrel. Shall we go for a walk?"

Elisa pulled on her skirt. "Miss Lou, Miss Lou. I have a secret."

"Oh, do you?" Louise stooped to Elisa's level. "And what is that?"

"My sister is a pooper!" she shouted, unable to contain herself.

"That's enough, Tesoro. You need to eat. Take a few more bites of the spaghetti," Mariella said, allowing Louise to slip out quietly with Olivia. When she returned twenty minutes later, the baby was fast asleep.

"How?" Mariella asked, laying her back in the carriage.

"She was ready. Trust me."

"Thank you." Mariella motioned to the chair next to her. "Sit with me. Jack went to his office to get some money. He thinks his mother might not tip the waitresses enough."

"Well, that one is every bit a businesswoman. I'm sure she knows when she has to be frugal."

"But without them, there is no party. Imagine not appreciating the very people who worked so hard to make it happen."

Louise sat back. "Hmm. Sometimes, I think no one can understand what it's like to struggle until you've lived through what we've lived through."

"That is very true," Mariella said, warmed by her friend's touching remarks. She watched the two waitresses clearing the tables. When Mariella used to hostess, she worked with both of them. The younger one, named Caroline, had three boys at home and needed the job to help make ends meet. The other one was Sherry, a ten-year veteran of the restaurant. She was older, with premature wrinkles around her eyes that told the story of a tough life. Mariella hadn't spoken to her much because she was a no-nonsense woman—in for work and out right after. But she had a lot of respect for Sherry.

Once they cleared the last plate, Ma stood up, holding a glass of red wine, and everyone quieted. She searched the room for a moment, then relaxed when she spotted Jack, standing by the kitchen's swinging doors.

"I want to thank all of you for coming to Jack's daughter's first birthday." She lifted her glass, not for Olivia, who had just woken and sat yawning on Mariella's lap, but to her son.

Louise shot her a look. Mariella shrugged. She was used to it.

"Jackie, you may be my youngest son, but you make me incredibly proud!" she cooed, then shouted, "Chin chin!"

"Chin chin!" everyone cheered.

Suddenly, the lights went out.

"Mama!" Elisa cried. She had always been afraid of the dark.

Mariella patted her head. "Wait until you see what's coming!"

Jack ceremoniously opened the kitchen door, and Sherry emerged with a towering cake decorated in pink buttercream frosting. Each tier was adorned with thin candles and small sparklers perched on top. Despite the sparks flying into her face, Sherry didn't flinch once.

"Ta daaaaa!" Jack sang, following the cake to the table.

Everyone joined him in a spirited version of "Happy Birthday." Most sang casually while a group of friends from the church choir were melodic and operatic. Sitting wide-eyed on Mariella's lap, Olivia's chin trembled, as if she were unsure whether to laugh or cry. Once the sparklers dwindled out, Sherry placed the cake before her. The guests watched as she tentatively touched it with the tip of her finger. Laughter filled the room, giving her the courage to pluck a sugar rose off the top and inspect it. She looked up at her mother for guidance.

"Oh, go on and eat it!" Ma interjected.

"Go ahead, sweetheart," Jack joined in, crouching beside his daughter. "It's tasty!"

"Yes, Stellina," Mariella said, "you can eat it."

Olivia licked it once, giggled at the taste, then popped it in her mouth.

"Hooray!" everyone cheered.

"For she's a jolly good fellow!" Jack began to sing, kissing Olivia on the cheek. Everyone joined in, some clapped, while others blew paper horns that Carl had passed out. "For she's a jolly good fellow! For she's a jolly good fellow! That nobody can deny!"

Olivia's face changed from sheer joy to horror to joy again, as she clapped her hands together.

"Okay, okay! You can serve the cake now," Ma instructed the waitresses.

Sherry whisked it off to the kitchen. When it disappeared, Olivia looked around, then began to cry.

"Oh, no, no." Mariella bounced her daughter on her lap.

"Quiet that girl down," Ma said, becoming agitated.

Julia came over to the table and reached out for the baby. "Want me to take her?" Olivia shook her head back and forth as her face grew bright red. To add to the confusion, Julia's youngest boy, Rocco, ran up beside his mother and blew a paper horn in Olivia's face. Toot! Toot! Toot toot!

"Stop that!" Julia pushed him away, but it didn't deter him. He turned to his mother and blew the horn even louder. She took him by the ear and led him away.

"Let me take her," Jack said, lifting the baby from Mariella's arms. Just then, Olivia fell silent. Her eyes drew back into her head and her body jerked. She would have fallen out of Jack's arms if he hadn't been holding onto her tightly.

"Jackie, what's wrong with that baby?" Ma said, panic settling in her voice.

He studied her face carefully. "Olivia?"

Louise sprang to action. She made space on an empty table in the corner and Jack laid her down. Olivia's eyes were locked into the distance, her mouth hanging open.

"Someone call an ambulance!" Pop cried.

Carl ran to the phone booth by the bar. Ma tried to get close to Olivia, waving a napkin to cool her off, but Mariella stepped in between her and the baby. Then, almost as quickly as it had begun, Olivia returned to life, letting out a siren of a cry. Although Mariella had been through it before, each time felt like the first. She let out a breath.

Ma fell back in her chair and fanned herself with a menu. "That nearly killed me."

Pop stood just off to the side, trying to make sure his granddaughter looked okay but ready to jump into action if needed.

Pulling the baby into his arms, Jack glanced over at Mariella. "I'm sorry, I didn't realize."

"I was not telling stories," Mariella said. She inspected Olivia, whose cry began to settle. "It is okay, Stellina. You are okay."

"How long for the ambulance?" Willie called out to Carl.

"Ambulance? There's no need for an ambulance," Ma shouted.

"Well, now," Pop said, "maybe just to be sure she is okay."

Julia returned to the table. "Pop is right, just to be safe. She should see a doctor at least."

"She's fine. Just a temper tantrum," Ma grumbled.

"No, Ma." Jack's forehead wrinkled with concern. "This was not a tantrum."

"Yeah, Ma," Julia joined in. "That little girl was as limp as a noodle."

"Come on, she wanted more cake. She was, without a doubt, kicking up a tantrum," Ma said. "You used to be like that when you were young. You all were. But I made sure you knew what's what. Jack, you need to be firm with that girl."

Mariella had heard enough. She gathered her things, sat Olivia in her carriage, and took Elisa by the hand. "I do not have to take this from family," she said to Jack. "We are leaving."

"What? What did I say?" she could hear Ma ask the room as she headed for the door.

While Mariella was waiting for Jack to bring the car around, Sherry slipped outside and joined her. She lit a cigarette, then offered it to Mariella.

"Thank you."

"No problem," Sherry said, lighting another for herself.

Mariella took a long, hard drag, then let it out. "Also, thank you for everything. Even though it didn't end well, this was a lovely party."

"My pleasure. Your husband tipped us nicely. He always does."

Mariella flicked ash onto the sidewalk, as Elisa swung on her arm, humming the birthday song. "You worked hard. Somebody has to show you our appreciation."

Sherry nodded toward Olivia, sleeping in the carriage. "I think that baby needs to see someone."

"I've already been to five doctors. They all say the same thing."

"And what's that?"

"Apparently," Mariella said, a weary smile on her face, "I'm a terrible mother."

"You are not a terr-blue mama," Elisa sang.

"Thank you, Tesoro."

Sherry handed Mariella a piece of paper. "Jack told me about how you've been trying to find a doctor."

"He has?"

"Sure, he worries about you and the girls," she said.

Mariella looked at it. The name "Dr. Vero" and an address was scribbled on it in pencil.

Taking a drag of her cigarette, Sherry blew the smoke out into the cold air. "Look, I know she might be on the poor side of town, but she sure knows what she's doing."

"She?"

Sherry cocked her head. "Ya have a problem with a woman doctor?"

"Not if she can figure out what's going on," Mariella said. The prospect of speaking with a woman about her daughter, someone who might know what it was like to be a mother, was promising.

"Good. Now, she might not be working on this side of the tracks, but sometimes, we get a good one. And trust me, she won't blame anything on bad mothering." Sherry tossed her cigarette to the ground, then vigorously rubbed her arms "I gotta run back inside. It's freezin' out here."

Once she left, Mariella took her last drag. *Why can't a woman be in medicine?* she asked herself, looking down at her name. *And she's Italian, to boot!*

Chapter Thirty-Six

The next day, Mariella made an appointment for noon with Dr. Vero, knowing Jack would be out of the house by 11 a.m. She decided not to tell him the good doctor was a woman—at least, not yet.

"I wish I could go with you. If this doctor is as good as Sherry says he is, I'll want to shake his hand."

"It is okay, amore. Louise will drive us. It is not too far from here," she lied, knowing he wouldn't like her going into a "bad section" of Asbury Park.

Jack let out a laugh. "I hope she drives well. You know what they say about women drivers."

"Amore, she has been driving for two years. She is a fine driver."

"Okay, sweetheart, but promise you'll call me at my office when you get home?"

"Of course."

As Louise navigated her powder-blue Chevrolet to the doctor's office, Mariella marveled at what she saw. Although it was January, children played on the street while mothers chatted in front of their small, attached homes. It reminded Mariella of her neighborhood back home.

"Here we are!" Louise pulled up to a four-story building. Hanging above the entrance was a medical sign with an eagle at the top and two snakes climbing up on either side. There wasn't a name, just the number 328 etched onto the glass door.

The building had no elevator, so they left the stroller with several others lining the lobby and climbed to the third floor. At the end of the hallway there was a door with a brass sign that read "Dr. Vero." Mariella shot Louise a hopeful look and went in. The large waiting room was filled with crying babies and toddlers squirming in their mothers' laps. Mariella signed in where she was told and waited.

"Mrs. Valentino?" a nurse called out forty-five minutes later. She was a black woman with short, neatly pinned hair and kind eyes.

"Good luck!" Louise said. "I'll keep Elisa entertained, but let me know if you need help with anything you might not understand."

Mariella followed the nurse down a long hallway.

"Mar-Ella," she said, reading the file.

Now that she had been in the United States for almost five years, Mariella didn't hesitate to correct people, but this woman was careful with her name. "Eh, it's Mar-e-ella."

"Mar-e-Ella?"

Mariella smiled, touched by the woman's effort. "Yes, thank you. Most people get it wrong."

"Well, it's your name. People should learn to say it properly." The nurse smiled, leading them into an examination room with purple elephants dancing across the walls. "The last part reminds me of my grandmother. Her name was Ella. I love that name. Okay, you can sit here while I weigh the baby." She picked Olivia up. "Hello, little one!"

Olivia smiled, gumming a teething ring.

"Oh, yes, you are a sweet one." The nurse laid a blanket on the metal platform and gently sat Olivia on top. Eyeing the scale, she slid a weight over a half inch, then back a quarter inch until it was balanced. "Good lord, you're a little one indeed."

Mariella furrowed her brow. "She doesn't eat as much as I would like."

"That's okay, she's small but mighty. And she has time to grow. You don't have to worry. Right, sweetie?"

Olivia offered the nurse her fist.

"No, thank you, darlin'. I've already had my lunch and don't want to spoil my dinner!" The nurse laughed as she placed the baby back on Mariella's lap. "Okay, sit tight. The doctor will be with you as soon as she can."

Taking stock of the room, Mariella was pleased to see the necessary equipment, plus a basket of toys and a colorful mobile with ballerinas suspended above an examination table. *Of course. Only a woman would make sure the room was child-friendly*, she thought.

"Is this my next patient?" someone said outside the door.

Recognizing the woman's accent, Mariella's spine straightened. Before she could do anything, a tall, blonde, fair-skinned woman wearing a white coat and stethoscope around her neck entered the room.

"Mrs. Valentino?" she said. "Nice to meet you."

Mariella's heart pounded in her chest as panic rendered her paralyzed. The desire to scoop up her daughter and run clawed at her, but she was trapped.

Her fear must have been obvious because the doctor's smile quickly faded. "I can imagine what you are thinking, Mrs. Valentino. My nurse told me about your Italian accent. I am certain you have heard mine."

Mariella's cheeks flushed as she touched her face but remained silent.

"It's okay," Dr. Vero continued. "I understand. Yes, I am

German, but I am not what you think. I was never for Hitler's regime." The woman hesitated, as if deciding whether or not she wanted to relive the past. She went to close the door for more privacy, but thought twice and left it ajar. "I joined the resistance, along with some others at my university."

It was true, everyone had their own story, but Mariella was still on guard. Germans were prone to lying when they needed to. Still, the woman's voice was comforting, her eyes soft and caring when she looked at them. Mariella sat quietly at the edge of her chair.

Dr. Vero continued. "Unfortunately, my fellow countrymen caught me early on. I was sent to a work camp. That is how I met my husband, Mario Vero."

The doctor rolled her r's perfectly when she said her husband's name, softening Mariella's guard.

"He was there too. In the camp. And although under those awful conditions we suffered tremendously, we promised each other if we survived the war, we would marry and come here to America." Dr. Vero looked like she could cry, but quickly regained her composure. "Now, if you want to leave, I will understand. But I want to be Olivia's doctor, if you let me."

The war had affected so many people, even the enemy. Mariella's schoolteacher, who had joined the Nazi party, cornered her on the street the night she was looking for Papa. Before the war, he had been so kind. He told the class even though he came from Germany, his wife was Italian, making him one of them. But on that horrible night, he'd almost raped her. The influence of alcohol couldn't wash away his shame. "Run," he'd yelled at her. She knew her teacher had become a broken man. But it was clear the woman standing before her had fought back.

After a moment's hesitation, Mariella spoke. "Thank you for telling me your story. I would very much like for you to be my children's doctor."

Dr. Vero's face relaxed. "Terrific. Now, let us see what is happening with this little miss." She gently took Olivia from Mariella's arms and sat her on the table. Allowing the baby to play with her stethoscope while listening to her heartbeat, the doctor sang an Italian lullaby. She said she had learned it from her husband and sang it to her own children. She examined Olivia's ears and nose, then checked her reflexes one by one. After she finished, Dr. Vero handed Olivia back to Mariella. "She looks wonderful to me."

Mariella pursed her lips. "Of course," she muttered.

"Now," Dr. Vero said, narrowing her eyes, "tell me what has been happening."

For the next five minutes, Mariella told Dr. Vero about her daughter's episodes of breath holding that she considered seizures. She explained how none of the doctors had taken her seriously and instead blamed it on bad mothering. Dr. Vero took notes on her daughter's appetite, sleeping habits, and energy levels.

"Now, could you tell me about your family history?" the doctor asked.

The question caused Mariella to catch her breath. The thought of Olivia having a tumor sat just under her skin. "There *is* something I need to tell you." She went into detail about her sister's first seizure, the diagnosis and the slow march to death, all while trying not to cry. Dr Vero listened carefully, sympathetic eyes encouraging Mariella to tell her every detail needed. When she was done, the doctor left the room. Olivia nuzzled her face into her mother's neck, trying to soothe herself to sleep. Mariella held her close. *Talcum powder and oatmeal,* she thought, happy her daughter smelled just like any other child.

A few minutes later, Dr. Vero returned with a thick, hard-covered medical book and opened it to an earmarked page.

"After careful consideration, this is what I think Olivia has." She pointed to a strange word Mariella had never heard. "Epilepsy. It is a disorder in which nerve cell activity in the brain is disturbed. Symptoms can be things like staring spells, temporary confusion, and seizures, which you call breath-holding spells."

"Ep-ei-lepsy?" Mariella asked. Having a diagnosis was a

double-edged sword. She wasn't sure whether to hug the doctor or fall apart in tears. "Is it curable?"

Dr. Vero patted her shoulder. "Don't worry, Mother. She will be alright. Most of the time, children grow out of it. But for now, we can treat it with medicine." She wrote out a prescription and handed it to her. "Now, have this filled in the pharmacy downstairs."

"That is it?" Mariella asked, waiting for the doctor to add something more complicated.

"Let us see how she responds, shall we?"

"Okay."

As the doctor turned to leave, Mariella grabbed her by the arm. "Thank you, Dr. Vero. Thank you so much for taking me seriously."

"You are very welcome. And thank *you* for trusting me to care for your daughter."

Mariella examined the small, orange-tinted bottle filled with white pills as Louise drove them home. The nurse had explained how she needed to give her daughter two crushable tablets with food each day. She suggested sprinkling them in applesauce or pudding so the taste wouldn't put Olivia off. Then Dr. Vero carefully went over instructions for Mariella to report any odd reactions to the medication. Although it was a lot to take in, her confidence soared, knowing she had been right all along. Olivia wasn't merely having a tantrum to get her way. It wasn't bad parenting like the other doctors said. Her daughter was having seizures—it was an illness.

"Isn't it amazing?" Louise said, stopping at a red light on their way home.

"What do you mean?"

"Well, you have been dismissed by several doctors, all men, all from the area."

Shifting in her seat, Mariella's anger and frustration reappeared. "A few of them never even asked one thing about Olivia. They blamed it on me. Can you imagine? I am a good mother. I am sure of it."

The light turned green, and Louise stepped hard on the gas. It was clear she was just as frustrated. "Oh, yes, you are. If you weren't, you would have stopped long ago, but you didn't. You searched high and low until you found a doctor to listen to you. But the most wonderful part? She's a woman! Ha!" Louise's face lit up as she gripped the steering wheel tight.

Mariella laughed. "You are right!"

They sped down Corlies Avenue, a long stretch of road flanked by a dense wood of pine trees. Mariella covered her hair with a scarf then rolled down her window. Louise followed suit, letting the wind blow her neatly pinned chignon into a mess.

"Not only that!" she continued, excitedly. "The doctor was a foreigner just like us!"

The irony of it dawned on Mariella and suddenly she felt like a part of something special. Louise glanced over at her. They shared a knowing smile and continued home.

Chapter Thirty-Seven

Four and a half years passed with the absence of seizures. Although at the end of each day there was relief, Mariella didn't trust her daughter wouldn't meet her demise the same way her sister did. She spent hours in the evenings reasoning with herself. *Elisa died so quickly, surely Olivia wouldn't be here four years on. But she is just a child, maybe when she gets older it will come back again. Maybe the medicine is just putting off the inevitable.* These conversations with herself went on until exhaustion forced her to give up and sleep.

Then, Dr. Vero announced that Olivia was ready to be weaned off her medication. Those first weeks were the toughest. Mariella would hear a strangled breath, real or imagined, halfway through the night and run to her daughter's side to find Olivia curled up in a ball, sleeping peacefully. Still, she would pull up a pillow and lie on the floor next to her until Jack returned home from work and coaxed her back to bed. But after a full month without any seizures, Mariella finally began to relax.

The timing was perfect; Olivia was about to start kindergarten. Despite Mariella's broken heart, she sent the girls off to school three blocks away, tearfully waving goodbye as they skipped down the street. When she returned home, the house felt different. Olivia had been her shadow, always around to help with the cooking, or gardening, or laundry. Mariella enjoyed hearing her daughter practice the alphabet while she helped with chores, felt a sense of tradition when she lifted Olivia onto a chair to help knead dough for pasta. Now, the house felt unfriendly and sad. Thankfully, Louise was just across the street. Those first few days, Mariella drank more tea than ever, trying to fill the void.

Once spring rolled around, she began counting the days until June when school let out and she would feel whole again. Summer had become her favorite time of the year, and she was determined to make this one extra special. She planned to take her daughters shopping for new swimsuits and sundresses, spend long days on the beach in Asbury Park, teach them how to bake biscotti, and sign them up for a reading club at the Wanamassa library.

In June, the school had a small kindergarten graduation ceremony for Olivia's class. The children wore black paper caps with long tassels at the top. They sang songs about what they'd learned that year, then pledged their allegiance to the flag. The whole time, Olivia blew kisses to Mariella and Jack sitting in the audience. Although her daughter was supposed to be paying attention to the teacher, Mariella couldn't care less. Olivia wasn't just cured—after years of uncertainty and worry, she was thriving. On the ride home, Mariella and Jack decided to throw a party and celebrate.

"How many customers will we have?" Olivia asked her mother as they prepared the backyard.

Brushing the hair off her daughter's sweaty brow, Mariella gave her a curious look. "Customers?"

"For our restaurant."

"Stellina, these are our friends, not customers. And we're having a barbecue party."

"Yay! A party!" Olivia exclaimed, then skipped around the yard singing, "We're having a party! We're having a party!"

Elisa helped her mother set up the backyard with vinyl-strapped lounges and a few Adirondack chairs borrowed from Louise They covered the picnic table in a red-checked tablecloth, set out paper plates, plastic knives, forks, spoons, and napkins folded into triangles, then surrounded the patio with citronella candles.

Scanning her decorated yard to be sure everything was in its place, Mariella realized she had come a long way from those first months living in Jack's parents' house. Back then, everything was unfamiliar. Now, she was finally beginning to feel American.

As guests arrived, Jack prepared at the barbecue. Louise and Charles came a half an hour early to help with last-minute tasks. Charles took over the bar and quickly made a stiff martini for himself. Julia arrived with her boys in tow soon after. Mariella was relieved that Julia's husband, Tony, couldn't come. They only saw him at holidays but she never liked the way he leered. Still, with three boys, her sister-in-law could have used the help. Within the first five minutes, her eldest threw a ball into his younger brother's face, causing his lip to burst. A horrible fight between the boys ensued and although Jack tried to calm the situation, it was no use. Julia piled everyone back into the car and left. It would have helped if Jack's parents had come to the party, but Ma made a big production about being at the restaurant and said the world didn't stop just because they were having a party. Carl and Willie also worked that night, so Jack didn't have to worry.

Mr. and Mrs. Johnson, a sweet older couple from Eisle Avenue Mariella had met while taking the children trick or treating, showed up carrying a freshly made cherry pie. Clara arrived with her sister, Millie, her brother-in-law, Butch, and a large bowl of ambrosia salad, something Mariella had never heard of. Upon further inspection, she discovered it wasn't a salad at all. It was a delightful mixture of pineapple, grapes, marshmallow, and coconut all bound together with cream. Rachel came for an hour, driving up in Carl's Cadillac. After years of trying to conceive, she and Carl had decided having another child wasn't in the cards for them so they bought the car instead. Besides, with Frankie playing sports, she needed to be able to bring him to his games. Mariella was impressed after her sister-in-law got a driver's license. Now that the girls were in school, she vowed to get one too.

The backyard buzzed with activity as the party hit its stride. Children ran wild, holding out jars in one hand and lids poked with holes in the other, trying to capture lightning bugs. Multi-colored lanterns strung across the brick patio laid by Jack's father added to the festive atmosphere. The smell of Jack's sausages grilling next to juicy green peppers and caramelized onions permeated the air and the yard was alive with neighbors, family, and friends happily chatting away.

Earlier in the week, Mariella had been excited to see a new couple move into the corner house, so she left them an invitation. When they arrived, she was thrilled that it was an American man married to a tall, shapely woman with a Spanish accent.

"You Mariella?" The woman stood at her front door rolling her R perfectly, then finished the rest of her name like a song. It reminded Mariella of home.

"Yes, welcome." Mariella put out her hand, then thought twice and kissed the woman on each cheek.

"Thank you. I Bibiana, but you call to me Bibi." She beamed.

Her husband shook Mariella's hand. "Hi there, I'm Aaron. Thanks for the invite! We just moved in so it's nice to meet some neighbors." He was the opposite of Bibi—tall, slim, and blonder than some Germans she had encountered.

"I am so happy to have you here," Mariella said, showing them into the house.

Bibi held out a basket of something that looked like a pastry. "Here, these from my land—empanadas!"

"How lovely. And where is that?" Mariella asked, leading them through to the kitchen to the back door.

Bibi let out a throaty laugh then proudly said, "Brazil!"

"Wonderful! I am from Italy, and Louise here is from England. And she must stop cleaning and come outside," Mariella scolded.

Louise had been busy washing dishes. She pulled out a soapy hand and waved hello. "Just wanted to get this last one. I promise I'll be right out!"

"Okay, but the next time I see you your hands better be out of those rubber gloves!"

Mariella brought Bibi and Aaron out the back door. Everyone's gazes turned to their exotic new neighbor as she made her way over to Jack.

"Jack, these people just moved in on the corner. This is Aaron and his wife, Bibi."

"Hello there." Jack absentmindedly held out a barbecue fork with a sausage on the end. "Oops! Let me make a sandwich for you!"

"Thanks. They smell great," Aaron said.

Jack opened a roll and pressed it onto the grill. "So, where are ya coming from?"

"We just moved back to the States."

Bibi laughed. "No back for me. It me first time here."

Jack adjusted his hearing aid as he tried to decipher her accent. "Colombian?"

"Oh, you are treading on dangerous ground, sir," Aaron joked.

"I am Brazilian," Bibi said proudly.

Once her new guests were settled, Mariella returned to the kitchen to coax Louise to join the party.

"That one is a firecracker!" Louise commented, drying her hands on a dish towel.

Mariella watched from the door, intrigued by the prospect of another "foreign" friend in the neighborhood. "I am so happy they came. It is never easy being new, is it?"

"You've got that right."

"Come on, let's get to know our new neighbor!"

Mariella linked arms with Louise and went into the backyard, but Millie intercepted.

"Who's that loud woman? My goodness, if she isn't soaking up all the attention here. Did you invite her?" she asked Mariella, shooting Louise a knowing look. It was obvious she did not have the same disdain for an English-speaking immigrant.

"She's my guest, and I find her charming," Mariella said, hardly concealing the grin that formed on her face.

"Charming?" Millie pursed her lips, then swatted at a mosquito. "Can't you do anything about these bugs? They're all over the place. Honestly, I don't think we can stay long if they keep biting. I might be allergic. Didn't you have someone come and spray today?"

"Spray?"

"Yes, so they're not attacking your guests? We always have our yard sprayed. It's just common courtesy. I'd give you his name, but he's ridiculously expensive..."

"That is okay," Mariella said, casually. "They are only biting you, Millie. I guess you are just too sweet."

Millie shot her a look.

"Don't you worry, dear," Mariella continued. "We

understand if you need to leave. I can have Jack wrap up a couple of sandwiches to go. We do not want your legs to get any more—how do you say—scarred than they already are. With your pale skin, it really shows up more than others. You might end up looking like you are infected with some horrible disease." As Millie's mouth fell open, Mariella patted her arm. "Close your mouth, dear, you do not want to catch a fly," she said, then walked away.

Louise quickly followed her behind the shed at the far end of the yard where she plucked a pack of cigarettes from her apron and lit one up. Taking a long, hard drag, Mariella blew the gray smoke out of her nose.

"That woman."

"Oh boy. You weren't joking when you told me those stories about how awful she was. That woman is a cow," Louise agreed. "But you were perfect. I mean, how you stood up to her. Terrific!"

"I have been so polite with her, I have just had it. I am at the end of my foos."

"Foos?" Louise thought a moment, then smiled. "You mean fuse. You are at the end of your fuse."

"Well, you know what I mean."

"Of course, but you were brilliant. And she was speechless!"

Mariella leaned against the fence, watching Millie complain

to her husband. She pointed to the back gate. He shook his head a few times, then they said their goodbyes and left. But a sense of relief made Mariella lighter on her feet.

"Excuse me, Louise. I should go see if Jack needs help." Mariella crossed the yard and sidled up to her husband, who was laying more sausages onto the grill.

"Where've you been, sweetheart? Millie and her husband had to leave," Jack said, his disappointment obvious.

"Did they? Why?" she asked, avoiding his gaze.

"Ah, something about their son being sick so they couldn't stay. Funny, they didn't mention it when they arrived. Anyway, I think they're missing out on a pretty fantastic party, wouldn't ya say?"

Mariella laughed, happy to discard the conversation about Millie altogether. "I think it is the best of parties."

"And the kids," Jack said, throwing his arm around her, "would ya look at them! They seem to be having the most fun."

Watching Olivia giggle, holding her sister's hand as they hid from whoever was "it," made Mariella hopeful for the future. She leaned into Jack. "Yes, they do."

He kissed her cheek. "None of this would be possible without you, honey."

"What do you mean? You are the one cooking."

"That's the least I could do. Look at this place." He

pointed to their garden in the corner of the yard that was full of ruby-red tomatoes ready for canning, heads of lettuce, and a few small zucchini. "That's your doing."

"Amore, you built the gate," Mariella said.

"What about all of these people here? All friends you've made while I was at work."

"Yes, amore, but they like both of us."

"Then what about them?" he asked, pointing to the girls.

Mariella raised her eyebrows. "Our children? I think you had something to do with that too."

"Sure, but you're the one really raising them. You're with them every day. They're all you."

Watching Elisa huddling with her sister behind a tree, Mariella had always marveled at how thoughtful and kind they were. How they made her laugh with their questions and how they seemed to sense her loneliness just when she needed some company. But that wasn't taught. "We are lucky to have wonderful girls."

Jack looked into her eyes, his love and appreciation obvious. "I love you, sweetheart."

"I love you, amore," Mariella said. Caught up in their own world, for a moment she forgot they were throwing a party.

"Mama!" Olivia said, suddenly by her side and pulling on her skirt. "Ellie and I got caught by 'it.'"

Mariella stroked her daughter's thick, black hair. "It's okay, Stellina," she said, kissing the top of her head.

"Can we have dessert? I'm hungry."

Jack pointed to the grill. "How about another sausage?"

"My belly doesn't want that, it wants dessert!"

"Oh!" Mariella slipped out of Jack's arms. "I guess it *is* time for dessert. Let me go get it."

As she turned to walk away, Clara crept up behind her, almost making her jump out of her skin.

"Cheers!" she slurred, holding up a glass of red wine before swiftly descending into sobs.

Jack seemed alarmed, but Mariella knew there had been something bothering Clara. She'd been hinting at it, talking about how lonely she was, for the past month.

"Come help me with dessert." Mariella pulled her inside. "Tell me, what is going on?"

Clara wiped her eyes with a cocktail napkin, then shook her head. "Nothing. I'm just feeling emotional."

"But you have been odd for a long time. What is it?"

"Nothing, really. I'm fine."

Mariella narrowed her eyes, "We are friends, are we not?"

Clara smiled through her tears.

"Then tell me, what is it?"

"I've joined the Peace Corps," Clara said, her voice heavy

with trepidation.

"What? But why?"

"Let's face it, except for my occasional visits to you, I have nothing here. And I can't live with my sister for the rest of my life. Fighting over my father's house is killing me."

"But, the Peace Corps? Where are you going? What will you do?"

"I found out this morning they've assigned me to Malaysia for the next year. I'll be teaching English!" Suddenly, Clara became more upbeat.

"And just when I was going to learn to drive so I can come visit more often," Although Mariella's heart sank at the prospect of losing her friend, she knew this would be good for her. Clara needed to get out from under the shadow of her sister's demands and find her own life. "But I think it sounds wonderful. And do not worry, I will be waiting for you to come back and tell me all of your exciting stories about malaria."

"It's Malaysia, not malaria!" Clara said. "Malaria is what you get if you're bitten by a diseased mosquito."

"Hmm. Let us hope your sister will not come down with that either!"

"What?"

"Never mind," Mariella said with a laugh. She pulled out a chair at the kitchen table. "Now, sit. I'll make you an espresso just like old times."

For the rest of the evening, Mariella and Jack chatted with their guests while Olivia, Elisa, and the other neighborhood kids played tag, running barefoot in the grass. They indulged in a dessert of ice cream, apple pie, and marshmallows toasted over the barbecue. Once the sun went down, Jack handed out sparklers to the children. He lit them one by one for a brilliant show while they sang "America the Beautiful." Mariella had never been prouder to be living in her adopted country.

Chapter Thirty-Eight

"What are we doing, Mama?" Olivia asked, watching her mother go into the garage.

"I am just feeding my little friends," Mariella said, emerging with a large bag of seeds.

"Come on, Liv! You're it! You have to find me," Elisa complained.

" 'Kay, Ellie, but first, I'm gonna help Mama feed the birds." She gave her mother a toothy smile. "Okay?"

Mariella patted her head. "Of course you can help." She took down the feeder, which was shaped like a small British cottage—a gift from Louise after a visit back home to England. "Now, you pour the seed in the top, here." She took off the roof and pointed inside.

"I got it, Mama," Olivia said impatiently, then poured the seeds too quickly and spilled them all over the lawn. "Oh, no!"

"Never mind, it will not go to waste." Mariella tried to sound light. Olivia was not only stubborn but also very hard on herself. "The birds love sweeping down to the ground in search of food."

Olivia's face brightened. "They do?"

"Sure they do. Not right now, because we are here. But you can watch from the kitchen window when we go inside. They sing their songs while they do it, too."

"Liv!" Elisa scolded. "Come on!"

Mariella put the bird feeder back together and hung it up. "A little patience, Tesoro. Your sister was helping me. Now, would you two like to plant some seeds in the garden? You've always liked to do that."

Although she was only seven, Elisa was tall for her age and sometimes didn't seem at home in her body. Especially since she towered over most of her friends. She sighed. "Okay, Mama. But then Liv has to play with me."

"Yes. First we plant, then, we play," Olivia explained to her sister, as if it were her idea.

Mariella went into the garage and brought out a spade and a few packets of seeds. "Do you remember how we did this last year?"

"Yeah," Elisa said, distracted by something. "I remember."

But Olivia watched intently as Mariella dug a little hole,

then dropped a few seeds inside. "What are we planting?" she asked.

"Oh, these are the carrots."

"For the bunnies?"

Mariella tickled Olivia's belly. "You mean this little bunny?" she asked, smiling at the sound of her daughter's giggles. "Here, give it a try."

She handed her the spade and pointed to a spot. Olivia stuck her tongue out as she concentrated on digging the hole. When it was deep enough Mariella placed a few seeds in her hand. Olivia carefully placed them at the bottom, then buried them with dirt.

"Now, we have to give them some water so they grow. Can you get the watering can for me?"

"Yes, Mama! Right away!"

As Olivia ran over to the shed, Mariella noticed Elisa watching three blonde girls playing two houses over. "Who's that?" she asked.

"I think it's Charlotte! Yoo-hoo! Charlotte! Is that you? It's me, Ellie!" Elisa jumped up and down, waving until she caught the girls' attention.

"Hi, Ellie! Wanna come play?" Charlotte called over.

"Just a second." Elisa turned to Mariella, her hands clasped in prayer. "Mama, can I go over to Charlotte's? Please? Please? Please?"

Mariella glanced over at the girl's house. Their yard was a mess: the grass was high, and weeds crept up the chain-link fence dividing the properties. She wished she knew more about her family. They had moved in at the beginning of the school year and Mariella had only spoken to her mother once, during a holiday pageant at the elementary school. The woman seemed a bit scattered and not interested in speaking with the other parents. But Elisa was always talking about Charlotte, and how pretty she was with her golden locks and blue eyes; something so classically American. With Mariella's strong accent, she could tell that her daughter was beginning to feel embarrassed of her.

Despite her misgivings, she reluctantly agreed. "Make sure to tell me if you girls go anywhere else."

Elisa squealed. "Okay, okay! I promise! Love you, Mama!" She hugged her mother, then shouted over the fences, "Be right over!"

Mariella walked Elisa out front and watched her skip down the sidewalk. When she returned to the backyard, she found Olivia dragging a metal watering can behind her.

"I've got the water, Mama!" she said, just as a phone began to ring.

At first, Mariella thought it was coming from her neighbor's house. By the third ring, she realized it was her own.

"Stellina, stay here. Mama has to answer the phone."

"Don't worry. I'll water the plants for you."

"No, you wait until I get back!" Mariella called out, running into the house. She picked up the phone by the sixth ring. "Hello?"

A crackle of static greeted her on the other end of the line.

"Hello?" she said again, but there was no answer.

She placed the phone back on its cradle, wondering who it could have been; then, a shriek came from the backyard. Mariella dashed outside and found her daughter battling with the hose as it snapped back and forth, water gushing like a fountain. When Olivia noticed her mother watching her, she froze.

"Olivia Helena Valentino!" Mariella cried. She dodged the stream of water, grabbed the hose by its neck, then twisted the faucet shut. Drenched from head to toe, Olivia stood casually, trying to look as innocent as possible. "What did I tell you?"

"You told me 'Olivia Helena Valentino'!" she cried, mimicking her mother.

Mariella gave her a stern look. "Stop being silly. I told you not to touch the hose. Why do you not listen to me?"

Olivia held her hands out and shrugged. "I don't know, Mama. I think it's naughty Olivia. She always tells me to do bad things."

"Oh, I think I am looking right at naughty Olivia." The phone rang again. "Go. Sit in the sun and dry off." Mariella stooped to Olivia's level. "And you better not move. Do you understand?"

Olivia nodded, then obediently sat on a chaise lounge.

Mariella ran back in the the house and answered the phone.

"Hello?" she said, speaking loudly through the static. This time, she could hear a small voice calling her name. "Mama? Mama, is that you?" Mariella said.

"Yes, can (crackle) (crackle) Mari-(crackle)?"

Mariella went rigid. "Mama, I will call you back, okay?"

The static became so loud she could hear nothing else. It seemed to scratch the tender inside of her ear. She hung up, then called back. Her mother picked up on the first ring.

"Mariella?"

"Oh, thank God, Mama. I can hear you as clear as day now. Is everything okay?"

When Mama fell silent, Mariella's heart dropped.

PART THREE

Chapter Thirty-Nine

The 747 gradually tilted, bringing Rome into view. Against the backdrop of blue skies, scattered puffy white clouds clung to majestic gold domes while marble landmarks across the city glimmered in the morning sun. Mariella swallowed hard. She had never seen Rome from above, and it was even more beautiful than she remembered. She glanced over at her daughters, both slumped in their seats, fast asleep. The gingham dresses freshly pressed at the start of the journey were now a crumpled mess. It wasn't surprising. To get to Italy, they had taken four flights: New York to Boston, Boston to Ireland, Ireland to Paris, before finally arriving in Rome. The whole thing was daunting. Mariella had never flown before and Jack couldn't leave the restaurant so she'd had no choice but to get on with it.

Mariella listened to the creaking sound of landing gear maneuvering into place and, with a lurch and a thud, they were on the ground. Cheers and claps erupted throughout the plane while tears filled her eyes. She nudged her daughters awake.

"Are we here?" Elisa asked, craning her neck to look out the window.

"Yes, Tesoro, we're here."

Olivia resisted waking up. "Take me home! I wanna go home now!" she whined groggily.

Mariella held her daughters close and thought, *I am home.*

After setting her large case onto a cart and allowing the girls to sit on top, Mariella quickly made it through customs. Cheers filled the terminal as they stepped through the large double doors. Mariella eyed her brother first. Matteo certainly wasn't a baby anymore. Tall with dark curly hair slicked back into place, his big brown eyes lit up. Lia jumped up and down with joy, while tears rolled down Mama's face, her arms opened wide ready to have her daughter close again. Mariella abandoned her cart and ran to them. They clung together, crying, laughing, and kissing each other as time seemed to stand still.

"Mama!" Olivia whined. She ran to her mother, her arms stretched out. When Lia tried to pick her up, she howled louder. "Mama! Mama! I want Mama!"

Elisa was more curious.

Matteo stooped to her level and said hello. "I you cousin,"

he told her.

"Not cousin, dummy. You are her uncle," Lia corrected, speaking perfect English.

"Lia! I can tell you've been studying. And look at you! You're practically a woman now," Mariella noted, admiring her stylish dress.

"Thank you." Lia twirled around, then touched her hair, cut into a bouncy bob. "You like it? I had it done a few weeks ago."

Mariella touched her sister's face. "You are beautiful."

"How about me, Mariella?" Matteo stood next to her. "Ha! I'm the same height as you!"

"Yes, you are!" Mariella said with a laugh.

Olivia threw her head back dramatically and stomped her feet. "I'm tired."

Mama stooped down to Olivia's level. "Tesoro, I am your nonna," she said in Italian, trying to hug her.

Olivia pulled away. "I am not Tesoro. I am Stellina."

"It's okay," Mariella said, scooping her up. "This is my mother. Can you please say hello? For me?"

"No."

"Stellina."

As Olivia peeked over Mariella's shoulder, Mama gently kissed her hand. She clung to her mother.

"Ciao, Nonna," Elisa said sweetly.

"Oh, Tesoro mio," Mama cried. She kissed her cheeks, then looked at her. "She is the spitting image of you."

Mariella smiled. "I know. She's got the same temperament, too."

"Mama, I'm tired!" Olivia whined. "I wanna go home."

"Poor little one. Let's get you home." Mama took Elisa by the hand, Matteo pushed the luggage cart, and they all headed for the exit.

Getting a taxi right outside wasn't a problem, but fitting everyone into a Fiat 500 was a fiasco. Matteo sat in the front, while Mariella, Mama, and Lia smooshed themselves into the back with Olivia and Elisa perched on their laps. Driving through the streets of Rome, Mariella was happy to see nothing had changed, but the energy was different. Men bustled down sidewalks on their way to work while others gathered at the bars in cafes to throw back their morning espresso.

Although she was exhausted, when the taxi dropped them off at the bottom of the street, Mariella felt reinvigorated. It could have been the smell of wood burning in ovens across the city permeating the air or the fact that the Colosseum loomed behind them as they walked to their building. With each step, a new memory reappeared. They passed the fountain where she and Elisa queued for hours during the war, just to fill their tin buckets with rusty water. She remembered returning with her father after the supplies they'd picked up at her grandparents' farm were stolen. She would never forget that night. It was the first time she realized her papa was not invincible.

But there were happy memories too, like when Rome was liberated and the whole family walked outside to a new world, or the fateful day she passed a man walking on her street and realized Jack had returned for her.

"Mariella," Matteo grunted as he hefted her overstuffed suitcase, "what have you got in here?"

Mariella's face lit up. "I've brought something special from America for all of you! Mama, I know Giada is expecting, but will she come visit soon? I can't manage traveling with the girls to visit her." Her sister had married Salvatore the year before and moved down south to be close to his family. She was anxious to meet her new brother-in-law and see her sister, but the two-hour train ride would be too much.

Mama nodded, but seemed preoccupied with a group of women chatting outside a flower shop. "Make yourself small, so they don't notice you," she whispered, ducking her head until they passed. "I want you all to myself. At least for now."

As they approached their building, Signora Manetto called down from her window. "Ciao Bella! Welcome home! Oh my, you look so chic! America has been good for you! And are those your children? Bella! Bella ragazze!"

"I wish she would hush up," Mama complained. "Can't she wait until we get inside?"

"It's okay, Mama. We're like family to her. She is to me, too," Mariella said, trying to ignore the faint outline of Mother Superior's blood stained into the cobblestone. Years had passed, yet it was still there, as if the woman's spirit protected it from fading along with her memory.

When they arrived on their landing, Signora Manetto was waiting, a dish towel in one hand and a sauce-stained wooden spoon in the other. "It's so wonderful to have all of you home!" she cheered, pulling Mariella in for a hug. "And who is this?" she asked, trying to get a look at Olivia.

Olivia hid her face in Mariella's skirt.

"Okay, Sylvia, let's give the girls some space. They're here for a while. You'll have plenty of time to get to know them." Mama herded everyone into the apartment, leaving Signora Manetto in the hallway complaining about the taralli she'd made for Mariella's homecoming.

"Papa?" Mariella called out, looking around the apartment. "Mama, where's Papa?"

"He's not here, Tesoro," she said in a voice filled with shame. Lia and Matteo stood awkwardly in the center of the room.

"What do you mean? Where is he?"

"Why don't we put the girls down for a nap? They could use some sleep. Let's put them in your old bed. Then I'll make an espresso for you."

"That's a good idea," Lia interjected "We can have an espresso and talk."

Mariella's eyes darted between them, searching for answers. "What's wrong with all of you? I don't want to have a coffee. I came all this way to see my papa."

"I understand, Tesoro. And we will. But I need to talk to you about his..." Mama paused, choosing her words carefully, "condition."

It took a half hour to get the girls to sleep. With the windows opened, strange sounds coming from outside frightened them. Mariella had to reassure Olivia several times that she would be there when they woke.

Once they were finally settled, Mariella joined her family in the kitchen. She pulled out a chair, its legs scraping across the hardwood floor, and couldn't fight the sense of unease gnawing at her nerves. She was used to having the rug pulled out from under her, especially in their tiny kitchen. Lia made coffee while Matteo explained he had a soccer game he couldn't miss and quickly left.

Mariella watched her mother gulp her coffee down as if it could power her through. "Your father is in the hospital," she said bluntly.

"I don't understand. When you called you said you wanted to fly us here to cheer him up. You said he was having problems remembering things. But that isn't something a doctor can cure," Mariella said, biting at her thumbnail.

"It wasn't so bad at first, just moments of forgetfulness. That went on for years. I thought he was just being lazy," Mama's voice cracked, "not taking the time to remember things. We all get forgetful as we age. It was small things like forgetting keys, losing his wallet, not remembering appointments. I guess it was all so gradual. But a few weeks ago, the day before I called you, he got lost on his way home. We were out looking for him for hours. We traced and retraced his steps, but he had wandered."

"Where was he?"

"Across town where his grandparents had an apartment. You can imagine his confusion when he knocked on the door and a strange man answered. That was the day he made a costly mistake while at work..."

"Did they fire him? Papa gave his life to that bank."

"Tesoro, he hasn't had that job for over a year. His boss spoke with me first. He didn't want to let your father go, but he couldn't be trusted with money so they allowed him to do janitorial work. That morning, he had left the water on and flooded the basement. It was a good thing they let him go. Within a week, more of his memory had vanished."

Trying to put the pieces together, Mariella's mind spun. She wished Mama had told her it was more serious. She'd just thought he was sad. Over the past few years, Mariella hadn't really spoken to him much. He would get on the phone to say hello or sing happy birthday, but he always sounded tired. Although she worried, she had her own life to manage. Now, Mariella wondered how she let it go without demanding to know why he seemed so removed. If she had known her father was in the hospital, she would have insisted Jack come with her. But thinking he needed cheering up wasn't enough to ask him to leave the business—especially since they were struggling. They had to take advantage of the summer tourists or possibly close the restaurant for good.

"I want to see him. Now," Mariella demanded.

"There's one more thing you need to know. We can visit him, but he may not remember you."

Lia abruptly rose from her seat and left. Mariella turned to Mama. It was the first time she had really taken her in since she'd arrived. Hardened wrinkles defined her forehead, and bags swelled under her eyes. But the most shocking thing was her mother's mouth, now turned down on both sides, even when she tried to smile.

Chapter Forty

While the children slept, Mama and Mariella took a taxi to the hospital.

"You must not overwhelm him. Give him time to figure out who you are. If you run in expecting a hug, you will scare him," Mama explained. "And try not to cry. That will scare him, too. He's still your father. He doesn't want to see anyone sad, even strangers."

As Mariella entered the stark room, her father sat at the window looking smaller than she remembered. His gaze drifted aimlessly over the courtyard below, his fingers rhythmically tapping his knee as if they danced a ballet to a song in his head.

"Signore DeRosa," the nurse said, gently patting his back, "you have visitors."

"Oh?"

When Papa turned to Mariella, she fought the urge to rush

into his arms, longing for the comfort of his embrace. She yearned for him to tell her everything would be okay like he did when she was a child. Instead, she bit her lip.

"Hello," Papa said, his mannerisms turning formal.

"Hello," Mariella replied.

Mama went over to him and leaned against the window. "How are you feeling today?"

Papa nodded. "I'm fine. Are you a nurse? You're not wearing your uniform. Why aren't you wearing your uniform?" He glanced over at Mariella, wrinkling his brow, then turned away. "What is that girl doing here?"

"This is Mariella. She's come to visit."

Mariella tried to smile, but her face felt numb. "Papa," she whispered.

He looked back at her, cocking his head to one side. A flash of recognition warmed his face, but only for a second. "I don't know you," he said, challenging her.

She knelt at his feet. "Papa, I'm your daughter."

Mama tried to stop her, but it was too late.

"Don't you remember me? I'm your Tesoro." Mariella tried taking hold of his calloused hands but he pushed her away.

"I told you! I don't know you!"

The anger in her father's voice broke her heart, but nothing was worse than not being able to comfort him.

"It'll be alright, Signore," the nurse said softly. "You're okay."

Looking to her mother for support, Mariella noticed Mama's face had no emotion. It was the same blank face when Elisa was dying. Despite traveling hours to be home, she felt like she was in a room of strangers.

"Mariella," Mama said. "We should go."

"Okay, okay," Mariella murmured, stealing one last glance at her father before leaving the room. They walked down the hospital corridors in silence, just like the final days of her sister's life. When they got to the street, she turned to her mother. "I'd like to walk home if you don't mind."

"Of course."

Soft light filtered through the towering stone pines as the sun lowered. The weight of a lifetime of tragedies constricted Mariella's heart. Now, she understood why her mother kept the truth from her, but if she'd known before leaving America, Jack could have helped her make sense of it all. Her mother said he had dementia, a condition that caused her father's brain to slowly deteriorate until all the things that made him Papa disappeared. It was cruel.

Traveling through the park, she felt her sister walk alongside her. They had done it often during the war, scavenging for fruit and firewood. Back then, the entire world seemed upside down.

Today wasn't any different. Guilt weighed Mariella down once again. She hadn't just left Italy for love. She had abandoned her family. Matteo seemed to be struggling the most. *A boy needs his father,* she thought, wondering how many soccer games he'd played without Papa cheering from the sidelines.

How could I? I should have been here. If I had been here, Papa wouldn't forget me like he does. Why didn't anyone stop me?

Mariella sat down on a splintered wooden bench. Despite her efforts, tears welled up and couldn't be contained. She wouldn't dare go home without pulling herself together. But she didn't want the pain to stop either. She deserved to feel miserable.

The sun retreated behind the moon, and the stars began to appear in all their glory. Mariella glared at them. She might not have fallen in love with Jack if they didn't twinkle like they do. She might have been more sensible.

Mariella entered the apartment with caution. She'd thought it strange that from the street, there was no light coming from their window. "Mama? Elisa? Olivia? Anyone home?" she called out.

"Ciao Bella!" Signora Manetto stood in their doorway. "Come, come! I've cooked a large lasagna and must share it with someone."

"Do you know where everyone went?"

"They were worried you hadn't come home, so they took the girls to look for you. Never mind, though. I'm sure they'll be back soon."

"Okay." Mariella shuffled over to her neighbor's apartment. The smell of her neighbor's rich, silky lasagna reminded her of the last time she had eaten it. It was with her family and Jack, right before she'd left for America and everything changed.

"Signora, did you know about Papa?"

Signora Manetto quietly set the lasagna in front of Mariella, but was suddenly at a loss for words.

"Signora?"

"Oh, Mariella," she sighed, wiping her hands on a dish towel. "I'm so sorry about your father. I don't think we realized until it was too late."

"That's what Mama said. I just wish I had been here."

The sound of footsteps, some running and others weary, came from the stairs.

"There they are!" Signora Manetto said, happy to change the subject.

She opened the door just as Matteo vanished into their apartment. Lia appeared with Olivia and Elisa chatting excitedly about America as they followed Matteo inside. Mama came up last, stopping in their neighbor's doorway.

"Oh, Sylvia, we haven't found her. I can't imagine how she

must feel—"

"I'm here, Mama," Mariella said. Noticing the relief on her mother's face when she finally saw her, she apologized. "I'm sorry. I didn't mean to give you a scare."

Mama sunk into the chair next to her and sighed. "You don't need to be sorry, Tesoro."

"But I am. I should have never left Italy. If I were here with you—"

"The same thing would have happened."

"But if I only—"

"Tesoro." Mama patted her hand. "There is nothing we could have done. I've been here the whole time. If he doesn't recognize me, why would he recognize you?"

Mariella let her mother's words sink in. Despite feeling that she had abandoned her family, she knew Mama was right. But regret was hard to digest.

The following morning, Mariella woke up to a nudge. Giada stood over her, offering a silly smile.

Mariella sat up and threw her arms around her sister. "You came!"

"Of course I came. My big sister is here all the way from America! How could I not?"

"I'm so happy you're here! Let me see your belly."

Standing up, Giada turned sideways and patted her stomach.

"My goodness, you look like you swallowed a watermelon!"

"They say it's going to be twins. Can you imagine?"

"Twins? Or maybe triplets?"

Giada glanced over at her nieces sleeping peacefully in her old bed. "Oh, Mariella, they're beautiful." She tiptoed over and gave them each a kiss. "I can't wait until they wake."

"I can't wait for you to meet them." Mariella got out of bed and slipped a bathrobe on. "C'mon, let's go have a coffee."

"We live in a little village outside of Naples. It's small, but I like it," Giada said, as Mariella set the espresso pot on the stove. "I didn't think I would, but everyone is so kind and they all take care of each other. It feels … I don't know."

"I know," Mariella said. "You like it because it feels safe."

Giada nodded.

Since they would never escape the scars developed from the war, Mariella figured why fight it? Finding peace living in a small village made sense.

"Oh, Giada, how did all of this happen? How did he get so bad without anyone noticing?"

"It's hard to explain. I can't even pinpoint when everything changed, but when it did, the difference was glaring. He began to stumble on his words and forget where he was. We would try and joke, but there was nothing funny about it. His brain was working strangely but... he was still Papa. After I moved away, I would visit and have to remind him of who I was married to and where I lived. Now, he doesn't know who I am..."

"But maybe we can help him," Mariella suggested. "Are you coming with me to see Papa today?"

Giada looked away. "I-I just can't bear to."

"What? Why not?"

"He thinks I'm a stranger."

"But he's Papa. Are you giving up on him?"

"Mariella," Giada said, speaking in a small voice. "I'm not strong like you. I never was."

"But what about Mama?" Knowing how hard it was to see her father in his condition, Mariella tried to stay calm. "She needs you."

Giada searched her eyes. "I'm here now."

"For how long?"

"Salvatore wants me back tonight. I help take care of his mother. She's a real bear. I almost didn't marry him because of her. But then, she took ill and everything changed."

"What do you mean?"

"Her bark softened, now it's gone. She had to move in with us."

"His mother lives with you?"

"Yes, but it's okay. She stopped speaking right before. Just sits in her room and stares into space."

Mariella shot her a look. "Is she the same as Papa?"

"No, I think she went crazy," Giada said. "I know what you are thinking. But it's much easier when it's someone you don't care about."

Olivia skipped into the kitchen with bleary eyes, breaking the tension. Elisa followed.

"Oh, my! Are these your little princesses?" Giada asked in English.

Elisa frowned. "I'm not a princess."

"Yeah," Olivia said, putting her hands on her hips. "We're not princesses."

"Well then, what are you?"

"We're just little children."

"Ah! So you must be Olivia, yes?" Giada asked, poking her stomach.

Olivia giggled.

Giada turned to Elisa, who had slipped into the chair next to her. "And you are Elisa."

"Yes."

"Well, it's wonderful to meet both of you."

Mariella was happy to watch her sister interact with her girls, but couldn't help feeling disconnected. There was no excuse not to see their father. Especially while caring for someone else's mother.

For a few hours, Giada visited with everyone. She regaled Elisa and Olivia with stories of the first time Mariella laid eyes on their father. The girls took turns feeling the babies kicking and rolling inside her stomach, then told her all about life in America. Elisa explained how they ate eggs or pancakes or a bowl of cereal for breakfast. They bragged about how they had a television set in the living room with four channels to choose from. They described the big, yellow school buses that took them to camp in the summer. By the end of the visit, Elisa decided that Zia Giada was her favorite because they both had a love for books.

"Are you sure you don't want to come with me to the hospital?" Mariella asked one last time. She wasn't trying to make her sister feel bad. She just didn't want her to have regrets.

"I'm sorry," Giada said. "But I promise to pray for him."

Mariella walked her to the bottom of the street and helped her get into a cab. She hugged her sister tightly, then kissed her belly. "Good luck. I'm not sure what it is like to deliver twins, but I don't think it will be easy."

Giada laughed. "No, I don't think it will be. I'll send pictures when they come!"

"You better!"

"I love you, sister!"

"I love you too!"

Giada waved from the back seat as the taxi pulled away, her expression tinged with sadness. *At least she feels safe,* Mariella thought.

Chapter Forty-One

After Giada left, Mariella searched for things to stir Papa's memory. She found the dress he'd brought home during the war to cheer her up. She also retrieved the cigar box still hidden under her bed. Her father gave it to her to keep her treasures safe, but it was the sweet, smoky scent Mariella loved. It reminded her of the nights when he puffed on the cigars in front of the building because Mama wouldn't allow him to smoke inside. Thankfully, the smell was still there. Lastly, she picked out a photo of the two of them, taken on her wedding day. His eyes were full of tears as he proudly stood next to her. On her way to see him, she made a stop at a bar to buy his favorite breakfast, a Ciambello.

In a special wing for people with mental health conditions, Mariella walked down the hallway, desperate to drown out moans emanating from one of the patients' rooms. It was something out of a nightmare. Before she went into her father's room, she took a moment to gather herself.

Papa lay in bed, flat on his back, when Mariella entered. He stared at the ceiling for a moment, then startled when he noticed her.

"Nurse? Where have you been? I've been lying here all day. My back hurts."

"You've been in bed all day?"

He reached out for her. Mariella quickly helped him sit up.

"How am I supposed to…to…?" His voice trailed off once he was upright. He looked around the room suspiciously, then whispered, "They may be coming. We have to prepare."

She searched his face, hardened by whatever he imagined coming for them. "Who is coming?"

"Those, those…" His voice trailed off again as his eyes darted around the room. "Those dirty bastards. They stole food from me and my girl."

"Your girl?" Mariella asked, her heart racing. "You mean your daughter, Mariella?"

"I'll kill 'em. They can't do that to my sweet little girl. I'll kill the dirty bastards." His mood suddenly shifted when he noticed the basket hanging on Mariella's arm. "Is that my lunch?"

"Yes, yes, it's your favorite, Pa—" Mariella caught herself and gave her father the donut. He devoured it, not stopping until he swallowed the last crumb.

"I'm so hungry," he whined.

"You are?"

He nodded.

"I'll be right back."

Mariella went to the nurses' station, where a young woman smoked a cigarette and spoke on the phone about a patient from the main hospital who had burned seventy-five percent of his body.

"Poor guy. I give him a day."

"Excuse me," Mariella interrupted. "My father says he hasn't eaten yet. Has anyone been in there to see him?"

The nurse glanced over at her, sighed, then stubbed out her cigarette. "I'll call you right back, Mama," She hung up. "What do you need?"

"My father is in room #204 and needs to eat."

"Oh, they've already been fed. Never mind what he says. Most of them aren't even aware of what they're babbling about."

"I think my father would know if he is hungry."

The nurse laughed. "Oh, I doubt that. Most of these people couldn't even tell you their names. Besides, they're hungry all the time. Just tell him to be patient. Lunch is in an hour."

Giving up on the nurse, Mariella ran down to the corner market. She bought two crusty rolls and three slices of prosciutto. But when she opened her wallet, she grew red in the face. Since she had arrived home, her focus was on Papa, and she hadn't exchanged her American dollars for lire. Thankfully, the owner was delighted to see the green money. She was sure he charged her double, but Mariella didn't care. She just wanted her father to have something to eat.

"Here you are," Mariella said, returning to his room. She offered Papa the sandwich but he waved it away.

"What do I want that for?"

Mariella unwrapped it, worried he might not know what it was.

He looked at her, eyebrows stitched together. "I said I'm not hungry."

"I don't understand, Papa. You told me you were, not thirty minutes ago. You said you hadn't eaten yet. Don't you remember?"

Her father's eyes glazed over, a look of confusion clouding his expression. He grumbled about something but Mariella couldn't make sense of it.

"Papa?"

"I'm not your papa!" he bellowed. "Don't you call me that! I'm not your father. Nurse! Nurse! Get in here!"

As the nurse hurried into the room and tended to her father, Mariella was overcome with jealousy. He continued to carry on, piercing her heart with each word he spoke.

"Get her out of here! She's crazy. Calling me Papa. Who does she think she is? She doesn't know me!"

"You need to leave now," the nurse said firmly, pushing Mariella out of the room.

Alone in the hallway, she listened to her father's gut-wrenching sobs. "How dare she say she is my daughter. My daughter isn't here anymore. She left me and never came back."

"It's okay, Signore. You are fine. Now, lay back and relax."

When he finally calmed down, Mariella left the hospital. She walked home in a daze. When she arrived at her building, her eyes traveled to their fourth-floor apartment but she couldn't bear to go inside just yet.

Instead, she turned back down the road and noticed an odd-looking woman standing by the convent. Although a red scarf concealed her face, Mariella could feel the woman's eyes on her. Then, with one leg horribly deformed, the woman limped up the road.

Mariella continued walking down the hill to the ring road that circled the Colosseum, traveled past to the Forum, then Piazza Venezia, Piazza di Spagna and on and on for the rest of the day until the sun began to set. Before returning home, Mariella stopped at her church, lit a candle, and said a prayer for her father.

Chapter Forty-Two

As soon as Mariella entered the apartment, she could tell Elisa sensed something was wrong.

"Mama, when am I going to meet Nonno?" she asked, her eyes full of worry.

"Yes, Mama! I wanna meet Nonno, too," Olivia chimed in, skipping around her mother.

Mariella went to the sink and poured herself a glass of water, chugged it down, and then filled up another. She wasn't sure if she was actually thirsty or simply wanted to avoid addressing her daughters' questions.

Matteo came in from the bathroom, pulling on a T-shirt. "Where were you? We've already had dinner."

"Where's Mama?"

"She and Lia went to look for you."

Mariella sighed. "Again? I'm not a child. And I know this city like the back of my hand."

"She's just worried about you."

"Well, she doesn't have to," Mariella snapped, then apologized when she saw the hurt on her brother's face. "I'm just tired."

"I understand." Matteo turned to Olivia and stooped down to her level. "You want come play with me and me friends for gaming to soccer?" She nodded, then her turned to Elisa. "You come, too?"

"Do your friends talk funny like you?" Elisa asked.

Matteo grinned. "They English worse to mine! But no matter. You in Italy now. You talk Italian."

Elisa shrugged. "Okay."

"Will you let me kick the ball?" Olivia asked, looking up at her uncle.

Matteo patted her on the head. "All things you want."

"Oooh! Can I pick flowers?"

"Yes."

"And hug the little boy?" she asked, referring to the statue of a boy happily peeing into a fountain in the corner of their courtyard.

"Yes," Matteo said, then turned to Mariella. "Mama left a piece of chicken for you in the oven."

Mariella mouthed thank you to him as he left with the girls.

Once they were gone, Mariella wet a dishcloth, laid it on the back of her neck, and sat at the table. The oppressive weather didn't help her dismal mood. As she glanced around the apartment, a kaleidoscope of memories played out before her: Papa on all fours giving her horse rides when she was the only child in their life, smiling faces welcoming each new sibling after Mama gave birth in her bedroom, the loud sounds of family dinners in the kitchen, a worn oak table at the center of it all. Then there were the cries of her mother when she lost her son, then a second time when Elisa died. Although her brother was a baby and her sister had more years on this Earth, there was no difference in the heartbreaking sound that came out of Mama. She remembered the smell of her childhood—espresso and lavender—wafting through the apartment. Mama used to have sprigs of lavender in each room and every day, like clockwork, a pot of espresso bubbled on the stove. Now, the air was stale.

Mariella let out a yawn. Jet lag coupled with the fact that she'd barely slept the night before caught up with her. Taking advantage of the empty apartment, she went to her bedroom, lay down, and fell quickly asleep.

The phone rang twice before Mariella opened her eyes. She took a moment to fully wake. Noticing the soft light filtering through her window and the girls curled up in bed, she realized she had slept through the night. The phone rang again. She hurried into the kitchen and picked it up.

"Pronto? Hello?" Mariella whispered her words so she wouldn't wake Lia and Matteo sleeping in the next room.

"Hello, darling." It was Jack, his voice transporting her to another life. "Did I wake you? I thought you might be awake by now."

Mariella tried to focus her eyes on the oven clock. "Amore, it's six a.m."

"Six? Gee, I thought it was eight. I'm sorry, darling. I'm just missing you something awful. How are things?"

"Oh, Jack. Things are horrible."

"They are?"

"Yes," she replied softly, sinking into a chair. Mariella explained how debilitating Papa's illness was and how she wished it was some other horrible disease. She would hate to see him suffer, but the pain of not being recognized by him, having him fear her, his familiar traits slowly disappearing, was another form of torture.

Jack was quiet, listening intently to each word she spoke. When she was done, he didn't say a word.

"Jack?"

"I'm here, sweetheart. I—" He went quiet again and

Mariella knew he wished to be with her at that moment. "You two were so close. I mean, 'are,'" he corrected himself.

"It's hard because I just want to hug him and talk and laugh about the past."

"I bet you do," Jack said, then lowered his voice. "I'm sorry I took you away from him."

Now Mariella was the quiet one. Jack said the words she had been thinking since arriving in Italy. And although they had both made the decision for her to move to America, she had battled with second thoughts. "Jack, we better get off the phone, this is costing a lot of money."

"I just wish I could hold you in my arms and make it better."

"I know, amore."

"And my girls? Do they still remember their papa?" Jack chuckled softly but his voice sounded heavy.

"Amore, of course they remember you. They wish you could be here too."

"I want to be, I really do. If I could, I would drop everything and board the next flight. But you know I have to be here, don't you?"

"Of course," Mariella said quickly.

"Okay, sweetheart. Please, take all the time you want. I'm sure Mama needs you."

"She does. I worry about her too, but she just carries on."

"Give her a hug and kiss from me, please."

"I will."

"And give a kiss to my sweet girls. Tell them their papa loves them. And tell them to keep writing! I love getting their letters."

"Yes, I will." Mariella contemplated waking the girls up, but it would only make them miss home.

"Sweetheart?"

"Amore?"

"I love you more than you can ever know."

Mariella swallowed hard. "I love you too, amore. Ciao, ciao ... ciao."

After they hung up, she couldn't help but feel let down. He had said all the right things, but it didn't help her situation; nothing could. She decided to take a walk. Instead of heading down the street, she walked through the park. It had rained overnight, and while the pathways were slick, with the air free of humidity, everything felt fresh. She walked over to the water clock. As a child, she remembered how it loomed above her, ticking in all its glory. Now, it signified the beginning of an end. Glimpses of Jack proposing to her underneath it were bittersweet. Even though her parents had given them their blessing, it wasn't the start of her happily ever after. It was far from it.

She considered what life would have been like without Jack. Perhaps she would have noticed Papa's deterioration and gotten the help he needed sooner. Mama always had too much on her plate to notice anything. She was constantly treading water. But without Jack in her life, something far more important would be missing—her daughters.

Still, after years of living in America, it didn't feel completely like home. It was nice to have other immigrants like Bibi and Louise as neighbors. But the thing that bonded them were the very things making her feel like an outsider. And although Mariella was fluent in English, her accent let her down. She was reminded every time she spoke. Trying to decipher the nuances of what people said versus what they actually meant was tiring. In Rome she knew that a lively group happily chatting as they walked through the cobblestone streets of her neighborhood were generations of one family. The eldest surrounded by the young ones, eager to help them along. Or that the prices at the markets were only meant as a starting point for bargaining. Or when you went to someone's house for a party, dinner was at a table instead of served as a buffet and free-for-all seating.

After wandering around aimlessly, Mariella sat down on a bench. In the hushed early morning hours, the park was mostly deserted except for a mysterious figure shrouded in red, hobbling along the path. Upon closer inspection, she realized it was the woman she had eyed the day before. But this time she limped toward Mariella with purpose. Despite her heart quickening, fearful of what would happen next, something caught her eye. It was a gold Star of David hanging around her neck and suddenly.... everything fell into place.

It couldn't be, Mariella thought even as the woman removed her scarf. Her face was harder than she remembered, but her dark eyes and gentle smile were the same.

Helena.

Chapter Forty-Three

"So, I guess she'll be there awhile." Jack leaned against his car speaking to Louise in his driveway. "Ah, don't mind me. I'm just sad I couldn't be there with her," he said, shoulders slumped in disappointment.

She patted his arm. "Oh dear. I'm sure she knows you would be there if you could. But Mariella is exactly where she should be—surrounded by her family."

"I thought I was her family," Jack said, quietly.

Pulling up to the restaurant, Jack eyed his mother's car and was overcome with dread. Ma had been exceptionally upbeat since Mariella left, making it obvious she preferred having her son all to herself. He couldn't bear to see her so cheery.

"Jack!" Ma sang when he walked through the door. Sitting in a booth by the front, she ate a bowl of linguini with clams. "Come, sit with me. Have some lunch."

Jack shook his head. "I can't, Ma. There's too much to do."

"Oh no, you need your strength. Sit." She waved to Sherry, who was folding napkins in the dining room. "Bring my Jack a plate of spaghetti."

"No, Ma, I really can't—"

"And tell Carl to cook him a nice, thick piece of veal," Ma instructed.

Sherry nodded, then disappeared into the kitchen.

Jack reluctantly took a seat across from his mother.

"You go to the bank today?"

"Sure, I made the deposit. I also went to the supply store for more small forks."

"The ones for lobster? Good! I swear someone's been stealing them."

"Ma, who would be stealing your forks?"

"You can never trust anyone, Jack." Ma glanced around the restaurant suspiciously, then twirled the linguini onto her fork and ate it.

Jack shook his head. With business slumping, his mother had become suspicious of everyone. He watched her eat lunch hunched over as if someone might steal that too.

After several minutes, Sherry appeared with a plate of spaghetti in red sauce and a piece of breaded veal. "Anything else?"

"No," Jack said. "Thank you."

Sherry gave Jack a wink before returning to the dining room.

"Is it hot enough for you?" Ma asked, inspecting his food. "That doesn't look hot enough. Sherry can bring it back if it's not."

"Ma, it's fine."

She sat back and made a sour face. "Why are you in such a foul mood? What's going on?"

"What's going on?" Jack asked. "My wife and children left over a month ago, and you haven't even asked about them. Don't you understand? I miss them."

Ma shrugged. "Of course you miss them. Why do I have to ask?"

"Because maybe then I would think you cared," Jack said, narrowing his eyes on her. "Mariella is going through something awful. Her father doesn't even remember who she is. I can't imagine what that would be like."

"It can't be easy," Ma said, her voice softening. "How's her mother doing?"

"She's okay, I guess."

"Let's face it. That family lived through a war. They can survive anything."

Jack put his fork down. "Hasn't her family had enough tragedy?"

"Of course, Jack, but they're strong ..." Ma's voice trailed off, suddenly distracted by someone standing at the bar with her back to them.

"Is Jack here?" the woman asked the bartender. Dressed in a powder-blue suit with a pink scarf around her neck, the sound of the woman's voice was all too familiar.

Jack wiped his mouth with a napkin, giving him time to process, then went to her. "Hello, Lauren."

Since they broke up, he had only seen her a handful of times and she was always with her husband. They were respectful, but that was it. Until now, she had never once come into the restaurant. He looked over at his mother, the scowl on her face reminding him of the threats Lauren's father made to sue when Jack called off the wedding.

"Long time no see."

Lauren turned to him, her eyes misty. "Can we talk?"

"Sure."

Jack led her through the kitchen, passing a gambit of stares from Carl and Willie. They went into his office and he quickly closed the door behind them. "What can I do for ya, Lauren?"

"Well, I assume everyone knows I'm a divorcée now!" she said, dissolving into tears.

Jack was baffled. He knew Lauren and her husband were headed for divorce, but had no idea why she was there. He offered her a seat and sat at his desk across from her.

She blinked her swollen, doe-brown eyes at him and sniffled. "Do you have a tissue?"

"Sorry." Jack handed her his handkerchief. She dabbed gingerly at her eyes, careful not to ruin her makeup. "What happened?"

Lauren complained about how her husband was hardly ever at home. She suspected he was unfaithful, but he'd stormed out of the house when she finally confronted him. "That was when I knew. Oh, Jackie, I never thought in a million years that I would be in this situation."

"Well, gee, Lauren, how long has it been?"

"This whole mess started almost a year and a half ago, but we just today finalized the divorce."

"I'm sorry," Jack said, running his fingers through his hair. "I'm sure you'll find someone else."

Lauren looked up at him. "And who on this earth would be interested in a divorcée? Only questionable characters, I bet."

"I don't know about that."

"I do."

"Lauren," Jack began, leaning in.

"Yes?" She sat up, a slight smile forming on her face.

"Why are you here?"

Lauren twisted his handkerchief into a corkscrew. "Oh,

Jackie. Was I that horrible when we were together?" Her perfectly assembled facade couldn't make up for the weariness in her eyes. She looked at him, desperate for his reassurance.

"You were fine. It wasn't you, Lauren. It was me. All me."

"But why wasn't I enough?"

Jack shook his head. The night of their engagement party, she had only been interested in parading him around. He didn't feel love the way he felt with his wife. Mariella wanted to be a part of Jack's life, cared about what he was thinking and always had that glint in her eyes that showed she wanted him. With Lauren, he was just a prop, used to complete her appearance. "You were just, not for me."

"I would have been a good wife. I wouldn't have left you for weeks on end," Lauren said, growing more confident. "I would have treated you like a king."

"Hold on, now." Jack raised his eyebrows. "Who told you that my wife was gone?"

Lauren shrugged. "Oh, you know how gossip travels around this town."

"Of course," Jack said curtly. "Well, she's not on vacation. Her father is sick."

"Oh. I just thought maybe she was missing home. I mean, you did take her away from everything she knows. And I'm sure it's not easy being married to a foreigner."

"Lauren—"

"Millie did say she wasn't very happy living here."

Jack hesitated. "She said that?"

"Something like that." Lauren shifted in her seat. "I hope you know that I am here for you. Let's face it, it's hard for a man to live on his own. I can always come over and—"

Jack held up his hand. "That's okay, I'm doing just fine."

"Well, then." Lauren folded his handkerchief then gave it back, stood up and straightened out her skirt. "If you need anything, don't hesitate to ask. Toodles!"

"Bye, Lauren." As Jack watched her walk to her car from his street side window, wondering what she was up to, Carl stood in the doorway.

"Hey buddy, what was that about?"

He shrugged. "Beats me. I'll never understand women."

"All I know is if you want your marriage to continue, you better stay away from that woman," Carl said, then ducked back out, closing the door behind him.

Jack glanced at the silver-framed photo on his desk, the one he'd taken at Olivia's christening. Mariella had sewn a frilly pink outfit for Elisa complete with a hat and gloves. His daughter was thrilled at the way she looked and insisted on wearing them in the car. Unfortunately, when they arrived at the studio and she got out of the car, the lace that lined the skirt of her dress tore off.

Although Mariella reassured her that she could fix it, Elisa was inconsolable. By the time they took the photo, her face was crimson red and she was in no mood to smile. Jack's heart ached. Despite his daughter's misery, Mariella had never looked more proud. He wished he knew when they were coming home.

"Jack! Where's Jack?" he heard Ma calling from the kitchen.

"On my way," Jack said under his breath. He took one last look at his family, then left his office to start the day.

Chapter Forty-Four

Mariella stared in disbelief at the woman standing before her. It was almost too much to comprehend. The face, frozen in her memory for years, was suddenly alive. When she finally spoke, her voice came out as a whisper.

"Is it you?"

Tears filled Helena's eyes as she nodded.

"I can't believe it. You're alive!" Mariella's joyful words shattered the early morning quiet.

Helena laughed. "And so are you!"

Taking a step back, Mariella studied her to be sure. Helena's petite frame, twisted from a broken leg that hadn't healed properly, didn't match her chic reddish-brown hair resting just above her shoulders. The jagged scar across her neck from one ear to the other seemed unfathomable. They embraced, neither wanting to let go.

"Helena," Mariella repeated, as if conjuring up ghosts. "Come, sit down with me." They sat on the bench as golden rays of the rising sun peeked through the trees. Mariella tried to form questions, but the words tangled in her mouth. "Where have you... I saw them shoot...Oh, Helena. They killed Mother Superior."

"I know," Helena said quietly.

"You must have been so scared. I watched from our living room window. Saw them take you and the others away. What happened after that? Where were you taken?" Mariella asked in quick succession, then lowered her eyes and whispered, "I thought you were dead."

"I should have died," Helena said, solemnly. "They brought us to the north, a camp near Modena, where we stayed for a few days. The soldiers took the nuns somewhere else. We never saw them again."

When Helena paused, Mariella slipped her hand into hers.

"After three days, they piled us onto the back of another truck. We went further north."

"Oh my," Mariella said. "How did you stay warm?"

"There was a canvas covering the back, but it didn't keep the snow from hitting us sideways. We put the young ones between us older children so they wouldn't freeze. They drove in a convoy of sorts. The Allied bombings must have disabled all of

390

the trains. That made me hopeful. But then I realized they didn't care if we arrived dead or alive."

Mariella was reminded of what the rabbi had said, how Jews didn't matter.

"The first night, the driver slept in the cab while we were forced to sleep in the back with another soldier who kept his gun aimed at us. The two youngest died on the second night." Helena caught her breath, then continued. "We couldn't keep them warm—we tried, but we couldn't. I'll never forget the relief I felt when … when their cries grew weaker and they finally drifted off."

Mariella pulled up the bottom of her skirt and wiped the tears falling from Helena's eyes.

"Do you remember Gabriel, the oldest boy?" Helena asked.

"Yes, of course. I remember for someone so young, his face was full of sadness."

"That's because he had seen his parents gunned down. Sister Gabriella told me. He had to stay strong for the younger children and never spoke of it. But late at night, while everyone slept, his whimpers echoed off the walls throughout the convent."

She thought of Helena hearing the poor boy's pain late at night when her own heartache at losing her parents was sharpest. In an instant, it brought back the anger Mariella felt toward Mama for sending her friend to live with the nuns.

"By the third night," Helena continued, "Gabriel couldn't sleep. The poor thing was in so much pain from the cold. The soldier was also sick and didn't want to be outside either. So, when he'd had enough of Gabriel's whining, he tried pulling him off the truck, but I grabbed hold of him and wouldn't let go."

"Oh Helena, you were so brave."

"I don't know if it was bravery or I was just ready to give up. Gabriel would die either way, but I couldn't let him die alone. So the soldier marched the two of us over to a tree about a hundred feet into the pines. When he put his rifle to the back of Gabriel's head, I held his hand and promised he would see his parents soon. It was over quickly. He didn't even cry. His body went limp, and that was that."

"Poor Gabriel. At least we know he is with his mother and father."

Helena nodded, looking off in the distance as if searching for her own parents. Mariella put an arm around her, but she pulled away, determined to finish her story.

"Once he was dead, the soldier aimed his rifle at me. I held my breath and he pulled the trigger. It clicked, but nothing happened. He did it another time, then over and over, it was maddening. Finally, I prayed for a bullet to end it all, but the gun was jammed."

Mariella looked at Helena's scar. "What did he do?"

"He left."

"He left?"

Helena nodded. "I waited for him to return, but he never did."

"What did you do?"

"I cleared a spot free from snow and, well, ... I put on Gabriel's coat and laid his body on mine. He was still warm and... I guess I fell asleep because when I woke up the sun had risen and the trucks were gone. Gabriel's poor body had become as cold as ice. So I buried him in pine needles. Before I left, I carved his initials into the ground next to him. Just in case..."

As a silent understanding passed between them, they honored Gabriel and the children with their tears.

"How did you survive?" Mariella asked after a while.

"I spent days walking through the woods, eating pine bark, and drinking melted snow. Eventually, I stumbled into a small village. It was shocking how everyone went about their day, as if a war wasn't brewing right under their noses. I hid behind a woodpile and noticed a farmer pull up in a wagon filled with large tin vats."

"Milk?"

"Yes!" Helena's eyes brightened. "It was a sight! I hadn't seen milk for ages. I spied the farmer take his ladle from the side of the cart, fill a small tin container, and walk it up to a house. At

393

that point, I was dizzy from hunger. I certainly was not thinking straight, so I snuck over to his cart while he spoke to the woman inside the home, ripped the top of the vat off, scooped the milk with my hands and poured it into my mouth. When he didn't notice, I scooped another, then another, until I heard him scream." Helena ran her fingers along her neck.

"Did he do that to you?"

"He grabbed me from behind. I was so focused on the milk I didn't even see him. Slit me from ear to ear, then left me on the road to die. I remember thinking, 'Okay, this is how it ends,' like I'd thought many times before. But I wasn't too sad, I felt relief. At some point I blacked out. When I woke up, I was warm, lying by a fire with a heavy quilt on top. I was sure I had arrived in heaven!"

"Where were you?"

"It was the woman in the house who saved me. She thought I might be dead and waited until dark to bring me in. Although there was blood everywhere, the wound turned out to be superficial. She was so kind."

Mariella's heart warmed at the idea of a stranger helping her dear friend. "Did you stay there?"

"Oh, no, no. I couldn't. It would have been too risky if I stayed. The farmer came to deliver milk the following day and asked where my body had gone. I hid in the cupboard, listening.

The woman yelled at him about not wanting a dirty Jew lying dead in front of her home and carried on about having to hire someone to drag me in the back and burn my body. Boy, was she convincing. She got so angry, the man gave her an extra cup of milk for her troubles."

"God was certainly watching over you, my friend."

Helena narrowed her eyes. "And where was he for everyone else?" she asked defiantly.

Mariella was quiet. She knew some things would never make sense.

"I was lucky. It turned out the woman worked with a network of good Samaritans helping to hide Jews. I owe them an enormous debt. When I was well enough to travel, a friend of hers shuttled me away at night. I'm not sure where they brought me because they kept me hidden in cellars and tunnels. Some places were downright scary. But I eventually arrived in Geneva, Switzerland, where I live now."

"Why? Italy is your home. And why did you come back?"

Helena's expression changed from sadness to joy. She leaned in. "I met my husband in Geneva. He's the son of the last family that I stayed with. At first, they were going to send me away again, but we'd fallen in love. Oh, how he fought for me! They couldn't keep us apart. His name is Peter, and he's not so handsome, but I've never met anyone with a bigger heart than my Peter. You would like him too."

"I'm sure I would," Mariella said, beaming happily for her friend. "So, then, why are you in Rome?"

"Peter and I tried for a few years to have children, but it wasn't in the cards for us, so I joined the Red Cross. We're here all week for a convention. I saw you by your building yesterday, but I lost the nerve to say hello."

"Why?"

Helena let out a nervous laugh. "All these years I've worried that something might have happened to your family. Those Germans seemed to know so much, and your parents were so kind taking me in. I've really regretted going to your house that night." She seemed to hold her breath, waiting to hear news of their fate.

"Oh, Helena." Mariella hugged her tightly. "We did what we had to do. But we came out of it alright."

"Thank goodness," she said. "I could have looked your family up, searched any death records, but I don't think I could have forgiven myself if something happened."

"It wouldn't have been your fault. We only did the bare minimum," Mariella admitted. Her mother had been a coward, folding the minute the neighbor below them threatened to turn her in. But then Mariella thought of her daughters and her anger softened.

Helena reached for her hand and smiled. "You did enough."

Chapter Forty-Five

Over the next several days, Mariella met Helena for an espresso at a bar close to the hospital. It was a relief to spend time with her friend, especially after spending hours listening to her father talk nonsense and avoid eye contact. But hearing about what happened to Helena's parents after they were caught squirreled away in an attic broke her heart.

Helena returned to her old apartment in the Jewish ghetto and ran into a neighbor, who had been transported with her parents to a camp in the east. Getting back to their daughter was all they talked about and during transit her father quickly developed a plan to make their escape. The neighbor considered fleeing with them, but decided it was too risky. She was right. Helena's mother was shot just as she made it over the barrier fence. Her father, who trailed behind, got caught up in barbwire at the top of the fence and was left there to die a slow, agonizing death.

Mariella thought about the night Helena's mother pushed Helena out the window when the Germans came for them. Despite breaking her leg, she was free.

"You were inconsolable when you arrived at our house," Mariella reminded her.

"Oh, I don't remember much of that time. I guess I was in shock."

"That's understandable."

"There is one thing…" Helena touched the Jewish star around her neck. "The Shabbat ceremony in your living room. And, of course, when you and I prayed in our windows across from each other after I moved to the convent. You can't imagine how much that helped."

"It was a comfort to me too. The whole ceremony made me feel connected to you."

"You mean, connected to our old life."

"You're right," Mariella agreed, realizing why those moments were so special to her. It was the one thing that they did together before their world turned upside down. She spent many Friday nights at Helena's kitchen table, giggling at the funny words her father sang before they ate. Then, when everything changed and there was no more school, no playing at the Colosseum, nothing to whisper about or books to discover.

When they had been reduced to animals, burning wood in their living room to keep warm or drinking clear soup made from a few leftover chicken bones, celebrating the Sabbath became of symbol of their past lives.

"Tell me, what happened to the nuns? Sister Gabriella came back but she wouldn't tell Mama anything."

Helena's eyes glossed over. "Those sisters were like angels. They huddled around to keep us warm and worked so hard to protect us, but the soldiers didn't like their kindness. They barked at them like dogs. When we got to the camp…" Helena grew quiet.

"We can talk about this later," Mariella said.

"No." Helena shook her head. "I'd rather tell you now, then forget about it. Those animals ripped us from the arms of the sisters and sent them away. We were all crying, especially the little ones."

"Did you ever find out where they went?"

"I wish I knew. There are rumors… many convents were hiding Jewish children. Rounding up the nuns wasn't uncommon."

"And the rumors?"

Helena swallowed hard. "The soldiers had their way with them. Then, they were shot in the head and discarded."

"I hope the world never sees evil like that again," Mariella said.

"Let's hope so."

The year before Hitler sent soldiers into Rome, Mariella remembered her parents talking. Germans occupying Italy was unfathomable. No one believed it could happen. But now she was painfully aware that anything was possible.

Watching a street cleaner push a broom across the road, sweeping up dirt and trash, Helena gave Mariella a weary smile. "Can we talk about happy things? You said your mother had the baby?"

"Oh, yes! A sweet boy named Matteo. He's not little, though. He's my height!"

"Time does fly, doesn't it? How are your sisters?"

Mariella hesitated. "Lia is, well, the same as she was as a child—stubborn and sure of herself. But she's grown into a lovely young lady. And Giada is expecting twins!"

"Twins! Who did she marry?"

"I've never met the man, but Mama says he's lovely. She moved to his village just outside of Naples. When she came to visit, I could tell she was happy."

"And Elisa?" Helena asked, an expectant look on her face. "How is she?"

Having to explain what happened to her sister made the color drain from Mariella's face.

"Mariella?" Helena asked, reaching for her. "What is it?"

"I'm sorry, I forgot."

"Forgot what?"

Mariella looked at Helena, afraid to say the words that she hadn't had to say in years. "Elisa died."

"Oh."

"Not from the war, afterwards, when we finally felt safe..." Mariella's voice trailed off.

"I'm sorry. I remember what a good sister she was to you."

She never had time to be anything else, Mariella thought, the familiar ache crawling into her heart. "I often wondered where God was when she became ill."

"It isn't fair. But your father being ill isn't either." Helena nodded. "Tell me about your Jack."

Mariella was happy to change the subject. She told Helena about the American with the lopsided smile she met while selling postcards after they were liberated. Back then she was only fifteen, but there was something special about him. Helena couldn't believe he returned for her eight years later.

"Do you remember how we used to dream when we were young? Remember went to play underground in the Colosseum?" Helena laughed. "I was always the king and you were the queen and we forced your sisters to be our servants. They would get so angry at us ordering them around!"

"I remember sending them all the way home to bring biscotti back for us. Mama was so mad!"

"How silly we were!"

"Yes, we were," Mariella said wistfully, remembering those lazy afternoons when their imaginations got the best of them.

On Helena's last night in Rome, Mariella invited her to the apartment for dinner. Matteo tried to help Olivia set the table, but she was too stubborn to take his advice. In the end, she set the plates haphazardly, with a fork and knife on top and a napkin puffing out of each glass.

"Tada!" she said, beaming.

Matteo cheered. Over the course of their stay he had become her biggest fan. "You am very good."

When Helena arrived, the knock on the door was much different compared to when she sought refuge so many years ago, but Mama's face was the same. She had been out of sorts the whole day and when their guest arrived, she quickly retreated to the bathroom.

Helena brought dolls, purchased from a posh store on Via Veneto, for the girls. Each was dressed in silk clothing with fancy hats and gloves. They had delicate, porcelain faces painted with intricate detail.

"Grazie signora, che bello!" Elisa replied quickly. Mariella's face lit up, but it took her daughter a moment to realize what she had done. "I speak Italian now!" she bragged to everyone.

"I'm Italian too!" Olivia whined.

Helena stooped to her level and smiled. "Of course you are," she said in Italian. "You understand me?"

Olivia nodded, then skipped to the table.

Mama returned to the kitchen and said a quick hello to Helena, then shooed everyone to the table. She had gone to great lengths to make a magnificent dinner, including a bolognese sauce stewed with wine and chops of veal. But as Mama quietly served the spaghetti, a tear rolled down her cheek.

"What's wrong, Mama?" Lia asked.

Mama set the bowl down and wiped her face with a dish towel. "I'm sorry," she said.

"Sorry about what?"

"I'm sorry," Mama repeated, turning to Helena with glossy eyes. "I'm so sorry."

The polite smile on Helena's face faltered as she tried to make out what Mama was talking about. "It's okay, you've made a beautiful meal. I know it must be difficult with your husband in the hospital. Having guests over is probably not the best thing right now."

"That's not what I'm sorry about." Mama's voice trembled as she glanced over at their front door. "When you arrived on our doorstep that night, I wanted to turn you away."

"Signora." Helena raised her hand to stop Mama from apologizing any further. "It was a hard time for everyone."

Mama firmly shook her head. "No, no. If it were up to me, we wouldn't have let you in. I was so scared for my family that I would have left you on the street without a second thought. The only reason we didn't was because of my husband. But when our downstairs neighbor found out we were hiding you, I was consumed with fear like never before." She paused a moment, and it was clear Mama was choosing her words carefully. "It was me who made the decision to send you away, no one else," she said in a whisper.

The atmosphere in the room shifted as Mama's words hung heavily in the air. Mariella glanced over at her daughters, their innocent faces reminding her how tough the decision must have been for her mother. But at the time Helena was only a few years older than Elisa. The idea of sending a child away when they needed protection was hard to get her mind around. She tried to avoid the glaring fact that if Helena hadn't been sent to the convent, she wouldn't have been rounded up with the children and nuns that terrifying evening.

"I would never blame you for wanting to keep your family safe," Helena said.

Mama tried to smile, but it didn't matter what words Helena had for her. Mariella knew her mother's regret had already been stitched into her soul.

"It's okay, Mama," Mariella said, "you did what you had to do." As she pulled her in for a hug, the feel of Mama's small, frail body caused Mariella to dissolve into her own set of tears. She quickly wiped them away, hoping not to upset her daughters.

Everyone watched Mama sit down, her face still wet from crying. No one spoke until Olivia became bored, popped a strand of spaghetti into her mouth, puckered her lips, and sucked, creating a loud whistle as it disappeared.

"Mama Mia!" Elisa exclaimed, throwing her hands up in the air and everyone laughed, breaking the tension in the room. Even Mama couldn't resist joining in, the corners of her mouth turning upward for the first time that evening. However, Mariella noticed her mother's smile fade halfway through. She wished there was something she could do to ease her mother's pain, but the damage had already been done.

After Helena left, Mariella put her daughters to bed.

"Mama," Elisa said, "why was Nonna crying tonight?"

Mariella busied herself tucking a crisp white sheet around the girls, but she couldn't avoid the question. "Tesoro, it was nothing you should worry about."

"But, but, why was Signora Helena hiding with you? Was there a monster outside? Was it scary?" Olivia asked, gasping dramatically.

"It certainly was," Mariella said without thinking.

Elisa shrieked, then covered her head with the sheet. Olivia followed suit.

"Is it still downstairs?"

"Don't let it get us!"

"Make it go away!"

"Oh, no, girls. You don't have to be afraid. Signora Helena was talking about a long, long time ago," Mariella said. "There's no more monster. I promise."

"Are you sure?" Elisa said through the sheet.

Olivia peeked out with one eye. "Yes, Mama, are you sure?"

"I'm positive," Mariella said, smiling when her daughters finally emerged. She kissed each one on the forehead. "And if there ever was one, I assure you I would do whatever it takes to protect you, my loves."

Chapter Forty-Six

Jack rubbed the back of his neck. It was 2 a.m. The restaurant closed at midnight, but he had taken to staying late, delaying the loneliness of returning to an empty house. That night he lingered in his office until it was morning in Italy, then raced home to call Mariella. Initially, he hadn't planned on calling often. She and the girls were only supposed to be away for a month. But, as one month turned into two, he began weekly phone calls. Despite their efforts, the time difference and their schedules made it hard. It had been over two weeks since they spoke last.

"How are the girls doing?"

"Olivia is charming everyone. All she has to do is smile, and the shop owners give her free gelato."

"Ha! That's my girl."

"And Elisa, she speaks Italian now. Full sentences, too."

"Full sentences? Boy, I wish I was there. I miss you all so much." Jack knew his longing was obvious, but it was hard to conceal.

"Yes, amore. I-I'm sorry. I miss you too. We all do. But I need to be here." Mariella's voice trembled, making him feel awful.

"I understand. You don't have to explain. I do worry though." Jack hesitated, but the practicalities had to be addressed. "It's September. The girls are missing school."

Mariella took a deep breath, making him wonder if she was hiding something. "Yes, I know, but ... I just can't leave yet. You understand, no?"

Jack considered putting his foot down and telling her no, but she had sacrificed enough to be with him. If she needed to stay longer, they would figure it out. "Of course I do. How's Mama?"

"She is as well as she can be. The girls have been a wonderful distraction for her."

"I bet." Just the thought of them lifted Jack's spirits. He missed their little dances, their giggles when he pulled funny faces, or the snuggles they gave him when he read a bedtime story. "Make sure to give them a big hug and kiss from their papa. And tell them I love them. And miss them. Very much."

"I will."

"And, of course, tell Mama and the rest of the family I'm sending a good ole American hug!"

"Okay, amore."

"I love you, sweetheart."

"I love you too."

Jack hung up and poured himself a glass of bourbon. The amber liquid reflected light from the moon filtering through his living room window. He quickly threw it back, then filled the glass again. His situation felt impossible. It wasn't just missing his family; business had been downright brutal. Getting people into the restaurant was like pulling teeth. Jack poured one more bourbon to help him sleep then went to bed.

"Fire officials have opened an investigation into the cause of the blaze that lit up the Asbury Park boardwalk. It occurred this past August, resulting in the destruction of Sunset Pavilion along with twelve storefronts, and has cost the city over one million dollars and five hundred and fifty feet of boardwalk," the morning news blared from the clock radio sitting on Jack's night table.

He hit the button and turned it off. The fire had been on everyone's lips since it happened and he was sick of hearing about it. Word on the street was that the owner of one of the businesses involved had started it, just another sign of desperation as tourists bypassed the city for beach towns further down the parkway.

He shuffled to the bathroom, plopped two tablets of Alka-Seltzer in a glass of water, and drank it in one gulp. Jack wasn't used to drinking bourbon, and his head felt like someone was squeezing it. He looked at his bed, yearning to crawl back in, but there was no time. Instead, he dressed for work and headed out to pick up his father.

Jack and Pop drove down Route 35 in silence until they reached the Belmar basin. His father led the way out onto the pier and approached a burly fisherman.

"Hello, Domenico," the man said in a rough voice. Although he was familiar, Jack had never learned his name. Pop advised him not to, saying it was much easier to make a deal that way.

"What you got?" Pop asked. He was all business when bargaining for the best catch of the day. At over six feet tall, he could be intimidating, but more importantly, he excelled in the art of negotiation.

The man uncovered a plastic bucket brimming with flounder.

"How much for all?" Pop asked casually.

The fisherman stroked his graying beard. "I'll take fifty dollars."

"Fifty?" Pop picked a small fish from the bucket and held it in the air. "What am I supposed to do with this?"

"Oh, c'mon, Domenico. Most are nice sized."

Pop shrugged then dropped the fish back in the bucket. He looked past the man's shoulder, as if searching the harbor for another boat returning with a better haul.

The man took his cap off and wiped his brow. Jack couldn't help but feel bad about his father's cold demeanor toward him. Although they weren't friends, Pop had done business with him several times before. And fifty dollars was a fair price during normal times. But these weren't normal times.

"Look," the man said, waving his cap, "gimme forty-five, and I'll be happy."

Pop's expression hardened. He looked back down at the bucket, unimpressed, but remained silent. The fisherman shifted on his feet, nervously looking around the empty parking lot adjacent to the pier.

"What you thinking, Giacomo?" Pop asked.

Normally, Jack enjoyed playing a character in his father's negotiations. "I'd say that's fair."

"Fair?" Pop said with a chuckle. "You look again, son."

Jack sighed. He looked down into the barrel and watched the fish on top sucking air. "I think maybe, uh, thirty-five?"

"Thirty-five, huh?" Pop stroked his chin.

They stood on the pier without saying a word for a few

drawn-out seconds. Pop had taught him that the first person to speak would lose. Jack shoved his hands deep in his pockets, waiting for the silence to break.

Finally, the fisherman threw up his hands. "I'll do forty and no lower."

Pop took a beat, then said, "Thirty-eight and we make deal."

The man clenched his jaw as he watched Jack and his father walk off with the barrel of fish. When they got back into the car, Pop handed Jack the receipt for his accounting.

"Gee, Pop, you got a good deal," Jack said on the ride home.

"What good deal?" Pop's face screwed up with worry. "We be lucky to sell these."

That summer had been brutal for the restaurant. In the past, their dining room had filled up quickly on weekends and stayed that way until closing. Even the summer before was better. But now, they were cutting back on staff due to the lack of customers.

"I'm trying to get creative with my promotions, Pop. Tonight should be okay. We have dinner and tickets to *Laurence of Arabia* at the Strand. I'll put the fish, Mom's lasagna, and maybe pizza on the menu. I think the margins are good."

"Va bene, Giacomo. You know what you doing."

Jack turned on the radio, jiggling the knob around for a station, but only got static. He turned it off. "I talked with Mariella this morning."

"Oh?" Pop smiled. "How is her father?"

"Not great. He doesn't recognize anyone anymore. Not even her mother. It's a real shame. He was such a stand-up guy. You would have liked him."

"Certo. This man is Italiano, no?"

Jack laughed. "He woulda liked you too, Pop."

"When you think Mariella and the girls come home?"

"Well, that's still up in the air. Mariella doesn't want to leave her father just yet. I understand. Her family needs her."

"Ma, Giacomo, you need you family, too."

Jack contemplated his father's words. Sure he needed his wife, but not because she took care of him. Jack was managing fine by himself. Every so often, Louise checked in, offering to iron his shirts or cook a meal. Charles invited him over for cocktails on his nights off too. It was nice to have someone to talk to. Jack had taken for granted how much he relied on Mariella's input. She would often stay up until the wee hours of the morning when he returned home from work, to discuss their days. He would bounce off new campaign ideas or vent about rowdy bar patrons. He yearned to hear about her day too and the amusing anecdotes of their daughters. Like Elisa, who always breezed through her homework and then complained of boredom, or Olivia, who went on about a boy named Owl from her class, but when Mariella and Jack tried to figure out who he was, they discovered the boy's real name was Al. They both had a good laugh that night. Although he was managing fine, Jack missed the everyday joys of his family.

Chapter Forty-Seven

A phone rang in the distance, then a voice speaking low and somewhat muffled disappeared when Jack opened his eyes the next morning. He lay in bed, listening to the birds chirping outside. Mariella had insisted he hang the bird feeder by the bedroom window so she could wake to their music. Soon, the clock downstairs in the kitchen chimed. Jack reluctantly dangled his feet off the bed, slipped into his slippers, and shuffled to the bathroom.

"Yoo-hoo! Jack?" A woman's voice, all too familiar, traveled up the stairs.

He stiffened. "Lauren?"

"Of course it's me, silly."

He listened to the clacking of her heels as she moved around the house, from the bottom of the stairs to the kitchen and back again. Thankfully, she didn't venture up.

"Lauren," Jack said, popping his head out of the bathroom, "how'd you get in?"

"Everyone leaves an extra key hidden under the doormat! Now, hurry down. I've got breakfast for you. I stopped at Friedman's bakery on the way over. Oh! I also bought some fresh eggs from the Carlton farm. Come on down and I'll cook 'em right up."

Jack splashed water on his face, wondering if he was dreaming. The last time he'd spoken with her, she was in tears about not having anyone to love. He knew he hadn't led her on, so why was she in his house?

"Jack?" Lauren sang from the bottom of the stairs. "Are you coming down?"

He gazed at his reflection in the bathroom mirror, wincing at his disheveled appearance. Dark circles had formed beneath his eyes as a result of lack of sleep, his hair was sticking up in odd places, and stubble lined his jaw.

"Just give me a moment," he called back. He took his razor out, cleaned up his face, combed his hair into place, then brushed his teeth. It wasn't to impress Lauren; he didn't want her to think he was falling apart without his wife at home.

After dressing, he went down to the kitchen and found Lauren ready for a garden party. She wore a lavender cap-sleeved shirt with embroidered daisies decorating the Peter Pan neckline and a pair of pink capri pants. Her hair was perfectly styled and sprayed to keep from collapsing. She stood next to a beautifully set table offering sliced bagels, a rectangle of cream cheese, and orange slivers of lox lined up on a silver serving dish he and Mariella had received for their wedding. A vase with a bouquet of yellow roses sat in the center. He was sure they were from the bush by their driveway that he'd surprised Mariella with one Valentine's Day. On top of everything, the dirty whiskey tumbler he'd left in the sink the night before was washed and put away.

"Oh, you poor man!" Lauren pulled out a chair. "You look like you haven't eaten a proper meal in ages!"

As Jack sat down, she got busy toasting a bagel for him. "Lauren, my family owns a restaurant. I am not malnourished."

Lauren's cheery expression quickly disappeared. "I'm sorry, Jack, I just... I..." She began to sob, although it was more sniffling than anything else. "Oh boy, I can't do anything right, can I?" she said, sitting down next to him.

"No, Lauren, it's fine. I'm just surprised to find you here," Jack said, trying to keep her from falling apart in his kitchen. "Okay, I'll admit it, I am exhausted."

"That's why I'm here, silly!" Lauren's mood brightened as she jumped up and fished his bagel out of the toaster, then spread a healthy amount of cream cheese on one side and layered lox on the other. "Let's face it, I don't have much else to do. Since the

417

divorce, I've moved back home, and Mother and Father are far busier than I am!" She placed the bagel in front of him. "Here, I hope you like it."

"Mm-hmm," Jack mumbled, devouring the sandwich.

After breakfast, he convinced Lauren to leave. But not before allowing her to return later in the week with one of her famous casseroles. He agreed, not because he wanted it, he just felt bad for her.

"Don't worry, Jack. I'll keep you fed!" she said, walking out the door.

Jack scratched his chin, where the skin was irritated from shaving without Barbasol cream. "I'm sure my wife will be back in a few weeks."

"Well, until then!"

"Oh, Lauren, before I forget—"

She quickly turned back. "Yes, Jack?"

"Did the phone ring? I could have sworn I heard it ring this morning when I woke up."

"Nope," she replied without a beat. "It was probably just a dream."

Watching her walk away, Jack glanced around the neighborhood, wondering if anyone saw her come in. With Mariella gone, gossip about an affair could run rampant. But maybe that was what Lauren wanted. He'd be more direct the next time he saw her.

Chapter Forty-Eight

Mariella grew pale as she hung up the phone, then checked the time, counting back six hours. It was morning in Wanamassa Gardens. What on earth was Lauren doing in her house? She mulled over the conversation they'd had.

"No, he's still asleep. Can I take a message?" Lauren had asked, even though Mariella was sure she knew who she was speaking to.

"This is his wife," she said, still in shock.

"Oh, hello. It's Lauren, remember me? From the luncheon?"

"Uh-huh." Mariella couldn't understand why she sounded so comfortable.

"Jack told me you're in Italy, so I figured someone needed to do the heavy lifting around here. Don't you worry about him, though. Everything is fine. Take all the time you need!"

He's doing just fine without me, Mariella thought, *just fine with Lauren around.* Ever since Jack returned to her, she had never considered him untrue. She'd always felt his love, even when they were apart. Now, her world in Italy was crumbling, and her life in America was uncertain. She waited by the telephone, but Jack didn't call back. Several times, she picked up the receiver to be sure lines hadn't crossed as they often did in Italy. But fearing what she would discover, Mariella didn't dare call back.

"What's wrong, Mama?" Elisa asked that evening when it was time for bed.

"Nothing, Tesoro."

Olivia ran into the bedroom, singing and dancing around. "Traveling circus, traveling circus! La di da di da!!!"

"You don't even know the words," Elisa said, slipping her nightgown over her head.

"Yes I do." Olivia twirled in circles and continued to sing. "Traveling circus! Traveling circus! So many aminals!"

Elisa bowled over in laughter. "It's animals you dum dum!"

"Mama!" Olivia cried, still twirling.

"Okay, girls, it's time for bed."

"Off she ran to la da da!" Olivia sang. "And never came back again!"

Mariella sighed, pushing a strand of hair behind her ear. "Come on, Olivia, let's get to bed."

"Ta da, da da, di daaaaaaa!"

Losing her patience, Mariella grabbed her by the arm. "Stop it. Stop it now."

Olivia's mouth fell open. Then, moving around the room like a drunk, she began to cry. "Mamaaaaaaa!"

Mariella took a deep breath. "I'm sorry, Stellina."

"But . . . but you used your meanie voice!"

"You are right," she said, picking up her daughter. "Mama was not being nice using her mean voice. Now, let's get under the covers."

Elisa slid into bed without hesitation.

"Mama?" Olivia said, holding her head. "Mama, I don't feel so good."

"Of course, you do not." Mariella laid her down next to her sister. "With all of that spinning, your brains have been scrambled."

"Scrambled?" Olivia said. "Like eggs? I don't want eggs on my brain."

Mariella pulled the sheet up to their chins. "Do not worry, it will go back to normal in a few minutes. Now, try and get some sleep."

Olivia popped her thumb in her mouth and nodded.

"Buona notte, Tesoro," Mariella said, kissing Elisa. "E Stellina." She kissed Olivia goodnight, then slid into her own bed with a book, hoping to keep her mind off what was happening at home, but she couldn't concentrate. As soon as the girls fell asleep, Mariella slipped out of the encasement window and crawled onto the roof.

An early fall breeze blew her nightgown around. She gathered it at her ankles and leaned back on the terracotta tiles. Looking out at the Roman skyline, Mariella realized it had been nine years since she left Rome. Nine more years separated Italy from the war. Nine additional years for Italians to recover. Suddenly, she felt like a coward who'd run off when times got tough. *How could I have been so selfish?*

A window across from her illuminated, and an elderly man wandered into view. He looked tired as he hunched over the sink, filling a glass with water. Then, his wife, a petite woman with long, silver hair, shuffled in and gently coaxed him back to bed.

Mariella thought about her mother, who had counted on growing old with Papa like the woman in the window. It should have been that way. Mama knew how to care for the man she married, but a stranger who didn't trust her was another thing altogether.

Her mind wandered to Lauren answering *her* phone at Wanamassa Gardens as if she belonged there. That morning, Mariella decided to bury it in the back of her mind. Treated it like an errand she would run tomorrow or the next day. But the facts were evident. She had left home, and someone had taken her place. *Where is my place?* she wondered, crawling back into her bed.

Mariella watched her daughters sleep, curled up into each other. Before they arrived in Italy, the idea they had become too American and wouldn't like her home country worried her. It was bad enough when Mariella saw the women at school pick-up laughing at her accent. But having her own children tease her was unbearable.

"It's not 'little bug,' Mama! It's a litter bug. Litt-ER bug!" Elisa scolded one afternoon.

When she put them to bed at nighttime, she would repeat the pronunciation hoping it would stick. But there was always another oddly pronounced word or a reference that didn't make sense.

Sleepovers were another American thing Mariella would never get used to. Why any parent would let their child sleep at a house that was not their own was a mystery to her. When Elisa's friend's mother pushed for it, Mariella tried to explain her uneasiness. Then, Elisa slyly asked her father, and without a beat, he agreed. Jack said it was a fun thing for children to do, but Mariella was furious. It wasn't that she felt her daughter would be in danger, but the more she gave in to "American tradition," the more she disappeared.

Now that her girls had spent time in Italy, that fear had

dissipated. They'd grown accustomed to late-night dinners and afternoon naps. Hearing her language fall off their tongues was something she thought she could only dream of. Watching them kissing each cheek to greet everyone was too. Or sitting by a leg of prosciutto, waiting for a slice. Or helping out with the daily shopping at the market. Or playing in the Colosseum like she had at their age. It was all reality now, and suddenly she wondered if she could ever return to America.

Chapter Forty-Nine

Jack drove past Steinbach's department store on Corlies Avenue late in the afternoon. Normally, this part of town hummed with shoppers, but now only a few people wandered about. They were having a heat wave and the new shopping center on Route 35 offered fifty stores with state-of-the-art air conditioning. Although the signs outside Steinbach's advertised "Cool Deals for Hot Days," it wasn't enough to draw in the crowds.

Arriving at the restaurant, Jack expected to see his pop waiting in front. Instead, the sidewalk was empty. He went inside and found Carl setting up the bar.

"What's going on?"

"Nothing. What's going on with you?"

"Pop's not outside. Where is he?" Jack and his father had been trying to find a new bakery to supply bread at a better price.

They had three appointments set up.

"He called earlier. Didn't think it was worth going today."

"Not going? But it's Friday," Jack said, running his fingers through his hair.

"Look around, Jackie boy." Carl gestured to the empty tables. "The place is dead. Besides, we've got plenty of leftover bread in the freezer we can pull out for the few customers we'll get tonight."

Back in his office, Jack pored over the ledger. Pop was right. Since business was on a steady descent, they needed to make do. He picked up the phone to cancel the appointments, and heard a jiggling sound coming from his office door. Jack looked over to see the mail slot open and a letter dropped inside. It was from Italy.

Amore,

How are you? We have had a miracle here! I found Helena! She was in Rome for a conference with the Red Cross. All these years, I was certain she had died! It has been wonderful to visit with her. Our girls love her already!

But there is no good news for everyone. Mama worries all the time. She never complains, but I see it on her face. Papa gets a little worse each day. Sometimes, he is angry that I am there and I have to leave. Most times, he sees me as a nurse and is okay. One day, though, he looked at me, and I could see his eyes change. It was small, but something made me believe me he was still there. That is why I cannot leave him. I know the girls must return to school, so if we stay to September, I will sign them up here. They speak Italian so well, it should be fine, and they can make some friends.

I am sorry, amore. I wish I could tell you when we will be home, but I do not know. My parents cared for me as a child, and I cannot sit back and watch them struggle alone.

All of my love,

Mariella

Jack examined the postmark. It was dated back in August. Mariella had already told him all about finding Helena in the park. But she never mentioned anything about getting the girls enrolled in school. He worried she was slipping away.

Bringing the envelope close to his face, Jack inhaled. The fresh scent of citrus, roses, and sandalwood brought him closer to Mariella. She had promised to spray her envelopes with her favorite perfume, one she could only get in Italy, a reminder of the day he'd returned for her and held her close. Everything lately

428

reminded Jack of her. Even the things he was missing, like the sound of Italian conversation coming through static on their portable radio as she cooked, the rich aroma of sauce, or the fresh vegetables she grew in her tiny garden and tossed in pasta or a salad. Without her, the garden had weeds and brown stalks of whatever she had started to grow. Jack knew he should have kept up with the watering, but he was distracted and then it was too late.

At the bottom of the envelope, he spotted one more letter.

Dear Papa,

I miss you, my sweet Papa! Did Mama tell you I speak Italian now? She says I speak fluent. I make my Zio Matteo laugh! He is a good football player. Did you know they call soccer football here? Isn't that funny? I am getting good at it, too. Maybe I can play in school when I come back to America.

a hug, a kiss and a smile to my favorite Papa.

Love,

Elisa

Then, further down, a few more sentences were carefully printed. Some letters were large while others were much smaller and half of one fell off the page.

Dear Papa,

I miss you and love you and want to hug and kiss you for ever and ever!

Love,

Olivia

The letters were bittersweet. Jack knew months were like years when it came to children and his girls were growing fast. A knot of sadness and uncertainty formed in his chest. For the first time since Mariella left America, he worried she would not come back.

Chapter Fifty

"But I don't want to go to school." Elisa's face screwed up with worry. "I don't know any of the kids here. Besides, I miss my friends back home."

"Tesoro," Mariella said, "it would just be for now, while we are here."

"I wanna go!" Olivia said, enthusiastically. She had been excited at the prospect of going to school, mostly because of the royal-blue smock that was part of their uniform. "I look like an artist!" she said when she tried it on. Holding her hand in the air as if it held a paintbrush, Olivia did a ballet. "I look like an artist, like Papa!"

Mariella's stomach ached when she thought of Jack. She had spoken to him a little over a week ago, and wanted to ask about Lauren, but with her father growing weaker, she couldn't bear more heartbreak. Still, Jack didn't seem different. If anything, he sounded sad and went on about missing her and the girls.

"Oh dear, it's getting late," Mariella said, slipping on her shoes. "Nonna will come home as soon as I get to the hospital and if you need anything, your aunt and uncle are doing their homework in the kitchen. But please don't bother them unless it's important."

"Ciao, Mama!" Olivia said.

"Ciao, Stellina." Mariella gave Olivia a kiss, then went to Elisa, who sat in the window gazing out somberly. "We can talk about this later, okay, Tesoro?"

Elisa shrugged. Mariella knew her daughter was upset, but she was running late. She kissed the top of her head and left.

Lately, Papa slept most of the time Mariella visited. It didn't make a difference, though. During the scant moments he was awake, he lived in the vast recesses of his mind. Sometimes, she sat by his bedside for hours without him acknowledging her. Other times, he outright avoided her, shifting over to the far side of his bed or asking the nurse to seat him at the window. It broke her when he recoiled at her touch. Entering his world where she was no longer his daughter, Mariella felt like an impostor.

She had spent long, drawn-out days and lonely nights in the hospital mourning her father. His face, which had once belonged to a powerful man who protected his family at all costs, was now that of a ghost. Large, deep wrinkles around his eyes, pasty skin stained with age, and a grayish, coarse beard robbed him of any familiarity. Mariella tried to keep him neatly groomed, but without his trust, it was impossible. An odor of urine, stale breath, and moldy coffee lingered in the air. He shuddered every now and then, as if lost in some odd dream.

She hated watching her father exist this way, but recently Mama's visits had become shorter. She insisted Matteo and Lia needed her more at home so Mariella took her mother's place. Although it was painful to be in the room while her father ignored her, she couldn't imagine what it was like for Mama to watch the man she loved all her life reduced to nothing.

Early one morning, Papa woke up and looked over at Mariella. She gave him a smile, but he averted his eyes as usual.

Fighting the urge to tell him she loved him, Mariella asked, "Do you need anything, signore?"

"What?" Papa inspected her. "Who are you?"

Mariella swallowed hard. "I'm your nurse. Do you remember?"

"No, no, no." He sat up, frantically shaking his head. "You're lying. You're not my nurse."

"It's okay, signore."

"No! No, it is not okay! Why are you here?"

"I told you, I am your nurse." Watching him grow more agitated, Mariella wasn't sure what to do. But suddenly, as if someone had changed the channel, he became eerily calm.

"Tesoro, you're supposed to be in America," he said.

"America?" Mariella whispered, unsure she'd heard right.

Papa nodded, a familiar twinkle brightening his eyes. He reached for her hand. "Tesoro, why are you here?"

"Papa?" Mariella held onto his hand with two of hers. "You recognize me? You know who I am?"

Tears began rolling down his cheek as he nodded again.

"Oh, Papa, I'm here to be with you. The girls are here too. We've been here all summer."

A slight smile formed on his face, but he struggled with his words. She curled up in his arms.

"I'm not leaving again. I won't ever leave you, Papa. Never again. As long as you need me, I'll be here. We'll get through this. I promise. You'll get better, you'll see. I'm here now to take care of you."

When he didn't respond, Mariella pulled back, studying his expression carefully. The familiar glimmer was fading fast. "Papa? Papa? Where did you go?" She grabbed his shirt and shook him.

He shoved her away, his chest heaving with each breath. "Get out of here!" he growled, spitting out his words. His thick hands clenched into tight fists. "You don't belong in this place."

The anger in his voice caused all the emotions Mariella had tried to quiet for months to come pouring out. She sobbed as she spoke about his granddaughters—how much they talked about him, though they'd never even met. Tears streamed down her face when she confessed the guilt she carried for leaving Italy to be with Jack. She considered returning to America and explained to her father that all he needed to do was ask, and she would stay with him forever. Papa's face contorted trying to understand her, but it wasn't long before he pushed her away again.

"Get out of here. I don't know who you are. Get out! Go home. You don't belong here." His voice cracked, and Mariella realized that deep down inside, past his twisted brain, his heart was still the same. He knew exactly what he was doing. She watched his eyes glaze over, and he slowly retreated into another world.

While every fiber of her wanted to stay and fight, it was clear he wanted her to leave. She gathered her things and rose. As she reached the door, he finally quieted down.

"Goodbye, Papa," she said, her voice trembling. "I won't come again. I promise. I'll leave you alone. But I hope you'll always know how much I love you."

She waited for a response, but he didn't say a word.

Olivia slept sprawled across Mariella's lap as they flew over Gander, Nova Scotia. One of her braids had come undone, the chocolate brownie dessert she'd eaten a few hours earlier was still smudged on her cheek, and a shoe had gone missing. At that point, Mariella didn't care. Their journey had been exhausting, not helped by an unplanned landing due to mechanical issues. They had to deboard in England and wait almost five hours in the terminal for the problem to be resolved.

For their last leg, they flew over a series of little islands, and the vast darkness of the Atlantic gave way to clusters of lights. Mariella wondered what life was like in the villages below. Were families sitting together at dinner tables sharing stories of their day? Could someone be getting ready for work? Or returning from an evening shift? Or dying? Anything was possible.

Leaving Rome had proved much more challenging than the first time. Mama didn't plead with her to stay. She understood it was time for Mariella to return and make her family whole again. Matteo and Lia said they would miss her, but also liked the idea of coming to America when they were older. Lia even discussed moving to New York City to work at the UN after finishing her studies. Mariella could see her there, too. Fearless and determined, Lia would make a great representative.

No one beckoned her to stay, but her father had done enough to convince her to leave. Although trapped in his own mental prison, for a moment, he'd broken free to demand she go home. Papa had always fought for Mariella to claim her happiness, and he had done it again one last time. She knew he felt her love. But he was right; it was time.

Over the last several months, Papa's health had steadily worsened, proving his time on Earth was growing short. Mariella made peace with that.

Chapter Fifty-One

"Papa! Papa!!"

Elisa was the first to eye her father. He stood outside customs, craning his neck in search of his family. Before Mariella could grab her, she took off running.

"Papa!" Olivia shrieked, following her sister past the customs officer and out of the secure area.

"Hello, darlings!" Jack exclaimed, his voice softening. He scooped each girl up and hugged them tight.

Mariella pushed her hair behind her ears when she caught up with them. After such a grueling trip, she worried she must look ghastly. She said hello, gave him a quick kiss, then attended to their luggage.

"Let me get these monkeys off me and help you," Jack joked, tickling Elisa into hysterics.

"My turn, Papa! Tickle me! Tickle me!" Olivia cried, pulling

438

on his collar.

"It's okay, Jack." Mariella pushed the luggage cart past him. "I can manage."

Jack led them to the car, settled the girls into the back seat, and helped Mariella put the suitcases in the trunk. He opened the passenger side door but before she got in, he pulled her close.

"Boy, have I missed you," he said, nuzzling his face into her neck.

Mariella pulled back and searched his eyes for any hints that he had been unfaithful. Instead, she found the same Jack she'd met while selling postcards at the Colosseum. When he kissed her, it was filled with passion and possibility all wrapped together. Exactly the same as when he came back for her. And in his arms, she got the Jack that she'd left, the one who loved her, accent and all. The Jack who was truthful to a fault.

"I'm so happy you're back," he whispered.

It was 4:30 a.m. when they finally arrived in Wanamassa Gardens. The sight of their cheery yellow house was bittersweet. Mariella realized two things at once: that she really had missed her little piece of America, and that her father would never see it.

Jack carried Elisa up the stairs, and Mariella followed, holding Olivia in her arms. They tucked them into bed and pulled down the shades. When they left the room, Jack stopped in the doorway.

"Would you look at that?" he whispered, watching his daughters fast asleep. "Gee, it's good to have my girls back." He gently closed their door, then turned to Mariella. "How about you, sweetheart? Are you happy to be home?"

"I will be when I get some sleep," she said, trying to avoid his gaze as she walked to their bedroom.

Jack followed, slipping his arms around her waist from behind. "I can't tell you how much I missed you," he breathed into her ear.

Mariella fought the urge to give in until they had a chance to speak about what happened while she was gone, but the warmth of his body was hard to ignore. She turned to him and searched his eyes. "Oh, Jack. What was she doing here?"

"Who?"

"Lauren," Mariella said, the woman's name leaving a bad taste in her mouth. "I called one morning and she answered."

"You called?"

Mariella nodded.

"That was—?"

"Yes. How could you?"

"Oh, honey, it's not what you think. I swear." Jack shook his head as he paced the room. "I don't know why she came by. It was a surprise to me too. But…see, she's been divorced for a while and I guess…"

"What happened?"

"Nothing," he said quickly, turning to her. "I swear, she found our key under the mat, the one for emergencies, and let herself in. Believe me, I was shocked to see her in our kitchen cooking eggs and toasting bagels."

Jack's face screwed up and Mariella could see he was hurting. Not only from her mistrust; she could tell her absence had taken a toll on him.

He sat down on the edge of the bed. "I don't even know how I could have ever been with someone like that. She's pushy and superficial and she's not interesting or clever or—" He looked up at her and swallowed hard. "You. She's not you. She'll never be you."

"Oh, Jack." Mariella stood in front of him, wiping the tears forming his eyes. "I'm sorry I was gone so long. Staying was the only way I knew I had done enough. I know you missed us. And I never wanted to keep the girls from you. I love you more than you can know."

"And I love you more than that."

In those early morning hours as the sun rose, Jack quietly made love to Mariella with a passion that proved another woman could never capture his heart. An ordinary man might have ventured elsewhere, but she was certain Jack wouldn't. All he ever wanted was to love her.

At noon, when everyone woke, Jack cooked a batch of pancakes for his daughters. To their delight, he made smiley faces using chocolate chips and topped them off with a dollop of Cool Whip.

"Grazie, Papa," Olivia said, then giggled. "That means thank you!" She spooned a heaping mound of cream into her mouth.

"You're welcome, sweet pea."

The sound of thunder rumbled in the distance, the sky darkening quickly.

"Looks like it will be an inside day today, girls," Mariella said. She closed the kitchen window, leaving an inch open for some air.

"That's okay, Mama. I've got to get started on my pictures for Zio Matteo," Elisa chatted happily.

"Pictures?"

"Yes, Papa. Matteo wanted me to make him a picture of our house, then one of the backyard because he doesn't have one. Oh! Maybe I'll draw one of our school. He wants to see what America is like."

"Ah." Jack kissed the top of her head. "Well, it's best to get right on it." He turned to Mariella, snaking his arm around her. "I'm sorry I have to run, but I promise to be home for dinner. Are you going to be okay today? You must be tired."

"I'll be fine, amore," she said.

Outside, sheets of falling rain made the house feel cozier than Mariella remembered. Once Jack left, she brought out paper, crayons, and colored pencils for her daughters. They drew elaborate sketches of houses, yellow school buses, traffic lights, and the milkman. Olivia ran to look at the garden from the back door, then back to the table to draw. Although it was overgrown with weeds and little else, she drew purple eggplants, oversized ruby-red tomatoes, and a single orange pumpkin with a jack-o'-lantern face.

"That's because the poor Italian children don't have Halloween there," she told her mother sadly.

Afterward, they went to the living room and read books until the girls fell asleep, jet lag catching up to them once more. Mariella covered each one with a sheet and was about to start her housework when there was a knock at the door. Since Louise had just left for England and they wouldn't be seeing Jack's family until Sunday dinner, Mariella wondered who it could be. She opened the door and was met with the top of a pink umbrella and a pair of kitten heels underneath.

"I swear, Jack, this weather is the pits! Hurry up and open the screen door so I can get out of this mess. Jack?" When Lauren peeked out from under her umbrella, the color drained from her face. "Oh. You're back."

443

Reminding herself *she* was the one who Jack loved, Mariella felt emboldened. "Hello, Lauren," she said, surprised at how calm she sounded.

Lauren stood in a puddle crouched underneath her umbrella looking small. "I, uh, I thought—"

"You thought I was out of the way, did you? Well, I am back." Mariella teased a warm smile, but it didn't stay on her face long.

"I see," Lauren said, her voice hardening. "Well, I was just bringing a casserole by for Jack. I mean, you've been gone for months, and someone had to look after him. We don't want Jack to starve, now, do we?" She mustered her own phony smile.

"Of course not," Mariella said. Leaning against the doorframe, she gazed down at the dish in Lauren's arms and laughed. "But we also want him to eat well, now, do we not?"

"Jack happens to like my tuna casserole," Lauren said with a huff. "I delivered one just last week."

"Is that what I spotted in the trash?" Mariella leaned in, then narrowed her eyes. "Now, you listen to me, Lauren. Jack is my husband, not yours. I know the games you are playing, trying to convince him that I might not return. But I am back, here, in *our* home. And he only has eyes for one woman. Me. So, take your sad-looking tuna casserole back where you came from. I do not want to see you on my doorstep again."

Lauren's eyes flickered. After a moment's hesitation, she retreated down the stairs and gingerly walked across the lawn, careful not to sink into the grass with one of her heels. Just before she got to the sidewalk, she stumbled over a root from the elm tree but quickly regained her composure. She passed the metal garbage can sitting at the edge of the road, then turned back and dumped the casserole in, dish and all. Once she reached her car, Lauren closed her umbrella and threw it in. The rain had soaked her perfectly coiffed hair, causing it to droop around her face. She paused a moment, looking back at the house.

Mariella gave her a cheery wave goodbye, then firmly shut the door on Lauren forever.

Chapter Fifty-Two

"Are you ready, sweetheart?" Jack called upstairs.

"Just a moment. Elisa? Are you dressed?"

"Yes, Mama. But Olivia is being stupid."

"I am not!"

"Then why aren't you dressed, dummy?"

"Stop calling me dummy!!! I'm not a dummy. You are!"

"Olivia! Get dressed. Now."

"But Mama."

"Now!"

"Okay."

A few moments later, they went down to the living room and found Jack, eyes misty with pride. "Look at my beautiful girls."

Mariella wore a dark blue suit with a matching pencil skirt, white blouse, and a brooch of an American flag on her lapel. She had wanted to make something special for the girls, but at ten and eight years old, they refused to wear matching outfits. Elisa looked sweet with a long, flowery skirt and white blouse, while Olivia stayed true to her tomboyish self in bell-bottom jeans and a T-shirt with an American eagle on it.

"I'm more nervous than I thought," Mariella said, checking her complexion in the mirror.

Above the living room couch, she glimpsed the large painting of the Colosseum that hung next to it. Although oversized for the space, the sight of it made Mariella smile every time.

She traced her lips in red lipstick, then took a deep breath. "Okay, I'm ready."

Heavy, dark clouds hung in the distance as Jack pulled up to the Municipal Courthouse. He quickly escorted Mariella and the girls to the front before parking the car, then joined them outside the courtroom.

Mariella looked tentatively at the crowd inside. "I guess all of these people are ahead of us. Well, that's okay. I need to rehearse my oath some more."

"Mama, you've practiced it for hours. You know it by heart! Don't worry, you'll do great," Elisa said, patting her mother's shoulder.

That morning, a call from Italy had punctuated the

importance of the day. Mama sobbed into the phone talking about how proud she was that her daughter would become an American. She also reminded her that Papa would have been proud, too. After another excruciating year in the hospital, he had passed away peacefully. And while Mariella mourned his absence, her father's exit was comforting. He was no longer suffering.

Mama wasn't the only one who had rejoiced on the phone; Matteo and Lia chimed in with their congratulations as well. Giada had called the night before, joining Salvatore and their twins, Andrea and Tomasso, in a hearty congratulations.

A lanky, young clerk welcomed Mariella, Jack, and their daughters, plus two more families into the courtroom twenty minutes later. It had a regal atmosphere, with dark wood paneling, a few large, brass seals hanging on one wall, and a raised wooden platform similar to an altar in the center where the judge sat in his black robe.

"Mrs. Valentino? You're first. Step up to the witness box, please," he instructed.

Mariella prayed her trembling legs wouldn't give out as she took her place beside him.

"Okay, then." The judge turned to Mariella. "Are you ready, Mrs. Valentino?"

Mariella nodded.

"And you have your oath prepared?"

"Yes, sir, I think I do," Mariella said, cautiously.

"It's okay, Mrs. Valentino. If you forget anything, I can help guide you along. It's not as if we'll revoke your citizenship."

The room filled with laughter, helping Mariella relax.

"Now, raise your right hand and begin."

"I hereby declare, on oath, that I absolutely and entirely renounce and abjure all allegiance and fidelity to any foreign prince, potentate, state, or sovereignty of whom or which I have heretofore been a subject or citizen; that I will support and defend the Constitution and laws of the United States of America against all enemies, foreign and domestic; that I will bear true faith and allegiance to the same; that I will bear arms on behalf of the United States when required by the law; that I will perform noncombatant service in the Armed Forces of the United States when required by the law; that I will perform work of national importance under civilian direction when required by the law; and that I take this obligation freely without any mental reservation or purpose of evasion."

Upon finishing, she let out a breath of relief. But when she turned to the judge, he looked at her expectantly.

What did I miss? she wondered, reciting the oath once more in her head.

"So help me, God," he finally said.

"Oh!" Mariella blushed. "So help me, God."

Jack, Elisa, and Olivia watched proudly as the judge presented a certificate of naturalization, made official with a gold stamp pressed on it, confirming Mariella's citizenship.

"Ladies and gentlemen, I present to you our newest American citizen," the judge said.

The room erupted in cheers and applause. Mariella shook the judge's hand while Jack snapped away with his 8MM camera. After a few shots, the clerk motioned for Jack and his daughters to join Mariella. He took the camera as they moved into place, allowing Mariella to take center stage. "Say American cheese!"

"American cheese!"

When they returned to the car, the sun had come out. A light blue sky made a beautiful backdrop to the fluffy white clouds.

"What a day! Should we celebrate with dinner at the restaurant?" Jack asked.

Mariella hesitated. It wasn't that they ate at the restaurant often, but it didn't seem appropriate for such an occasion. "Amore, why don't we eat something American?" she asked.

"American, huh?" Jack grinned. "Spoken like a citizen of the good ole United States of America!"

On the drive over to the Asbury boardwalk, he led the family in a chorus of "God Bless America." Everyone sang enthusiastically, except for Mariella, who was overcome with emotion and had to stop a few times to collect herself. They found a parking spot right in front of the Howard Johnson restaurant with its towering pentagon-shaped windows and bright orange railings. Mariella couldn't think of anything more American.

They were quickly shuttled to a round table by a window overlooking the ocean. Despite the weather clearing, the boardwalk was deserted, but Mariella didn't mind. As they feasted on cheeseburgers, fried chicken, French fried potatoes, and ice cream floats, she knew she was exactly where she belonged.

Chapter Fifty-Three

"That is all for now, Tesoro," Mariella said in a weary voice. "I am quite tired." She had been talking for three hours straight.

Elisa folded her tripod and stood it in the corner of the room. "It's okay, Mama. I can come back tomorrow to do some more, okay? I can bring lunch." She packed away her equipment and a notepad filled with questions that had gone unasked. Her mother's recollections were so vivid, she didn't need any prodding.

"I can walk you down," Mariella said, pushing herself out of the recliner.

"No, Mama. You're tired. Stay here. We can let ourselves out," Olivia pleaded.

Mariella clicked her tongue with resolve. All her life, she had been resilient. That wasn't about to change now. Instead of using the chair, let Olivia hold her arm as they carefully navigated the stairs down to the living room. She paused when they reached Jack's painting of the Colosseum and turned to the girls. "Did I tell you that your father and I met at the Colosseum?"

Olivia and Elisa locked eyes, silently conveying their worry to each other.

"Yes, Mama," Elisa said, patting Mariella on the shoulder.

"Mama, will you be okay?" Olivia's voice always went up an octave when she worried.

"Of course I will."

"And you'll take your chair back up the stairs? You need to use the chair."

"Mama's not a dummy," Elisa said. She gave her mother a big hug, then narrowed her eyes at her. "You'll use the chair, right, Mama?"

Mariella pushed the hair out of her daughter's eyes. "You both worry too much. I love you, Tesoro. You made me a mother." She took Elisa's face into her hands and kissed her forehead.

"Thanks, Mama. I love you too."

Mariella turned to Olivia. "And you, Stellina. My little star. You made us a family. I love you to the moon."

Olivia smiled, hugging her mother tightly. "I love you back to Earth, Mama."

Standing in the doorway, Mariella watched her girls walk to

their cars. They smiled at her through worried eyes. *What would I do without them?*

She closed the door, shuffled to the stairs, and slowly positioned herself in the chair, then pressed the button and rose up until she arrived on the second-floor landing. Bedtime was always the same routine; she changed into her pink silk nightgown, brought the silver-framed photo of Jack to her lips and whispered goodnight, then sat on the edge of the bed. After reciting the same prayers she had done since childhood, Mariella reached into her nightstand and pulled out a small paper note.

No matter where you are,
No matter what you do,
I will always be with you.
…Until we meet again.

The curved lines of Jack's handwriting always brought a smile to her face. She had found the note in her jewelry box a week after they buried him. His kidneys had failed for almost a year before he passed. She held the paper to her heart and whispered, "I love you, amore." Slipping it back into her drawer, Mariella curled up in the bed she'd shared with him for sixty-one years and drifted off to sleep.

After a few hours, her breathing became labored. Her eyes

squeezed shut. She furrowed her brow as if trying to get somewhere, determined to make the trip. Gasp, gasp, gasp, then silence. The house in Wanamassa Gardens took on an eerie stillness.

No more screen doors slammed as kids ran in and out of the house on balmy summer days.

No babies crying from their cribs in the room beside theirs. No doorbell echoing through the house, announcing a dear friend carrying over a baked dish to help out—with a family death, a birth, or a trying time.

At 4 a.m., the house came alive again, but only briefly. Birds chirped throughout the living room, announcing the time.

Then silence again.

Gone are the whispers of sweet nothings from him to her those first days in the house. Or the nights they made love, determined to make a family of their own and erase her yearning for the one she had left.

No more sobbing in his arms when the calls to Italy ended, his heart breaking with hers. The days of sausage and pepper parties under a canopy of festive lanterns, neighbors arriving with anticipation for his tasty sandwiches—all long gone. The backyard grill Pop had built for them using leftover red bricks from his own house was now overgrown with weeds.

No more carols playing on the radio as each daughter

marched down the stairs on Christmas morning while Jack filmed with his 35MM movie camera, their eyes filled with wonderment at the sight of colorful lights twinkling on the tree, announcing that Santa had come.

Or Halloween scares, or Easter egg hunts, or Valentine's cookies baked for teenage crushes.

It was all over now.

In the light of the day, Mariella's weary body would be discovered. The one that had survived the horrors of war, journeyed miles from everything she knew to be with her love, straddled two vastly different cultures the best she could, raised her daughters with the fierceness of a lion, then, as her heart broke in two, tenderly cared for her love as he took his final breath. Until then, the house at Wanamassa Gardens, holding precious memories tucked away in its far corners, sat peacefully amidst the stillness of night.

The End

Thank you for supporting my work! If you've enjoyed this book, please leave a review on Amazon or Goodreads. It really helps a lot.

Also, check out my **website** @ luiginavecchione.com

Follow me on **Instagram** @ lvecchioneauthor

Facebook @ Greetings fromAsbury Park

TikTok @luigina.vecchione

www.ingramcontent.com/pod-product-compliance
Lightning Source LLC
Chambersburg PA
CBHW021840010726
47493CB00005B/1490